LOVECRAFTIAN PROCEEDINGS 4

S. T. Joshi, *Primal Sources: Essays on H. P. Lovecraft* (2003)

————, *The Evolution of the Weird Tale* (2004)

————, *Lovecraft and a World in Transition: Collected Essays on H. P. Lovecraft* (2014)

————, *The Recognition of H. P. Lovecraft: His Rise from Obscurity to World Renown* (2021)

Robert W. Waugh, *The Monster in the Mirror: Looking for H. P. Lovecraft* (2006)

————, *A Monster of Voices: Speaking for H. P. Lovecraft* (2011)

————, *The Tragic Thread in Science Fiction* (2019)

————, *A Monster for Many: Talking with H. P. Lovecraft* (2021)

Scott Connors, ed., *The Freedom of Fantastic Things: Selected Criticism on Clark Ashton Smith* (2006)

Ben Szumskyj, ed., *Two-Gun Bob: A Centennial Study of Robert E. Howard* (2006)

S. T. Joshi and Rosemary Pardoe, ed., *Warnings to the Curious: A Sheaf of Criticism on M. R. James* (2007)

Massimo Berruti, *Dim-Remembered Stories: A Critical Study of R. H. Barlow* (2011)

Gary William Crawford, Jim Rockhill, and Brian J. Showers, ed., *Reflections in a Glass Darkly: Essays on J. Sheridan Le Fanu* (2011)

Steven J. Mariconda, *H. P. Lovecraft: Art, Artifact, and Reality* (2013)

Massimo Berruti, S. T. Joshi, and Sam Gafford, ed., *William Hope Hodgson: Voices from the Borderland: Seven Decades of Criticism on the Master of Cosmic Horror* (2014)

Donald R. Burleson, *Lovecraft: An American Allegory–Selected Essays on H. P. Lovecraft* (2015)

Mark Valentine and Timothy J. Jarvis, ed., *The Secret Ceremonies Critical Essays on Arthur Machen* (2019)

Lovecraft Annual

Dead Reckonings

Lovecraftian Proceedings

Penumbra

LOVECRAFTIAN PROCEEDINGS 4

Select Papers from the Dr. Henry Armitage Memorial Scholarship Symposium, NecronomiCon Providence: 2019

Edited by Dennis P. Quinn and
Elena Tchougounova-Paulson

Hippocampus Press

New York

Published by Hippocampus Press
P.O. Box 641, New York, NY 10156
www.hippocampuspress.com

Cover illustration by Pete Von Sholly.
Cover design by Barbara Briggs Silbert.
Hippocampus Press logo designed by Anastasia Damianakos.

First Edition
1 3 5 7 9 8 6 4 2

ISBN 978-1-61498-361-3 (paperback)
ISBN 978-1-61498-364-4 (ebook)

Contents

Foreword 7
    NIELS-VIGGO S. HOBBS

Introduction: Haunting Phantasms—A Bookworm Edition 9
    ELENA TCHOUGOUNOVA-PAULSON AND DENNIS P. QUINN

Żaḥḥāk Beside Cthulhu: Philosophizing with Monsters in Persian
    Mythology and American Horror 17
    ROBERT LANDAU AMES

The Influence of The Great Game on the Writings of H. P. Lovecraft:
    The Opening of Tibet and the Creation of Leng.................................... 41
    BENJAMIN DAVIS

The *Necronomicon Yalensis* and Lovecraft in Connecticut......................... 52
    EDWARD GUIMONT

Lovecraft's Archive: Materiality and Readership in Lovecraft's Fiction 70
    COLE DONOVAN

The Outsiders: Mapping Lovecraft's Loathing 84
    PAUL NEIMANN

The Ebb of Sanity: "The Night Ocean" and Bipolar Disorder 100
    KYLE GAMACHE

The Weird Within the Real: Common Territories in Lovecraft's Fiction
    and Southern Literature.. 111
    HEATHER POIRIER

A Lover of Past Phantoms: Lovecraftian Reflections in R. H. Barlow's
    Life and Work 126
    THOMAS SCHWAIGER

American Frankensteins: George Porter and George Poe, and Their
    Attempts to Reanimate the Dead in New England................................ 149
    MICHAEL J. BIELAWA

Encounters in the Mountains of Madness: H. P. Lovecraft and Werner
    Herzog at the World's End 161
    LÚCIO REIS-FILHO, LAURA CÁNEPA, AND JAMER DE MELLO

Fear and (Non)Fiction: Agrarian Anxiety in "The Colour out of Space".... 174
  ANTONIO ALEJANDRO BARROSO

Nathaniel Hawthorne and Herbert S. Gorman's Shadows over Innsmouth 189
  JEREMIAH DYLAN COOK

Neo-Gothic Decadence as a Pervasive Challenge in the Works of
  H. P. Lovecraft, Arthur Machen, and Alexander Blok............................ 202
  ELENA TCHOUGOUNOVA-PAULSON

Lovecraft's Accursed Share in Bataille's General Economy: Antiutilitarian
  Cosmologies and Anti-capitalist Social Visions 219
  CHRISTIAN ROY

A Sequence of Paintings So Horrible: Montage in Visual Adaptations
  of "Pickman's Model" 237
  NATHANIEL R. WALLACE

Contributors.. 261

Appendix: Abstracts from the Fourth Biennial Dr. Henry Armitage
  Memorial Scholarship Symposium of New Weird Fiction and Lovecraft-
  Related Research, Providence, RI, 23–25 August 2019 267
  DENNIS P. QUINN, CHAIR

Index 297

Foreword

Niels-Viggo S. Hobbs
Director, Lovecraft Arts and Sciences Council
Providence, Rhode Island

I am deeply honored to provide a brief foreword for the 2019 proceedings of the Armitage Symposium. But, while pleased by the honor, beyond that, I feel a great sense of personal joy and immense accomplishment because this is now the fourth installment of what was, at one time, merely a figment of my imagination. Coming from an academic background and having been involved in planning various international science conferences, where research from various fields and many minds comes together to advance knowledge, I felt it was natural to incorporate something similar within NecronomiCon Providence as it began to be formed in 2013. Now the Armitage Symposium has proven itself to be the preeminent platform for Lovecraftian and weird scholarship, an academic field long overdue for expanded thought, new viewpoints, and an opening of the gates of inclusion—all while maintaining a rigorous and professional standard. So, while the research presented at the Armitage Symposium, and thus the papers included in the present proceedings, come from a mix of scholars of all ranks—professional and amateur, well-established and entirely new to the field, professors and lay people, and known and unknown—this diversity of background is central to the success of the Armitage Symposium and is core to its growing relevance.

Given the now proven and enduring value of the symposium, and the proceedings that come from them, it's important to give some recognition and thanks to the folks who are most making this both possible and so successful and important. As chair, Prof. Dennis Quinn has been a guiding light, a calm rudder, and a workhorse! As you read the following scholarship and, hopefully, have your thinking expanded on various subjects, and perhaps even consider making your own contributions, please thank Dennis—and then get doing that research! It's also important to acknowledge the reviewers who have worked to ensure a fitting standard of academic rigor that is demanding without being excluding: thank you for your hard work. I must extend a heartfelt appreciation to Ken Birdwell, the man who was so impressed with the first Armitage Symposium in 2013, or the Emerging Scholarship Symposium as it was called then, that he signed on to provide the crucial monetary support needed to cover the various expenses related to putting on such a large operation within an even larger complex event. Finally, I should thank both the scholars who have put their hearts and minds into the works contained herein and those of you who have attended talks at NecronomiCon (often packing the room) or are now holding in your hands this iteration of the proceedings. Thank you—all of you.

With warmest regards from hoary Providence.

Introduction: Haunting Phantasms—
A Bookworm Edition

Elena Tchougounova-Paulson
Independent Researcher
Cambridgeshire, England

and

Dennis P. Quinn
Chair of the Dr. Henry Armitage
Memorial Scholarship Symposium
Professor and Chair of the Interdisciplinary
General Education Department
Cal Poly, Pomona, California

This collection of essays comes from the conference talks and presentations delivered at the Henry Armitage Symposium, NecronomiCon Providence, R.I., on 23–25 August 2019. Every two years researchers visit the place that combines every facet of what the horror/weird fiction scholar should look for: the city of Providence, the main land of its genius loci and the Old Gent, H. P. Lovecraft. As we all know, Providence created everything mighty and phantasmagorical for its most famous citizen—remember the Fleur-de-Lys Studios, where Henry Anthony Wilcox, the young, anxious artist and sculptor of "The Call of Cthulhu," resided, or Prospect Terrace, featured in *The Case of Charles Dexter Ward*, or the Samuel B. Mumford House (now at 65 Prospect Street), mentioned in "The Haunter of the Dark." We can say that Providence is as real as it is imaginary in that its physical presence cannot be envisioned without its fictional layer.

But where exactly do those two worlds intersect? One could argue that it is elsewhere in the city, but surely there must be places where the Lovecraftian *Zeitgeist* is the most powerful and the atmosphere produces utterly weird and wonderful things. Certainly all these locations are connected to one another during NecronomiCon, from the Providence Athenaeum, one of the oldest libraries not only in the city itself but also in the country, to the newer John Hay Library at 20 Prospect Street, "next-door," as Lovecraft called it in a letter to Elizabeth Toldridge (15 December 1935), continuing to Brown University (Miskatonic in the Lovecraftian universe) and Ladd Observatory, where he read "endlessly in the observatory library" (letter to Duane Rimel, 29 March 1934).

Once in Providence, you cannot miss visiting these sites during the Walking Tour over College Hill. Indeed, the university, the libraries, and bookstores full of antiques (old books, maps, and memorabilia) shaped Lovecraft's universe. Wandering around various cities with pen friends and literary colleagues was the most Lovecraftian thing one could imagine doing: let us remember how carefully, with a keen interest to the slightest detail, Lovecraft describes his book hunting in antique bookstalls together with *the Boys*,[1] as, for example, in his letter from Brooklyn to his aunt Lillian of 22 January 1925:

> Monday I rose late, & accompanied Loveman on a tour on Fulton St. (Bklyn.) bookshops. Here we obtained some unbelievable bargains, though Loveman insisted on treating me to those I wanted most. Among my "hauls" are the first edition of Fitzhugh Ludlow's "Hasheesh-Eater" (a reprint of which I have always envied Kleiner) & an 1800 copy of Walpole's "Castle of Otranto" on large paper, with long ſ's, & with a fine set of engraved illustrations coloured by hand. (*LFF* 239)

In a sense, all the scholars at NecronomiCon—especially at the NecronomiCon book fair known as Grand Emporium of Weird that occurs simultaneously with the Armitage Symposium (and do not forget that Dr. Henry Armitage was the chief librarian at Miskatonic University in Arkham!)—repeat this Lovecraftian obsession: like the Old Gent and the Boys, they seek for treasures, they hunt the rarities, they exchange, and they contribute to literary research.

But one cannot forget about the locations of the NecronomiCon venue itself, the two hotels where everything—including the Armitage Symposium, the book fair, weird readings, gaming, and the H. P. Lovecraft

---

1. I.e., the members of the famous Kalem Club in New York: Rheinhart Kleiner, George Kirk (a book collector), Samuel Loveman, Everett McNeill, and James F. Morton. For more about them, see Mara Kirk Hart and S. T. Joshi, ed., *Lovecraft's New York Circle: The Kalem Club, 1924–1927.*

Original art created for this volume by Brennan Quinn.

Historical Society's *Dark Adventure Radio Theatre* performances—takes place: the Graduate (formerly the Biltmore) and the Omni. Both are connected to Lovecraft in one way or another, but the Biltmore[2] in particular: Lovecraft's wife, writer, journalist, and businesswoman Sonia Greene, stayed there regularly while traveling on business to Rhode Island from New York, and the hotel was where she met Lovecraft and his aunts:

> Before we were married, on my trips to Boston I'd invite him and his aunts to take their meals with H. P. and me. In Providence we would eat mostly at the Hotel Biltmore. I loved music, soft lights and good service. His aunts and he thought me extravagant for this. But both they and he always enjoyed these jaunts. (Davis 13)

Around that time and later, the Biltmore started gaining the reputation of being one of the most haunted hotels in the United States:[3] as much as we can take the story with a touch of humor, let us not forget that hotels—especially macabre hotels full of grotesquery—hold a special place in Lovecraftian geography. One of these is, of course, "a tall, cupola-crowned building with remnants of yellow paint and with a half-effaced sign proclaiming it to be the Gilman House" (CF 3.176), the hotel in Innsmouth, in all its decaying grandeur. The audience remembers what happened (or, rather, *almost* happened) there, and to some extent one could argue that every Lovecraftian scholar should be ready to face eerie things, once stepping into the corridors of either the Biltmore or Omni during NecronomiCon.

Given how exhaustively everyone who participates in this volume has worked on their themes, there is no doubt that they would definitely face

---

2. We decide to go for its former, glorious name.

3. "Over the years, paranormal activity has been reported at the hotel, in the form of laughter from parties that can't be found, locks turning on their own, and ghostly apparitions. These reports have given the hotel a reputation as one of the most haunted hotels in the United States. In fact, elements of the Biltmore may have inspired some fictional hotels, namely the Bates Motel from Robert Bloch's *Psycho* and (along with the Stanley Hotel in Colorado) the Overlook Hotel in Stephen King's *The Shining*. While it might be a coincidence, the name of the main protagonist of *The Shining*, Jack Torrance, sounds a lot like Dorrance, the street on which the Biltmore is located." ("Providence Biltmore, Providence, Rhode Island: Rumors of the occult haunt this upscale 1920s hotel." www.atlasobscura.com/places/providence-biltmore-graduate. Accessed 19 December 2020).

any of the sinister Lovecraftian ordeals: the variety of topics they focused on in these *Proceedings* is more than impressive. As we look at them more close-ly we can see that Robert Landau Ames analyses a monstrous deity, Żaḥḥāk, from classical Persian literature to connect it through an intertextual per-spective to Lovecraftian Cthulhu; in his paper "Fear and (Non)Fiction: Agrarian Anxiety in 'The Color out of Space,'" Antonio Alejandro Barroso reflects on how certain agrarian locations in Rhode Island inspired Love-craft to write one of his most dystopian tales. Meanwhile, Michael J. Bielawa follows traces of the Gothic motifs focused on an "undead entity" with superpowers that emerged in Mary Shelley's *Frankenstein,* in Love-craft's story "Herbert West—Reanimator" and beyond; Cole Donovan gives his own approach of how readers could interpret the symbolism of Lovecraft's *Necronomicon* in a semiotic way, as something that cannot be entirely completed ("intradiegetic texts as *use* rather than *reading*").

In his paper "Nathaniel Hawthorne's and Herbert S. Gorman's Shadow over Innsmouth," Jeremiah Dylan Cook juxtaposes fictional/imaginary and semi-real locations in the works of Hawthorne and Lovecraft from the folk-horror perspective, whereas Benjamin Davis gives a panoramic view of the Tibetan motives and reminiscences in Lovecraft's compendium, including the analysis of a possible influence on Lovecraft's works of Helena Blavat-sky's *Isis Unveiled* and *The Secret Doctrine.* Kyle Gamache in his article "The Ebb of Sanity" looks at the novelette "The Night Ocean," a collaborative work of H. P. Lovecraft and R. H. Barlow, from the psychological point of view, as a subtle manifestation of the stages of bipolar disorder, in which case "The Night Ocean" could be seen as "more of a personal and lonely exploration of human emotion rather than cosmic horror." In his paper "The *Necronomicon Yalensis* and Lovecraft i(a)n Connecticut" Edward Guimont explores the Connecticut references and literary liaisons within the Cthulhu Mythos lore, and Paul Neimann in his work examines the re-evaluation of values in Lovecraftian universe, shown in the early stories, which "systematically engage a conundrum about how to hang on to behav-ioral and social standards amid modernity's profound 'shifting of values.'"

Heather Poirier investigates how Lovecraftian mythological territories intersect with the literary landscapes of Southern Literature on the basis of Gothic, and Lúcio Reis-Filho, Laura Cánepa, and Jamer de Mello show the encounters between Lovecraft's *At the Mountains of Madness* and Wer-ner Herzog's Antarctica project, *Encounters at the End of the World.* Chris-tian Roy examines Lovecraft's cosmic horrors from Bataille's concept of "cosmic," or "solar economy" ("a reversal of all verticality into terrifying abysses that stand for the depths of the sky as the foul, bottomless pit of wasteful expenditure of the universe's chaotic energies"). Thomas Schwaiger examines the "possible posthumous influence" of Lovecraft on Barlow's linguistic studies in Mesoamerican history, languages and culture, whereas Elena Tchougounova-Paulson explores Neo-Gothic Decadent traces in works of Lovecraft, Arthur Machen, and Russian poet-Symbolist Alexander Blok, and Nathaniel R. Wallace reviews a variety of visual adaptations of "Pickman's Model" by Lovecraft in comic series.

As we see, the multiplicity of topics in regard to the works of H. P. Lovecraft is as opulent as it is conventionally academic, and we are certain that there is much more to come later.

We want to express our endless gratitude to all the people who have been involved in both the Armitage Symposium and the *Lovecraftian Proceedings*. First of all, many thanks to Niels-Viggo S. Hobbs, who is the main organizer of NecronomiCon Providence and one of the founders of the modern art-Lovecraftiana. Without him and his endless, excellent efforts, none of the Armitage Symposiums would become a reality. We also want to thank David E. Schultz, whose academic and editorial knowledge is immense. We are also grateful to Derrick Hussey whose belief and support of the *Lovecraftian Proceedings* is greatly appreciated. And, of course, we must thank eminent and prolific S. T. Joshi, without whom modern Lovecraftiana as an academic field could hardly be possible. A special thanks to the nameless peer reviewers whose anonymity will not overshadow their hard work and dedication to this project. They were instrumental in in helping maintain the highest standards of academic scholarship contained herein. We would also like to thank Cal Poly Pomona student assistant Whittni Wibisono, who helped early on with preliminary editing, as well as Brennan Quinn for his remarkable artwork for this volume.

We hope to see all our contributors, authors, and speakers at the next NecronomiCon—and perhaps you, dear reader. Because we all know that stars will be right again one day.

Works Cited

Davis, Sonia H. *The Private Life of H. P. Lovecraft*. Ed. S. T. Joshi. West Warwick, RI: Necronomicon Press, 1992.

Hart, Mara Kirk, and S. T. Joshi, ed. *Lovecraft's New York Circle: The Kalem Club, 1924-1927*. New York: Hippocampus Press, 2006.

Lovecraft, H. P. *Letters to Family and Family Friends*. Vol. 1. Ed. S. T. Joshi and David E. Schultz. New York: Hippocampus Press, 2020.

Providence Biltmore (Providence, Rhode Island): Rumors of the occult haunt this upscale 1920s hotel. www.atlasobscura.com/places/providence-biltmore-graduate. Accessed December 19, 2020.

Abbreviations

HPL	H. P. Lovecraft
RHB	R. H. Barlow

AG	*Letters to Alfred Galpin and Others*, ed. S. T. Joshi and David E. Schultz (Hippocampus Press, 2020)
AT	*The Ancient Track: Complete Poetical Works*, ed. S. T. Joshi (Hippocampus Press, 2013)
CE	*Collected Essays*, ed. S. T. Joshi (Hippocampus Press, 2004-06; 5 vols.)
CF	*Collected Fiction: A Variorum Edition*, ed. S. T. Joshi (Hippocampus Press, 2015-21; 4 vols. [citations to vol. 4 are taken from the revised edition of 2022])
CLM	*Letters to C. L. Moore and Others*, ed. David E. Schultz and S. T. Joshi (Hippocampus Press, 2017)
DS	*Dawnward Spire, Lonely Hill: The Letters of H. P. Lovecraft and Clark Ashton Smith*, ed. David E. Schultz and S. T. Joshi (Hippocampus Press, 2017)
DW	*Letters with Donald and Howard Wandrei and to Emil Petaja*, ed. S. T. Joshi and David E. Schultz (Hippocampus Press, 2019)
ES	*Essential Solitude: The Letters of H. P. Lovecraft and August Derleth*, ed. David E. Schultz and S. T. Joshi (Hippocampus Press, 2013)
ET	*Letters to Elizabeth Toldridge and Anne Tillery Renshaw*, ed. David E. Schultz and S. T. Joshi (Hippocampus Press, 2014)

FLB   *Letters to F. Lee Baldwin, Duane W. Rimel, and Nils Frome,* ed. David E. Schultz and S. T. Joshi (Hippocampus Press, 2016)

IAP   S. T. Joshi, *I Am Providence: The Life and Times of H. P. Lovecraft* (Hippocampus Press, 2010)

JFM   *Letters to James F. Morton,* ed. David E. Schultz and S. T. Joshi (Hippocampus Press, 2014)

JVS   *Letters to J. Vernon Shea, Carl F. Strauch, and Lee McBride White,* ed. S. T. Joshi and David E. Schultz (Hippocampus Press, 2016)

LL   S. T. Joshi and David E. Schultz, *Lovecraft's Library: A Catalogue,* 4th ed. (Hippocampus Press, 2017)

LLF   *Letters to Family and Family Friends,* ed. S. T. Joshi and David E. Schultz (Hippocampus Press, 2020)

MWM *Letters to Maurice W. Moe and Others,* ed. David E. Schultz and S. T. Joshi (Hippocampus Press, 2018)

OFF   *O Fortunate Floridian: H. P. Lovecraft's Letters to R. H. Barlow,* ed. S. T. Joshi and David E. Schultz (University of Tampa Press, 2007)

RB   *Letters to Robert Bloch and Others,* ed. David E. Schultz and S. T. Joshi (Hippocampus Press, 2017)

RK   *Letters to Rheinhart and Others,* ed. S. T. Joshi and David E. Schultz (Hippocampus Press, 2020)

SL   *Selected Letters,* ed. August Derleth, Donald Wandrei, and James Turner (Arkham House, 1965–76; 5 vols.)

Żaḥḥāk Beside Cthulhu: Philosophizing with Monsters in Persian Mythology and American Horror

Robert Landau Ames
Adjunct Assistant Professor, Global Liberal Studies,
New York University

This paper aims to apply the terms in which recent exponents of speculative realist tendencies in (post-)continental philosophy have analyzed horror and monstrosity to the study of classical Persian literature. Just as Graham Harman adopted Lovecraftian fiction as the poet laureate of his philosophical project (*Weird Realism*, per the title of his book), I ask what positions might result from a similar attempt to philosophize with Żaḥḥāk, the serpent-shouldered king who features prominently in the Iranian national epic, the *Shāhnāmah* (*Book of Kings*) of Firdawsī (d. 1019 or 1025), rather than Cthulhu. To that end, I devote much of what follows to a close study of the language used to describe the monstrous elements of Żaḥḥāk in order to read this monster alongside these recent philosophical adoptions of both weird fiction and horror more broadly. The *Shāhnāmah*'s historical context in general and the interplay between kingship and monstrosity in the Żaḥḥāk story in particular lead to different philosophical priorities from the speculative realist adoption of H. P. Lovecraft. In light of its medieval Perso-Islamic context, a philosophical reading of the Żaḥḥāk cycle in the *Shāhnāmah* points toward ethics, while such a reading of Lovecraft lends itself to ontology.

Note: There are many systems for transliterating Persian into English. This paper uses the Library of Congress system. Some of its secondary sources, however, use other systems, which has led to some inconsistencies in the spelling of Persian words. Parts of this paper appeared previously in the author's "On Monstrosity in the Shāhnāmah: Philosophizing with Żaḥḥāk," 355–76.

Much of Żaḥḥāk's monstrosity rests in his body's fusion of royal and dragon-like elements. This fusion derives from his violation of Persian norms of kingship; the interplay between monstrosity and monarchy is thus central to the Żaḥḥāk cycle. The question posed to Żaḥḥāk by the blacksmith Kāvah, "*tu shāhī va-gar azhdahā paykarī/bi-bāyad bidīn dāvarī*," or, in Dick Davis's English translation, "A king then, or a monster? Which are you? Tell us, your majesty, which of the two?" encapsulates this interplay (Firdawsī 49; Davis 19). Unlike ancient accounts that minimize or deny Żaḥḥāk's human origins and portray him more strictly as a dragon or demon, in Firdawsī's circa 1010 C.E. telling, Żaḥḥāk's kingship and monstrosity are not only closely linked, but also specifically reflect a medieval, rather than antique, cultural context: in Firdawsī's account, the pre-Islamic, pre-medieval Persian demon (or dragon) is given a human origin and then proceeds down the path of monstrosity by opting to violate medieval Perso-Islamic norms of kingship and subsequently suffering a bestial hybridization instead of simply entering the narrative as a purely destructive and inhuman force, as is the case in pre-Islamic sources.

An Introduction to the *Shāhnāmah*

The New Persian literature of Firdawsī's period was central to the preservation of Persian linguistic and cultural identity after the Islamic conquest of Greater Iran; while this conquest led in many cases to the replacement of local languages with Arabic, it led in Greater Iran to the creation of New Persian (sometimes called *Fārsī*), a language that featured Arabic loanwords and used the Arabic script, but retained a grammatical structure largely continuous with the pre-Islamic Middle Persian. In the popular mind, Firdawsī's *Shāhnāmah* often enjoys a reputation as the text that "saved" Persian language and culture after the Islamic conquest by retelling pre-Islamic Iranian legends and by using few Arabic loan words. Firdawsī composed it more than three centuries after the Islamic conquest of the Sassanian Empire following the Battle of al-Qādisīyah in 636 C.E. A poem, the text consists of 50,000 couplets and purports to chronicle the history of Greater Iran from the time of the world's creation until the aforementioned fall of the Sassanian Empire at Qādisīyah. Secondary scholarship usually divides the poem into three sections and three corresponding ages of humanity, the mythic (*ustūrah'ī*), the heroic (*pahlavānī*), and the historic (*tārīkhī*).

The rise of poetry composed in New Persian like Firdawsī's *Shāhnāmah* also parallels political developments in the wider Islamic world. In the Umayyad period (661–750), privilege within the new Islamic polity extended to, and only secondarily through, Arab genealogy, with non-Arab converts needing Arabic patronage (and symbolic adoption into their patrons' lineage) to safeguard their position in the new order (this was known as the *mawālī* system). The Abbasid revolution in 750, which was spurred by, among other things, a rebellion in the far eastern province of Khurāsān (later the birthplace of New Persian poetry), saw a major shift in caliphal preferences, with the new Abbasid caliphate establishing its capital, Baghdad, in what was previously the territory of the Persian empire and adopting a number of royal customs and habits of literary-intellectual patronage modeled on those of earlier Persian monarchs. Throughout the ninth and tenth centuries C.E., this also led to the rise of semi-dynastic Persian families like the Barmakids and the Buyids as administrators and as the "power behind the throne," which was accompanied further east in Greater Persia by the rise of Persian-speaking dynasties like the Saffārids (861–1003) and the Sāmānids (819–999). The latter, a dynasty that claimed descent from Bahrām Chūbīnah (a Sassanian general and character in the *Shāhnāmah*) and patronized the first great New Persian poet (Rūdakī, c. 859–941), ruled basically autonomously in Khurāsān, where Abū al-Qāsim Firdawsī was born in 940.

Firdawsī was from the *dihqān* class—a native Persian class of landholders who, despite having lost much of their power after the Islamic conquest, still viewed themselves as the heirs to elite pre-Islamic Persian culture and who aided in the reconstruction of Persian culture in the Islamic period by, among other things, continuing to transmit pre-Islamic Persian literature, serving as likely sources for Firdawī and his immediate predecessors (Ashraf). Between his *dihqān* status and the rise of dynasties willing to support Persian literary production (like those discussed above), Firdawsī was well positioned to produce a poetic retelling of Iran's pre-Islamic mytho-history. Written and oral sources also preceded Firdawsī's *Shāhnāmah* and helped shape his output. Aside from oral transmission by *dihqān*s and other elder storytellers, there were also a number of written precedents. The first of these is a Middle Persian text, the *Khwadāy-nāmag*, which no longer survives, but which informed both Arabic histories of Persian kings and subsequent *Shāhnāmah*s. Earlier New Persian precedents included the prose Abū Manṣūr *Shāhnāmah*, composed for the

Sāmānid court by Abū Manṣūr Maʿmarī in 957, and the first attempt at a verse *Shāhnāmah*, the Daqīqī *Shāhnāmah* (composed c. 977), which Firdawsī cites as a source. Firdawsī legendarily sought (and was denied) the patronage of the ethnically Turkic Ghaznavid dynasty (977–1186), who were also active patrons of Persian literary production (Browne; Hodgson; Rypka).

The Żaḥḥāk Cycle in Brief

According to Firdawsī, Żaḥḥāk is an Arab prince whom the devil convinces to commit patricide. After killing his father, the good king Mardās, he invades and conquers Iran and commits his second regicide, this time against the legendary Persian king Jamshīd. Żaḥḥāk executes him in a particularly gruesome fashion, sawing him in half. Following Żaḥḥāk's conquest of Iran, the devil appears again, this time in the form of a cook, and uses his culinary skills to ingratiate himself with Żaḥḥāk, after which he kisses the king's shoulders. This causes a serpent to grow from each shoulder, and, when Żaḥḥāk tries to remove the snakes, they grow back. None of his court physicians knows a treatment for this ailment until the devil appears once more, this time as a doctor, who informs the king that the only treatment for his new ailment is to feed the serpents the brains of young men. Żaḥḥāk rules Iran for a millennium, attempting to satiate the snakes' hunger by feeding them the brains of Iranian youths all the while. A rebellion instigated by the blacksmith Kāvah eventually overthrows Żaḥḥāk and a native Iranian, Faraydūn, subdues Żaḥḥāk, imprisons him beneath Mount Damāvand (a mountain in Iran's Alborz range with a cultural significance comparable to that of Mount Athos or Mount Fuji), and claims the throne, becoming the epic's next hero-king (Tafazzoli).

Lovecraft, Horror, and Philosophy

Horror in general and Lovecraft in particular have, over the past decade or so, come to be adopted by a number of philosophers including Eugene Thacker, Graham Harman, and Reza Negarestani. These adoptions usually lead to ontological conclusions, feeding speculation about the nature of being and the limits of human access to the Real. Much of Lovecraft's oeuvre focuses on presenting the cosmos as, at best, indifferent to humanity, but moreover, all too capable of destroying life and sanity whenever people encounter its real contents. For example, the horror in Lovecraft's story "The Colour out of Space" is not simply that an alien lifeform lands on earth, kills some of those it encounters, and then drives the survivors insane. The true horror of the story is that the titular being is completely unrecognizable as a lifeform at all. It has no body as such and is barely even a color, but is rather only a tint that subtly colors the objects it affects. This lends itself fairly conveniently to the central themes of Speculative Realism, a philosophical current that basically posits that objects' existence exceeds their complete comprehension or perception by human subjects, that objects are nonetheless capable of acting on humans, and that figurative or indirect language can best convey the reality of such objects, given their incomplete accessibility to human consciousness or perception.

In *In the Dust of This Planet*, Eugene Thacker frames horror as a genre that discloses "the unthinkable world," in which we find "the thought of the unthinkable" (2). Because philosophical discourse is unable to present the unthinkable in its own terms, horror can supply figurative language better suited to expressing such a thought. In Thacker's case, horror serves to express the collision of the human and non-human worlds represented by the threatening ways that the non-human can take on a life of its own, linking this to the non-human actors of the climate crisis: "we are increasingly more and more aware of the world in which we live as a non-human world, a world outside, one that is manifest i[n] the effects of global climate change, natural disasters, the energy crisis, and the progressive extinction of species worldwide" (Thacker 9). For Thacker, Lovecraft's cosmic horror is the horror writing most relevant to his project because it depicts human beings' responses to the intrusion of the unknowable or non-human, the "misanthropic" Real, upon human lifeworlds. To this end, Thacker employs a famous line of Lovecraft's article "Supernatural Horror in Literature" ("The oldest and strongest emotion of mankind is fear, and the oldest and strongest kind of fear is fear of the unknown" [CF 2.82] in the introduction to *In the Dust of This Planet* (9).

Graham Harman, the founder of Object-Oriented Ontology, has meanwhile dedicated a book to Lovecraft, presenting him as the literary forebear of the book's titular *Weird Realism*. There, Harman takes Lovecraft's description of the idol in "The Call of Cthulhu" as a jumping-off point for his adoption of Lovecraft in service to his object-oriented ontology. The description he selects reads as follows:

its impressionistic execution forbade a very clear idea of its nature. It seemed to be a sort of monster, or symbol representing a monster, of a form which only a diseased fancy could conceive. If I say that my somewhat extravagant imagination yielded simultaneous pictures of an octopus, a dragon, and a human caricature, I shall not be unfaithful to the spirit of the thing. A pulpy, tentacled head surmounted a grotesque and scaly body with rudimentary wings, but it was the *general outline* of the whole which made it most shockingly frightful. (CF 2.23–24)

The philosophical significance of this description rests in its indirectness; because Lovecraft "downplays" the idol of Cthulhu's appearance "as merely the result of his own 'extravagant imagination,'" "evasively terms his description 'not unfaithful to the spirit of the thing' rather than dead-on correct," and "asks us to ignore the surface properties of dragon and octopus mixed with human and to focus instead on the fearsome 'general outline of the whole,'" Lovecraft produces a gap "between an ungraspable thing and the vaguely relevant descriptions that the narrator is able to attempt" (24). This gap is central to Lovecraft's stylistic world, which matters, philosophically, because it is "a world in which (1) real objects are locked in impossible tension with the crippled descriptive powers of language, and (2) visible objects display unbearable seismic torsion with their own qualities" (27). For Harman, this world bears a resemblance to the one that follows Heidegger's radicalized phenomenology, which, following his tool-analysis, reoriented phenomenology by noting "that we usually deal with things insofar as they *do not* appear," unlike the call for philosophers to return to the things themselves issued in Husserl's original phenomenological project, which directed philosophical study to objects as they appear as given to human consciousness (28).

So, in *Weird Realism*, the Lovecraftian style of description matters philosophically because it reflects the gap between objects and the power of language to describe them. To return to the description of an idol of Cthulhu, Harman emphasizes that it is the specific language of the description that highlights the gap between things as they are and things as they can be comprehended by the human subject; simply saying that the idol "looked like a dragon, an octopus, and a human, all rolled into one" would, for Harman, "ruin the passage" (57). Speaking more philosophically, a description that leans so heavily on the individual qualities of the idol, could lead to an absurdly Humean account of the idol, which would insist "When we think of Cthulhu, we only join three consistent ideas, *octopus*, *dragon,* and *human,* with which we were formerly acquainted" (Harman 58). It is, instead, the particular language of Lovecraft's description that "makes us *feel* the difference between an object and its qualities by framing the description of those qualities as contingent upon a palpable if unspeakable "'spirit of the thing' and 'general outline of the whole' irreducible to cheerful bundles of octopus, dragon and human" (Harman 58–59).

Żaḥḥāk in Cyclonopedia

The use of Persian mythology in service of the philosophical adoption of horror is not entirely unprecedented: Reza Negarestani in fact uses Żaḥḥāk as one of the literary devices in *Cyclonopedia,* his 2008 work of theory-fiction. Adopting the basic speculative realist premises discussed above, Negarestani uses *Cyclonopedia* to explore the notion that the Middle East is itself an entity that has, through its material avatars (including dust, oil, and archaeological remains), been acting on and through humanity for its whole history. In service of this notion, he frames Żaḥḥāk as one manifestation of the "draco-spiral," a symbol he uses to represent one of the Middle East's ability to confuse, corrupt, and ensnare humans within itself. For Negarestani, "the dragon, or as in ancient Persian and Babel (Babylonia), *Azhi,*" is "the archeo-demonographical figure of this spiral" (itself a visual rendering of the spiraling "thirst to hunt that exists within each warmachine" and is "the simulation of the radical frenzy of war to hunt all warmachines" (Negarestani 131). Negarestani borrows the concept of the "war machine" from Deleuze and Guattari, for whom it refers to "a collection of nomad-warriors engaged in resistance to control," a collection that "is not influenced by the economic and political concerns of the State" and which "which bubbles up from common concerns for freedom to move" (Heckman). He elsewhere terms this figure "the divergent spiral or diffusive axis of Az," the "corkscrewing motion" of which is based on "spiraling unlocalizability, inexhaustible becomings of perversion, deviations, and insurgent creativities" (Negarestani 176). Negarestani later gives the name "the Seal of Azhi" to the entanglement of the "strains of the draco-spiral," fictively attributing this entanglement to a "middle-eastern occult" tradition according to which the Seal "is simultaneously the impossibility of external influence and the movement of the draco-spiral as the blade of impossibility" (221). Here, it bears noting that in pre-

Islamic sources considered Żaḥḥāk an *Aẓhi*, or dragon; in fact, the New Persian word Żaḥḥāk derives from the Avestan term *Aẓhi Dahaka*.

While Negarestani's discussion owes more to Deleuze and Guattari than it does to Firdawsī, it merits pointing out that actual historical and linguistic scholarship on ancient Persian has highlighted a link between *āz* ("greed") and *Aẓhis* like Azhi Dahāka. The "Avestan Āzi [. . .] derives from the root *āz-* 'Strive for, endeavor to,'" while Middle and New Persian use *āz* "without mythological significance," to refer to the psychological, rather than mythological dimensions of this demon of "Greed, Lust, Avarice, Avidity, Concupiscence," which is to say that they refer to those vices as "realized in man" (Asmussen). One Middle Persian source identifies greed as one of Dahāg's defects and other Middle Persian sources also link dragons in general to greed. For example, "in the *Bundahišn* the snake-like (*mār homānāg*) Gōčihr and Mūšparīg with the tail (*dumbōmand*) and wings (*parrwar*) are said to be the evil opponents of the sun, moon and stars. These two harmful beings were bound to the sun so as not to run free and cause harm" (Skjærvø). This Guchihr is probably ultimately derived from the Avestan *gaociθra*, which is "mentioned in connection with Āzi, the demon of greed," in the Avesta (Skjærvø). Elsewhere, the *Bundahishn* also mentions an "evil that is from the seed of Greed (Āz) and is a snake," further contributing to an association between serpentine creatures and greed (Askari 189).

Elsewhere in *Cyclonopedia*, Negarestani includes a version of the Żaḥḥāk myth with some similarities to Firdawsī's, in which

> Ashemogha (the false mage, deceiver, imposter, quack), messenger of Ahriman [the supreme evil in Zoroastrianism, the imperial religion of the Sassanian empire], appears to Zahak, the king of Persia, as a cook who taints the vegetarian Zoroastrian cuisine with meat. As a culinary felon bent on defiling the Persian diet, Ashemogha executes his scheme by secretly adding small quantities of meat to his meals and over time increasing the quantity of meat, then replacing it with human meat so as to get Zahak addicted. After ten years, Ashemogha finally comes up with a cuisine composed entirely of meat, to complete Zahak's initiation into the carnivorous realms. As Ashemogha (the cook) kisses Zahak's shoulders after his initiation (the Gift of Ahriman), two giant worms or snakes grow out of the kiss marks.
>
> The pain of the growing worms can only be alleviated by feeding them with human brains of both sexes. The demonic is only attainable by becoming-chef or by returning to the culinary aspects of matter. (Negarestani 189)

The above paragraphs' focus on the link between "the demonic" and a return "to the culinary aspects of matter" is one of the points where Negarestani's retelling of the Żaḥḥāk myth resembles Firdawsī's most closely (see below). However, in making Żaḥḥāk an icon, Negarestani appeals more to a possibly constructed pre-Islamic mythology than to Firdawsī's telling of the myth. While Negarestani's use of Żaḥḥāk makes sense in light of his particular theoretical-fictional project, in what follows, I aim to attend more closely to the actual text of Firdawsī's version of the Żaḥḥāk story. This is, in part, the result of an attempt at a sort of object-oriented thinking; I would argue that attending to the language in my particular object of study is an attempt to recognize the independent existence of that object and let it dictate its own philosophical concerns—if we are to let objects act on us, and if the particular object in question is a text, the text's specific linguistic content may be the closest we can come to a raw material that can exert influence upon us as readers. To that end, my major inspiration from Harman is methodological, in that it has directed me toward a focus on the style in which our monsters are described. These descriptions, however, point us toward different philosophical genres; if, according to Harman, Lovecraft's monsters lend themselves to ontology, Firdawsī's Żaḥḥāk lends himself to ethics. I would, moreover, argue that this ethical concern and Firdawsī's humanization of Żaḥḥāk's origins are historically significant, as they reflect the medieval-Islamic context of the *Shāhnāmah*'s composition and thereby distinguish the *Shāhnāmah*'s account of Żaḥḥāk from both its antique-Zoroastrian predecessors and Negarestani's twenty-first century adoption of it. In assigning Żaḥḥāk demonic, rather than human, origins, Negarestani's version does share certain similarities with pre-Islamic accounts of the myth.

Żaḥḥāk in Antiquity

In Firdawsī's telling, Żaḥḥāk is first a human usurper who only later turns into a monster, and most modern scholarship tends to focus on his human status as bad king of foreign origin rather than as a snake-shouldered monster. However, in pre-Islamic Iranian mythology, Żaḥḥāk appeared as a dragon or demon without these strictly human origins; in Avestan Persian, he was known as Azhī Dahāka, from which both the word Żaḥḥāk and the New Persian word for dragon, *azhdahā*, derive. In Avestan, *azhī* could mean "snake," "worm," or "dragon," but, already in Middle Persian, specific, unrelated terms (*mār* and *kirm*, respectively) had come to refer to snakes and worms, giving dragons a monopoly on *azhī* (Skjærvø). In the *Avesta* (the earliest available Zoroastrian sources), our subject appears as "a dragon-like (*aži*) monster with three mouths (*θrizafanəm*), three heads (*θrikamarəδəm*), six eyes (*xšuuaš.ašīm*), with a thousand viles (*hazaŋrā.yaoxštīm*), very strong (*aš.aojaŋhəm*), a demoniac devil (*daēuuīm drujim*)" (Skjærvø). Elsewhere in the *Avesta*, Azhī Dahāka prays to Arduuī Sūrā and Vaiiu, the Zoroastrian deities of wind and water, for the power to depopulate the entire world (Skjærvø). Late antique Middle Persian sources offer more detail on these vices and begin to cast Żaḥḥāk as a sort of anti-king (though he is still more demon than man), a figure representing the opposite of human virtue, which idealized kings embodied.

The *Bundahišn* gives an immediate, physical dimension to Żaḥḥāk's counter-kingship, stating that he and his brother sawed the king Yīma (Jamshīd) in half after the *khwarnah* (New Persian *farr*) for his kingship departed Yīma. Another late antique source, the *Dēnkard*, identifies Dahāg as the founder of the "bad religion" (an anti-Zoroastrianism the *Dēnkard* at one point identifies with Judaism) and claims that Dahāg issued "ten bad, counter-counsels" in contrast to the "ten good counsels to mankind given by Jam [Jamshīd]" (Skjærvø). Elsewhere, the *Sūdgar nask* attributes to Dahāg five defects (greediness, want of energy, indolence, defilement, and illicit intercourse) that oppose what it frames as the best virtues, "wisdom, instructed eloquence, diligence, and energetic effort." The *Dādestān ī dēnīg* calls Dahāg "one of the seven worst sinners ever, i.e., those who are close to Ahriman himself" and presents him as "the first who lauded (*stāyīd*) sorcery (*jādūgīh*)" (Skjærvø).

These late antique sources historicize and humanize our monster somewhat; they tend to locate him within the line of the Pīshdādīān, the mythical rulers of Iran that descended from Hūshang, succeeded Jamshīd, and preceded Faraydūn (Skjærvø). However, the genealogy provided by the *Bundahišn* traces his lineage to "the Evil Spirit himself" (Skjærvø). This same period's sources also give Azhī Dahāka an eschatological significance; upon defeating him, Faraydūn does not kill Dahāg, but only incapacitates and binds him, for fear that upon his death, Dahāg's body would flood the world with noxious creatures. These texts, however, predict that Dahāg will break his fetters and return to wage war against all life on earth at the coming of the millennium (Skjærvø).

Żahhāk in Modern Secondary Sources

Żahhāk tends not to figure as prominently as the *Shāhnāmah*'s heroes in the scholarship on it and subsequent Persian literature. Those sources that do mention him seldom focus on him, usually limiting their attention to Żahhāk's status as a tyrannical usurper of the Iranian throne, his foreignness, or his position in the genealogy of heroes in the *Shāhnāmah*'s later heroic age and, with the exception of Laurie Pierce's "Serpents and Sorcery," they generally have little to say about his monstrosity as such.

In her 1984 study, "The Development of a Literary Canon in Medieval Persian Chronicles: The Triumph of Etiquette," E. A. Poliakova argues that Żahhāk became a literary device in subsequent medieval Persian chronicles, noting that "the Żahhāk type" became a model "evil genius" upon whom later Persian chroniclers patterned their accounts of historical figures, claiming, for example, that Juvaynī represents Chingīz Khān along this pattern (246). Similarly, Mohamad Tavakoli-Targhi's 1996 discussion of Żahhāk focuses on his identification as a non-Iranian in post-*Shāhnāmah* histories, noting that *Niẓām al-tavārīkh*'s "chapter on Persian kings (*mulūk-i Furs*) [. . .] included the non-Persian rulers Żahhāk, Afrasiyab, and Istihan" (160). Jerome Clinton and Marianna S. Simpson only mention Żahhāk's role as an "evil usurper" in passing when observing that Rustam's combat with the white *dīv* "seems to hark back to an earlier stage of mankind's development when, as recounted by Firdausi, mankind was pitted against monsters," though this passage is useful for our purposes in that it at least recognizes Żahhāk as a monster (191).

Fraser Clark's discussion of Żahhāk in his 2010 article, "From Epic to Romance, via Filicide? Rustam's Character Formation," limits its focus to Żahhāk's position in the genealogy of Rustam, the great hero of the *Shāhnāmah*, terming the marriage of Rustam's father Zāl to Rūdābah (a descendant of Żahhāk) "the Żahhāk controversy" (56). This controversy 'shocks' Zāl's father Sām, who has an "instinctive recognition of taboo in any union between Zal's 'antidote' House of Faridun and Rudaba, the daughter of Mihrab's 'poison' House of Żahhāk" (56). In another article from the same year, Sebastiaan den Uijl also focuses on Żahhāk's genealogical link to Rustam, limiting his discussion of the former to the observation that the descent from Żahhāk also connects Rustam to the primeval and chaotic world (74). Cameron Cross makes a similar observation in a 2015 paper, noting, "Although the physical Żahhāk is long dead by"

Rustam's time, "both Rostam and Sohrāb are of his demonic lineage, and it is clear that his legacy of *āz*–avarice, pride, and concupiscence–can still wreak much suffering upon the world" (412). Mohammad Jafar Amir Mahallati focuses on Rustam's descent from Żaḥḥāk in another 2015 article, where he writes, "Rostam, the main hero, is a descendant on his mother's side of Żahhāk, a demonic king" (Mahallati 910).

In her monograph from 2014, *Faramarz, the Sistani Hero*, Marjolijn van Zutphen also attributes Żaḥḥāk's significance to his status as the ancestor of later heroes in the Sīstānī cycle of epics, a collection of medieval Persian poems that followed Firdawsī's *Shāhnāmah*, highlighting, for example, Sām's initial objection to his son Zāl's marriage to Rudābah on the grounds of her descent form Żaḥḥāk (154). As its title suggests, Edmund Hayes's 2015 paper "The Death of Kings: Group Identity and the Tragedy of *Nezhd* in Ferdowsi's Shahnameh," focuses on lineage (*nizhād*) in its discussion of Żaḥḥāk. Hayes argues that "the death of the king is explicitly seen in terms of *nezhād*," noting that the focus on lineage in the text's condemnation of the killer of the last Sassanian king, Yazdgird, is particularly noteworthy in contrast to its discussion of Żaḥḥāk: whereas "Yazdegerd, is the epitome of glorious lineage (*farrokh-nezhād*)," his killer "is the epitome of evil lineage (*bad-nezhād*) [. . .] and he is also known as 'shepherd-born' (*shabān-zādeh*)" (381). For Hayes, the "intense focus on a character's evil lineage and low origin is unparalleled in the Shahnameh, even in the case of the demon-king Żaḥḥāk who is, after all, the son of a noble king" (381). Lineage is similarly prominent when, slightly later, a Zoroastrian priest warns Yazdgird's killer that "Żaḥḥāk's murder of Jamshid was avenged by Faridun 'of glorious lineage' (*farrokh-nezhād*)" (382).

Dominic Parviz Brookshaw addresses Żaḥḥāk only in relation to Jamshīd in his 2015 study of later poets' use of the latter, "Mytho-Political Remakings of Ferdowsi's Jamshid in the Lyric Poetry of Injuid and Mozaffarid Shiraz." There, Żaḥḥāk serves to move Jamshīd's story to its conclusion: noting that "for many in the pre-modern Iranian world, Jamshid simply was Solomon," Brookshaw points out that "this association ignores the disparity in the outcome of the Jamshid and Solomon narratives–Jamshid never regains his *farr* [divinely-ordained kingly glory and mandate to rule], does not reestablish his legitimacy to rule, and is succeeded by the demonic Żaḥḥāk" (467). When "Jamshid [. . .] grows overly proud at his many civilizing achievements," he "turns away from God (*ze yazdān pichid*), becomes ungrateful (*nā-sepās*), and loses his *farr* (and with it his right to kingship)," at which point, "the people turned against Jamshid, and the evil Żahhāk headed for *takht-e Jamshid* (Jamshid's throne, or possibly Persepolis), seized the royal throne and crown (*takht o kolāh*), and thus became the king of the Iranian lands (*shah-e Irān-zamin*)" (465). Charles Melville's 2016 study of the use of the *Shāhnāmah* in a later medieval chronicle (Rashīd al-Dīn's *Jāmiʿ al-tawārīkh*), notes only that Rashīd al-Dīn's reliance upon the *Shāhnāmah* peaks with his discussion of Żahhāk, who only appears as someone Iranians sought out after Jamshīd's "*farr* and his glory (*shukūh*) disappeared" and Żahhāk had "had killed his father and seized the kingdom" (212–13).

Medieval Kingship: Perso-Islamic Norms

Despite the apparent antique or late antique pedigree of Firdawsī's *Shāhnāmah*, it also reflects its more immediate medieval Perso-Islamic milieu and its norms of kingship. Żahhāk, in violating these norms, is considerably more human (and less demonic) a monster-king in this telling than the above-discussed Zoroastrian ones, which itself may reflect these medieval, Perso-Islamic norms as much as the more demonic, earlier descriptions of him reflected the norms of Zoroastrian antiquity. Of course, as even the "Perso" in "Perso-Islamic" suggests, these norms (and the status of kingship itself) are the result of an interaction between pre-Islamic Persian elements and subsequent Islamic influences, the fusion of which led to the development of the high culture of the great Islamic empires from the ʿAbbasid period onward. However, that culture is more likely the distinctly medieval result of a fusion and mutual influence between these two elements rather than a unidirectional influence of antique sources upon a medieval artifact.

A. C. S. Peacock's recent study "Firdawsi's *Shahnama* in its Ghaznavid Context" concludes that Firdawsī's *Shāhnāmah* is more comparable to other Ghaznavid sources in form and content than is usually recognized (2–12). Moreover, in her *Medieval Reception of the Shāhnāma*, Nasrin Askari has argued that its medieval reception indicates that "the *Shāhnāma* was primarily understood as a book of wisdom and advice for kings and courtly elites," in which light it "enhances our understanding of the development of major concepts related to kingship and statecraft in later Perso-Islamic literature of wisdom and advice for rulers" (5). The *Shāhnāmah* advises kings in favor of virtues including honesty, calmness, trustworthiness, softspokenness, and humility (Khaleghi-Motlagh). It additionally dictates that a "good man must wish for the world what he wishes for himself" and that "food should be taken sparingly" (Khaleghi-Motlagh). As we will see, Żaḥḥāk violates many of these directives: he not only kills his father, but does so by trickery (proving himself to be dishonest in addition to ambitious), eats to excess rather than taking food sparingly, reacts with violence rather than calm, and ultimately wishes destruction for the world and survival for himself.

Describing Żaḥḥāk

Żaḥḥāk enters the *Shāhnāmah* in fully human form as the son of the Arab king Mardās. This early description is hardly flattering, even if it affirms his humanity: where his father is pure-hearted (*pākdil*), Żaḥḥāk is impure (*nāpāk*): "this pure-hearted one (*īn pākdil*) had a bad son [*pisar-i bad*] to whom there was not but a little kindness (*kish az mihr bahrah nabūd andakī*). This ambitious one had the name Żaḥḥāk (*jahānjūī rā nām-i Żaḥḥāk būd*). He was impetuous, unsteady, and impure (*dalīr u sabuksār u nāpāk būd*)" (Firdawsī 27–28). At the outset, it bears noting that, unlike in Harman's reading of Lovecraft, in Firdawsī, the language used to describe our monster does not admit a gap between description and reality; rather than saying Żaḥḥāk was *like* something (or someone) bad or impure, the passage says he simply *was* bad or impure, repeatedly using *būd*, the simple past tense form of the Persian verb "to be," where it could, conceivably, have used another verb (provided, of course, that that verb abided by the rules of rhyme and meter demanded by classical poetics).

One day, Satan (called Iblīs, an Arabic term ultimately derived from the Greek *diabolos* in this passage) appears to him as a well-wisher (*bi-sān-i nīkkhʷāh*) (Firdawsī 28). While the reader knows that the well-wisher is in fact Iblīs, Żaḥḥāk does not: as the text says of his first conversation with the devil; "He so welcomed his [the devil's] words [that] he was not aware of his evil behavior (*Hamānā khush āmadash guftār-i ūī/Nabūd āgah az zisht kardār-i ūī*)" (Firdawsī 28). With his eloquence, Iblīs convinces Żaḥḥāk that he would be a worthy advisor, but makes him swear to obey his advice on becoming king before offering details of the specific advice, taking advantage of Żaḥḥāk's aforementioned stupidity and ambition. Żaḥḥāk thus consents to patricide before he even knows rising to the throne would require him to kill his father (Firdawsī 28–29). While his agreement to commit patricide and regicide initiates the narrative motion of the story and begins Żaḥḥāk's transition to monstrosity, before analyzing Żaḥḥāk himself any further, it may make sense to pause here to discuss the significance of the devil in this account.

After Żaḥḥāk kills his father and takes "the Arab crown," the devil returns in the form of a young man offering his services as a cook, who impresses Żaḥḥāk with his skills in cooking meat and eggs, which fortify Żaḥḥāk's constitution (Davis 10). He offers to pay the cook with whatever gift he requests. To this, the cook only requests to kiss Żaḥḥāk's shoulders. Then, "Two black snakes rose from his shoulders. It turned painful and he sought help from every corner (*daw mār-i sīyah az daw kitfash birust/ghamī gasht vaz har su'ī chārī just*)" (Firdawsī 32). Seeking a relief from the pain caused by these serpents, "He finally cut both from his shoulder (*saranjām bi-burīd har daw zi kift*)" (Firdawsī 32). However, upon their removal, "Like the branch of a tree those two black snakes rose another time from the shoulders of the king (*Chaw shākh-i dirakht ān daw mār-i sīyāh/bar āmad digar bārah az kift-i shāh*)" (Firdawsī 32). In the face of these snakes' reappearance, the available court physicians were left clueless, and the devil took this opportunity to return to the court in the form of a doctor. He then told the king that there was no removing the snakes and that instead, feeding them would be the only way to manage the pain they caused.

This account of Żaḥḥāk's origins distinguishes Firdawsī's telling from earlier sources. In the pre-medieval Zoroastrian accounts, Żaḥḥāk enters the narrative as a demon, dragon, or descendant of Angra Mainyu, but here he instead starts out as a human and then acquires his monstrosity when the snakes grow from his shoulders (though his moral and intellectual shortcomings can probably be figured as the seeds of his monstrosity). Laurie Pierce notes that "the *Shahnameh*'s narrative of Żaḥḥāk is unique and compelling in its own right" because, unlike the earlier Zoroastrian accounts, Firdawsī's telling, "portrays the demonic as something the king *becomes*, not as something that he *is*" (355). I, however, read this transition as one to monstrosity, instead of a process of "demonification," as Pierce terms it, because the terms the text uses to refer to Żaḥḥāk describe him as a human-dragon (or human-serpent) hybrid rather than a demon (355). It is not unreasonable to read demonic elements into Żaḥḥāk, as Pierce does, but the text does not explicitly call him a demon, while it does call him "dragon-bodied" and "dragon-natured."

To return to this paper's opening question ("a king or a monster?"), it is worth noting that the Persian phrase used in that passage hints at certain elements Davis's English does not. If we proceed from the assumption that a monster is, among other things, a human-animal hybrid, the Persian line *tu shāhī va-gar azhdahā paykarī/bi-bāyad bidīn dāvarī* suggests this hybridity more strongly: a more literal translation into English would ask not if Żaḥḥāk is a king or a monster, but instead if he is a king, *shāh*, or someone "dragon-bodied," *azhdahā paykar*. This term, *azhdahā paykar*, also speaks to a certain ambiguity between kingship and its representation; while here it refers directly to Żaḥḥāk, it can, according to the *Encyclopaedia Iranica*, also refer to a military banner depicting an *azhdahā* to frighten opposing forces (Skjærvø). Regardless, inasmuch as Żaḥḥāk fuses kingly and draconic elements and is monstrous in his hybridity; elsewhere, the Firdawsī describes him as "dragon-natured" (*azhdahā-fash*; Firdawsī 35).

Neither kingship nor the conquest of Iran sate Żaḥḥāk's bloodlust; as king he "knew nothing other than wickedness, killing, plunder, and burning (*Nadānast juz-i kazhī āmūkhtan/Juz az kushtan u ghārat u sukhtan*)" (Firdawsī 35). His impulses to destroy, moreover, intersect with his monstrous compulsion to eat:

> [Zaḥḥāk was] so bad that every night, the cook would bring two young men, whether minors or from the seed of champions, to the shah's court in order to make the shah's cure. He would kill them and remove their brain to prepare food to feed that dragon (*Chinān bad kih har shab du mard-i javān chih kihtar chih az tukhmah-yi pahlavān/Khurishgar biburdī bih īvān-i shāh vazu sākhtī rah-i darmān-i shāh/bikushtī va maghzash bipardākhtī mar ān azhdahā rā khurish sākhtī*). (Firdawsī 35)

As in the above passage where the devil's culinary abilities make way for Żaḥḥāk's monstrous transformation, this section links the violent impulses represented by the text's claim "knew nothing other than wickedness, killing, plunder, and burning" to Żaḥḥāk's immoderate appetites, here represented by his nightly need to feed his snakes. The text explicitly links his compulsion to eat, the need for a "cure" (the passage's *darmān*) to monstrosity by also calling that cure "feeding the dragon" (*azhdahā rā khurish sākhtī*). In linking his need to "feed the dragon" to the fact that he was so bad, this passage highlights the connection between Żaḥḥāk's moral failures as a prince and king and the physical dimension of his monstrosity, the shoulder snakes and the related comparisons to a dragon (both in this passage and in the passage where Kāvah asks if he is a king or a dragon). Moreover, this description is again quite direct in linking Żaḥḥāk's evil to his monstrosity; it does not say, "Żaḥḥāk was so bad that it was *as if* he were a dragon who ate youths' brains;" it says Żaḥḥāk "[was] so bad that every night, the cook would bring two young men [. . .] to the shah's court [. . .] He would kill them and remove their brain to prepare food to feed that dragon," simply identifying Żaḥḥāk as a dragon rather than something dragon-like. It not only links Żaḥḥāk's evil and his monstrosity, but does so without hinting at a tension between Żaḥḥāk's reality and those aspects of it that can be described.

Arnavāz and Shahrnāz

Żaḥḥāk's evil is not limited to physical violence, either. After his conquest of Iran, Żaḥḥāk corrupts Jamshīd's two daughters (or sisters, depending on the edition of the text), Arnavāz and Shahrnāz, by teaching them magic: "Two pure [ones] from the house of Jamshīd were taken out trembling like a willow [leaf] (*Daw pākīzah az khānah-yi Jamshīd/Burūn āvarīdand larzān chaw bīd*)" (Firdawsī 35). These two were "both sisters to Jamshīd and were like officers among ladies (*Jamshīd rā har daw khʷāhar budand/Sar-i bānuvān chaw afsar budand*)" (Firdawsī 35). After they were brought to Żaḥḥāk's court, he "Trained them in the way of wickedness [and] taught them trickery and magic (*Biparvardishān az rah-i bad khūy/Biāmūkhtishān tunbul u jādūī*)" (Firdawsī 35). Once introduced, the link between magic and Arnavāz and Shahrnāz persists without further influence from Żaḥḥāk.

One of the sisters next appears when Żaḥḥāk sees Faraydūn, the hero who eventually defeats him, in a dream, extending the link between women, magic, and dreams. Late one night, while Żaḥḥāk "was asleep with Arnavāz (*bi-khʷāb andarūn būd bā Arnavāz*)," "thus he saw: that from the branch of kings, three warriors were suddenly coming (*Chinān dīd kaz shākh-i shāhanshahān/Sih jangī padīd āmadī nāgahān*)" (Firdawsī 37). One of these, "with the height of a cypress and the visage of a king (*bi-bālā-yi sarv u bi-chihr-i kīyān*)," who "went quickly toward Żaḥḥāk for war" (*damān pīsh-i Żaḥḥāk raftī bi-jang*)," "struck his head with an ox-shaped mace [Faraydūn famously wields an ox-headed mace] (*zadī bar sarash gurzah-yi gāv-rang*)" (Firdawsī 37). When Żaḥḥāk tells Arnavāz of his dream, she first comforts him, assuring him that there are no threats to his power, but then suggests that he summon astrologers (*akhtar-shināsān*) and priests (*mawbidān*) to interpret his dream (Firdawsī 38). After this scene, neither woman appears again until Żaḥḥāk's defeat.

Shahrnāz appears by Faraydūn's side when defeats Żaḥḥāk, but even in siding against Żaḥḥāk (who taught her magic in the first place), her association with sorcery remains. When Żaḥḥāk returned to his palace, "he saw that black narcissus Shahrnāz, full of magic, hidden with Faraydūn (*bi-dīd ān sīyah nargis Shahrnāz/pur az jādūī bā Farīdūn bi-nāz*)" (Firdawsī et al. 59).[2] Thus, even after siding with Faraydūn against Żaḥḥāk, Shahrnāz's link to magic persists, as she appears "full of magic" when spotted with Faraydūn.

Killing Barmāyah

Żaḥḥāk's reaction to the priest's interpretation of the dream he has in bed with Arnavāz further cements his reputation for violence and distinguishes him from his father, which in turn further opposes him to royal virtue. On first hearing his dream, the assembled astrologers and priests find themselves unable to speak for fear of his reaction to their confirmation of the dream's truth, but eventually, one, Zīrak, first attempts to remind Żaḥḥāk that all kings are mortal, but then identifies the figure who defeated him in his dream as the soon-to-be-born Faraydūn, who would be nursed by the mythical cow Barmāyah (Firdawsī 39–40). This leads Żaḥḥāk to order a search for Faraydūn, with the hope of killing his would-be enemy before he is old enough to rise against him. When Żaḥḥāk's men capture and kill Faraydūn's father, his mother sends him into hiding, giving him to the keeper of the meadow where Barmāyah lives. Knowing that Barmāyah would help raise Faraydūn, upon learning of Barmāyah's location, Żaḥḥāk again indulges his violent impulses; although Faraydūn and his mother had already fled, Żaḥḥāk destroys the meadow and kills the cow.

The description of Żaḥḥāk in this passage likens him to an animal, which may serve as additional evidence of his monstrosity, given that monsters are often figured as human-animal hybrids. When news of Barmāyah and the meadow reached Żaḥḥāk, "he came, full of malevolence like a furious elephant" and "crushed that very cow Barmāyah (*Bīāmad pur az kīnah chūn pīl-i mast/Mar ān gāv Barmāyah kard past*)," after which, "everything, whatever he saw on four legs, he scattered and finished (*Hamah*

---

2. In some editions, this couplet concludes *bi-rāz* rather than *bi-nāz*. This lends itself to a more obvious translation of "in secret," as *rāz* mainly means "secret" or "hidden," while the most familiar use of *nāz* refers to coquetry rather than hiding or concealment. However, *nāz* can also be used as "dissimulation."

har chih dīd andarū char pāy/Bīafgand u zīshān bipardakht jāy)" (Firdawsī 42).
In addition to the specific language in this passage describing Żaḥḥāk's an-
imalistic ferocity, this activity may deepen the contrast between Żaḥḥāk
and a virtuous king.

The association of his monstrosity with his drives to consume flesh
and kill animals links Firdawsī's Żaḥḥāk to Negarestani's, who, as discussed above, symbolizes "the demonic," which "is only attainable by be-
coming-chef or returning to the culinary aspects of matter" (Negarestani
189). In this, Żaḥḥāk is simply one example of *Cyclonopedia*'s broader
theme, since, as a text in general, "*Cyclonopedia* stuffs a 'Good Meal or
ambrosia plaue [. . .] gourmandized in the abattoir of openness,' a spicy
immolated synthesis of what divinity eats 'up there' and punishes the
world with 'down here'" (Masciandaro 185). Negarestani thus makes
Żaḥḥāk an avatar of the demonic by presenting his transgressions as one
particular iteration of a wider cosmic tendency toward butchery and consumption; something metaphysical, and therefore ontological. In contrast,
Firdawsī's Żaḥḥāk still has human origins, which leads to an assessment in
ethical, rather than ontological terms: for Firdawsī, he is a bad prince who
becomes a bad king, with his monstrous blending of the human and the
animal indexing his transition into tyranny and violence.

While in Firdawsī we have already seen that Żaḥḥāk's consumption of
meat occasions his transition from man to monster by creating the conditions under which the devil, disguised as the cook that introduces him to
meat-eating, can kiss his shoulders and thereby make serpents grow from
them, but in this passage, Żaḥḥāk kills a cow, which may represent a definitive break with his father, Mardās, who raised cattle for dairy rather than
killing them for meat.

Firdawsī links Mardās's ability to preserve animal life to the virtue of
his kingship: "of the four-legged creatures fit for milking he had, from
each one a thousand would come" (*Mar ū rā zi dūshīdanī-yi chār pāy/Zi har
yik hizār āmadandī bi-jāy*); his herds, moreover, served as evidence of
Mardās's generosity, as this passage goes on to say he "had given [these
thousands] to the shepherds," whether they were "goats, camels, or sheep
(*Buz u ushtur u mīsh hamchawnīn/Bi-dūshandigān dādah bud pākdīn*) (Firdawsī
28). Rather than giving them to shepherds for milking, Żaḥḥāk chooses to
eliminate all this same class of animal ("four-legged" or *chār pāy* beings)
from the meadow where Faraydūn had hidden. Thus, the text defines
Żaḥḥāk's relationship to livestock in terms of his murderous drives while it

uses the relationship between Mardās and livestock as evidence of his generosity. However, even if to contrast him with his father Mardās, Firdawsī still references Żaḥḥāk's *human* parentage, breaking with both pre-Islamic myth and Negarestani, which ascribe to Żaḥḥāk demonic (and thus fully inhuman) origins.

Żaḥḥāk as Counter-Sovereign

As seen above, the recent adoption of modern horror fiction by contemporary philosophers associated with speculative realism has granted a new philosophical significance to the language used to describe monsters, and this significance may extend to Żaḥḥāk, if only indirectly. The philosophical adoption of modern horror fiction (including Lovecraft) by thinkers like Eugene Thacker, Graham Harman, and Reza Negarestani has tended toward the ontological; they view it as particularly capable of revealing the limits of human thought and the Real's ability to both exceed and intrude upon these limits, while Askari's recent study of the *Shāhnāmah* has interpreted it as ethical literature. However, identifying Żaḥḥāk as a counter-sovereign may be the best way to synthesize these two apparently disparate intellectual trends. Speaking historically, if we accept the hypothesis that medieval audiences received the *Shāhnāmah* as a mirror for princes, the text's focus on Żaḥḥāk's many vices suggests that it frames him in opposition to the kings whose virtues it lauds. Thacker's conception of the counter-sovereign (for him a particular class of demon) may provide an additional link between the *Shāhnāmah* and recent theory. In *In the Dust of This Planet*, Thacker takes Dis, the "giant, grotesque, brooding, arch-emperor" in Dante's *Inferno*, who is as "centralized and transcendent to that which he governs" as the divine sovereign, to be the paradigmatic counter-sovereign (31–32). Żaḥḥāk's father Mardās and his people were pastoralists who mainly subsisted on dairy, but Żaḥḥāk's meat-eating (to say nothing of his snakes' brain-eating) and killing of the legendary cow Barmāyah represents a break with this lifestyle: Iblīs ingratiates himself with Żaḥḥāk in the form of a cook, who takes to feeding meat to Żaḥḥāk, in the process ending humanity's original vegetarianism. This shift, alongside Żaḥḥāk's other vices, may serve to frame Żaḥḥāk as a counter-sovereign: where Mardās was a wise, generous, just, ruler who led his people in a *modus vivendi* that did not necessitate taking life, Żaḥḥāk, the ambitious, patricidal fool, starts living off of the flesh of others. Just as Dis is as central to the order of his section of the *Inferno* as the divine sovereign is to Paradise, Żaḥḥāk is as central to this section of the *Shāhnāmah* as the Iranian kings that precede and follow him are to theirs, and like Dis, Żaḥḥāk finds himself led, by his vices, into a "cycle of transgression and blasphemy against the Creator": he is wrathful, foolish, and gluttonous, where, according to the norms of medieval Persian literature on kingship, kings were expected to be magnanimous, wise, and moderate in their consumption (Thacker 31–32).

Like Harman, I see our chosen authors' style of description as philosophically significant. However, in Firdawsī's case the language tends to emphasize questions of vice and virtue rather than the question of the accessibility of objects to human subjects (as is the case for Harman's study of Lovecraft). We could imagine Firdawsī relying entirely upon the earlier Zoroastrian descriptions, emphasizing Żaḥḥāk's physical qualities and demonic origin, presenting him as "a dragon-like (*aži*) monster with three mouths (*θrizafanəm*), three heads (*θrikamarəδəm*), six eyes (*xšuuaš.ašīm*), with a thousand viles (*hazaŋrā.yaoxštīm*), very strong (*aš.aojaŋhəm*), a demoniac devil (*daēuuīm drujim*)," as in the *Avesta*, or, according to the genealogy provided by the *Bundahišn*, descended from "the Evil Spirit himself" (Skjærvø). But, because the *Shāhnāmah* is about how kings are supposed to act and can be situated within the medieval mirrors for princes genre, Firdawsī instead emphasizes the moral dimension to the Żaḥḥāk story and presents Żaḥḥāk as a figure with human origins. In this account, Żaḥḥāk is not descended from "the Evil Spirit" himself, but is the "impure" (*nāpāk*), "bad son" (*pisar-i bad*) of the pure-hearted (*pākdil*) king Mardās. He is not born a dragon, but instead, the snakes rise from his shoulders at a specific point in the narrative, making his body mirror the escalation of his violence. Despite Firdawsī's reputation for having "rescued" Iran's pre-Islamic myths, I would argue that this description of Żaḥḥāk is considerably more Islamic (and therefore medieval) than its predecessors. Those predecessors situated Żaḥḥāk within Zoroastrian's intricate angelology and demonology and in many cases avoided discussing human origins, or at least included Ahriman in his genealogy. Firdawsī, meanwhile, gives Żaḥḥāk a specifically human genealogy and situates his evil not in Zoroastrian demonology, but instead, personal shortcomings, and, notably, deception by the specifically Islamic devil designated by the term Iblīs.

The differences in the descriptions of their monsters may also reflect the differences in genre between Lovecraft and Firdawsī; the late Marxist theorist Mark Fisher once hypothesized that the Lovecraftian Weird could be distinguished from the fantastic on the following grounds: "Fantasy [. . .] is set in Worlds that are entirely different from ours"; if, in some fantasy writing, "there is an egress between this world and the other," in "Lovecraft, there is an interplay, an exchange between this world and others" (Fisher). Unlike modern fantasy or horror fiction, though, Firdawsī purported to be writing about this world; even if Żaḥḥāk appears in the first, mythic portion of the *Shāhnāmah* rather than its later historical section (roughly the last third of the text), it still claims to narrate the formation of the world of human history, which also happens to be the location of the conflict between good and evil. This may, in part, be why Żaḥḥāk can be distinguished from other people on ethical grounds rather than ontological ones; unlike a Lovecraftian monster, he is a human too, from the same order of being as other people, and as a result, his monstrosity is the result of his choices, and not the result of the fact that he exists on a completely different cosmic scale than humans as is the case with Iblīs in this text or with Cthulhu in Lovecraft.

Works Cited

Ames, Robert Landau. "On Monstrosity in the Shāhnāmah: Philosophizing with Żaḥḥāk." In Albrecht Classen, ed. *Imagination and Fantasy in the Middle Ages and Early Modern Time Projections, Dreams, Monsters, and Illusions.* Berlin: de Gruyter 2020. 355-76.

Ashraf, Ahmed. "Iranian Identity: iii. Medieval Islamic Period." *Encyclopaedia Iranica*, 2012. iranicaonline.org/articles/iranian-identity-iii-medieval-islamic-period. Accessed 4 December 2019.

Askari, Nasrin. *The Medieval Reception of the Shāhnāma as a Mirror for Princes.* Leiden: E. J. Brill, 2016.

Asmussen, Jes Peter. "Āz." *Encyclopaedia Iranica*, 1987. iranicaonline.org/articles/az-iranian-demon. Accessed 4 December 2019.

Brookshaw, Dominic Parviz. "Mytho-Political Remakings of Ferdowsi's Jamshid in the Lyric Poetry of Injuid and Mozaffarid Shiraz." *Iranian Studies* 48 (2015): 463-87.

Browne, Edward Granville. *A Literary History of Persia.* Cambridge: Cambridge University Press, 1956.

Clark, Fraser. "From Epic to Romance, via Filicide? Rustam's Character Formation." *Iranian Studies* 43, No. 1 (2010): 53-70.

Clinton, Jerome W., and Marianna S. Simpson. "How Rostam Killed the White Div: An Interdisciplinary Inquiry." *Iranian Studies* 39 (2006): 171-97.

Cross, Cameron. "'If Death is Just, What Is Injustice?' Illicit Rage in 'Rostam and Sohrab' and 'The Knight's Tale.'" *Iranian Studies* 48 (2015): 395-422.

Fisher, Mark. "Lovecraft and the Weird: Part I." *K-punk*, 2007. k-punk.org/lovecraft-and-the-weird-part-i. Accessed 8 December 2019.

Harman, Graham. *Weird Realism: Lovecraft and Philosophy*. Alresford, UK: Zero Books, 2012.

Hayes, Edmund. "The Death of Kings: Group Identity and the Tragedy of Nezhād in Ferdowsi's Shahnameh." *Iranian Studies* 48 (2015): 369-93.

Heckman, Davin. "Glossary." *Rhizomes* 5 (2002). www.rhizomes.net/issue5/poke/glossary.html. Accessed 4 December 2019.

Hodgson, Marshall G. S. *The Venture of Islam: Conscience and History in a World Civilization, Volume Two: The Expansion of Islam in the Middle Periods*. Chicago: University of Chicago Press, 1974.

Khaleghi-Motlagh, Djalal. "ADABP i. Adab in Iran." *Encyclopaedia Iranica* I (April 1983): 432-39. An updated version is available online at iranicaonline.org/articles/adab-i-iran (last accessed 5 April 2019).

Mahallati, Mohammad Jafar Amir, "Ethics of War and Peace in the Shahnameh of Ferdowsi." *Iranian Studies* 48 (2015): 905-31.

Masciandaro, Nicola. "Gourmandized in the Abattoir of Openness" In Eugene Thacker et al. *Leper Creativity: Cyclonopedia Symposium*. Brooklyn: Punctum Books, 2012. 181-91.

Melville, Charles. "Rashīd al-Dīn and the *Shāhnāmeh*." *Journal of the Royal Asiatic Society* 3 (2016): 201-14.

Negarestani, Reza. *Cyclonopedia: Complicity with Anonymous Materials*. London: Re.press, 2008.

Peacock, Andrew Charles Spencer. "Firdawsi's *Shahnama* in its Ghaznavid Context." *Iran: Journal of the British Institute of Persian Studies* 56 (2018): 2-12.

Pierce, Laurie. "Serpents and Sorcery: Humanity, Gender, and the Demonic in Ferdowsi's Shahnameh." *Iranian Studies* 48 (2015): 349-67.

Poliakova. E. A. "The Development of a Literary Canon in Medieval Persian Chronicles: The Triumph of Etiquette." *Iranian Studies* 17 (1984): 237–56.

Rypka, Jan. *History of Iranian Literature*. Dordrecht: D. Reidel, 1968.

Skjærvø, Prods Oktor, Djalal Khaleghi-Motlagh, and James Russell. "Aždahā." *Encyclopedia Iranica* 3 No. 2, iranicaonline.org/articles/azdaha-dragon-various-kinds. Accessed 5 April 2019.

Tafażżolī, Ahmad. "Ferēdūn." *Encyclopedia Iranica* IX (May 1999). iranicaonline.org/articles/feredu-. Accessed 4 December 2019.

Tavakoli-Targhi, Mohamad. "Contested Memories: Narrative Structures and Allegorical Meanings of Iran's Pre-Islamic History." *Iranian Studies* 29 (1996): 149–75.

Thacker, Eugene. *In the Dust of This Planet*. Alresford, UK: Zero Books, 2011.

den Uijl, Sebastiaan. "The Trickster 'Archetype' in the *Shahnama*." *Iranian Studies* 43 (2010): 71–90.

van Zutphen, Marjolijn. *Faramarz, the Sistani Hero: Texts and Traditions of the Faramarzname and the Persian Epic Cycle*. Leiden: E. J. Brill, 2014.

The Influence of The Great Game on the Writings of H. P. Lovecraft: The Opening of Tibet and the Creation of Leng

Benjamin Davis
Independent Scholar

Geopolitical events surrounding the Great Game and the opening of Tibet in the nineteenth and early twentieth centuries shaped literature in profound ways, from inspiring Rudyard Kipling's *Kim* to James Hilton's *Lost Horizon*. The Great Game was the geopolitical competition for wealth and power in Asia between the Russian and British Empires (*TGG* 102). It saw both empires' holdings vastly expanded, the eventual creation of new countries, and the opening of previously closed ones, such as Tibet. *Kim*, the most famous example of literature inspired by the Great Game, was published in 1901, when Lovecraft was eleven years old. In 1907 the Great Game was considered concluded with the establishment of borders between the two empires and the opening of Tibet to the West. Tibet had been a place sealed off from outsiders for more than a century (*TRW* 56). However, its opening provided inspiration for various occult movements throughout Europe and the Americas, especially the Theosophical Society. Occult writings, literature, and art all drew on inspiration from Tibet's unique culture, mythology, and religious beliefs. The influence of the Great Game and the opening of Tibet provided critical inspiration for many of the works and settings created by H. P. Lovecraft.

Imperial Competition

As the British and Russian Empires vied for control of Asia, they began to conquer or control more and more territory. Britain did so to develop trade routes into the Asian heartland and to create buffer states out of fear for its valuable Indian possessions. Russia did so out of a desire for prestige and wealth as well as to potentially make itself able to threaten India if needed in wartime. The Golden Age of the Great Game lasted from the 1860s to 1907, though it had begun decades before. During this time as it became more widely discussed in newspapers, more and more amateur adventurers began to explore and map out previously unknown corners of Asia for their own prestige, for king and country, and for missionary efforts. Many wrote books or published accounts in newspapers, romanticizing their adventures. This only spread knowledge of British and Russian activities, which further fueled more adventurers to try their luck in filling out what to them were blank places on the map.

There was far less control of borders and migration at the time, and an enterprising adventurer could get quite far in their own explorations. Tsar Nicholas I of Russia is recorded as saying, "Where the imperial flag has once flown, it must never be lowered." Therefore, many enterprising Russians moved to "raise the two-headed eagle first, and ask permission afterwards. Those who did just that found that they were rarely, if ever, repudiated" (TGG 295). Many on the British side published their travelogues and tales of adventure. One popular account was *A Ride to Khiva* by Frederick Burnaby, published in 1876. Burnaby, a man of enormous size and strength, a polyglot with a taste for adventure, made a name for himself in the British Army and press. On multiple occasions while on military leave, he would visit faraway locales and write reports for British newspapers. During one such period of leave he decided to visit Central Asia, with his book being a product of that visit. It became a bestseller at the time and subsequently fueled interest by others in Britain and around the world to take their own adventure. These published accounts also piqued the interest of another set of adventurers. Missionaries from Victorian-era Europe sought to spread the gospel to these isolated and exotic lands. Some also published their own accounts. Two of the more famous ones include Annie Royale Taylor's *Pioneering in Tibet* (1898) and Susanna Carson Rijnhart's *With the Tibetans in Tent and Temple* (1901).

The latter part of the Great Game, from 1890 to 1895, saw the British and Russian Empires exchanging notes that defined their individual spheres of influence in Central Asia, later codified by the Pamir Boundary Commission in 1895 (TGG 499). What remained though was Tibet and the exploration of it. Tibet had been periodically closed to foreigners throughout the preceding centuries and had been completely closed since 1795. This meant that on most maps it remained *terra incognita*. The British desired to fill in the blank spaces on the map because they feared the recent Russian advances put their holdings across the Indian subcontinent in jeopardy. Protecting these holdings required understanding access across the mountains and deserts to the north (*TGG* 329–32). The Russians desired to explore Tibet following the Treaty of Tarbagatai they signed and updated 1864, which brought Russian borders to Central Asia. After this, the British eventually came upon the idea of using "native explorers to carry out clandestine surveys of the lawless regions beyond India's frontiers" (*TGG* 329). These efforts which began in the 1860s, only intensified over the ensuing decades.

The rush of adventurers continued as Tibet became known as the place to reach, with accounts of these attempts filled with the supernatural and mystical. Because of difficulties with weather and geography, or simply being turned away by Tibetan border guards, some explorers tried several times. Attempts by private citizens to reach Tibet illegally decreased after Britain ended up waging a punitive campaign against Tibet from 1903 to 1904. In the 1904 Convention Between Great Britain and Tibet that the two countries signed, the British set up trade posts in several cities, and the Tibetans had to allow foreign travelers, as approved by the British, access to the country (*TRW* 190–91).

Occultism and the Arts

At same time, the United States was facing a wave of religious upheaval. Professor Bruce F. Campbell, in *Ancient Wisdom Revealed: A History of the Theosophical Movement*, described it thus:

> the religious situation was one of challenge to orthodox Christianity. The forces that had surfaced in spiritualism included anticlericalism, antiinstitutionalism, eclecticism, social liberalism, and belief in progress and individual effort. Occultism, mediated to America in the form of Mesmerism, Swedenborgianism, Freemasonry, and Rosicrucianism, was present. Recent developments in science led by the 1870s to renewed interest in reconciling science and religion. There was present also a hope that Asian religious ideas could be integrated into a grand religious synthesis. (20)

One of these forms of occultism, Theosophy, was in part inspired by its founder's alleged travels into Tibet. In November 1875, Helena P. Blavatsky and Henry Olcott formed the Theosophical Society in New York City. Olcott hoped "that the society would 'aid in freeing the public mind of theological superstition and a tame subservience to the arrogance of science'" (Campbell 29). Initially the society's goals were for the "study of Occultism, and Cabbala, etc." (Campbell 27). The society and its leadership also had an interest in studying Eastern Religious traditions and in 1879, Blavatsky and Olcott moved to India. Theosophy spread rapidly, with twenty-three countries founding National Societies in its first thirty years of existence.

Furthering this expansion and interest in Theosophy, Blavatsky published a number of books and papers from the 1870s until her death in 1891. The most important included the founding texts of Theosophy, *Isis Unveiled* and *The Secret Doctrine*. These works fueled interest across the Western world of Theosophy, occultism, and Tibet. Blavatsky's own stories of Tibet, which excited the imaginations of many, were only part of the allure. Until 1907 Tibet had been a forbidden and unknown land to most people in the West (*TRW* 1–2). It developed a highly unique culture and belief system because of its unique geography, climate, and religions. Buddhism is the most well-known religion in Tibet, but Bon, the "devil-worshipping, shamanistic religion practiced by Tibetans before the arrival of Buddhism" (*TRW* 12), provided ample material for occultist books. These were all strange and exotic to Western audiences. Some practices such as sky burials, whereby the dead are dismembered to feed vultures and wolves or tops of skulls are used as drinking cups and bowls, were exciting to audiences at the time and are still considered in most parts of the world to be highly unusual and exotic (*TRW* 16–18). Furthermore, Tibetan mythology and folklore included stories of the ability of certain holy monks to fly, to use their minds to heat their bodies so as to survive without clothing in the high mountains, or of sorcerers reanimating the dead. One of Blavatsky's students published a popular book relating these tales. *Magic and Mystery in Tibet* (1932) by Alexandra David-Néel recounts her own travels to Tibet and her experiences with the supernatural and mystical.

While interest in occultism was rapidly growing and Tibet was opening to the West, the Russian painter Nicholas Roerich was introduced to Theosophy by his wife, Helena, in St. Petersburg. Their interest in Eastern religions, Theosophy, and the occult grew with the outbreak of World War I and the Russian Revolution. These events fueled apocalyptic and occult followings throughout Russia. This influence can be found in his paintings, short stories, and poems written following his introduction to occultism in the early 1900s and accelerating through 1914–17. Initially part of the Gorky Commission and the Petrograd Soviet, he moved to the countryside near the Finnish border due to illness; after the rise of the Bolshevik Party, Roerich and his family emigrated to Finland. From there they moved through Scandinavia, settling eventually in London. There they joined a chapter of the Theosophical Society and founded their own school of mysticism, Agni Yoga (Andreyev 293). Shortly afterward they decided to emigrate to the United States, and from his painting work in London he gained the attention of the Art Institute of Chicago, which offered to arrange a tour of the United States. The Roerichs lived in the US from 1920 to 1923, where Roerich toured extensively. During that time, Nicholas and Helena envisaged his

> "Great Plan," of unification of millions of Asian peoples through a religious movement using the Future Buddha, or Maitreya, into a "Sacred Union of the East." Here, the King of Shambhala would, following the Maitreya prophecies, make his appearance to fight a great battle against all evil forces on Earth [. . .] According to Roerich, the same Mahatmas revealed to him in 1922 that he was an incarnation of the Fifth Dalai Lama. (Andreyev 294)

This inspired the Roerichs to move in 1923 from New York to Darjeeling, India, where Nicholas began to paint the Himalayas and to meet many influential British and Tibetans, including some who were part of the opening of Tibet. But within a year, they decided to return to the US, stopping in Berlin on the way. There Nicholas approached the Soviet Embassy and asked for assistance in conducting an expedition through Soviet Central Asia into Tibet. Through 1924, the Roerichs remained in New York, founding various institutions of the arts, civics, spiritual groups, and even an art school (Andreyev 293).

In 1925, with Soviet assistance confirmed, the Roerichs left New York yet again. Traveling to Russia, they crossed Siberia and entered Mongolia. The expedition lasted from 1925 to 1929. They made it to Tibet but not to Lhasa. They once were held captive by the local government but were eventually allowed to depart south into India. There they founded a spiritual research center, the Himalayan Research Institute. Roerich painted all the while during this expedition and returned again to New York in 1929 (Andreyev 311–16). Following the Roerichs' return to New York, the art school they had founded five years before was converted into a museum for his artwork. His fame grew and from his membership in the Theosophical Society, he became close with President Franklin Delano

Roosevelt's Secretary of Agriculture, Henry Wallace. He also created the Pax Cultura, which was to serve as a sort of cultural and artistic Red Cross. He wished to preserve humanity's art and culture after seeing so much of it destroyed in World War I and the Russian Revolution. For this work he was nominated for the Nobel Peace Prize in 1929 and again in 1932 and 1935. Roerich continued expeditions to the Himalayas, and eventually settled in northern India.

Lovecraft's Connections

H. P. Lovecraft lived in New York from 1924 to 1926 while Roerich was on his four-year expedition, and moved back to Providence before Roerich returned. However, he visited New York on a few occasions over the next several years. In May 1930 while in New York, Lovecraft discovered Roerich's museum. He appreciated weird art, from Francisco Goya to Clark Ashton Smith, and after discovering Roerich added him to his list of admired artists. His first visit to the museum was with his friend Frank Belknap Long. He described their visit in a letter to August Derleth:

> The other day Belknap & I explored the new Roerich Museum [. . .] for the first time, & were fairly knocked out by the exotic impressiveness of the paintings therein displayed. Doubtless you know of Roerich—the Russian who has captured the mystery of remote & forbidden Thibetan uplands in art of a highly strange & original technique. (*ES* 263)

Lovecraft was so amazed by the museum that he recommended it to several of his correspondents. In a subsequent letter to Derleth, Lovecraft provided additional insight into the inspiration the museum provided him. He wrote that the museum

> is wholly devoted to the strange & mystical paintings of [. . .] Nicholas Roerich, who draws his inspiration & scenic subjects from the daemon-haunted uplands of forbidden & half-fabulous Thibet. Some of these things have a bizarre, cosmic, & eerily two-dimensional quality which allies them wholly with the land of dream as opposed to the objective world—so that they make a tremendous appeal to any lover of outré *outsideness*. (*ES* 265-66)

Roerich's paintings fired Lovecraft's imagination and helped him fuse together various ideas and subjects he had studied. In his early years he had a fascination with Antarctica and the exploration attempts going on at that time.

Tibet. Himalayas (1933) by Nicholas Roerich.

The Range (1924) by Nicholas Roerich.

Lovecraft claimed to love astronomy more than any other subject, but previously he had studied geography and geology extensively. Beginning around 1900, when Lovecraft was ten years old, he "became a passionate devotee of geography & history, & an intense fanatic on the subject of Antarctic exploration" (*RK* 69). Lovecraft reports "the *Antarctic* was my favourite region—wonder and the unknown being my ideal" (*MWM* 432). Lovecraft regarded "a fascinating land for fictional composition precisely because so little was then—and for many years later—known of it. One might imagine almost anything existing in that bleak world of ice and death" (*IAP* 76). These three subjects—Antarctica, geography, and geology—coalesced when Lovecraft saw Roerich's works. The next year he wrote *At the Mountains of Madness*, which, being set in Antarctica, uses extensive geological and geographic references. He mentions Roerich six times in the story, remarking that "something about the scene reminded me of the strange and disturbing Asian paintings of Nicholas Roerich" (*CF* 3.17–8). And "great low square blocks with exactly vertical sides, and rectangular lines of low vertical ramparts, like the old Asian castles clinging to steep mountains in Roerich's paintings" (*CF* 3.28). In describing the Plateau of Leng, he writes

> how disturbingly this lethal realm corresponded to the evilly famed plateau of Leng in the primal writings. Mythologists have placed Leng in Central Asia; but the racial memory of man—or of his predecessors—is long, and it may well be that certain tales have come down from lands and mountains and temples of horror earlier than Asia and earlier than any human world we know. (*CF* 3.51)

The scenery Roerich depicted may have compelled Lovecraft to move the Plateau of Leng to a different locale. In "The Hound," Lovecraft placed the plateau in Central Asia. Joshi wrote that this change may have occurred because Lovecraft was

> so struck by Roerich's paintings—which seemed to embody his own conception of the Plateau of Leng—that he bodily transferred both the mountains they depicted (recall that the "mountains of madness" are explicitly declared to be taller than Everest) and the plateau to the ice-bound south. He probably did not set the tale in the Himalayas themselves both because they were already becoming well known and because he wanted to create the sense of awe implicit in mountains taller than any yet discovered on the planet. Only the relatively uncharted Antarctic continent could fulfil both these functions. (*IAP* 784)

Lovecraft was also interested in Tibet and enjoyed reading about some of the strange and alien rituals performed there. These include tales from Alexandra David-Néel's book. Regarding her book, Lovecraft had written to Clark Ashton Smith:

> Thanks prodigiously for the Thibetan article, which I herewith return. I must get hold of that book somehow—it must be a veritable mine of lore. The *rolang* (ugh!) has vast fictional possibilities—I've made a note about it in my hellish book of plot-germs (*DS* 423).

At that time, Lovecraft wrote the following entry (192) in his commonplace book:

> Thibetan ROLANG—sorcerer (or NGAGSPA) reanimates a corpse by holding it in a dark room—lying on it mouth to mouth & repeating a magic formula with all else banished from his mind. Corpse slowly comes to life & stands up. Tries to escape—leaps, bounds, & struggles—but sorcerer holds it. Continues with magic formula. Corpse sticks out tongue & sorcerer bites it off. Corpse then collapses. Tongue become a valuable talisman. If corpse escapes—hideous results & death to sorcerer (*CE* 5.231).

The story is fantastic enough that he copied it almost virtually word for word from what David-Néel had written.

Finally, he mentions his fondness for geography and his attempts to make his settings as real as possible so as not to distract the reader from the story. Also, Lovecraft took ample inspiration from his own travels to spark ideas. In letters he described the power scenery had on him. For him it did not matter whether he saw it in person, in dream, or in a painting. This power over him is what led him to write

> illusions of some future ability to get down on paper that quintessence of adventurous expectancy which the sight of a sunset beyond strange towers, or a little farmhouse against a rocky hill, or a rocky monolith in Leng as drawn by Nicholas Roerich, invariably excites within me. (*SL* 3.321)

Both scenery and architecture provided critical inspiration for most of his stories. As has been written by many others, New England provided ample material for him. He wrote that inspiration for both "The Dunwich Horror" and "The Whisperer in Darkness" came from his travels around New England. He used these travels as material to be able to give his "weird tales a minutely realistic setting as a sort of foil for the unreal extravagancies of the central theme" (*JVS* 16).

As noted, Roerich's works helped to fuse ideas, and Lovecraft used such moments of serendipity or clarity and connection:

> I imagine that all arts involving a free play of fancy have much the same sort of stimuli. Stories often result from the oddest & most seemingly irrelevant ideas & glimpses. I am most often moved to composition by vague landscape, atmospheric, & architectural effects—either first-hand or in pictures—though stories, newspaper cuttings, dreams, & all sorts of other things have lain behind many of my efforts. [. . .] I think my own imagination is predominantly *geographical*, for to me there is nothing so fascinating as antiquity & unreality as manifested in the aspect of some strange *region*. (SL 4.84)

While using Roerich as an influence in his later stories, Lovecraft was also aware of the Theosophical Society and mentioned using their material for inspiration as well. In particular, he mentions Blavatsky's works, even using the supposed ancient Tibetan *Book of Dzyan*, which Blavatsky claimed inspired her *Secret Doctrine*, in "The Haunter in the Dark."

Yet of all these influences, Lovecraft shied away from setting his stories firmly anywhere in the East. When asked of submitting stories to the magazine *Oriental Tales*, Lovecraft wrote:

> *Oriental* doesn't look like much of a market for me, for I've never seemed to get captivated by the conventional "Spell of the East." To my mind the Orient is so remote that its happenings lack the sense of substance needed to produce an impression of reality. (DS 252)

If the Orient was so far removed that even Lovecraft could not visualize it when reading about it, he understood that his audience would be unable to as well. During Lovecraft's time, tales set in "the East" tended to have the same settings, culture, etc. This is another reason why Lovecraft shied away from writing about the East, as he thought few could create anything close to a convincing setting or capture its mysticism.

In his last, unfinished letter, Lovecraft wrote:

> There is no drawing a line betwixt what is to be called extreme fantasy of a traditional type & what is to be called surrealism; & I have no doubt but that the nightmare landscapes of some of the surrealists correspond, as well as any actual creations could, to the iconographic horrors attributed by sundry fictioneers to mad or daemon-haunted artists. If there were a real Richard Upton Pickman or Felix Ebbonly, I am sure he would have been represented in the recent exhibition by several blasphemous and abhorrent canvases! Better than the surrealists, though, is good old Nick Roerich, whose joint at Riverside Drive and 103rd Street is one of my shrines in the pest zone. There

is something in his handling of perspective and atmosphere which to me suggests other dimensions and alien orders of being—or at least, the gateways leading to such. Those fantastic carven stones in lonely upland deserts—those ominous, almost sentient, lines of jagged pinnacles—& above all, those curious cubical edifices clinging to the precipitous slopes and edging upward to forbidden needle-like peaks! (JFM 404)

The Great Game opened the way for adventurers, missionaries, and occultists to access previously isolated and forbidden parts of Asia. This occurred at a time of spiritual restlessness and awakening across Europe and the Americas. These ideas spawned countless spiritual and occult movements, including the previously mentioned Theosophical Society. Roerich, inspired by these movements, traveled extensively across Asia, producing hundreds of paintings in his lifetime. Lovecraft, having studied multiple fields and read widely, was aware of some of these events and had already begun writing extensively by the time Roerich established his museum. Lovecraft coming into contact with Roerich's art helped to influence future stories and fuse disparate ideas together. He came prepared, so to speak, to be influenced by Roerich's art. It helped him visualize settings for his stories, on which he placed great importance.

H. P. Lovecraft took inspiration from a wide variety of sources and expertly crafted them together. He read widely and voraciously as well as had extensive travel writing experience and personal travel across the United States. The ideas he gained from reading, correspondence, and his travels were pivotal in his creation of At the Mountains of Madness and settings such as the Plateau of Leng. Lovecraft's appreciation of geography, the occult, and Antarctica allowed him to understand and embrace ideas and art developed from the Great Game and the opening of Tibet.

Works Cited

Andreyev, Alexandre. Soviet Russia and Tibet: The Debacle of Secret Diplomacy, 1918–1930s. Leiden: E. J. Brill, 2003.

Campbell, Bruce F. Ancient Wisdom Revived: A History of the Theosophical Movement. Berkeley: University of California Press, 1980.

Hopkirk, Peter. The Great Game: The Struggle for Empire in Central Asia. New York: Kodansha International, 1994. Cited in text as TGG.

———. Trespassers on the Roof of the World: The Secret Exploration of Tibet. New York: Kodansha International, 1995. Cited in text as TRW.

The *Necronomicon Yalensis* and Lovecraft in Connecticut

Edward Guimont
University of Connecticut

Introduction

Of all the memorable phrases written by H. P. Lovecraft, "I am Providence" is not only one of the shortest, but also one of the most personal. It is the one chosen not only as the title of the definitive biography of him, but also as the inscription on his gravestone in the city's Swan Point Cemetery. But Lovecraft was not merely a Providence patriot, or even a Rhode Islander; he was a true New England Yankee. Consider that of the major works of the Cthulhu Mythos, its most notable locations (Innsmouth, Dunwich, Kingsport, Arkham with its Miskatonic University) are all in Massachusetts, and "The Whisperer in Darkness" (1930) is set in Vermont. Yet on no less than hplovecraft.com, the section on "Lovecraftian Sites in New England" has no entry for Connecticut (Loucks, *Archive*). In Jason Eckhardt's *Off the Ancient Track: A Lovecraftian Guide to New-England and Adjacent New-York*, Connecticut is truly off the ancient track, appearing only as part of the map of New England on the final page; meanwhile, Lovecraft's detested New York City gets three pages (Eckhardt 15–18). As Will Murray stated at the 1990 H. P. Lovecraft Centennial Conference, "If you are familiar with Lovecraft's stories, you know that all the great fictitious cities are in Massachusetts; there are no fictitious cities in Rhode Island or, for that matter, in Maine or New Hampshire or certainly not Connecticut—I don't think Lovecraft ever wrote of Connecticut" (Murray 15).

This, of course, is not true. Explicit references to Connecticut appear in a number of Lovecraft's stories. Connecticut remained one of the two places (along with Massachusetts) outside Rhode Island that Lovecraft had been to by the age of twenty-five (MWM 47). Further, he had several personal connections to the Nutmeg State. Most prominently, but not exclusively, his friend Robert Moe lived in Bridgeport (*ET* 300) and his friend and fellow amateur journalist Michael White lived in Torrington (Faig 88). Friend and occasional co-author Henry S. Whitehead attended seminary in Middletown and served as rector of Episcopal churches there as well as in Torrington and Bridgeport at various points over the period 1912–25 (Barlow vii–viii). Although Lovecraft was dismissive of New London (*MWM* 84), it had been home to the playwright Eugene O'Neill (Richter 25–26) and the Frank Munsey magazines (Richter 10–11), both admired by Lovecraft (Waugh 311–68; Callaghan 69–71).[1] Most dramatically, Lovecraft and his wife Sonia saw each other for the final time in 1933 on a visit to Hartford and its environs (*IAP* 853). And it is well documented that "The Dunwich Horror" (1928) incorporates two of the better-known tales of Connecticut folklore, the Moodus Noises and the Devil's Hopyard of East Haddam, the latter of which was also the basis for the "blasted heath" of the Gardner farm as described in "The Colour out of Space" (Joshi 411–12n16–17). Lovecraft read about those legends in Charles M. Skinner's *Myths and Legends of Own Land*, which he owned (*LL* no. 878; Skinner 241–45). They were also mentioned in Charles Fort's *New Lands*, which Lovecraft read in September 1927 (*DS* 145; Fort 93).[2]

Murray mentions the Moodus Noises briefly in his story "The Sothis Radiant," where they are identified as the cosmic drumming of Azathoth (295). This brings up a related point. While Connecticut is not absent from Lovecraft's writings, the state remained largely absent from pastiches until the 1990s. The first Mythos story firmly set in Connecticut seems to be Joseph Payne Brennan's "Jendick's Swamp," but its references to both the Mythos and Connecticut are slight (189, 198–99). In 1991, John H. Crowe III published "The House on Stratford Lane," a *Call of Cthulhu*

---

1. HPL must not have been totally dismissive of New London, as he gave it a brief, but narratively important, appearance in *The Case of Charles Dexter Ward* (CF 2.258).

2. East Haddam is also notable for being the home of William Gillette, one of the most important Sherlock Holmes authors and actors of the early 20th century (Rosenfeld and Harrison 11–13), something that HPL must have known as a Holmes aficionado (AG 191). Gillette himself has actually been briefly linked to HPL by Andy Lane in his 1994 novel *All-Consuming Fire*. A three-way crossover between *Doctor Who*, Sherlock Holmes, and the Cthulhu Mythos, the novel opens with a quotation from a conversation between Gillette and Sir Arthur Conan Doyle on how to write Holmes (Lane vi).

role-playing scenario involving a Mi-Go incursion in early 1920s Hartford that gets several key aspects of the city's geography wrong. Peter Cannon's alternate history biography *The Lovecraft Chronicles* is somewhat better, opening with Lovecraft on the bus from Hartford to Providence following his final meeting with Sonia. Indeed, Cannon's entire alternate history divergence comes from Lovecraft making friends with another passenger departing Hartford whom he did not actually meet (Cannon 1–8).

But more recent years have seen a flowering not only of pastiches but also of scholarship in what might be called Connecticut Mythocartography. Stephen Olbrys Gencarella and Michael J. Bielawa have respectively proposed expanded inspiration of East Haddam lore in "The Dunwich Horror" (Gencarella 1–10, 39–47) and Bridgeport history for "Herbert West—Reanimator" (Bielawa 38–51). Faye Ringel has drawn from recent work by Connecticut State Historian Walt Woodward (75–92) to propose that Joseph Curwen was based on John Winthrop, Jr., colonial governor of Connecticut who founded New London as a center of alchemy (Ringel 142–43). Ringel, professor emerita at the US Coast Guard Academy in New London, is one of several current Lovecraft scholars who have either matriculated from or teach at Connecticut universities. In addition to Ringel and Brennan (who was a librarian at Yale), there is the University of Connecticut[3] (Richard Bleiler, Michael A. Torregrossa); Central Connecticut State University (Anthony Conrad Chieffalo); Wesleyan University (Horace A. Smith); and Southern Connecticut State University (Byron Nakamura, Troy Rondinone).

Sam Gafford's debut novel *The House of Nodens* (2017) opened the era of Connecticut-set Mythos novels. Gafford achieves what Brennan did not. Not only does the novel incorporate the Nodens cult with Dudleytown, Connecticut's most legendary ghost town (Gafford 18, 61, 211, 231; Gencarella 190–98), it also includes extremely detailed accounts of the history and geography of Bridgeport, on the level of Lovecraft's attention to Providence in *The Case of Charles Dexter Ward* (Gafford 193–200). The year 2017 also saw the *Skype of Cthulhu* podcast perform "The House on Stratford Lane." The renaissance is even interactive; in 2018, Mystic Seaport put on "Nautical Nightmares: Madness on the Mystic River," a Lovecraft-inspired interactive theater performance during which the audience joined a group of alienists from Arkham to investigate eldritch occurrences on

---

3. An institution prominently featured in "The House on Stratford Lane" (Crowe 37).

the whaling ship *Charles W. Morgan* and in the recreated nineteenth century seaport town. The choice of the *Morgan* is apt, as Lovecraft and Bridgeport resident Robert Moe visited the vessel together in 1935, at its former museum site in Massachusetts (*DS* 605).

We have evidence of increasing attention to Connecticut by modern scholars and authors alike, as well as an overview of Lovecraft's personal ties to the state. But what of its actual influence in his fiction? I believe that the influence Lovecraft derived from Connecticut history and folklore was beyond the Moodus Noises and Devil's Hopyard, and have spent several years attempting to document the wider net that Connecticut has cast on Lovecraftian fiction. Listing all such Connecticut connections would far exceed the space allowed here. I focus instead on the impact of what is perhaps Connecticut's most famous institution: Yale University in New Haven. The Yale connections will serve as a stand-in for Connecticut's role in the Mythos at large, and will be approached in three sections. First and foremost will be a look into Yale's role in what might be the most durable Lovecraftian hoax, the persistent claim that the university library contained an entry for the *Necronomicon* in its card catalogue. Second will be an overview of potential explanations for the origins of that hoax claim. Finally, I will examine the roles that Yale, and New Haven more broadly, have played in the Mythos.

Searching for the Yale *Necronomicon*

Of all the Connecticut connections to either Lovecraft or the Mythos, the claim that the Yale library card catalogue had a *Necronomicon* entry is perhaps the most prevalent. As of the final editing of this chapter in July 2020, the claim is prominently featured at the top of the grimoire's Wikipedia entry, citing L. Sprague de Camp's 1976 volume *Literary Swordsmen and Sorcerers* (101). What is interesting about that reference is that de Camp does not mention the supposed Yale hoax in his biography of Lovecraft published the previous year. Similarly, in his essay "Books That Never Were," in the section on the *Necronomicon*, while de Camp claims that some people asked librarians and booksellers for copies, neither hoaxes nor Yale are mentioned (de Camp, *Scribblings* 82–83). It seems that the claim of what might termed the "*Necronomicon Yalensis*" reached de Camp between his writing of the Lovecraft biography and *Literary Swordsmen* sometime in the mid-1970s. But whence did de Camp learn of it?

Lovecraft himself did not include Yale in his list of libraries where the *Necronomicon* could be found at the end of his faux essay "History of the 'Necronomicon'" (CF 2.407–08), but libraries of two Massachusetts universities (Miskatonic and Yale's rival Harvard) are included. Lin Carter's "H. P. Lovecraft: The Books" covered fifty-nine real and fictional books used in the Cthulhu Mythos to date. In the second paragraph, Carter claims to be aware of two unknowing "H. P. L.-ophiles" who advertised for Abdul Alhazred books in "learned journals," but these were neither hoaxes nor involved libraries (Carter 212). Mark Owings's chapbook *The Necronomicon: A Study*, a work inspired by Carter's article (Owings 4), includes an updated listing from the then-current Mythos of all the libraries where the *Necronomicon* could be found, but again there is no entry for Yale (Owings 20). Indeed, Yale is not mentioned in Owings's chapbook at all. It does, however, contain the claim that "While it might be difficult, if not impossible (and justly so) for the layman to see the copy in the Widener Library at Harvard, the book is listed in the master card catalogue/index on the public floor, and is open to all" (Owings 12). This appears to be the earliest claim that the a *Necronomicon* entry could be found in the card catalogue of a New England Ivy League library. Although only 600 copies of the chapbook were printed, Owings received assistance from such figures as August Derleth, Frank Belknap Long, and Manly Wade Wellman while researching and writing it, which could account for its being circulated around the upper circles of Lovecraftian authors in the late 1960s (Owings 4, 31).

However it happened, the late 1960s appears to be the turning point. In 1969, Harry Warner, Jr. published a history of 1940s science fiction fandom. Referencing the "sentimental gesture" of a rare book dealer who put the *Necronomicon* into his catalog, Warner added that "Another Lovecraft devotee somehow smuggled reference cards into the catalog of the Yale University Library, causing repeated false alarms about the book in that institution" (11). This appears to be the earliest published claim of a Yale *Necronomicon* hoax, yet it also is the only one to claim *multiple* such hoaxes, with the suggestion that they were also widespread by the time this apparently-first account was written.

In 1993, Joan L. Stanley published an overview of the books stated by Mythos authors to have been held in the Miskatonic library. As with Owings's chapbook a generation earlier, in her entry on the *Necronomicon* there is no indication that any source at the time recorded Yale owning a copy (Stanley 49–59). She does, however, note Yale owning fragments of the *Book of Eibon* (46). But 1993 would finally see the *Necronomicon* directly linked to Yale, in George Alec Effinger's short story "Maureen Birnbaum at the Looming Awfulness." A parody of the Mythos with Yale sitting in for Miskatonic, its titular heroine discovers that the (fictional) "Omega Collection" of Yale's (real) Sterling Memorial Library includes a *Necronomicon* hand-copied from Dr. John Dee's original English translation "sometime in the last two or three centuries" (Effinger 137–38). The next year, while not referencing Yale (or any institution) specifically, Kendrick Kerwin Chua's online "NecronomiCON REFerence file" does state that there are "many entries in catalogs, library systems, and cross-references to books with the title Necronomicon, most of which are pranks or inside jokes." However, Chua's file has also been noted for being "notoriously misleading" (Loucks, "Wollheim" 217).

Nor was Yale explicitly referenced in the entries in *The Necronomicon*, a collection of fiction, essays, and commentary edited by Robert M. Price. The closest is Price's introduction to de Camp's "Preface to the Al-Azif" (1973), in which Price states: "It used to be that *Necronomicon* hoaxes were limited to bogus ads in book dealer trade journals or fake card catalog entries. No more" (183). Yale also is absent from either of Daniel Harms's two essays in *The Necronomicon Files*, one of which was specifically about *Necronomicon* hoaxes. Dan Clore's article "The Lurker on the Threshold of Interpretation: Hoax *Necronomicons* and Paratextual Noise" mentions the hoax in passing, stating that his article would "not deal here with such matters as [. . .] the card catalogue entries that a number of university libraries (Yale, UC Berkeley, etc.) have sported at various times." Clore's article was the basis for a passage in Jason Colavito's book *The Cult of Alien Gods* claiming that "Both Yale and the University of California at Berkeley once sported listings for the work of the Mad Arab, Abdul Alhazred" (171, 358n7).

In 2014, Nate Pedersen published *The Starry Wisdom Library: The Catalogue of the Greatest Occult Book Auction of All Time*, an anthology of entries on Mythos books written as if an 1877 catalogue by an Arkham auction house preparing to sell off the occult library of the Church of Starry Wisdom. The entry on the *Necronomicon* is simply Lovecraft's essay, with some annotations and a preface by Pedersen, and does not mention Yale (Pedersen et al. 66–69). And as late as 2019, after his Armitage Symposium presentation "In Search of the Lost Kitab *Al Azif*," Lars Backstrom claimed to have found no link to Yale in either real-world or in-universe history of the *Necronomicon*.

In terms of extant fiction and nonfiction pertaining to the Cthulhu Mythos, at least by major authors publishing in the field, this appears to be the totality of references to the *Necronomicon Yalensis*. Going by this literary path, at some point by 1967, the *Necronomicon* was being associated with the card catalogs of New England Ivy League universities, and within two years hoaxes at the Yale Library were being mentioned. Which leads to two subsequent questions. Did such a hoax actually exist? And if not, what was the basis for the legend?

In Search of the *Necronomicon Yalensis*

In the summer of 2019, I asked Daniel Harms about the Yale claim and why he did not include it in his sections of *The Necronomicon Files*. His response was that while he was not sure, the likely reason was that he could not authenticate the claim, with de Camp being the only person he knew of to have written about it. As we have seen, this is incorrect, although it does point to de Camp being the major vector for popularizing the *Necronomicon Yalensis*. Harms suspected that the rumor might have originated in fanzines, which would be difficult to research. Both thoughts had also occurred to me. As a librarian, Harms proposed that it was possible that the card could have been both inserted and removed from the catalog without any Yale librarians aware of either action.[4] If such a hoax were perpetrated in the catalog unbeknown to the librarians, then a study conducted by Ben-Ami Lipetz in 1969–70 gives some insight into who the culprit might be. Lipetz and research assistants approached 2,134 people near the card catalog at Sterling Memorial Library and asked them what they were about to do. Eighty-four percent had a specific author, title, or other goal in mind; only sixteen percent said they wanted to browse a set of subject cards. Graduate students used the catalog the most, followed by undergraduates, with faculty using it the least (Baker 163–64).

Just going from the statistics of Lipetz's study, therefore, an assured graduate student would be the most likely culprit of the hypothetical hoax. That said, there is one employee of Yale who stands out as a potential culprit: the fantasy and horror author Joseph Payne Brennan (1918–1990). Brennan, born in Bridgeport, spent almost his entire life in his parents'

---

4. Although I attended his Delta Green panel at NecronomiCon 2019, I regretted not being able to approach Harms to talk to him in person. As far as I am aware, he did not attend the Armitage talk from which this essay is adapted.

hometown of New Haven. From 1941 onward—barring three years spent in the US Army in World War II—he worked at the Yale Library. His wife Doris, whom he married in 1970, also worked there (Brennan, "Autobiography" 6-7).[5] Brennan used his position at Yale to research and publish an early bibliography and biography of Lovecraft in 1952 and 1955, respectively. However, he stated that "While I am a great admirer of Lovecraft, and have been mentioned as a 'disciple', I think he had only incidental influence on my early work and that his later influence was limited" (Brennan, "Autobiography" 7). It is tempting to suggest a *Necronomicon* card catalog hoax might have originated with the Lovecraftian librarian working there, but there is no evidence—on the basis of either a devotion to Lovecraft or a lack of devotion to his lifelong career—that Brennan would have been tempted to engage in such a hoax. (This still leaves open the possibility that Brennan's association with Lovecraft may have inspired a student to carry out the hoax.)

That raises the question: if the actual Sterling Library card catalog was not involved, then what might have hypothetically been the origin of the hoax? Out of interest, I did a search for the *Necronomicon* on the Yale library online catalog, and sure enough, a hit came up—the Simon *Necronomicon*. For a moment, I thought that this might explain it, given the persistent belief among some (and promoted by the book itself) that the Simon *Necronomicon* was the "real" *Necronomicon* and Lovecraft's claims that the book was fictional were simply a cover. A Yale student believing that, and seeing a copy of the "real" Simon *Necronomicon* in the bookshelves, might have been the seed from which the urban legend germinated. However, I quickly realized this was impossible, as Simon's *Necronomicon* was first published in 1977, years after de Camp's claim, let alone Warner's (Simon viii; Harms, "Volume" 39-48; Davies 268).[6]

Another possibility that came to mind was a hoax review of the *Necronomicon* that Donald A. Wollheim published in the 12 September 1935

5. In keeping with the *Necronomicon* hoax reference, Brennan's Wikipedia entry lacks details from, and includes details contradictory to, his autobiographical statements.

6. The Simon *Necronomicon* was part of a separate hoax in Connecticut, however. Self-proclaimed demonologists Ed and Lorraine Warren had a copy of it in their Occult Museum in Monroe, CT (16 miles west of New Haven). Ed believed it was a supposedly legitimate medieval "Book of Shadows" translated into English, and helpfully marked it as such with a Post-it Note affixed to the cover.

issue of the *Branford Review and East Haven News*, a local newspaper, which Willis Conover later passed on to Lovecraft himself in September 1936. Although Harms had been unable to find the article in 1998, Donovan K. Loucks unearthed and reprinted it in 2015 (Loucks, "Wollheim" 215; Harms, "Volume" 30). The town of Branford is 8 miles east of New Haven, with East Haven separating the two. Loucks noted that Wollheim's review is unique, as it was not only the apparent first *Necronomicon* hoax, it was also the only one that occurred within Lovecraft's lifetime and the author knew of (Loucks, "Wollheim" 218). What led to New York City resident Wollheim publishing a hoax review in a small-town newspaper east of New Haven remains unknown, though Loucks speculates it may be due to family connections in the town or the summering in Branford of fellow New Yorker and Lovecraft acquaintance Otis Adelbert Kline (Loucks, "Wollheim" 216-17). However, even though the hoax occurred in such proximity to New Haven, there is no apparent connection to Yale, or indeed, other universities or libraries of any sort. Whatever copy of the *Necronomicon* Wollheim's fake reviewer Dr. W. T. Faraday got his hands on, it was not the *Necronomicon Yalensis*—though perhaps Wollheim meant to imply that "Dr. Faraday" was a faculty member of nearby Yale.

However, there is another candidate for a Yale-owned *Necronomicon*. This is the Voynich Manuscript, a famous untranslated fifteenth-century codex that has inspired all manner of hypotheses and conspiracies since it was first mentioned in a letter of 1639 to scholar Athanasius Kircher. In 1969, the Voynich Manuscript was donated to Yale's Beinecke Rare Book Library. That same year, Colin Wilson published "The Return of the Lloigor" in Derleth's anthology *Tales of the Cthulhu Mythos*. In Wilson's story, the Voynich Manuscript is stated as not only being a real copy of the *Necronomicon*, but that it actually inspired Lovecraft to write about the *Necronomicon* in his fiction (Wilson 356). Wilson's use of the Voynich Manuscript and its association with the *Necronomicon* has remained popular in Mythos pastiches since (Harms, "Rumors" 65-66; Stanley 60-61). This seemed like a potential explanation for me: someone believed Wilson's claim that the Voynich Manuscript was the real *Necronomicon*, at the same time Yale announced acquiring the actual Voynich Manuscript. However, these events both occurring in 1969 would make this too quick to have been documented in Warner's book. In his study of grimoires, Owen Davies suggested that it was "possible that Lovecraft's interest in mysterious occult books, and that of his fellow writers of weird tales, was also influenced by the public interest in and controversy over the Voynich manuscript." However, Davies does not suggest that the Manuscript was ever actually believed to *be* the *Necronomicon*, nor does he reference the Yale card catalog (or Wilson's story) despite briefly mentioning post-Lovecraft *Necronomicon* hoaxes.

With the Voynich avenue a dead end, I approached Mark Branch, executive editor of the *Yale Alumni Magazine*, to ask if he knew of any stories published in the magazine by Yale alumni related to the *Necronomicon*, or Lovecraft more generally. Branch kindly checked the indices of the magazine's bound volumes from 1965 to 1977, finding nothing. Branch believed there was a chance it may have been mentioned but not made it into the index, but that this would be very unlikely. In any case, the lack of digitized records makes deeper searches of the magazine prohibitively time-consuming, although such digitization may happen in the future and allow for such a deeper examination (Branch).

With this seeming exhaustion of potential origins at Yale itself, I must agree with Harms that the likely cause of this hoax rumor was in the fan press, which would also explain why Warner, the chronicler of fan culture, was seemingly the first to report it in a more conventional publication. I would like to take time to search through fanzines from the era at some point in the future, though at the present such a wide-ranging and in-depth search is not possible for me. But although the search for the *Necronomicon Yalensis* wound up with no entry in the proverbial catalog, that does not mean that Yale University itself played no part in Lovecraft's fiction.

Other Yale and New Haven Appearances

At the start of the Miskatonic University entry in *The Lovecraft Lexicon*, Anthony B. Pearsall claims that it is "plainly modeled on such great Ivy League institutions as Harvard, Yale, and Providence's Brown University" (281). As far as I can tell, there is no written evidence to support Pearsall's claim that Yale influenced Miskatonic's creation. However, A. Merritt's story "The People of the Pit" (1918) has been seen as an influence on *At the Mountains of Madness*; the discoverer of the prehistoric Arctic city in that tale identifies himself as "Sinclair Stanton. Class 1900, Yale" (Merritt 103). If this story is indeed an *At the Mountains of Madness* influence, then not only the idea of a polar expedition by a New England Ivy League university finding an ancient city, but that New England Ivy League itself, could indeed originate with Yale, given that Lovecraft did not invent Miskatonic until writing "Herbert West—Reanimator," three years after the publication of Merritt's story.

It is true that, at first glance, Lovecraft's connection to New Haven overall is slight. Lovecraft speculated that his great-great-great-granduncle, Sam Casey Jr., may have relocated to New Haven after escaping the Newport hangman's noose for counterfeiting in 1770 (OFF 93). Lovecraft passed through the city on the train often; in a 1922 letter to Maurice Moe (Robert's father), he wrote that New Haven "seems alert and metropolitan from the station angle" (MWM 84). But Lovecraft never visited New Haven proper until 8 October 1935, when he and his aunt Annie Gamwell spent seven and a half hours touring the city. They made the trip in a friend's car, the one-hundred-mile drive going by in two and a half hours of "autumnal Conn. scenery [. . .] delightful" (JVS 278). In a letter to J. Vernon Shea, Lovecraft told how

> I visited ancient Connecticut Hall (1732—the oldest Yale College building, where Nathan Hale of the class of 1773 roamed), old Centre Church (1812—with an interesting crypt containing the grave of Benedict Arnold's first wife), the Pierpont house (1767—now Yale Faculty Club), the historical, art, & natural history museums [New Haven Colony Historical Society, Old Yale Art Gallery, and Peabody Museum of Natural History], the Farnam & Marsh botanic gardens, & various other points of interest—crowding as much as possible into the limited time available. [. . .] I wandered for hours through this limitless labyrinth of unexpected elder microcosms, & mourned the lack of further time. Certainly, I must visit New Haven again, since many of its treasures would require weeks for proper inspection & appreciation. (JVS 278)

Despite his plans, Lovecraft does not seem to have ever returned to New Haven. However, Yale may have inspired aspect of two of his most celebrated works. First is his visit to the Marsh Botanical Garden, established in 1899 from the personal collection of the famous Yale paleontologist Othniel Charles Marsh, who died that year. Marsh was famous for his ruthless collection of dinosaur fossils during the late nineteenth century "Bone Wars" (Mayor 182-84). Although Lovecraft visited the garden named after Marsh years after writing "The Shadow over Innsmouth," he would have certainly known about Othniel Marsh and his association with ancient animals, and he may have influenced the naming of Obed Marsh.

But the possibility of a more substantive influence is illustrated by Lovecraft's visit to the Peabody Museum of Natural History, established at

Yale in 1866 at the urging of Marsh, its most prominent staff member. In *At the Mountains of Madness*, Dyer narrates how "As a geologist my object in leading the Miskatonic University Expedition was wholly that of securing deep-level specimens of rock and soil from various parts of the antarctic continent, aided by the remarkable drill devised by Prof. Frank H. Pabodie of our engineering department" (CF 3.13). In a response to Frederic J. Pabody's inquiry of 28 February 1936 to the name's origin, Lovecraft described how

> I suppose I hit upon the name *Pabodie* by a very indirect process. Most of my tales centre in an imaginary Massachusetts town (vaguely reminiscent of Salem [. . .] hence I am rather partial toward Essex surnames—Pickman, Royes, Derby, Peabody, Keezar, Wingate, Upton, &c. &c. It was probably this Essex County leaning which made me think—at first—of *Peabody* for my engineering professor; but upon reflection I decided that the great fame of this name (in museums, philanthropic foundations, &c.) made it a little too conventional for the realistic atmosphere I wanted. So I turned to a variant of it which used to be quite well represented in [Providence]. (CLM 327-28)

The reference to the Essex County Peabody name in conjunction with "museums, philanthropic foundations, &c." is certainly a reference to millionaire philanthropist George Peabody, who was from Essex County—specifically from Danvers, which was Salem Village (of Salem witch trial fame) until the mid-eighteenth century. The fossil-filled Peabody Museum of Natural History at Yale was named after him, as he had provided the funding; Peabody was also the uncle of Marsh, the museum's lead paleontologist (Little 151). As noted, Lovecraft visited the museum, albeit in 1935, years after the writing of *At the Mountains of Madness*. Nevertheless, it is likely that he knew of the museum beforehand, and it was that association which initially caused him to consider Peabody a name to be associated with fossil discovery.

In particular, the Peabody Museum was famous for containing seven hundred fossilized cycads cut down and imported en masse from South Dakota by George Wieland in the 1890s, almost completely deforesting the Fossil Cycad National Monument before it could even be granted that distinction in 1922 (Mayor 300). The widespread knowledge of the fossilized cycad forest in the Peabody could have served as inspiration for the Antarctic chamber containing fossilized "forests of Tertiary cycads" (CF 3.33), the use of cycad wood in the shutters in the windows of the Elder Things (CF 3.82), and the "waving, vine-draped cycad-forests" depicted in their carvings (*CF* 3.111). Cycads would also be noticed in the past several times by the narrator of "The Shadow out of Time" (*CF* 3.380, 422). The cycad shape may also have at least partially influenced the giant "rugose cone" form of the Great Race (*CF* 3.387).[7]

Outside the Peabody connection, it is likely that *At the Mountains of Madness* draws from Connecticut fossils in an additional way. Since at least 1802, dinosaur fossils—principally large numbers of footprints—have been found along the Connecticut River in Massachusetts and Connecticut (Little 49-64). The footprints were only identified as dinosaur tracks in 1845; before that, the religious farmhand who discovered them assumed they were the tracks left by Noah's raven. Across southern New England, Native Americans carved "devil's tracks" into granite, apparently intended to replicate the fossilized dinosaur footprints they saw along the Connecticut River Valley centuries before the European newcomers first saw them (Mayor 48-49). Both of these anecdotes—the religious New England provincials misidentifying records of ancient beings, and associating Native replications of them with devilry—have very Lovecraftian traits to them. The preponderance of fossilized footprints along the Connecticut River could, therefore, be an inspiration for the descriptions of the fossils, especially the "distinct triangular striated [foot]prints" found in Antarctica by Professor Lake (*CF* 3.35-36).

There is one further piece of New Haven lore that may have influenced Lovecraft. In 1648, the denizens of New Haven witnessed a "Phantom Ship," representing a trading vessel (manufactured in Newport, Rhode Island) that had vanished a year before during the passage from New Haven to London. The Phantom Ship was seen sailing in the clouds above New Haven's harbor before breaking apart in mid-air. The Phantom Ship not only is mentioned in Skinner's *Myths and Legends of Own Land* alongside the details Lovecraft took for "The Dunwich Horror," it is also mentioned in Cotton Mather's *Magnalia Christi Americana*, which Lovecraft owned (*LL* no. 645; Skinner 238-39; Mather 5-6). We can be sure Lovecraft knew of the legend; it bears similarities to his story "The White Ship" (1919), particularly the segment when the eponymous vessel appears

---

7. Peter Cannon presents a similar origin for "The Shadow out of Time" in his alternate history novel *The Lovecraft Chronicles*, in which the alternate version of the story is inspired by HPL seeing prehistoric animals at the La Brea tar pits and the strange vegetation of the California desert (Cannon 84, 155).

from the full moon (*CF* 1.106).

Although Yale and New Haven are not mentioned in any of Lovecraft's fiction, it should be noted they have occasionally been referenced in subsequent Mythos works. Outside of Effinger's parody, Yale is mentioned in Elizabeth Bear's story "Shoggoths in Bloom," as the school where protagonist Paul Harding received his Ph.D. (Bear 155–56). And Sam Gafford's novel *The House of Nodens* briefly (and accurately) mentions New Haven's heavy traffic (Gafford 221).

Conclusion

Although my search for the *Necronomicon Yalensis* proved fruitless (at least thus far), my efforts to track it down led to me uncovering new aspects of both Lovecraftian history and Connecticut folklore, and making connections with other scholars at the center of those overlapping fields. As a result, my search for this elusive volume of the *Necronomicon* was a perfect encapsulation of what Daniel Harms identified as "two elements of *Necronomicon* hoaxes. One is that there are people who will believe anything is real without bothering to look at it carefully, a fact that anyone preparing to put together a hoax should consider. The other is that performing a *Necronomicon* hoax is so enjoyable that even a debunker can easily be caught up in the fun" ("Volume" 58).[8]

Works Cited

Backstrom, Lars. Conversation. 24 August 2019.

Baker, Nicholson. *The Size of Thoughts: Essays and Other Lumber*. New York: Random House, 1996.

Barlow, R. H. "Henry S. Whitehead." In Whitehead's *Jumbee and Other Uncanny Tales*. Sauk City, WI: Arkham House, 1944. vii–xii.

Bear, Elizabeth. "Shoggoths in Bloom." 2008. In Ross E. Lockhart, ed. *The Book of Cthulhu: Tales Inspired by H. P. Lovecraft*. San Francisco: Night Shade Books, 2011. 149–68.

8. I would like to thank all the individuals who helped me with research for this paper, ranging from brief email replies to extensive archival searches: Lars Backstrom, Michael J. Bielawa, Richard Bleiler, Daphnée Tasia Bourdages-Athanassiou, Mark Branch, Jessica Dooling, Ken Faig, Jr., Stephen Olbrys Gencarella, Daniel Harms, Donovan K. Loucks, Sara Powell, Donovan Reinwald, Allison Rich, and Tim Vert.

Bielawa, Michael J. *Wicked Bridgeport.* Charleston, SC: The History Press, 2012.

Branch, Mark. Email orrespondence. 16–17 May 2019.

Brennan, Joseph Payne. "Jendick's Swamp." 1987. In Robert M. Price, ed. *The Ithaqua Cycle: The Wind-Walker of the Icy Wastes: 14 Tales.* 1997. Hayward, CA: Chaosium, 2006. 188–99.

———. "Joseph Payne Brennan in Brief: An Autobiography." *Newsletter–August Derleth Society* 2 (1978): 6–7.

Callaghan, Gavin. "A Reprehensible Habit: H. P. Lovecraft and the Munsey Magazines." In Robert H. Waugh, ed. *Lovecraft and Influence: His Predecessors and Successors.* Lanham, MD: Scarecrow Press, 2013. 69–82.

Cannon, Peter. *The Lovecraft Chronicles.* Poplar Bluff, MO: Mythos Books, 2004.

Carter, Lin. "H. P. Lovecraft: The Books." In H. P. Lovecraft et al. *The Shuttered Room and Other Pieces.* Ed. August Derleth. Sauk City, WI: Arkham House, 1959. 212–49.

Chua, Kendrick Kerwin. "NecronomiCON REFerence file." *The Arcane Archive* (20 May 1994). www.arcane-archive.org/faqs/nconref.php

Clore, Dan. "The Lurker on the Threshold of Interpretation: Hoax Necronomicons and Paratextual Noise." *The Official Dan Clore Homepage,* 1999. www.oocities.org/clorebeast/lurker.htm

Colavito, Jason. *The Cult of Alien Gods: H. P. Lovecraft and Extraterrestrial Pop Culture.* Amherst, NY: Prometheus Books, 2005.

Crowe III, John H. "The House on Stratford Lane." In Brian Appleton, ed. *The Resurrected: Out of the Vault.* Columbia, MO: Pagan Publishing, 2002. 33–47.

Davies, Owen. *Grimoires: A History of Magic Books.* Oxford: Oxford University Press, 2009.

de Camp, L. Sprague. *Literary Swordsmen and Sorcerers: The Makers of Heroic Fantasy.* Sauk City, WI: Arkham House, 1976.

———. *Lovecraft: A Biography.* Garden City, NY: Doubleday, 1975.

———. *Scribblings.* Boston: NESFA Press, 1972.

Eckhardt, Jason C. *Off the Ancient Track: A Lovecraftian Guide to New-England and Adjacent New-York, Revised Edition.* West Warwick, RI: Necronomicon Press, 1990.

Effinger, George Alec. *Maureen Birnbaum, Barbarian Swordsperson*. New York: GuildAmerica Books, 1993.

Faig, Jr., Kenneth W. *The Unknown Lovecraft*. New York: Hippocampus Press, 2009.

Fort, Charles. *New Lands*. New York: Boni & Liveright, 1923.

Gafford, Sam. *The House of Nodens*. Portland, OR: Dark Regions Press, 2017.

Gencarella, Stephen. *Spooky Trails and Tall Tales Connecticut: Hiking the State's Legends, Hauntings, and History*. Guilford, CT: Falcon, 2019.

Harms, Daniel. Email correspondence. 8-9 June 2019.

———. "Evaluating *Necronomicon* Rumors." In Daniel Harms and John Wisdom Gonce III. *The Necronomicon Files: The Truth Behind Lovecraft's Legend*. Boston: Weiser Books, 2003. 61-68.

———. "'Many a Quaint and Curious Volume . . .': The *Necronomicon* Made Flesh." In Daniel Harms and John Wisdom Gonce III. *The Necronomicon Files: The Truth Behind Lovecraft's Legend*. Boston: Weiser Books, 2003. 29-59.

Joshi, S. T. "Explanatory Notes." In H. P. Lovecraft. *The Thing on the Doorstep and Other Weird Stories*. Ed. S. T. Joshi. New York: Penguin Books, 2001. 367-443.

Lane, Andy. *All-Consuming Fire*. London: Virgin Books, 1994.

Little, Richard D. *Dinosaurs, Dunes, and Drifting Continents: The Geology of the Connecticut River Valley*. Easthampton, MA: Earth View LLC, 2003.

Loucks, Donovan K. "Donald A. Wollheim's Hoax Review of the *Necronomicon*." *Lovecraft Annual* No. 9 (2015): 214-20.

———. "Lovecraftian Sites in New England." *The H. P. Lovecraft Archive*, 2 October 2001. www.hplovecraft.com/creation/sites/

Mather, Cotton. *Magnalia Christi Americana: or, The Ecclesiastical History of New-England, from its First Planting in the Year 1620 Unto the Year of Our Lord, 1698*. London: Thomas Parkhurst, 1702.

Mayor, Adrienne. *Fossil Legends of the First Americans*. Princeton, NJ: Princeton University Press, 2005.

Merritt, A. "The People of the Pit." 1918. In Ann and Jeff VanderMeer, ed. *The Weird: A Compendium of Strange and Dark Stories*. New York: Tor, 2012. 101-9.

Murray, Will. "Lovecraft's Arkham Country." In S. T. Joshi, ed. *The H. P. Lovecraft Centennial Conference Proceedings*. West Warwick, RI: Necronomicon Press, 1991. 15–17.

———. "The Sothis Radiant." In Martin H. Greenberg and Robert Weinberg, ed. *Miskatonic University*. New York: DAW Books, 1996. 271–99.

"Nautical Nightmares." Mystic Seaport, 2018. www.mysticseaport.org/event/nautical-nightmares/

Owings, Mark. *The Necronomicon: A Study*. Baltimore: Mirage Associates, 1967.

Pearsall, Anthony B. *The Lovecraft Lexicon: A Reader's Guide to Persons, Places and Things in the Tales of H. P. Lovecraft*. Tempe, AZ: New Falcon Publications, 2005.

Pedersen, Nate, and H. P. Lovecraft. "The Necronomicon." In Nate Pedersen, ed. *The Starry Wisdom Library: The Catalogue of the Greatest Occult Book Auction of All Time*. Hornsea, UK: PS Publishing, 2014. 66–69.

Price, Robert M., ed. *The Necronomicon: Selected Stories and Essays Concerning the Blasphemous Tome of the Mad Arab*. 1996. Oakland, CA: Chaosium, 2008.

Richter, Robert A. *Touring Eugene O'Neill's New London*. New London: Connecticut College, 2001.

Ringel, Faye. "New England Gothic." In Charles L. Crow, ed. *A Companion to American Gothic*. Malden, MA: Wiley Blackwell, 2014. 139–50.

Rosenfeld, Lucy D., and Marina Harrison. *Architecture Walks: The Best Outings Near New York City*. New Brunswick, NJ: Rutgers University Press, 2010.

Simon. *The Necronomicon*. 1977. New York: Avon Books, 1980.

Skinner, Charles M. *Myths and Legends of Own Land*. Philadelphia: J. P. Lippincott Co., 1896.

Skype of Cthulhu. "421—The House on Stratford Lane 01." 17 October 2017. www.cthulhu.me/2017/10/421-house-on-stratford-lane-01.html

Stanley, Joan L. *Ex Libris Miskatonici: A Catalogue of Selected Items from the Special Collections in the Miskatonic University Library*. 1993. West Warwick, RI: Necronomicon Press, 2019.

Warner, Jr., Harry. *All Our Yesterdays: An Informal History of Science Fiction Fandom in the Forties*. Chicago: Advent Publishers, 1969.

Warren, Ed and Lorraine. *The Occult Museum*. YouTube, 10 March 2016. www.youtube.com/watch?v=QoReucY44Gc&t=7m41s

Waugh, Robert H. *A Monster of Voices: Speaking for H. P. Lovecraft*. New York: Hippocampus Press, 2011.

Wilson, Colin. "The Return of the Lloigor." In August Derleth, ed. *Tales of the Cthulhu Mythos*. Sauk City, WI: Arkham House, 1969. 351–401.

Woodward, Walt. *Prospero's America: John Winthrop, Jr., Alchemy, and the Creation of New England Culture, 1606–1676*. Chapel Hill: University of North Carolina Press, 2010.

Lovecraft's Archive: Materiality and Readership in Lovecraft's Fiction

Cole Donovan

Graduate student, University of Chicago

> "Original title Al Azif–azif being the word used by the Arabs
> to designate that nocturnal sound (made by insects)
> supposed to be the howling of daemons."
> —H. P. Lovecraft, "History of the 'Necronomicon'" (CF 2.405)

The question this article poses and the answers it hopes to provide emerged not as a direct response to Lovecraft's work but rather as a response to my prior reading of his work. Initially taking the form of a kind of lineage of ideas and materialities traceable in Lovecraft's work (with a particular focus on a kind of medieval reception visible in Lovecraft's fiction), my initial thoughts carried with them assumptions about readership in Lovecraft that, upon further examination, proved to be trickier and subtler than I had first realized, assumptions that colored my interpretation and hindered me from understanding a problem that I see as integral to understanding Lovecraft's stories: the problem of fictional books and the characters who read them.

Of H. P. Lovecraft's many lasting contributions to American pop culture, few have gripped the imagination of readers and artists as thoroughly or persistently as the dreaded grimoire, the *Necronomicon*. Though this one fictional text is undoubtedly his best-known, Lovecraft's short fiction is riddled with references to many arcane texts of his own invention as well as texts appropriated from history and other literature. Foregrounded in many of his most famous stories, these fictional and semi-fictional texts serve as semiotic anchors, grounding the events of the narrative around a central material object, and it is through these objects that Lovecraft develops his horror.

With the recent efforts in literary scholarship to explore readership conceptually and to engage critically with the practices of reading, Lovecraft's corpus presents a unique problem: despite cosmic horror's insistence on shrinking the role of mankind in the grand picture of eternity, Lovecraft's grimoire-driven narratives appear to insist on humanity's ability to interpret text and symbol accurately, or, more briefly, humanity's ability to read. As an issue of *reading*, this seeming paradox is irreconcilable. The ability to read and interpret immediately foregrounds the role of the human—interpretation is the product of the internal self and therefore it is the self and not the unknowable cosmic depths that bring about its inevitable demise.

Given the treacherous nature of attempting to differentiate clearly between varying types of readers and texts, I find it necessary to clarify some key terms I will be using to navigate the boundaries of fiction and reality. Following terminology developed by Paul Goetsch, characters within the texts who are seen to read or describe themselves as having read something will be referred to as "intradiegetic readers" (194). Similarly, texts that exist within the fictional world will be referred to as intradiegetic texts. Readers who exist outside the fictional texts (i.e., you, me, Lovecraft) will be referred to as external readers, and the fictional texts that they read (i.e., Lovecraft's stories) will be referred to simply as stories or fiction.

This essay suggests characterizing the Lovecraftian protagonists' interaction with intradiegetic texts as *use* rather than *reading*. The nature of the intradiegetic reading on display in Lovecraft is so utterly different from that of external reading that simply calling it reading does much to mischaracterize it. Lovecraft's intradiegetic readers' engagement with the texts of his archive (a term I will define more fully below) is essential and unmediated. It is the perfect transmission of information that, rather than relying on the interpretative abilities of his protagonists, supersedes any need for interpretation and highlights *not* the efficiency of man's reading processes but rather the inevitability of the cosmic.

Lovecraft's Archive: Texts, Fragments, and Materials

In much the same way that an academic creates and draws from an archive of materials to form an argument, Lovecraft's fiction relies on an archive of texts that share a continuity across stories to bolster dramatic effect. As a conceptual framework, an archive of intradiegetic texts is complex and amorphous. Unlike an actual archive, it is not constrained by limits of physical arrangement, subjected to the perils of preservation, or dependent on the materiality of the texts contained therein. It is a perfectly lossless collection that exists only in reference to itself and its emergence in the fiction.

As a solely virtual collection, Lovecraft's archive escapes what Markus Friedrich calls "the inevitably physical nature of written knowledge" (112). Rather, it exists much like Borges's "Library of Babel." It is both wholly complete and wholly endless. What does and does not exist both within one text and within the entirety of the archive is not determined by any material truth. A text in the archive, a text like the *Necronomicon*, exists in infinite variety, each ready to be deployed at any moment, and none being more complete than the next. Each is a token of the infinite, symbolic of its own multiplicity, and even texts within the archive that have external analogues maintain this degree of infinite variability.

The texts that are featured in Lovecraft's archive can be cursorily divided into three groups: texts that exist only within the lifeworld of those who have direct access to them (i.e., the diegetic world), texts that exist in their entirety within the world outside of the story (i.e., the external world), and texts that exist in some form in the external world but appear significantly altered in the fiction. These three distinctions can be loosely equated to the three modes of virtual objects described by psychologist James Gibson and concisely laid out in Thomas Natsoulas's essay "Virtual Objects":[1]

> There are both real "virtual objects" and "virtual objects" that are not real. Although some "virtual objects" have no existence, whether in the past, present, or future, (e.g., the legendary king Gilgamesh), others of them have existed for a time but no longer exist now (e.g., Mohandas K. Gandhi), and

---

1. For the purposes of this article, Gibson's framework, while helpful for understanding how modalities of virtuality are conceived of irrespective of any application to HPL's work, fails in one instance by relying too heavily on the temporal relationship of existence with nonexistence. While two of Gibson's categories track cleanly with two of the categories of texts I have described (namely, wholly fictional texts/objects that never existed and wholly external texts/objects that currently exist), the third category, the "in-between" category, does not align quite as neatly. It is for this reason that, rather than simply relying on Gibson's modes, I have introduced a new way of categorizing the texts that does not attend to their temporal existence but compares their physical or external existence to their existence within the fiction.

still other "virtual objects" do currently exist, not having as yet gone out of existence (e.g., the Great Wall of China). (358)[2]

However, whereas Gibson's modes of virtual existence rely heavily on their temporality, the texts of Lovecraft's archive are more clearly defined by the external objects upon which they are or are not fashioned. Although, as will be demonstrated, Lovecraft attempts to imbue certain texts from his archive with an external temporality, in most cases this temporality is a texture of the narrative rather than a texture of the intradiegetic object. Because the object (i.e., the intradiegetic book) is wholly submerged within the fiction, the question of the text contained within the objects is removed from the question of the materiality of the objects that contain the text.

Texts in the first category form one of the major pillars of Lovecraft's fiction: the topos of the forbidden book. These creations include the *Necronomicon*, Bloch's *De Vermis Mysteriis*, and the Pnakotic Manuscripts. These texts are not available to the external reader in any form and are marked by their disruption of the continuity of fiction and reality.[3] They alienate external readers through their intangibility. They are to be read, but not by the external reader. They are symbols of a kind of futility, a failing on the part of the external reader to access the written word, unavailable to the external reader except as fragments.

In the context of the fiction, these texts are often described as rare or obscure. Strange then is the frequency with which these books are read within the stories. The *Necronomicon* in particular is frequently, perhaps even suspiciously so, on the reading list of many ill-fated Lovecraftian readers. Even despite its in-text reputation for secrecy and arcaneness, it is not wholly obscure; consider the popularity of the text among the Antarctic expedition party in *At the Mountains of Madness* in contrast to the text's

2. For clarity, *virtual* here refers to the texts' (regardless of category) existence within the narrative world. They are virtual in the sense that they are representative of the essence of a thing yet separate from the extradiegetic thing itself (i.e., the texts' very existence within the narrative lends the text its virtuality).

3. While it is true that some of HPL's invented texts have been elaborated upon since his death, the conceit of his stories relies, to a large degree, on these texts' unknowability. While these fabricated texts are interesting in their own right, their existence has no bearing on the issues contained in this article. For information on texts like the Simon *Necronomicon*, see John Engle's "Cults of Lovecraft: The Impact of H. P. Lovecraft's Fiction on Contemporary Occult Practices."

framing. In that short novel, we learn that within a relatively small group of academics three members have definitely read it: "Dyer and Pabodie have read 'Necronomicon'" (*CF* 3.40) and "Danforth, indeed, is known to be among the few who have ever dared go completely through that worm-riddled copy of the 'Necronomicon' kept under lock and key in the college library" (*CF* 3.157). Given the aura of horror that surrounds the text and the disorienting fact that the academics in question are engineers and geologists rather than humanists, the fact that they have read the *Necronomicon* signals the strange way it functions in the fiction.

Bracketing momentarily the question of function, there is much to be said regarding the virtual materiality of these texts. The *Necronomicon*, the richest example from this category of texts, is rarely quoted at length in Lovecraft's work. In "The Dunwich Horror," external readers are given a glimpse into the pages of the oft-referenced tome in a strange and jarring passage:

> "Nor is it to be thought," ran the text as Armitage mentally translated it, "that man is either the oldest or the last of earth's masters, or that the common bulk of life and substance walks alone. The Old Ones were, the Old Ones are, and the Old Ones shall be. Not in the spaces we know, but between them, They walk serene and primal, undimensioned and to us unseen. *Yog-Sothoth* knows the gate. *Yog-Sothoth* is the gate. *Yog-Sothoth* is the key and guardian of the gate. (*CF* 2.433–34)

The excerpt goes on, and it is in this instance that the *Necronomicon* is realized in a meaningful way. It becomes a text to which the external reader has access,, and though it is limited by the length of Armitage's translation, that access fundamentally constructs the means by which the external reader can engage with it. No longer amorphous and unknowable, instances of quotation of wholly fictional texts *create* the texts and complete them. Through a simple project of copying and pasting one could, if so inclined, create a certain amount of the *Necronomicon* as it appears in Lovecraft's stories. Because it is wholly fictional, those fragments comprise the entire reality of the text. The fragment becomes the whole.

In describing this phenomenon, Sean Braune writes: "Lovecraft cites text from a book that does not exist; however, by citing textual fragments, Lovecraft is essentially writing the extant text into an imaginary topological space of hypertextual potential" (243). The fictional text becomes actualized in the quoting of it, and, to push Braune's suggestion farther, the fictional text becomes wholly defined by and made up of the fragmentary quotations attributed to it. The question then emerges as to whether Lovecraft's archive remains wholly fictional or whether, through citation, it emerges as a collection of external texts that, rather than being, as I propose, like Borges's Library of Babel, something more akin to an archeologist's collection of broken pots and tablets.

I have suggested that you could, if so inclined, create your own "*Necronomicon*" by pasting together all the quotations from it available in Lovecraft's work. While that is certainly true, that version of text, a patchwork collection of citations from various stories and sources, would only be one version of the *Necronomicon*. The existence of quotations does not, indeed cannot, account for the entirety of the fictional text.

This is borne out both narratively and conceptually through theories of virtuality. Returning to the source of the fragment quoted above, the text of the story clearly notes the intradiegetic text's incompleteness: "Wilbur had with him the priceless but imperfect copy of Dr. Dee's English version [and . . .] he at once began to collate the two texts with the aim of discovering a certain passage which would have come on the 751st page of his own defective volume" (CF 2.433). It is a matter of narrative fact that, firstly, the quotation provided in the story is only a small part of the text that the character is able to engage with, and secondly, that the source of the quotation is itself fragmentary of an imagined perfect text. The text, referenced only in fragments, achieves an unknowable completeness. Had intradiegetic readerly engagement been limited to *only* that fragment with no reference to a diegetically extant whole, the virtual archive would indeed crumble into ancient debris; however, there is an explicit understanding that the book, like an iceberg, extends well beyond its exposed side and has a voluminous, even infinite, body of submerged text.

Virtually the text extends into infinity. Sean Braune concludes with this description of the texts he is engaging with: "The fragment is fragmentary, but it is also an undecidable totality, providing all the evidence, while simultaneously pointing to the absence of all evidence. The fragment, in this sense, resists being counted: it is both singular and multiple, existing in a strange space of the supplemental" (254). Lovecraft's fragmentary fictional texts signal their own infinitude through their inaccessibility, and like Derrida's arche writing, they "cannot be reduced to the form of *presence*" (Derrida 57).

Texts in the second category, texts that exist completely both in the external world and the fictional world, include works like *Regnum Congo* and *Magnalia Christi Americana*. These are texts that, setting aside matters of rarity and practical availability, are theoretically available to a reader of Lovecraft's work. They are, in a sense, *shared* with the external reader and the intradiegetic reader and preserve a continuity between the experience of the real and the fictional.

"The Picture in the House" is a story that relies entirely on texts of this first category. Unlike stories such as "The Dunwich Horror" or *The Case of Charles Dexter Ward*, which rely on wholly fictional intradiegetic texts to produce their cosmic effect, "The Picture in the House" achieves horror through the blending of reality and fantasy and remains largely Gothic rather than cosmic. The text at the center of this story, *Regnum Congo*, has a bibliographic history that, though it does not enter into the narrative of the story, is a part of the archive. Given that the text is appearing within a fictional world, it has been stripped of its materiality, and therefore the relationship between that bibliographic history and the intradiegetic text that shares its name with an external text becomes unclear. Note the description of the physical book that appears in "The Picture in the House":

> The first object of my curiosity was a book of medium size lying upon the table and presenting such an antediluvian aspect that I marvelled at beholding it outside a museum or library. It was bound in leather with metal fittings, and was in an excellent state of preservation; being altogether an unusual sort of volume to encounter in an abode so lowly. When I opened it to the title page my wonder grew even greater, for it proved to be nothing less rare than Pigafetta's account of the Congo region, written in Latin from the notes of the sailor Lopez and printed at Frankfort in 1598. (CF 1.210)

The narrator explores in significant detail both the physical materiality of the book as well as some cursory bibliographic information. Enough information is provided here for an external reader, if he or she so desired, to hunt down a copy of the book being described.

To that end, it is worth noting that the print history described in the story is not fabricated. Monroe Work's 1928 *A Bibliography of the Negro in Africa and America* corroborates the narrator's description of its printing in Latin at Frankfurt in 1598, though the story refers to the text only by its shortened name of *Regnum Congo* rather than the title that would have presumably appeared on the edition's title page, *Regnum Congo ho est vera descriptioregni Africani*.

Despite the adherence of the intradiegetic *Regnum Congo*, in this instance, to the external *Regnum Congo*'s bibliographic history, it cannot be accurate to describe the intradiegetic instance as being the same as the external instance. It partakes of the truth of the external text, but Lovecraft's plot element cannot be said to possess the same degree of external reality. It is a material that is, of course, not a material. It exists only as a description of an object but not as an object itself. Like the *Necronomicon*, it has been pulled from the shelves of the virtual archive, and it also achieves no more reality. The effect produced by the story of blending reality and fiction is not because reality and fantasy have been in fact blended. Rather, the effect is produced because the fantasy contains within it virtual materials *suggestive* of external reality. It is no more *real* (in the external sense) than the table upon which it sits or the characters who discuss it. It is in this sense that the category of texts that exist in the external world proves to be a false identification. That they suggest an external reality is an effect of their virtuality; they are completely independent of their non-virtual instance. They are, in truth, creations that only exist in Lovecraft's archive and in the stories in which they feature.

Texts in the third category, texts that have external analogues that are significantly different from their intradiegetic forms, also exist only in Lovecraft's archive. Despite their tenuous relation to the external, these texts are wholly fictional.

The most striking example of this category of texts is the *Providence Gazette and Country-Journal*. Appearing prominently in *The Case of Charles Dexter Ward*, this newspaper receives minor bibliographical details (limited only to vague geography) when it first enters the narrative: "the old brick colonial schoolhouse that smiles across the road at the ancient Sign of Shakespear's Head where the *Providence Gazette and Country-Journal* was printed before the Revolution" (CF 2.223). Here, the narrative grounds the history of the text in the external history of the publication; however, as is evident from the "excerpts" that Lovecraft later provides from the *Journal*, the content is wholly Lovecraft's:

Nocturnal Diggers Surprised in
North Burial Ground

Robert Hart, night watchman at the North Burial Ground, this morning discovered a party of several men with a motor truck in the oldest part of the cemetery, but apparently frightened them off before they had accomplished whatever their object may have been.

> The discovery took place at about four o'clock, when Hart's attention was attracted by the sound of a motor outside his shelter. Investigating, he saw a large truck on the main drive several rods away; but could not reach it before the sound of his feet on the gravel had revealed his approach. (CF 2.289–90)

Despite appearing in a nominally external text, the narrative related by the *Journal* is entirely fictional, and unlike the detailed bibliographic sketch of *Regnum Congo*, there is little work done in the narrative to boost the realism of the text. If indeed there is realism, it is derived from the genre alone—newspaper articles are already assumed to be operating within the realm of reality and externality.

Further complicating this text is the fact that it is a newspaper. As such, there is no one external text to turn to as the model upon which Lovecraft bases his version of the *Journal*. Each edition is its own complete text. In the world of the fiction, Lovecraft has created an alternate timeline for the *Journal* in which the events detailed in the story are a part of the *Journal*'s output. This added effect of temporality, while perhaps unique to periodical texts, further establishes this entry in Lovecraft's archive as being wholly different from any external text—the only editions of the text we see are entirely fictional despite carrying the name of an external periodical.

Regardless the irregularity of the type of text, like texts of the second category (which has now been dissolved into the totality of the archive), this category too proves superficial and does little to describe the texts ascribed to it. Instead, the archive emerges as something that is wholly contained within the fiction, and therefore each text may be engaged by the intradiegetic reader in the same way: used.

Users and Readers

It is now time to turn to the question of reading and use in Lovecraft's fiction, the question of how texts are *used* by their readers, and the question of how we, as readers of Lovecraft, should understand the role of the intradiegetic reader.

A popularly held view (despite a lack of criticism on the subject) that the Lovecraftian protagonist is often a more or less fictionalized version of Lovecraft himself. Regardless of the validity of this claim, it is undeniable that his protagonists, like the man himself, rather than being dashing adventurers and bold "men's men," are more often men of a *subtler* variety: antiquarians, academics, artists, etc. Given the tendency of Lovecraftian protagonists to favor intellectual rather than physical pursuits, Lovecraft's stories are rife with descriptions of his protagonists' relationships with print/textual culture, and that relationship resembles a kind book use other than reading.

Book use, a favored term of book historians, refers to the functions books have or are made to have by those who engage with them; it is the "foundation of practice and experience [. . .] of memory and knowledge itself" (Cormack 2). Book historians such as Leah Price and Roger Chartier use the term to capture all the moments in the "life" of a book in which it is being engaged with in some way. In the introduction to her seminal work *How to Do Things with Books in Victorian Britain*, Price outlines three major operations of book use: "reading (doing something with the words), handling (doing something with the object), and circulating (doing something to, or with, other persons by means of the book— whether cementing or severing relationships, whether by giving and receiving books or by withholding and rejecting them)" (1). Within this framework, all engagements with the text of a book count as reading. For Price and others, reading is an amorphous category of action not bound by constraints of comprehension or activity.

Under this wide view of reading, it certainly cannot be argued that the Lovecraftian protagonist does not read the texts outlined above. There are clear and undeniable moments within the stories that demonstrate this reading: Dyer's references to having read the *Necronomicon*, Armitage's reading of the same, Carter's failed attempts to glean information from the Pnakotic Manuscripts. Let us examine the case of Randolph Carter's experience with the manuscripts in *The Dream-Quest of Unknown Kadath*. At the beginning of his quest, Carter is told of a set of manuscripts "too ancient to be read" (CF 2.105). Then, after seeking guidance from Atal in the city of Ulthar, Carter is noted to be "disappointed [. . .] by the meagre help to be found in the Pnakotic Manuscripts" (CF 2.106).

Whether Carter actually encounters the physical manuscripts or not, it is nonetheless true that he has, in some way, engaged with their text. According to Price's model, this would count as reading. To Price's credit, there is a great deal of concern in her book regarding the relationship between reading and handling texts. It is therefore not my intention to portray her work as shortsighted in this regard but rather to question characterizations of *reading* at large and suggest that available definitions are limiting.

The act of reading is largely understood as a process of exchange—the reader and the book engaging in a relationship in which both exhibit agency and, to some degree, autonomy and reading is "no longer characterized merely by an 'impertinent absence,' but by advances and retreats, tactics and games played with the text" (de Certeau 175). The idea of a "literal reading" has been characterized as an illusion produced and espoused by the social elite.

While that characterization may indeed be accurate, where does that leave the experience of reading within Lovecraft? Consider Dyer's "reading" of the Old Ones' ruins in *At the Mountains of Madness*.[4] The accuracy and completeness of the narrative that he produces from his engagement with the fragmentary texts relies on a hyper-literalization of the story presented. The degree to which he is able to extract the most specific of details is, though an interpretative act, an act of complete faith in the text being read. The degree to which Dyer's own *experience*—a key component of one's reading according to de Certeau and other reader-response theorists—influences and shapes his interpretation is only in its strict literalization of other texts he has consumed. Working backwards through his understanding of the *Necronomicon* (it too being a completely literal understanding), Dyer can only produce the diegetic truth of the Old Ones' story.

There seems to be no appropriate terminology to discuss this action aside from the already discarded term reading. In many ways, it seems indistinguishable from reading. Even as an action in this instance removed from an object recognizable as a book, there is a quality of Dyer's actions that powerfully suggests reading, and this quality is that it *is* reading, but not reading that we, as external readers, are able to do. It is intradiegetic reading—a process that contains all the necessary parts of reading *except* the act of reading itself. If reading suggests a kind of interpretation, intradiegetic reading is anti-interpretative. It is a non-mediated transference of ideas contained within one medium (a book, a fragment, a carving) into the mind and experience of its user.

Despite this, there remains the temporality of reading, the linguistic

---

4. Unlike other texts discussed here, what William Dyer reads in the ruins is not a book but rather carvings. Despite this seeming material difference, I see no reason to exclude it from this discussion of reading and materiality in HPL's work. Dyer engages with the text just as he would a book or manuscript (as evidenced by his similar interpretation of the *Necronomicon*).

processes of reading (phonics, syntax, eye-movement), and even some of the effects of reading. It is true that the text exerts some force on its reader, and that force is born out in intradiegetic reading. In fact, it is that force that creates the entirety of intradiegetic reading. The reader is wholly removed from the process of reading. William Dyer's understanding of the carvings is not clouded by ideological presuppositions or tempered by skepticism. Any doubts of the text's veracity are discarded by the text itself, and Dyer's role is minimized to receptacle rather than reader.

This mode of reading appears again in "The Call of Cthulhu" as Thurston concludes his tale: "That was the document I read [. . .] Cthulhu still lives, too, I suppose, again in that chasm of stone which has shielded him since the sun was young" (CF 2.55). He has so powerfully absorbed the texts he has read into himself that the text he has created is indistinguishable from them. His fear that his work may reach other eyes emphasizes his text's assumption of the truth he has found—meaning, for Lovecraft's readers (and by extension, his writers), slides easily from medium to medium without informational damage.

Similarly, Armitage's translation of the excerpted *Necronomicon* referred to above relies equally on the perfect transmission of meaning. Rather than, as translators are tasked to do, "destroy[ing] and replac[ing] the original text with a new one that eliminates the traces of the old," Armitage pulls the meaning into English without effecting it (Primavesi 54). The role of the author or reader or translator is minimized almost entirely, and all that remains is the power of the meaning contained.

Conclusion

Let us return to Lovecraft's archive one final time and sit among the texts and fragments, ruins and manuscripts. It is an archive of pure information only loosely containing its materials. It is an archive of materials only just holding on to the truths within them.

For all its conceptual complexity, Lovecraft's archive is an archive of the literal. It is, as de Certeau warns, a product of elitism. Only here, the elitism comes not from social prejudice but from the immutability of diegetic truth. The practices of reading that extend from the archive are practices that can only manifest themselves intradiegetically—the practice itself is a fiction of reading. The overbearing weight of the cosmic impedes interpretation and strips the reader of his readership. There is no room for games and tricks when the text itself is the abject undeniable truth. It is a kind of reading unachievable to the external reader. This is why *use* better identifies the practice. It is as if the reader, in using the text, becomes the text. Nothing about the text changes through its being read except the medium in which it is contained. Reading the *Necronomicon* does not let us know the *Necronomicon*; rather, we become the *Necronomicon*.

In this sense, Lovecraft's intradiegetic reading practices are not unlike those of the zealot, only magnified a hundred times over. There is an undeniability built into the text that, for the believer, is all-consuming. Denying even the possibility of exegesis, the text's truth is the only truth. It is a perfect, seamless, and irrefutable text.

Lovecraft begins what is arguably his most famous story with what is arguably his most famous quote: "The most merciful thing in the world, I think, is the inability of the human mind to correlate all its contents. We live on a placid island of ignorance in the midst of black seas of infinity, and it was not meant that we should voyage far" (CF 2.21). Lovecraft's readers are vessels. They mine the depths of knowledge and become the texts they read. The placid island of ignorance upon which they live is not their salvation but rather their undoing. Unable to question, unable to criticize, unable even to think, readers within Lovecraft's stories are able only to absorb. And in absorbing, they doom themselves to belief.

Works Cited

Braune, Sean. "How to Analyze Texts That Were Burned, Lost, Fragmented, or Never Written." *Symplokē* 21 (2013): 239-55.

Cormack, Bradin; Mazzio, Carla; and University of Chicago Library Special Collections Research Center. *Book Use, Book Theory, 1500–1700.* Chicago: University of Chicago Library, 2005.

de Certeau, Michel. "Reading as Poaching." In *The Practice of Everyday Life.* Berkeley: University of California Press, 1988. 165-76.

Derrida, Jaques. *Of Grammatology.* Tr. Gayatri Chakravorty Spivak. Delhi: Shri Jainendra Press, 1976.

Engle, John. "Cults of Lovecraft: The Impact of H. P. Lovecraft's Fiction on Contemporary Occult Practices." *Mythlore* 33, No. 1 (2014): 85-98.

Friedrich, Markus, and John Noël Dillon. "Places: Archives as Spatial Structures and Documents as Movable Objects." In *The Birth of the Ar-*

chive: A History of Knowledge. Ann Arbor: University of Michigan Press, 2018. 111–38.

Goetsch, Paul. "Reader Figures in Narrative." *Style* 38 (2004): 188–202.

Natsoulas, Thomas. "Virtual Objects." *Journal of Mind and Behavior* 20 (1999): 357–77.

Price, Leah. *How to Do Things with Books in Victorian Britain.* Princeton, NJ: Princeton University Press, 2012.

Primavesi, Patrick. "The Performance of Translation: Benjamin and Brecht on the Loss of Small Details." *TDR* [*The Drama Review*] 43, No. 4 (Winter 1999): 53–59.

Work, Monroe Nathan. *A Bibliography of the Negro in Africa and America.* New York: H. W. Wilson Co., 1928.

The Outsiders: Mapping Lovecraft's Loathing

Paul Neimann
University of Colorado, Boulder

Introduction

For many readers, H. P. Lovecraft's appeal lies in the sense of a mythology lurking behind his stories. This has meant, for Lovecraft's protégés and other writers, expanding his work or connecting and cataloging a common fictional universe.[1] While most scholars now reject August Derleth's interpretation of the Lovecraft "mythos," his suggestion nevertheless confirms a strong reality effect in the fiction.[2] Lovecraft's work has also suggested oblique or symbolic ways of describing the outside world. Recent "speculative realism," for example, treats his creations as philosophically mapping weird reality. Cultural historians find Lovecraft giving mythic scope to xenophobia or anxieties around science or modernity.

To the extent the writings suggest myths, it seems fair to draw inspiration from theorists who defined modern scholarship in that area. The structuralist movement, for instance, helped sideline unproductive treatments of myths as poetic or pseudo-scientific cosmographies. Instead of looking behind myths for originating ur-stories or historical events, anthropologists such as Claude Lévi-Strauss advocated comparing related, variant tales to see how cultures cognitively mapped their worlds and what problems they felt compelled to solve.[3] Roughly speaking, they treated

---

1. A work such as Chris Jarocha-Ernst's *A Cthulhu Mythos Bibliography and Concordance* will always lag behind this enterprise. For an overview, see S. T. Joshi, "The Cthulhu Mythos."

2. Key critiques of Derleth owe much to Dirk W. Mosig and Richard L. Tierney. See also Joshi, *Dissecting Cthulhu*, and Price, "Demythologizing Cthulhu" and *H. P. Lovecraft and the Cthulhu Mythos*.

3. I am also thinking of Vladimir Propp, Tzvetan Todorov, A. J. Greimas in semiotics,

folklore seriously, as evidence of thought patterns, rather than as an obfuscation of something else.

This impulse might supplement or correct efforts to translate horror fiction into philosophy or opinion (demythologizing), or more commercial treatments of an author's "world building" or quasi-real "universe" (overmythologizing). Taking a cue from folk studies, we might just methodically do what Lovecraft's biographers, readers, and critics already do anyway: compare texts to see what they have in common. That can still mean reconstructing a vision fragmented across different stories. But it also implies respecting fictional form as a source of meaning rather than something to be set aside once we have discerned a metaphysics, social context, or intellectual property.

The early stories examined here systematically engage a conundrum about how to hang on to behavioral and social standards amid modernity's profound "shifting of values" (CE 2.63). S. T. Joshi's commentary and judicious selection of letters have elsewhere made visible Lovecraft's desire to retain the civility of otherwise bankrupt religious, aristocratic traditions while respecting scientific enlightenment, apart from its emergence with "bourgeois capitalism" that "gave artistic excellence & sincerity a deathblow by enthroning cheap *amusement value* at the expense of *intrinsic excellence* which only persons of cultivated, non-acquisitive persons of assured position can enjoy." The stories likewise repudiate the intellectual dishonesty of both middlebrow cultural conservatives (a "herd of acquisitive boors" with "mawkish sentimentalities") and those who make a cultural virtue of profit, catering to masses "starved & crushed into a sodden, inarticulate helplessness through commercial & commercial-satellitic greed and callousness" (Joshi, "Introduction" 23-28; CLM 209). Lovecraft often claimed cheerful stoicism as an alternative, but his fictions outline a historical and economic dilemma immune to philosophical resolution. His more compulsive reaction, in contempt for various social outsiders, appears as a response in the wrong register—needless yet endemic to conditions he himself describes.

---

and the literary critic Fredric Jameson.

Lovecraft's Template

Lovecraft's early texts up to about 1925 (corresponding with the first volume of the Hippocampus Press variorum edition) make for a convenient, if semi-arbitrary, data set to explore. The stories suggest a neo-Gothic period, in that they use longstanding horror tropes Lovecraft also repudiated as "clanking chains" in "Supernatural Horror in Literature" (1927; *CE* 2.84). Indeed, his output during this formative period strongly adheres to one slightly varying structure, with repeated narrative units or mythemes that underlie more superficial changes in content. Paradoxically, derivative and repetitive material evolves into gratifying patterns that make Lovecraft a genre unto himself. Stripped to common elements, the tales offer a template with the following:

1. A male protagonist, often the last of his paternal line, suggests the exhaustion of patrician norms. He is often identified with Old World aristocrats or colonial American analogues.
2. His curiosity and sensitivity divide him from both elite conventions and plebian provincialism.
3. Esoteric "physical and metaphysical" researches, as in "From Beyond," mark his capacity to escape, question, or revivify culture (*CF* 1.192). Occult explorations are also equated with academic disciplines from physics to archaeology, or even just sea voyages; while material objects stand for accessing this knowledge (ancient volumes, a family tomb, magical objects, or Herbert West's "electrical machine" [195]). Lovecraft extends this pattern to artistic ventures, such as those of Erich Zann or, later, Richard Upton Pickman.
4. The protagonist stumbles upon a shattering reality that undermines conventional truths or authorities. He is frequently drawn into destructive confrontation with his past.

Along these lines, we find, to take a few examples, "The Alchemist" concerned with the "last of the unhappy and accursed Comtes de C——" (*CF* 1.27) and "The Tomb" with the lost heir to the "old and exalted" but corrupted Hyde family (*CF* 1.39). Arthur Jermyn is the "last" of a line that "put forth no branches" (*CF* 1.172); both "The Moon-Bog" and "The Rats in the Walls" feature descendants of ruling nobles. The dubious heroes (a "dreamer and visionary" in "The Tomb"; a "poet and a dreamer" in "Facts concerning the Late Arthur Jermyn and His Family") and sometime-villains question their corrupted or sterile origins to pursue knowledge. Herbert West's forbidden research into reviving corpses opposes, for instance, his "tradition-bound elders" (CF 1.298). Analogous ventures include the "researches into the unknown" in "The Statement of Randolph Carter," in which the sought after "nameless thing" (CF 1.132–33) is as good a name as any for occult or scientific discoveries in other stories. This esoteric knowing opposes the ignorance of "plebeian" peasants (CF 1.27), the "bulk of humanity" and "prosaic materialism" (CF 1.39). At the same time, new researches challenge the received, outdated beliefs of social aristocrats.

This narrative of esoteric discovery amid social decay features with more or less variation in stories like "The Beast in Cave"; "The Alchemist"; "The Tomb"; "Beyond the Wall of Sleep"; "The Transition of Juan Romero"; The Statement of Randolph Carter"; "The Terrible Old Man"; "Facts concerning the Late Arthur Jermyn and His Family"; "From Beyond"; "The Picture in the House"; "The Moon-Bog"; "The Outsider"; "The White Ship"; "The Lurking Fear"; "He"; "Herbert West—Reanimator"; "The Rats in the Walls"; "The Horror at Red Hook"; "The Unnamable"; "The Music of Erich Zann"; and "The Festival." A case can be made for including certain dream narratives such as "Celephaïs," "Hypnos," "The Other Gods," and "The Doom That Came to Sarnath." In short, the pattern fits most stories (in this sample to 1925) that qualify as horror, as distinct from sketches and outliers like "Sweet Ermengarde."

(Civilized) Tyrants and (Smart) Mobs

Mapping Lovecraft's thought this way reveals a kind of social allegory, repeated with minor differences across a number of tales. Common denominators, such as character types, point to real-world social correlates. Here Lovecraft's central concern lies in opposition between moribund or decadent paternalism and a visionary but perhaps equally debased nonconformity. The extremes, the outer corners of Lovecraft's mental world picture, suggest social dead ends balanced with equally flawed or deviant alternatives. The conflict in these stories might be simplified to a tension between high culture (sophisticated but inhibited and exhausted) and skeptical or revolutionary (rehabilitating but undisciplined) knowledge:

Culture   ⟵————————⟶   Knowledge

In this so-far simple schema, Culture, at its best, conjures the Augustan eighteenth-century England Lovecraft admired. It also suggests the Yankee America he praised, for instance, in the xenophobic and anti-Bolshevist allegory "The Street" as comprising "good valiant men of our blood who came from the Blessed Isles across the sea" (CF 1.113). We might guess that Lovecraft's notion of legitimate culture derives from his cruder impulses toward blood-and-soil nativism. But Lovecraft also undercuts admiration for Old World bluebloods and colonial founders with a sense of their stultification. We find that in his European-set tales and, for instance, in Herbert West's contempt for bourgeois pieties in the "chronic mental limitations of the 'professor-doctor' type—the product of generations of pathetic Puritanism; kindly, conscientious, custom-ridden, and lacking in perspective" (CF 1.299).

On the other side of the equation, Lovecraft shows the same ambivalence. He presents radical Knowledge as an antidote to moribund or sclerotic civility, yet one lacking social standards. Herbert West's Puritanical foes may be hidebound and blinkered—but they are also decent. They are kind and "high-souled characters whose worst real vice is timidity" (CF 1.299). In contrast, West's brave researches are horrific and tainted, in Lovecraft's prejudicial typology, by association with a brutish underclass. In a recurring gesture, his mad science appears mechanistic and utilitarian in the sense of showing no purpose beyond the transactional. A typical West specimen, "a sturdy and apparently unimaginative youth of wholesome plebeian type" (CF 1.295), lacks high cultural competence even before becoming a zombie.

West's unblinking materialism ("the so-called 'soul' is a myth" [CF 1.292]) mirrors Lovecraft's own views. Yet it stands against "soul" and, by implication, against living culture. Not much divides West, a "calm, blond, blue-eyed scientific automaton" (CF 1.305) from the "greed, ambition, vindictiveness, or misguided zeal" Lovecraft associates with, as he sees it, raw material ambitions of immigrants and bounders (CF 1.117). The scientist or occult explorer may correctly condemn traditional authority's decadence and bland orthodoxy. But West's efforts to revive thinking through advanced knowledge and working-class material produce something undead.

The stories speak to a conceptual failure to combine the "ancient spirit" of tradition and community with more modern or American individualism, skepticism, and science. Lovecraft generates fiction out of this tension, compulsively repeating an unsatisfied effort to find a way out. His own poses of genteel refinement, against ignorant mobocracy, and his freethinking, against Victorian constraint, sit together less well than we might assume. In his stories, dead conformity haunts the former; mindless commerce and technocracy dog the latter. Lovecraft's philosophical embrace of mechanistic determinism cannot be divided from his loathing for a modern society organized much in those terms—as an accidental by-product of economic growth and popular taste rather than conscious guidance. Neither, however, does he seem convinced that cultural guardians manage more than self-serving autocracy or complacent small-mindedness.

All the Others: The Primitive and the Peasant

Culture and knowledge are not, of course, strict logical opposites. Nor are they mutually exclusive. They merely seemed so to Lovecraft, at a moment in time. Or, rather, his work channels a certain inability to reconcile these hypothetical ideals in his era. The perceived opposition between (old) Culture and (new) Knowledge can be fleshed out by looking for other repeated elements in the stories. The resulting world picture is neither strictly factual nor merely subjective, and likely not fully conscious. On balance, we get a sense of Lovecraft as creatively *situated*. He depicts real-life social tendencies, mostly ones he abhorred, and conceptualizes them in available and sometimes limiting ways.

Charting the stories means empirically searching out opinions conveyed by recurring typological or quasi-allegorical elements. At the same time, as the structuralist tradition observes, employing any abstracted map of reality entails some automatic commitment to the map itself. We can predict, simply on the basis of logic and language, for example, that anxiety about losing Culture implies (roughly) a fear of disorder or primitivism. Also: idealizing Knowledge compels contemplation of its stricter logical negation in ignorance. A discerning reader, confronted with the basic dilemma, knows to look for a compromise or combination of tradition and truth. The tendency to think in such patterns tells us where to look for Lovecraft's ideas; actually finding them helps confirm that approach.

The stories here do, in fact, generate a schema, a cognitive framing, consistent with a basic tension between "real" civilization or Culture and unbounded Knowledge: nostalgia for Old World or colonial community, a civilized "inside," finds its contradiction in Lovecraft's xenophobic references to foreign, supposedly primal tribalism or devolution of Anglo types. Apart from the notorious anti-immigrant sentiment in "The Horror at Red Hook," one finds "Facts concerning the Late Arthur Jermyn and His Family" linking degeneracy, familial collapse, and suicide to African sub-humans. The titular "Terrible Old Man," a clipper ship captain, does supernatural violence associated with "obscure Eastern" places—while his antisocial victims have Eastern European or Italian names and are "not of Kingsport blood; they were of that new and heterogeneous alien stock which lies outside the charmed circle of New England life and traditions" (CF 1.141). Cannibalism is associated with the Congo (CF 1.213). In a slight deviation, exotic locales signify socially disruptive, if not strictly primitive occult habits: Juan Romero is "ignorant and dirty" but also of "noble Aztec" ancestry; the narrator's own cultic knowledge comes from "odd Eastern lore" (CF 1.96-7).

We find, I think, a separate and distinct version of social margins in American "peasant" characters, ranging from the Catskills "white trash" of "Beyond to the Wall of Sleep" to the backwoods grotesque in "The Picture in the House." Apart from prejudice about uncivilized foreigners, Lovecraft's fixates on the uncouth ignorance of rural English or Dutch descendants he also often praises. These are not failed cultures, but rather cultural failures. Joe Slater, in "Beyond the Wall of Sleep," is "one of those strange, repellent scions of a primitive colonial peasant stock whose isolation for nearly three centuries in the hilly fastness of a little-travelled countryside has caused them to sink into a kind of barbaric degeneracy." This corresponds "exactly to the decadent element of 'white trash' in the South" (CF 1.72) The otherwise admirable Dutch Martense family in "The Lurking Fear" similarly decays after fleeing English colonial rule: "Their life was increasingly secluded, and people declared that their isolation had made them heavy of speech and comprehension" (CF 1.363). The cannibal in "The Picture in the House" is a Puritan descendant typifying the "solitude, grotesqueness and ignorance" resulting from "morbid self-repression, and struggle for life with relentless Nature" (CF 1.207).

One might reasonably find an overarching bigotry that ostracizes comprehensively on the basis of race, class, religion, and geography. Structural mapping, though, finds this spite channeled into a more specific classificatory system. Lovecraft distinguishes, I suggest, between largely foreign milieux he reflexively treats as wholly uncivilized; those mark the outside or logical antithesis of proper socialization. On the other hand, he perceives an atavistic impulse within culture, especially in New England settings. Idealized colonial Enlightenment, seen to correct rigid European custom, carries the risk of socially incoherent individualism and isolation. Employing Greimas's efficient "semiotic square" style of matrix, the founding Culture–Knowledge split might be supplemented to read:

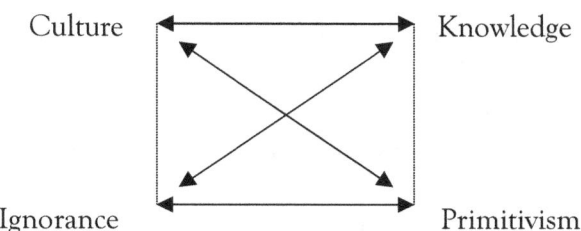

The lower coordinates here mark, on the diagonals, implied or inevitable logical negations of the original, more historically contingent Culture–Knowledge tension. The social map in these neo-Gothic stories, read as a movement from Culture to Knowledge, can be seen to compare older European aristocratic orders and newer American forms steeped in religious reformation, Enlightenment, and modernity.

The old order, distressingly, secures social harmony via aristocratic lies. But fictions about noble blood or feudal privilege conceal a supposedly excluded viciousness. The Culture–Primitivism axis, that is, designates conceptual-logical opposites, as seen in tales that locate the savage outside Europe. But the division is also an unstable construct. The stories show that claiming civility only guarantees ascribing barbarity to others. Similarly, regimes of modern Knowledge, while formally negating pre-modern Ignorance, can evolve their own philistinism, in social isolation, demeaning commerce, or Puritanical fanaticism.

Stated perhaps more intuitively, Lovecraft mirrors an older Gothic drama with a modern one. In the former, an *ancien régime* controls plebeian classes by enclosing them within feudal order or religion. Lovecraft hints approvingly at a hierarchy of learning and gentility that America lacks. Ignorance remains contained, and venturing outside the bounds of elite influence requires, as we have seen, leaving civilization itself. This contrast between Culture and alleged alien Primitivism suggests the political reactionary's sense of a forced choice between autocracy and primal chaos.

Lovecraft's unsavory anxieties around uncivilized contagion or miscegenation also confirm the supposedly foreign as a fantasy projection of the patrician's own repressed. These stories' scenes of revelation turn on Gothic tropes of internal rot, as in Walpole's *The Castle of Otranto* or Poe's "The Fall of the House of Usher." High cultural achievement comes at the cost of aristocratic tyranny (as in "The Alchemist" or "The Rats in the Walls") and intellectual stagnation. The aristocrat ends up peering at a savage already within. Tellingly, "The Outsider" offers a version of recognizing the monster inside that is stripped of any historical specifics. Inside and outside are, formally, just a matter of perspective.

Striking out from Gothic oppressiveness (in favor of Knowledge, on the right side of the diagram) suggests the colonial America Lovecraft admired, imbued with the possibilities of nonconformity and science. But, as noted, he also depicts craven materialism and, in a negation away from knowledge, debased vulgarity and superstition. Simply put, American elites, the grandees of Plymouth Rock or the Albany Convention, surrender the "soul" of communal custom and generate an ignorant peasantry reminiscent of Europe. The progress that makes colonial Providence makes Salem witch trials too. This complements the way the patrician order decays into frightful primitivism that Lovecraft also depicts as the underbelly of modernity.

Here we touch on what Greimas calls relations of implication or entailment (the axes Culture-Ignorance and Knowledge-Primitivism). In Lovecraft's view, traditional order, its hidden barbarity notwithstanding, at least contains provincialism within an inherited or educational hierarchy. In contrast, modernity—fluid and industrial, unrestricted and individualist—promises no link between authority and social education. Barely a generation divides colonial founder from backwoods rube, and both are entitled to rule.

Lovecraft's obsession with would-be markers of unworthiness—geographic, ethnic, pseudo-genetic—seems inversely proportional to an anxiety that, on America's own capitalist terms, nothing truly privileges him over the working class or the stranger. As a result, the stories try to define America's ideal, knowledgeable inside against an objectively "foreign" underclass. But in truth, Lovecraft's own cultural pedigree and self-education, as his life in New York showed him, were worth little, given that they were not worth money.

"The Rats in the Walls" and "He"

It seems possible to confirm this model by examining two stories, "The Rats in the Walls" and "He," in more detail. Both follow the outlines noted above; they clarify Lovecraft's thinking when seen in conjunction with patterns of other stories.

"The Rats in the Walls," along lines I have suggested, establishes the narrator as the American descendant of an "abhorred line" of corrupted English aristocrats: "Walter de la Poer, eleventh Baron Exham, fled to Virginia and there founded the family which by the next century had become known as Delapore" (CF 1.375). The story develops the noble ancestors as criminal tyrants detested by local peasants, "a race of hereditary daemons beside whom Gilles de Retz and the Marquis de Sade would seem the veriest tyros" (CF 1.379). In contrast, the renewed American family achieves the "the glories of a proud and honourable, if somewhat reserved and unsocial Virginia line" (CF 1.375). They appear as a social corrective, founded by an exceptional "shy, gentle" dissenter and avenger of the hidden crimes; he is classed by a fellow "gentleman-adventurer" as "a man of unexampled justice, honour, and delicacy" (CF 1.382). The family seems, in Lovecraft's terms, quintessentially American: they participate in the Civil War; the narrator achieves "ultimate wealth as a stolid Yankee"; his son fights in World War I and dies after a period as a "maimed invalid," though only after bringing word from Europe of "ancestral legends" and "sinister history" (CF 1.376).

The son's death prompts the narrator, Delapore, to recover the abandoned family seat at Exham Priory in England. He exemplifies ongoing skeptical and scientific reappraisal of the past, availing himself of "archaeologists and scientific men" (CF 1.390) and an anthropologist. His researches expose tyrant aristocrats as internalizing primitive pre-Anglo Saxon cults ("a Druidical or ante-Druidical thing" [CF 1.378]). Barbaric tendencies appear in the family's treatment of local serfs: a parallel descendant of local peasants who served in the war with Delapore's son, Capt. Norrys ("a plump, amiable young man"), relays "peasant superstitions" (CF 1.376). Delapore, now affecting the original de la Poer name, notes that "What the people could not forgive, perhaps, was that I had come to restore a symbol so abhorrent to them; for, rationally or not, they viewed Exham Priory as nothing less than a haunt of fiends and werewolves (CF 1.377–78). He confirms the hinted reversion to type with a dream of "a twilit grotto, knee-deep with filth, where a white-bearded daemon swineherd drove about with his staff a flock of fungous, flabby beasts whose appearance filled me with unutterable loathing" (CF 1.384). The dream conveys a hideous truth, the family's cannibalism of a stock of de-evolving peasants:

> The quadruped things—with their occasional recruits from the biped class—had been kept in stone pens [. . .] There had been great herds of them, evidently fattened on the coarse vegetables whose remains could be found as a sort of poisonous ensilage at the bottom of huge stone bins older than Rome. I knew now why my ancestors had had such excessive gardens—would to heaven I could forget! The purpose of the herds I did not have to ask. (CF 1.393)

This offers neatly condensed image of aristocratic violence and exploitation in which barbarism assigned to lower orders also resides within.

Tracking Lovecraft's conceptual habits locates the story within a bigger social picture too. The story includes Lovecraft's usual assessment of bankrupt tradition and admiration for new world reforms. At the same time, he remains suspicious of any future organized around a working or mechanical class: the descriptions of the "plump" Norrys, which foreshadow Delapore's regression to cannibalism, and Norrys's biological connection to livestock, hint at deficiencies in the "younger, stouter, and presumably more naturally materialistic man" (CF 1.389). Alternatively, the line of Virginia gentleman-scholars at least briefly combines the best of the old and new. Lovecraft idealizes a resolution between Culture and Knowledge. It is historically tenuous but potentially realized in his own stance as a cultivated visionary.

Without being overly programmatic, one might say that the drama between peasant-brutes and nobles exposed as savage cultists shows the abject combination of Ignorance and Primitivism. That seems confirmed by another cannibal figure, in "The Picture in the House," a character conspicuously linking intellectual decay in Puritan forbears and license taken from foreign, primitive rites; his anthropophagy results from reading neurotic Puritan texts together with imperialist accounts of a barbarous "Afriky." Relatedly, the cannibalistic cycle in "The Rats in the Walls" combines the serfs' dull passivity and the de la Poers' totally degenerate impulses.

Delapore's raving degeneration also returns to Lovecraft's bleak sense of decline. The family's Gothic consumption finds its modern equivalent or repetition in the mechanistic order pointedly identified as having "eaten" his son:

Why shouldn't rats eat a de la Poer as a de la Poer eats forbidden things? . . .
The war ate my boy, damn them all . . . and the Yanks ate Carfax with flames
and burnt Grandsire Delapore and the secret. . . . No, no, I tell you, I am *not*
that daemon swineherd in the twilit grotto! It was *not* Edward Norrys' fat face
on that flabby, fungous thing! Who says I am a de la Poer? He lived, but my
boy died! . . . Shall a Norrys hold the lands of a de la Poer? (CF 1.396)

Neither the revelation that Delapore is really a de la Poer nor the idea that
society still eats its own captures the ending's full disturbance. Delapore's
fury that Norrys outlived his son and is upwardly mobile targets modernity's Great War less than its erasure of hierarchy. Grief becomes trauma
because the wrong people are consumed. Reversion to patrician atrocity, a
circuit from old world to new and back again, makes for a horrific, impossible correction of the present with the past. That reflects the similarly
failed correctives in modernity we see elsewhere.

For example, "He," Lovecraft's autobiographical story of disillusionment in New York City, offers brief poetic hope for a civilized modernity.
New York's skyscrapers supply a fitting image of creativity underwritten by
knowledge and science, with "incredible peaks and pyramids rising flower-
like and delicate from pools of violet mist to play with the flaming golden
clouds" (CF 1.506). But this desire for new mythic culture, to be "one with
the marvels of Carcassonne and Samarcand and El Dorado and all glorious
and half-fabulous cities" (CF 1.506), gives way to disenchantment. There is
growth but no life, "the noxious elephantiasis of climbing, spreading stone."
Again, Lovecraft employs language of animate deadness, as in the Herbert
West series: "This city of stone and stridor is not a sentient perpetuation of
Old New York as London is of Old London [. . .] but [. . .] it is in fact quite
dead, its sprawling body imperfectly embalmed and infested with queer animate things which have nothing to do with it as it was in life" (CF 1.507).
The animate things are "swarthy strangers with hardened faces and narrow
eyes, shrewd strangers [. . .] who could never have aught to a blue-eyed
man of the old folk, with the love of fair green lanes and white New England steeples in his heart" (CF 1.507). Lovecraft figures a bleak endpoint
in equally racist terms, via magical glimpses of a future of vaguely Asiatic
cultic hordes, with "the yellow, squint-eyed people of that city, robed horribly in orange and red, and dancing insanely to the pounding of fevered
kettle-drums" (CF 1.515). Here "hateful modernity" produces a "corpse
city" (CF 1.514–15) reminiscent of Herbert West's researches.

The narrator's nostalgic retreat, in obsession with the city's older,

Georgian remnants and "archaic lanes and houses" recalling "when Greenwich was a placid village not yet engulfed by the town," fails to offer a real solution (CF 1.508). He meets a stranger, the "He" of the title, whose antiquarian "kindred seekings" (CF 1.509) exceed his own. This clear alter ego's revelations include the blunt admission that a colonial ancestor (likely he himself) murdered "mongrel" natives, serving them "monstrous bad rum" to steal their occult customs (CF 1.513).

The tale's denouement casts these hidden wrongs as worthy of justice or revenge. The "salvage" [sic] element already lies at the heart of the ancestral squire's will to power, in his researches into "qualities in the will of mankind" that flout "the sanctity of things as great as time and space" (CF 1.512). The city's dead future resembles this occult-elite past as much as any foreign element.

The historical problem appears to be repetition in altered terms, so that there is no social safeguard against decay into an inhuman calculus of power. The story's supernatural time shifts have the reader traversing a hopeless path from tribal and colonial devil-worship to an updated and more efficient Fordist or corvée labor of cosmic horror. The narrator's final return home, to "the pure New England" (CF 1.517) loses its appeal inasmuch as the idea of original purity—away from culture's degradation by directionless growth and raw self-interest, also has been destroyed.

In spite of itself, the story verges on a self-diagnosis of racist pathology. Lovecraft's instinct to play outsider-victim, a native displaced by foreigners, yields up horror of the self-regarding insider. The time-traveling squire dresses in "full mid-Georgian costume from queued hair and neck ruffles to knee-breeches, silk hose, and [. . .] buckled shoes" (CF 1.511). At best, the alter-ego makes for a wry, maybe intentional, image of Lovecraft's stubborn conservationism. But the ludicrous and perverse appearance also marks Lovecraft as an outsider mainly by virtue of being out of step and dysfunctional in a New York actually at a cultural high point. The story logic works similarly. Having presented no compelling alternative to modern tyrannies, the squire only makes for a dated iteration of a newly reconfigured horror machine.

All these occult researchers—ritualist natives, the squire, and cultic hordes from the future—suggest knowledge co-opted by selfish, senseless activity. Lovecraft's stories are replete with esoteric explorers: elites dabbling in tantalizing primitivism and, conversely, unwashed doomsday sects that out-know heroes only dimly grasping truths. These plausibly figure

Enlightenment split from order and then pressed into service of a pur-
poseless modernity. "The Horror at Red Hook," for example, features an
idealized detective-poet (Thomas Malone, "who united imagination with
scientific knowledge" [CF 1.485]) and a more dubious fearlessly educated
patrician (Robert Suydam, "a lettered recluse of ancient Dutch family" [CF
1.486]). Both are swept aside by a nihilistic mob only too happy to use
freedom or knowledge to dispense with culture entirely.

One might, with reference to the diagram, identify these occult savants
with the conjunction of Knowledge and Primitivism. An unappealing
hedge against this outcome takes shape in bourgeois or mid-Victorian
complacency Lovecraft hated, which preserves order by embracing oblivi-
ousness (combining Culture and Ignorance). Socially aspirant good taste—
one could say smarm—hobbles both progress and healthy peasant dissent.

Conclusion

Lovecraft's familiar fixation on cosmic indifference can be understood in
the social terms seen here, in the disjunction between Culture and
Knowledge: horror lies in civility's fragility or fraudulence and the inability, as he writes in "The Call of Cthulhu," to "correlate it" with uncom-
promising skepticism. Lovecraft's effort to identify failure with some
essentially foreign element is all the more unconvincing inasmuch as that
identity remains irrelevant to dynamics he actually explores. He writes, in
"Red Hook," that "modern people under lawless conditions tend uncanni-
ly to repeat the darkest instinctive patterns of primitive half-ape savagery in
their daily life" (CF 1.485). But he has also identified lawlessness—ruthless
extraction and malignant growth—as the hidden essence of both aristocratic and modern rationalities. A mechanical cosmos that blindly follows
"laws" likewise may as well be lawless. That might narrowly mean loathing
of outsiders is not "central" to texts that really blame decay on venerated-
but-antisocial establishments. But that leaves bigotry in arguably its most
noxious and essential form—as a personal way to salve insecurities or secure advantages while repressing knowledge of systemic problems.

The less troubling aspects of Lovecraft's legacy lie in his rejection of
both the Burkean conservative's tolerance for sublime lies about patrician
superiority and the pseudo-conservative's self-defeating affiliation with the
market of vulgar tastes. Truth cannot be found in a "hypocritical nineteenth-century view of the world" (CE 2.77). But neither can civility be

found in mercantile sensibility. Here Lovecraft's efforts to square the circle between culture and fearless knowledge, by rejecting these twin American idols, look like acts of self-sabotage: erudite pulp horror, predictably, endears itself neither to critics nor the general public. But for Lovecraft it is at the nexus of "a civilised condition" and "genuine ideas" (CE 2.76–77).

In one sense, this intellectual response to modernity, in "imaginative literature" (CE 5.48), clearly failed Lovecraft. It saved him neither from real-world indignities nor related compensatory hostilities. But the conceptual map latent in his work explains that failure as a misrecognition of socio-historical problems he saw. Structurally, the stories, like the letters quoted above, identify refinement not as an inherent quality of persons or places, but of (historically ill-gotten) leisure and economic security—the freedom of "non-acquisitive persons of assured position" to attend to it. The risks of mobocracy are conversely a contingent function of a populace "starved & crushed" by "greed" into frantic boredom and idiocy.

Lovecraft's wish for intellectual flourishing without drudgery or pandering requires, in other words, a security generalized to all. Along these lines, Joshi rightly, albeit vaguely, links a possible softening of Lovecraft's prejudices to the writer's late support for New Deal "socialism"—a dawning awareness, I suggest, of logic already in the early stories (Joshi, "Racism" 43).

Works Cited

Greimas, A. J. *Structural Semantics: An Attempt at a Method.* Tr. D. McDowell, R. Schleifer, and A. Velie. Lincoln: University of Nebraska Press, 1983.

Jameson, Fredric. *The Political Unconscious: Narrative as a Socially Symbolic Act.* Ithaca, NY: Cornell University Press, 1981.

Jarocha-Ernst, Chris. *A Cthulhu Mythos Bibliography & Concordance.* Seattle: Armitage House, 1999.

Joshi, S. T. "The Cthulhu Mythos." In S. T. Joshi, ed. *Icons of Horror and the Supernatural.* Westport, CT: Greenwood Press, 2007, 1:97–128.

———. "Introduction." In *An Epicure in the Terrible: A Centennial Anthology of Essays in Honor of H. P. Lovecraft,* ed. David E. Schultz and S. T. Joshi. 1991. New York: Hippocampus Press, 2011.

———. "Why Michel Houellebecq is Wrong About Lovecraft's Racism." *Lovecraft Annual* No. 12 (2018): 43–50.

————, ed. *Dissecting Cthulhu: Essays on the Cthulhu Mythos*. Lakeland, FL: Miskatonic River Press, 2011.

Lévi-Strauss, Claude. "The Structural Study of Myth." *Journal of American Folklore* 68 (October–Dececember 1955): 428–44.

Price, Robert M. "Demythologizing Cthulhu." *Lovecraft Studies* No. 8 (Spring 1984): 3–9.

————. *H. P. Lovecraft and the Cthulhu Mythos*. Mercer Island WA: Starmont House, 1990.

Propp, Vladimir. *Morphology of the Folktale*. Tr. Laurence Scott, rev. Louis A. Wagner. Austin: University of Texas Press, 1968.

Todorov, Tzvetan. "Structural Analysis of Narrative." *NOVEL: A Forum on Fiction* 3 (Autumn 1969): 70–76.

The Ebb of Sanity: "The Night Ocean" and Bipolar Disorder

Kyle Gamache
Community College of Rhode Island

Introduction

H. P. Lovecraft and R. H. Barlow's collaborative work "The Night Ocean" (1936) is one of the more poignant and atmospheric pieces in early weird fiction. Although the strength of the story lies in its subtlety and milieu, its minimalism provides the foundation whereby deeper meanings may be gleaned. Weird fiction commonly explores thematic aspects of mental illness or the disruption of reality. "The Night Ocean" is no exception, as mental illness can be clearly seen as a theme within the story. This paper argues that "The Night Ocean" can be used as an allegory for mental illness and, due to the shifting nature of the narrative, specifically for the classic presentation of bipolar disorder. This paper will present an overview of the story and identify which elements and symptoms of bipolar disorder are present within the mood and action of the piece. The intention is not to suggest that "The Night Ocean" is an outright case study in bipolar disorder. Instead, the intent is to show that the story is more of a personal and lonely exploration of human emotion rather than cosmic horror.

Knowing that mental illness permeated in Lovecraft's life and fiction makes it unsurprising that mental illness is a theme in "The Night Ocean." Lovecraft's parents were both institutionalized due to mental illness in Providence's Butler Hospital until their respective deaths, leaving Lovecraft isolated and lost. As a young adult, Lovecraft experienced a serious nervous breakdown and, for the rest of his short life, he would be stricken with bouts of depression and night terrors. A recurring theme in Lovecraft's work is the loss of sanity; believing that he was sensitive to the fragility of mental health and that his fear of madness influenced his work is reasonable. R. H. Barlow does not appear to have suffered the same afflictions as his friend (Abrams) but, as the future literary executor of Lovecraft's work, he was keenly aware of Lovecraft's themes of sanity and madness. In addition, the authors lived during turbulent times with significant social changes, changes with which Lovecraft himself felt particularly out of sync. The shifting nature of the environment and narrator of "The Night Ocean," in fact, may be the personification of both the authors' sense of displacement in their changing world and their feelings of being outsiders in their respective environments. Indeed, one of the more poignant lines at the close of the piece may suggest personal identification with the work: "[v]ast and lonely is the ocean" (CF 4.658).

Initial scholarship hypothesized that both authors evenly contributed to the writing; however, the recent discovery of Barlow's manuscript suggests that he was the primary author (CF 4.632; Joshi and Schultz).[1] Regardless, although mental illness is clearly a theme in "The Night Ocean," its presence is much more peculiar than other Lovecraftian works. Indeed, "The Night Ocean" stands out from Lovecraft's fiction, not just as his last completed work, but for multiple departures from his standard fiction. Compared to other pieces of weird fiction, supernatural occurrences are limited in the story, while an uncanny world is alluded to peripherally. Like the works of Poe, a major influence on Lovecraft, the story is more about the atmosphere and mood than eldritch monsters or evil gods. Instead, the simple piece is about an artist spending a lonely late summer isolated in a small seaside town. This simplicity allows the reader to see the story for what it is: a parable of bipolar disorder.

Summary of "The Night Ocean"

The unnamed narrator—an artist who arrives to the summer resort of Ellston Beach in August—hopes to rest his "weary mind" following the completion of a mural for an art contest. He takes up residence in a small beach shack on a sandy hill a mile from the touristy Ellston, and he spends the first weeks of his vacation swimming in the cold waters and walking on the beach. He enjoys his vacation, relishing being alone and

---

1. A facsimile of Barlow's typescript, with Lovecraft's corrections, appears in *Lovecraft Annual* No. 8 (2014): 84–110.

avoiding the tourists. The weather is wonderful and the sun, radiant. The narrator frequently contemplates the moods and changes of the ancient sea, thinking it a mysterious power from infant Earth capable of rejuvenating his mind (CF 4.632–36).

However, the idyllic summer turns stale as a series of events increase the narrator's anxiety. On one of his walks on the beach, the artist spies an odd animal bone with intricate carvings and a strange metal bead, reminding him of a half-forgotten myth of an underwater king whose love was stolen away by a strange ape-like creature. Later in the story, a series of drownings occur in Ellston, with the bloated bodies of the victims washing up on shore with signs of grisly trauma, increasing the narrator's sense of unease and making the sea a constant and ominous presence, which causes him to ceases his swimming (CF 4.638–42).

Later, after being caught in a sudden storm on his walk home, the narrator sees three dark shapes in the waves near his house. Bewildered by what they could be, or why people would be swimming during the storm, he calls out to them, but they abruptly disappear into the waves. When the narrator returns home, he remains confused by this event but eventually falls asleep. The next morning, his somber mood briefly abates due to the shining sun. Yet this elevated mood vanishes when he discovers what he thinks is a watery, decaying hand lying on the beach. The drownings, the dark shapes in the water, and the disembodied hand have a profound effect on the narrator and for the remainder of his stay in Ellston his mood continues to darken (CF 4.644–47).

Eventually, the summer comes to an end and autumn descends on Ellston. The tourists leave, and the narrator remains behind. He is notified that the mural he had worked himself into exhaustion over has won the contest, but he meets this news with no interest. His mood is dark as he has become afraid of the sea, now considering it an alien and unfeeling menace. When he prepares to leave Ellston he has a brush with the uncanny on his last evening. As he looks out at the night ocean, he sees a strange humanoid shape he describes as a "a dog, a human being, or something more strange" (CF 4.656). It bobs in the water before exiting laden with a "heavy burden" on its shoulder. The creature then bounds over the sand dunes out of sight, leaving the narrator to ponder the mysterious ocean and the darkness under the waves. No further events occur and the sea offers no more mysteries. The narrator muses that all things come from the sea, and to the sea they will return. The sea will remain until the end of the planet, its waves crashing on in the dusk of the world (CF 4.657–58).

Symptomology of Bipolar Disorders

The disorders now known as *bipolar disorders* have been studied and explored since the Classical period. The states associated with bipolarity, depression (termed *melancholia*), and mania were well known to ancient Greek philosophers and physicians. Aristotle and Aretaeus of Cappadocia both analyzed the heroes from Homer's *Iliad*, identifying states of rage and sorrow (Angst and Marneros). Plato also described "divine madness" (*theia mania*) as state of extreme mood and insight that caused sufferers to have increased inspiration. Hippocrates was the first to describe melancholia and mania as a disease, recommending salt baths and humor treatments (Angst and Marneros). Modern bipolar disorders can be traced to Emil Kraepelin's categorization of *manic-depressive insanity* in the late nineteenth century, linking the two as a single disorder (summarized in Angst and Marneros). Today, bipolar disorders include several different mental illnesses sharing similar symptomology: the presence of depressive states, with spikes of elevated manic episodes.

Today, the psychiatric category of "bipolar and related disorders" include classic examples of bipolar disorder such as *Bipolar I*, a disorder with severe depressive and manic states, as well as related disorders with similar features of affective distress (e.g., cyclothymic disorder, schizoaffective disorder), but with differences in the severity of either polar state, or the inclusion of cycling patterns, psychosis, or different course of symptoms (American Psychological Association [APA]).

Manic states are the most famous features of bipolarity. Mania is categorized as a state of elevated or energized mood. This mood creates a series of additional symptoms, often greatly increasing goal-directed activity, hyperactivity, distractibility, and decreased need for sleep (APA). Occasionally when gripped with mania, some patients channel this energy productively (Jamison), while most patients are heavily impaired (APA). In addition to manic episodes, bipolar disorders often include depressive episodes. Depressive episodes are marked by low mood and affect, fatigue, negative feelings of hopelessness or worthlessness, and anhedonia (APA). Episodes are similar to the traditional symptoms of major depressive disorder and other unipolar disorders (APA).

The course of bipolar disorder varies depending on the specific type and individual experiencing the illness. Symptoms usually begin in late adolescence or early adulthood, with the individual experiencing both manic and depressive episodes, often having multiple episodes of both during the course. Depressive episodes will often occur more frequently and last longer than manic episodes, and almost two-thirds (60%) of manic episodes will immediately proceed a depressive episode; however, there need not be an alternating pattern of mania followed by depression (APA). Occasionally, a person may experience psychosis during either type of episode. Individuals often experience periods of baseline functionality between episodes; but stress can decrease functionality during baseline (APA).

Bipolar Disorder in "The Night Ocean"

"The Night Ocean" is a perfect allegory for the symptoms of bipolarity. Both the narrator's thoughts and the description of the setting change between manic and depressive. The narrator describes frenzied activity followed by melancholy and lack of interest—common staples of bipolar disorder—and his mood during his adventure in Ellston fluctuates from elated to depressed. In describing the setting, the mood is constantly shifting between elation and dejection, an ebb and flow explored directly in the piece by the great attention placed on the passing of the tides and the changing of seasons within the setting.

The Narrator's Symptoms

The initial act of "The Night Ocean" suggests that the narrator is coming to the end of a manic episode. The narrator begins the piece describing that he is retreating to Ellston to rest his exhausted psyche, following the completion of his art project. He tells of the great amount of effort and attention he has given to his mural design, noting that the labor had driven him to near exhaustion (CF 4.632–33). This hyper-focus and exertion can be seen as the increased energy and intensive motivation of a manic episode, one that has drained the artist and brought him to the beach for relief.

Once in Ellston, the narrator is happy with his surroundings, greatly enjoying the cold ocean water and abundance of sunlight (CF 4.635). He describes spending all his time swimming and in the sunlight, feeling rejuvenated and protected by the sea (637). Though his lodging is isolated from the town and he mocks the tourists of Ellston (though he himself is one), the narrator describes that he is quite content with his vacation (638). This initial enjoyment of Ellston and the sea can be seen to be the end of the manic episode, or a brief period of baseline functioning.

A traditional presentation of bipolar disorder has the patient experiencing a depressive episode following the manic, and the narrator begins to feel such a change. The narrator makes early references to previous negative emotions (CF 4.633) and notes that he chose the isolated cottage as it was lonely "like [himself]" (634, 637), but the change of mood escalates. This change appears to be linked to the endings of the summer and the beginning of a stormy autumn (639), a common trigger for those with bipolar disorder between mania and depression (i.e., seasonal affective subtype of bipolar disorder) (APA). The narrator describes that the sea had "become abruptly strange" (CF 4.640) and that he is experiencing shifting dark moods throughout the day (640-41). He alternates from describing these dark moods to suddenly feeling "half of exultant pleasure" while being caught in the rainstorm (644).

The depressive episode fully descends following the first glimpse of the strange creatures in the ocean (CF 4.645) and finding the disembodied hand (650). The narrator describes that his mood quickly descends to fear, loneliness, and feelings of worthlessness (651). The sea, once the source of rejuvenation (641, 651), now is a source of fear (651). The narrator describes passive suicidal ideation, stating that he is a man "who no longer cares to live" (651) but is as fearful of death as he is of life (652). As the episode continues, the narrator is struck by a "curious apathy" (653) and is indifferent to the news that he has won the art contest he submitted to earlier in the summer. The narrator's reaction reflects anhedonia, a classic symptom of depressive episodes, by which the artist no longer feels joy about the art that had exhausted him nor any relief that he can now leave the recently cursed ocean (653).

A final symptom of bipolar disorders can be found in the narrator's possible psychosis. The limited supernatural experiences in the piece are indirect and murky, possibly able to be explained by paranoid delusion and brief hallucination. So much of the piece occurs wholly in the narrator's mind, with no dialogue or interaction with others. This could call all the events into question. Even if the reader assumes that the artist is a reliable narrator, the events described could still be interpreted as hallucinations or delusions.

Viewing the events through the lens of suspected psychosis, the sightings of the strange shapes in the water and the decomposing hand can be seen as hallucination. The first creatures the narrator observes are described as dark blobs of unknown shape (CF 4.645–46), which quickly disappear. The second sighting at the finale of the story is slightly more descriptive, but still confusing and strange (656). Ambiguous stimuli, confusion, and fear are common features of visual hallucinations (Dudley et al.), all present in the narrator's description of the events. The day after the first sighting, although the author sees a detached hand rotting at the shoreline, his description of it implies it is not wholly human. Overcome with fear and disgust, the narrator kicks it into the sea without looking long at it—reflecting that it was "too ambiguous" to report in town (CF 4.650).

Regarding delusional thought, the narrator may be subtly experiencing this as well, specifically ideas of reference. Ideas of reference are a form of delusional thought whereby the sufferer believes that innocuous events or situations have deeper, personal meaning (Grinnell; Kiran and Chaudhury). This can be seen with the discovery of the strange bone the narrator finds in the sand (CF 4.638), believing it different from the trash he normally picks up on the beach. The artist describes it as a bone inlaid with carvings unlike any he has ever seen. This may be a minor idea of reference, but the narrator is clearly experiencing the delusion when reflecting on the ocean itself. Though the narrator acknowledges that the sea does not change (652), he displays personification by projecting moods and emotion to the ocean (640–41). The sea is an alien presence that appears to respond to the narrator and influence him (636), and that perhaps his own moods are "only a reflection of the sea's own mood" (641). The ocean gives the narrator health, but then demands "recompense for the healing she had brought" (641). The narrator later reflects that "the once friendly waters [had] babbled meaningfully at me, and eyed me with strange regard" (652), but then offers nothing further (652). The sea holds sinister and forgotten secrets that could aid the narrator, but the sea jealously guards them (657). Such apophenia, the tendency to find meaning in unrelated phenomena, has been linked to the onset of psychosis (Mishara).

The Shifting Environment

The symptoms of bipolar disorder can be seen not just in the musings and thoughts of the narrator, but also in the setting in which "The Night

Ocean" takes place. The environment is ethereal and envelops the narrator during his summer convalescence in Ellston. Indeed, in classical romanticism the environment is a projection of the character's mood or fate. In "The Night Ocean," the environment shifts around the narrator. It is blamed for his changing mood and seems to respond to him. This change can be seen in three principal elements: the changing seasons, the weather, and the ocean itself.

The change of the seasons maps the narrator's change from mania to depressive states, indicative of a seasonal affective subtype of bipolar disorder. The bright sunlight and fresh air soothe him and encourage him to swim and spend his time outside (CF 4.637). But, as August becomes September, the season gradually changes (639). The year is growing colder, the tourists are beginning to leave—hastened by the grisly drownings (641). As September continues, the light of the sun alternates from its previous brilliance to being pale and weak. This change brings increasing feelings of loneliness and of anxiety (648). In late September, the summer is over and Ellston is empty and deserted (652). The narrator's mood is cynical and grim as the summer ends and autumn begins. The season is chilling the ocean water and the days are dreary: "Upon the beach and me alike had fallen a shadow" (652). The darkness of winter is coming and with it hopelessness and oblivion.

The weather shares this shifting pattern, changing with the season and being symbolic of the narrator's state. In the early parts of the story, the weather is ideal: an abundance of bright, golden sunlight in an azure cloudless sky (CF 4.635). However, as the summer fades, and the narrator's depressive state begins, the weather turns sour. The narrator describes that the days become progressively darker, with "long intervals of cloudiness" (639) that obscure the sun and leave the sky gray. This causes the water to grow chillier, and the beach becomes less pleasant (639). The day and nights are become marked by clouds that are "colourless and oppressive" (642), and the night sky is more a "carrion" and "sombre" color (642). The storm that brought the strange sea creatures left a long shadow over the beach (653). Moreover, like the change of the seasons, the weather becomes even bleaker as the narrator's depression descends, with the sky becoming dark and corpse-like (652).

The final environmental element of "The Night Ocean" that encapsulates the volatile nature of bipolarity is the titular character: the ocean itself. Expectedly, the ocean's mercurial essence is frequently described as "shifting" and ceaselessly changing (CF 4.635, 637-39). This constant change is found in rapidly cycling bipolar disorder (APA). The nature and influence of the sea changes throughout the story as well. Early in the piece, the ocean is viewed as a wondrous and peculiar thing, kindly healing the narrator (CF 4.637-38). As the season turns and the narrator's mind darkens, the ocean takes on an ominous state. "Something of the darkness and restlessness of the sea had penetrated my heart" the narrator claims, noting that the "dark, enveloping sea [had] grown slowly hateful" toward him (651).

Conclusion

Even though both Lovecraft and Barlow would have been aware of Plato's "divine madness" and contemporary explorations into affective disorders, the authors likely did not intend for "The Night Ocean" to be a case study in bipolar disorder. Nevertheless, the actions and thoughts of the narrator as well as the fluctuating mood and environment serve as examples of the features of bipolarity and deeper mental illness.

The intention of this paper is not to argue that "The Night Ocean" is a definitive exploration of bipolar disorder. In order to make such an argument, an avid reader of Lovecraft needs to ignore the obvious references to deeper Mythos elements. The curiously carved bone totem reminds the reader of the cursed idol of "The Temple" (1920). The gruesome drownings in Ellston allude to aquatic monsters, later suspected to be the humanoid figures the narrator watches. One cannot help but link these occurrences in "The Night Ocean" (1936) to the sinister Deep Ones of "The Shadow over Innsmouth" (1931). Finally, the narrator's reflections of a mysterious, undersea realm hints at the submerged and alien worlds described in "The Shadow over Innsmouth," "The Temple," "Dagon" (1917), and of course "The Call of Cthulhu" (1926). To have concrete use as a metaphor for bipolarity, one must ignore the supernatural weird in "The Night Ocean," even if it is present only faintly.

Additional limitations exist as well. "The Night Ocean" would be, at best, an allegory of stylized bipolarity and not an actual reflection of the illness. The narrator describes being devoted "during most of the year" (CF 4.632) to his work, much too long for a manic episode, and people can be focused on projects or goals intensely without having mental illness. Furthermore, while the narrator experiences a downward trend in the piece, hints of depression and low mood fill the onset of the story. This fits with the onset of unipolar depression rather than bipolar cycling however, as noted earlier, depressive episodes are more pervasive even in bipolar disorder (APA). Finally, this paper claims that the personifications of the ocean, season, and weather, are part of delusions of reference. It is likely just the nature of the style lends itself to such anthropomorphisms. To these points, "The Night Ocean" is better viewed as a reflection of mental illness and mood instability rather than a representation of classic bipolar symptoms.

"The Night Ocean" is a hauntingly poetic story that can be seen as a portrait of bipolar disorder. Its somber mood is beautiful, and sadly touching considering the story is Lovecraft's last completed work prior to his untimely death. Considering Barlow's own tragic suicide a little more than a decade later, the story stands our not simply because of the surreal prose but also for the deeper themes of depression and an indifferent world.

Works Cited

Abrams, H. Leon. *Robert Hayward Barlow: An Annotated Bibliography with Commentary*. Greeley: University of Northern Colorado, 1981.

American Psychological Association. *Diagnostic and Statistical Manual of Mental Disorders*. 5th ed. American Psychological Association, 2013.

Angst, Jules, and Andreas Marneros. "Bipolarity from Ancient to Modern Times: Conception, Birth and Rebirth." *Journal of Affective Disorders* 67 (2001): 3–19.

Dudley, Robert; Markku Wood; Helen Spencer; and Alison Brabban. "Identifying Specific Interpretations and Use of Safety Behaviours in People with Distressing Visual Hallucinations: An Exploratory Study." *Behavioural and Cognitive Psychotherapy* 40 (2012): 367–75.

Grinnell, Renée M. *Ideas of Reference*. Psych Central, 2018. psychcentral. com/encyclopedia/ideas-of-reference/ Accessed 23 June 2019.

Jamison, Kay. *Touched by Fire: Manic-Depressive Illness and the Artistic Temperament*. New York: Free Press, 1996.

Joshi, S. T., and David E. Schultz. *An H. P. Lovecraft Encyclopedia*. 2001. New York: Hippocampus Press, 2004.

Kiran, Chandra, and Suprakash Chaudhury. "Understanding Delusions." *Industrial Psychiatry Journal* 18 (2009): 3–18.

Mishara, Aaron L. "Klaus Conrad (1905–1961): Delusional Mood, Psychosis, and Beginning Schizophrenia." *Schizophrenia Bulletin* 36 (2010): 9–13.

Scully, Stephen. *Plato's Phaedrus: Translation with Notes, Glossary, Appendices, Interpretative Essay and Introduction.* Newburyport, MA: Focus Publishing, 2003.

The Weird within the Real: Common Territories in Lovecraft's Fiction and Southern Literature

Heather Poirier
Independent Scholar

> The past is never dead. It's not even past.
> —William Faulkner, *Requiem for a Nun*

> I have found that anything that comes out of the South is going to be called grotesque by the Northern reader, unless it *is* grotesque, in which case it is going to be called realistic.
> —Flannery O'Connor, "Some Aspects of the Grotesque in Southern Fiction"

Weird fiction would not seem to have much in common with Southern literature, especially that Southern literature written during and just after H. P. Lovecraft's life. For instance, Lovecraft famously argued that William Faulkner's story "A Rose for Emily" could not be considered weird fiction because, despite its bizarre events, the story was plausible and thus did not liberate the imagination (Joshi 49). Probably because of this apparent lack of common territory, literary critics do not offer much analysis of Lovecraft's weird fiction alongside Southern literature, which prevents us from understanding the commonalities shared by the two.

The lack of published commentary is understandable. Lovecraft's devotion to New England would lead most scholars to look toward other topics, while researchers in Southern literature have only concerned themselves with weird fiction recently. Given that Lovecraft's New England seems quite distant from the South, the barriers to research begin with the conceptual. Elements such as cultural divergences, images of conflict and war, and assumptions about the inhabitants of both New England and the South present obstacles. However, these barriers are not as high as they might initially seem.

Historically speaking, the South is defined by the well-worn grooves of slavery, oppression, and war. For a more literary definition of the South, Jay Ellis offers useful beginning observations in an essay on Southern literature's characteristics when he notes that "Southern and Southern Gothic have been configured through a regular trope of 'below'" (xvii). Both geographically and ideologically, the South has been seen as a place of darkness and fear, viscerally rendered, for example, by Harriet Beecher Stowe's *Uncle Tom's Cabin*, in which Uncle Tom's fate is determined by his sale down the Mississippi River, ultimately to Simon Legree in New Orleans. However, the literature of the South has wider origins than just America. It involves the Caribbean, Africa, and Europe, from the Middle Passage of the slave trade to the folk tales of Scottish and Irish immigrants to the literature of the settlers during and after the Age of Empire. It is helpful to keep in mind when drawing the various axes of Southern literature that Ralph Waldo Emerson holds New England as a universal center, with his famous "transparent eyeball," a master trope in his canonical work *Nature*, seeing the "ascendancy of Commerce" in the North over "Feudalism" in the South, with the implication in Emerson's time of the ascendance of an industrial North over a slave-borne South[1] (Ellis xxiv). Emerson's establishment of the trope of "below" plays out in the literature and commentary that follows him. Beyond geography, the South is defined in economic and mechanistic terms. Its agrarian economy, especially after the Civil War, could not compete with rising industrialism and westward expansion, and the South fell behind dramatically. Edgar Allan Poe characterized the South in terms that we would now think of as describing abjection, largely as a result of the association of abjection with the grotesque, both of which I will address.

An important context for both Southern literature and Poe is the Gothic. Poe's "work demonstrates how [American] Gothic"—which differs from Southern Gothic, which differs from the grotesque—"was ideally suited to the emerging artistic and political consciousness of the region"

---

1. Given the sheer amount of work done on race in the South, and race in HPL, this project does not allow the space for a full discussion of either. For race in HPL, S. T. Joshi has done extensive work for years on the topic. A consultation of his catalogue would be profitable, such as his early work *H. P. Lovecraft: The Decline of the West*, in which Joshi confronts the topic squarely, and shorter commentary such as "Why Michel Houellebecq Is Wrong about Lovecraft's Racism."

(Walsh 23–24).[2] In Poe's work, and in that of other Southern writers, we see what will eventually become the Southern Gothic used as a tool to deconstruct both the cultural narratives promoting the rational, progressive values held close by the North and the patriarchal, patrimonial values defended by the South. This use of the Gothic has been characterized as "a Gothic passage where what we would prefer to forget will not stay buried" (Ellis xxxiii). Just as the past is not the past, Southern Gothic reflects the South's ongoing struggle with its identity and its history, "investigating madness, decay, and despair, and the continuing pressures of the past upon the present, particularly with respect to the lost ideals of a dispossessed Southern aristocracy and to the continuance of racial hostilities" (Marshall 3). These struggles have shifted somewhat during the past century, but identity and history are still critical to an understanding of Southern literature.

Crucial to Southern identity is what Eudora Welty called a "sense of place" (8), with writers steeping their stories in numerous tropes dependent on Southern history and culture and developing new ones along the way. Still, the geographic delineations were only an idea, a creation of custom and a notion of who belonged where that was bounded by that historical struggle with identity and history, defining the South's inhabitants through race, caste, and class. Regardless of custom and notion, that identity was a fiction, real only so far as its unreality was accepted as authoritative. A real place and real people were transcended by an unreal idea. This idea of an unreal place is equally critical to Lovecraft's geographies. Both Lovecraft and Southern writers create literary geographies that are nonexistent yet crucial to their larger messages. As Mitch Frye notes in his article "Astonishing Stories: Eudora Welty and the Weird Tale," "The South that we hold collectively in our minds is not—could not possibly be—a fixed or real place. It both exceeds and flattens place; it is a term of the imagination, the site of national fantasy" (75). The New England of Lovecraft's stories is equally a place of imagination and fantasy. Grounded within a rational, everyday New England is Lovecraft's territory of the weird, populated with alien beings, time travelers, cultists, and other horrors. This unreality becomes an obstacle for both Lovecraft and Southern writers, defeating popular understanding and provoking caricature by outsiders.

---

2. A full study of the Gothic—even just American Gothic—would require more space than available for this article. Good places to start are Allan Lloyd-Smith's *American Gothic Fiction: An Introduction* and Leslie Fiedler's *Love and Death in the American Novel.*

Frye rightly observes that "empirical space is deformed in literary discourses that address the South through calculated caricature: representation via misrepresentation or anti-representation [. . .] critical terminology [in literary discourses] stages the discussion in [. . .] unreal cartographies" (76). Given the common territories of the weird found in both Lovecraft and Southern literature, these unreal cartographies become the basis for the authors' sense of place, which I will discuss later. Frye notes that "often the operative narrative mode of 'southern regional fiction' [. . .] is not precisely realism but a mutant form that borrows provocatively from the speculative fiction genres of dystopia, fantasy, science fiction, and the weird tale" (76).[3] The paradox is that caricatures in both Lovecraft and Southern literature arise out of a necessary process for both Lovecraft and Southern writers, a process that strengthened and solidified many of the respective works.

Arguably, the greatest of Southern writers to date is William Faulkner. The significance and effect of his presence in the Southern canon cannot be overstated. His Yoknapatawpha County is an unreal cartography that has become a permanent place in the Southern canon, not the least reason being its immersion within the Southern Gothic.[4] Allan Lloyd-Smith, in his study *American Gothic Fiction: An Introduction*, links Faulkner and Lovecraft through the Gothic:

> Faulkner is another profoundly Gothic writer also working out of a dispossessed region afflicted by loss of a grander history than its present condition. In Faulkner's southern Gothic the present can only be understood in terms of a working out of events from the past which emerge in uncanny interconnections and buried lineages, warped by the dark tangle of slavery and racial persecutions. [. . .] The vernacular of the New England locals, their ignorance and interrelationships, and the sense of family history shown here have "regional realist" parallels with Faulkner's ignorant but

---

3. Space does not permit examination of these genres within Southern literature. For dystopia, Cormac McCarthy's *The Road* is recommended; for the weird tale, Fred Chappell's *Dagon* is a reliable treat. Anne Rice's *Interview with a Vampire* is an urban fantasy, while science fiction is well represented by authors such as Samuel R. Delany and Octavia E. Butler. Afrofuturism is a relatively recent subgenre of science fiction that has numerous adherents.

4. Another example of unreal cartography would be Zora Neale Hurston's Eatonville, Fla., in her novel *Their Eyes Were Watching God*. Numerous examples exist in both Southern and African-American literature.

deeply embedded Southerners, similarly represented by a sophisticated informed consciousness beyond their own reach. (116–17)

Lloyd-Smith notes that Lovecraft and Faulkner share characters who use vernacular speech, who are ignorant, who have consanguineous relationships, who cling to their family history (and in some instances, regional history), and who inhabit haunted areas, lost plantations or family estates, forests, swamps, and decaying towns. The characters in both Faulkner and Lovecraft are bound by the past to the past, even as the present drags them into unknown and unwanted events.

In addition to the influence and use of the Southern Gothic, Faulkner has been cited as one of the most important writers of the Southern Renaissance, a movement started by a group of poets and literary critics at Vanderbilt known as the Fugitives after their eponymous publication. Eventually, these writers would become known as the Southern Agrarians, a group opposed to the post-World War I industrialization of the South who were galvanized by, because supremely annoyed by, the critic H. L. Mencken, whose essay "The Sahara of the Bozart" was highly critical of the South and its literary output and prospects. Primarily, the Agrarians believed that industrialization stifled creativity, that leisure was necessary for the full exercise of creativity, and that a return to an agrarian lifestyle would provide the kind of leisure needed. Although Lovecraft cannot be counted among the Agrarians, he does share opinions with them. In a letter to R. H. Barlow from September 1933, he writes:

As for the native rustic population and its psychological twists—it would seem, after all, that novelists like Faulkner and his school are essentially right about the decadence of the backwoods. It is probably true that the sounder and higher-grade American stock hastened to branch out in various adventurous ways, leaving the field of small-scale agriculture more and more to those feebler elements in whom repulsive abnormalities are most easily developed. That is one of the penalties of the machine age, which has broken up the relationship between the people and the soil and ruined the thrifty, sound-blooded agrarian element which flourished a century ago in all but a few parts of the country. Today, the hereditary small farmer is more and more in danger of slipping back from the yeoman status to the sordid condition of peasant or "poor white." It is so everywhere—my "Dunwich Horror" dealt with such a retrogressive region in Massachusetts, while the unpublished "Beyond the Wall of Sleep" [. . .] touched on a case in New York State. (OFF 79)

Other common elements in Lovecraft's work and in Southern literature involve the pull of ties of blood, as in "The Shadow over Innsmouth" (1931); a lack of economic or social justice; conflict between loyalty to family and adherence to justice; the necessity for concealment of motives; and the concealment of the truth. Additional characteristics include entrapment and despair, which we see in numerous Lovecraft stories; flight and pursuit; the inescapability of the past in the present, dramatically represented in such stories as "The Shadow over Innsmouth"; extreme pressure of racial hostilities, which brings "The Horror at Red Hook" (1925) to mind; and the notion of a lost mythos (Lloyd-Smith 61), which surfaces in Lovecraft as rediscovered ancient cults. Within this lost mythos of cults, we find the growing awareness that what was believed impossible is in fact real (Lloyd-Smith 117); Christ-haunted people and places (O'Connor, "Some Aspects" 44), which in Lovecraft becomes past-haunted; the styled intensity of violence (Lloyd-Smith 118), with Lovecraft's violence often deftly deferred and revealed at the same time; and the individual's relationship to the official past of memorialized statuary (Lloyd-Smith 118), most notably represented in both the famous bas-relief of Cthulhu in Lovecraft's story "The Call of Cthulhu" (1926), which comes to represent a past that has not remained in the past, and in the images found by the Antarctic scientists in *At the Mountains of Madness* (1931).

Through encounters with the weird, Lovecraft's narrators come to realize that beliefs held by scientific experts, authority figures, and others with similar status have been invalidated. This loss of the continuity of belief ultimately leads to cosmic horror, the result of encounters with the weird. Similarly, Southern writers in the early and mid-twentieth century struggled with the loss of traditions long held and the rapid influx of modernity brought about by technological advancement in the twentieth century, and for writers like Flannery O'Connor the grotesque was the best way to represent this sense of alienation and loss. Ultimately, the loss for both Southern writers and Lovecraft is linked to the loss of their respective forms of pre-industrial agrarianism.

This brings us back to the Southern Gothic. Certainly, there are aspects of Southern Gothic literature that find resonance in Lovecraft's work, but that is because both contain elements derived from American Gothic, which in turns owes fealty to European Gothic. Note that Lovecraft does not use the term "Southern Gothic"; it was not coined until 1935 by Ellen Glasgow in her *Saturday Review* essay "Heroes and Monsters." That same year, in a letter to C. L. Moore, Lovecraft states:

> Many people wonder why I don't exploit the traditional element of weirdness in the South—the brooding cypress swamps, the mouldering plantation-houses, the whispered negro lore, &c., &c. The fact is, however, that I can't feel the same deep, Gothic horror in any mild & genial region that I can in the rock-strewn, ice-bound, elm-shaded hillsides of my own New England. To me, whatever is *cold* is sinister, and whatever is warm is wholesome & life-giving . . . an echo, no doubt, of my own tropic-loving constitution. (*CLM* 47)

However tempting, we cannot limit Southern literature to Southern Gothic. Alan Spiegel, in "A Theory of the Grotesque in Southern Fiction," contrasts the elements of Southern literature with the Gothic, emphasizing that Southern literature focuses on normal, daylight settings of ordinary communal activity, people living within society in a normative manner, and the grotesque character as the reactionary, calling attention to the Establishment's failings (434–37). Because of 1) the reasons reviewed here; 2) the sheer diversity of works set in various places in the South; and 3) the caste, class, and social structures found therein, Southern literature more toward the grotesque than to the Gothic.

This connection to the grotesque becomes a connection to realism rather than to naturalism, as one might ordinarily expect. In addition to his parallels with Southern literature and the Agrarians, Lovecraft's emphasis on realism is one of his strongest connections to Southern literature. His affection for Enlightenment styling, values, and language—all highly realistic—is well established. As Spiegel observes, "the methods of the eighteenth-century novel [. . .] tended to cultivate the mimetic and the historical, the analytic and the normative. [. . .] The normative [. . . has] continued in our own time, in the work of the Southern writer" (433–34). Spiegel notes that the key differences between Southern literature and other American genres "involve far more than a setting; rather, they also involve technique, tone, mood, point of view—in short, a fundamentally different vision of life" (434). This different vision of life, based in similar adaptations of eighteenth-century stylings and expanded through the twentieth century into the present day, is the center of the common territory between Lovecraft and Southern literature: the realism that depends on the past for its energies. Also critical to the common territory is the return of the repressed, as described by scholars in multiple fields and predicted by Freud. The return of the repressed in Lovecraft is the arrival or return of figures who are not repressed and who cannot be suppressed. That is the real horror in Lovecraft: the eroding codes of control. Lovecraft's sense of place is not merely the history of New England, but also a landscape with its own history that is both looming and uncontrollable. Along with the different vision of life and the return of the repressed is the common territory of the grotesque, the gatekeeper to unvarnished reality.

If one were inclined to psychoanalyze Lovecraft's work, the return of the repressed does not bring forth guilt, responsibility, or violence, as it does in other writers. There is rarely a conventional villain in Lovecraft's work, and even those such as Wilbur Whateley are motivated by power derived from cosmic horror rather than conventionally evil motives. The violence in Lovecraft, if present at all, is often discovered after the return of the repressed, occluded by hints, or left off the page entirely and implied by such devices as the abrupt ending of a letter or diary entry.

The key to Lovecraft's realism is his skill with concealment of the most flagrant elements of violence and horror. Lovecraft reveals as he conceals, preserving mystery through uncertainty (Poirier). This use of the mysterious both contributes to and distances meaning. Similarly, in writing about how authors use mystery and meaning, O'Connor notes that

> if the writer believes that our life is and will remain essentially mysterious [. . .] then what he sees on the surface will be of interest to him only as he can go through it into an experience of mystery itself. His kind of fiction will always be pushing its own limits outward toward the limits of mystery, because for this kind of writer, the meaning of a story does not begin except at a depth where adequate motivation and adequate psychology and the various determinations have been exhausted. Such a writer will be interested in what we don't understand rather than in what we do. He will be interested in characters who are forced out to meet evil [. . .] and who act on a trust beyond themselves—whether they know very clearly what it is they act upon or not. ("Some Aspects" 41-42)

The term "mystery" is the key in O'Connor. In Lovecraft's fiction, mystery is occasionally deadly in its pursuit and revelation, frequently fatal, and rarely resolved satisfactorily (Poirier). Nevertheless, one can easily see that Lovecraft is a writer "interested in what we don't understand rather than in what we do" and whose work is "pushing its own limits outward."

This rejection of limits leads us back to the grotesque, a matter of no small interest to numerous writers, among them Mikhail Bakhtin, who placed the emphasis in the grotesque on both incompleteness and the human body (Donaldson 577). The grotesque rejects limits simply through its existence: the grotesque is a statement about limits placed on others by society, and its existence affirms both the social norm and the rejection of that norm. Grotesques live on the edges of society, metaphorically if not physically. This is certainly true in a story such as O'Connor's "Good Country People" (1955), which figures a woman who is grotesque in body, because she has a missing leg; in mind, because she has a Ph.D. in philosophy, far beyond the educational achievements of others in her small Southern hometown; and in attitude, because she changed her name from Joy to Hulga, rejecting any beauty and possible spirituality in her given name. In Lovecraft, the body in question is frequently that of the alien, the intruder, the one who threatens the narrator in some way. In "The Rats in the Walls" (1923), the body of Edward Norrys becomes grotesque both in its appearance and in its use as a kind of unholy communion material. For Bakhtin, the grotesque body pulls apart "the confines of the apparent (false) unity of the indisputable and the stable" (Donaldson 580) through its simultaneous rejection and affirmation of norms. The one who rejects and affirms norms has a place only on the periphery, as the grotesque does.

The shift from the Gothic to the grotesque in both Lovecraft and Southern writers is a shift from the external to the internal. The grotesque is not merely physical: it is attitudinal, spiritual, emotional. It is both an aesthetic category of art and literature and an epistemology (Moghadam 88). To live as a grotesque is to understand the world through its distortions, not simply because the grotesque himself is distorted but because the community around him is shaped by its response to him. The grotesque is "flesh made metaphor" (Moghadam 76). In terms of situations belonging to the grotesque, the grotesque can arise from the "sudden placing of familiar elements of reality in a peculiar and disturbing light" (Moghadam 80). The grotesque can thus result from some form of degradation: if physical, from deformities, physical defects, or distorted ugly appearance; if mental, from psychiatric disorders, nervous breakdowns, insanity, or aggression.

The grotesque is not limited to characters, however. In his essay "On Placing the Grotesque," Nahid Moghadam points out that its fluidity means the grotesque can be used in numerous forms and genres (88). This idea dovetails with one of O'Connor's observations on the widespread use of the grotesque: "When we look at a good deal of serious modern fiction, and particularly Southern fiction, we find this quality above it that is generally described, in pejorative terms, as grotesque" ("Some Aspects" 40). The grotesque is another bridge between the weird fiction of Lovecraft and the realism central to numerous Southern writers. As one researcher noted, "Rather than a sensationalist freak or horror show, grotesque literature cuts through the veil of civility, through decorum and oppressive normative fabrications to expose a harsh, confusing reality of contradictions, violence, and aberrations" (Bjerre). For some, the grotesque is a central character, such as Benjy Compson in Faulkner's *The Sound and the Fury* (1929), an intellectually challenged man who narrates one section of the novel. For others, the grotesque is a lesser character, as in O'Connor's story "A Good Man Is Hard to Find" (1953), where several characters are arguably grotesques, though to different degrees. The grotesque is not limited by social, caste, and class expectations; instead, the grotesque exists along the edges, between persons, groups, towns, and social structures. Two short stories, one by O'Connor and one by Lovecraft, reveal the common territories toward which the grotesque points us.

O'Connor's story "Everything That Rises Must Converge" (1961) shares tone and texture with weird fiction. Although it presents no monsters, it certainly presents the grotesque; the central character Julian is grotesque not in the way he looks but in the way he refuses to accept the values of those around him, especially those of his mother, even as he inwardly shares her values. The story does not rely on fear or terror, yet the readers of O'Connor's time, whatever their origins, could have been moved to recognize the degree of emotional force required to strike Julian's mother dead at the end of the story. For this text, weird ritual and science fiction have been replaced by the destruction of a publicly expressed yet changing social order through the single action of a woman on the street of a small Southern town.

The story is simple enough. Julian, a recent university graduate in English, is compelled to accompany his mother every Wednesday night to a reducing class at the local YMCA. As does the rest of his life, this weekly trip strains Julian's nerves; his mother's new hat, a purple and green monstrosity, is the first key point of conflict in the story. Julian's self-pity and accompanying snobbishness prevent him from accepting his mother as she is, a woman whose values can be charitably described as in retrograde. They also prevent him from taking seriously her comments about her blood pressure.

As he and his mother ride the bus the four stops to the YMCA, Julian's mood improves slightly when a well-dressed African-American man gets on the bus. Julian moves to sit by him not because he is genuinely interested in the man, but because he knows doing so will irritate his mother, who looks at him with reproach. At another stop, an African-American woman and her pre-schooler get on the bus, then sit directly across from Julian's mother. Both Julian and his mother realize within seconds that the woman is wearing the same purple-and-green hat. Julian cackles aloud at what he believes is his mother's loss of face, but soon her affect changes to a smirk toward the woman, then kindness toward the pre-schooler. Julian's mother praises the little boy both with her words and with a smile that O'Connor describes as a weapon: gracious because offered to an inferior. Julian's mother and the little boy play peekaboo while the boy's mother watches, fuming.

The next stop is the YMCA, and Julian, his mother, the woman, and the boy move to the street. In a gesture well known to those familiar with the pre-desegregation South, Julian's mother offers the little boy a shiny new penny. This enrages the woman, who punches Julian's mother, knocking her to the sidewalk. Julian lashes out at his mother, telling her she got what she deserved. Sitting upright on the sidewalk, she is immobile, struggling to speak, red and purple blotches on her face, and when she gets up with Julian's help, she walks only a little way before dropping her purse and falling to the pavement, dead from a stroke, her face purple and her eyes defocused. Julian cannot accept this unmooring of his life, and we leave him kneeling beside her on the sidewalk.

This story uses elements of the weird to move first toward the grotesque, then the abject, as described by Julia Kristeva in her book *Powers of Horror: An Essay on Abjection* (1982). For Kristeva, the abject is that which has been cast out through taboo. The abject is the forbidden that is still attractive, even though it is not acceptable to the group as a whole (1). The act of casting out a thing as taboo and the subsequent group acceptance of the taboo is what makes culture possible, because it introduces boundaries and limits (12–13). In Lovecraft, abjection works through human culture, which is in the symbolic (Lloyd-Smith 114). Human culture is an agreement among humans about how humans are and live; cultural variation can negate the symbolic if the differences between cultures are wide enough. The agreement is the symbolic, represented and delineated by that which is taboo. Things such as creatures, cultists, objects, places, histories, and events are all within the real, to use Kristeva's term, when they introduce, participate in, represent, or otherwise indicate cosmic horror, i.e., they indicate worlds, experiences, and creatures outside the human and the natural world (Kristeva 3–4). The real is outside the symbolic; the symbolic defines itself by that which is taboo. Thus, cosmic horror is the collision of the human symbolic and the alien real. Humans see the reality of alien beings, worlds, and experiences; they feel cosmic horror; and their response is a sense of abjection. In Lovecraft, abjection is the consequence of cosmic horror.

The plot of "Everything That Rises Must Converge" forces Julian's mother to see the reality behind the bride-like veil within which she lives, which is to say, seeing that her values are now taboo—those values are changing in her culture, but they have not changed within her. Her beliefs and values, which for her constitute the symbolic, cannot withstand this encounter with the real, as represented by the woman's rage and attack. This collision between the real and the symbolic, that is, the collision between that which is outside Julian's mother's cultural beliefs and values (the real) versus that which is agreed upon as culture (the symbolic) collide, generating the grotesque (Lloyd-Smith 114). Julian's mother changes from being a stereotypical Southern woman clinging to the past to a crumbling, crippled figure, destroyed by a challenge to her beliefs.

But threats to beliefs are Lovecraft's bread and butter. Sean Elliot Martin, in his study of Lovecraft and the grotesque, noted that "[t]he stories [in which Lovecraft critiques institutions of physical sciences] are most often narrated by characters who suffer mentally due to the violation of assumptions based upon the institutions to which they attempt to adhere" (93). In other words, these characters experience abjection when the real of the institutions of physical sciences collide with the symbolic of the violations of the assumptions insisted upon by those institutions. This results in destabilization of the paradigm, with the characters first attempting to defend the paradigm, as William Dyer does in *At the Mountains of Madness*, then stretching their beliefs further and further in an attempt to understand and rationalize the evidence before them.

Through those threats to beliefs, Lovecraft brings the grotesque into other stories. In "The Picture in the House" (1920), Lovecraft describes rural New England as where "the dark elements of strength, solitude, grotesqueness, and ignorance combine to form the perfection of the hideous" (*CF* 1.206). The main character is something of a mystery; as with many other Lovecraft stories, we do not know his name, but we learn about him through his reactions to the dilapidated, antique-filled house into which he is driven by a storm. Once inside, he is attracted to a book, Pigafetta's *Regnum Congo*, which, as he looks through it, opens up time and again to Plate XII, a depiction of a cannibal butcher's shop (CF 1.210). The owner of the house comes downstairs and is genial and kind in his speech, though his manner is as antiquated as his home. As the old man talks, leafing through the *Regnum Congo*, pausing with near reverence at Plate XII, the narrator realizes that the old man may have prolonged his own life by eating human flesh (CF 1.216). Spared from the potential danger of cannibalism by a bolt of lightning that destroys the house and apparently the old man, the narrator wakes up by the blackened ruins of the house.

In Lovecraft's story, the narrator's encounter with the grotesque old man is contextualized by its similarities with Southern literature. We see the significance of family, ties of blood, the necessity of concealing family truths from the community, and the complexity surrounding violations of family norms. A yeoman farmer becomes a poor white, the result of the lost relationship between people and the land; this loss of class and caste then becomes decadence as people and families grow isolated. Finally, we recognize the inescapability of the past in the present, as seen in the iconography in the *Regnum Congo*.

Stolen land and bartered bodies run through both Lovecraft's fiction and Southern fiction. In Lovecraft, humans have occupied the land that belonged to no one, at the time of humanity, anyway, and that was occupied by entities who brought structures, items, practices, and relics evoking cosmic horror. The grotesque in Lovecraft—whether a character or a situation—exists to bear witness about human insignificance in the light of a universe without grace, reflecting the inhumanity that is the context of the human. It is not merely non-human; it is inhuman and grotesque. The grotesque in Lovecraft is refutational in nature; this mode presents simultaneously an image of man's feebleness and an understanding of the impossibility of his beliefs about humanity and the universe. In Southern literature, especially in O'Connor and Faulkner, we see the impossibility of the views of both the dominant Southern culture—that of the landed wealthy—and those of characters subject to the power of the dominant culture.

The common characteristics between Southern literature and Lovecraft's fiction find their way to the grotesque and the abstract as rendered through the effects of industrialism, modernity, and loss. At the end of many of Lovecraft's stories, as well as the end of numerous texts in Southern literature, the reader is left with the understanding of that loss.

This article is only a beginning. Other work remains to be done—for example, a closer examination of the grotesque in Lovecraft; more extensive surveys of the common territories; and a look at where new Southern criticism could be profitably applied to Lovecraft. Future research in this area should bring to light new ways of looking at these topics and many more.

Works Cited

Bjerre, Thomas Ærvold. "Southern Gothic Literature." *Oxford Research Encyclopedia of Literature.* June 2017. DOI:10.1093/acrefore/9780190201098.013.304.

Donaldson, Susan V. "Making a Spectacle: Welty, Faulkner, and Southern Gothic." *Mississippi Quarterly* 5 (1997): 567–84.

Ellis, Jay. "On Southern Gothic Literature." In Jay Ellis, ed. *Critical Insights: Southern Gothic Literature.* Ipswich, MA: Salem Press, 2013. xvi–xxxiv.

Fiedler, Leslie A. *Love and Death in the American Novel.* New York: Stein & Day, 2nd ed. 1975.

Frye, Mitch. "Astonishing Stories: Eudora Welty and the Weird Tale." *Eudora Welty Review* No. 5 (Spring 2013): 75–93.

Joshi, S. T. *H. P. Lovecraft: The Decline of the West.* Mercer Island, WA: Starmont House, 1990.

———. *A Subtler Magick: The Writings and Philosophy of H. P. Lovecraft.* Mercer Island, WA: Starmont House, 1996.

———. "Why Michel Houellebecq Is Wrong about Lovecraft's Racism." *Lovecraft Annual* No. 12 (2018): 43–50.

Kristeva, Julia. *Powers of Horror: An Essay on Abjection.* New York: Columbia University Press, 1982.

Lloyd-Smith, Allan. *American Gothic Fiction: An Introduction.* New York: Continuum International, 2004.

Marshall, Bridget M. "Defining Southern Gothic." In Jay Ellis, ed. *Critical Insights: Southern Gothic Literature.* Ipswich, MA: Salem Press, 2013. 3–18.

Martin, Sean Elliot. "Lovecraft, Absurdity, and the Modernist Grotesque." *Lovecraft Annual* No. 6 (2012): 82–112.

Mencken, H. L. "The Sahara of the Bozart." In *Prejudices: Second Series.* New York: Alfred A. Knopf, 1920. 157–68.

Moghadam, Nahid Shahbazi. "On Placing the Grotesque." *Fantastika Journal* 1, No. 1 (April 2017): 73–90.

O'Connor, Flannery. "Everything That Rises Must Converge." In *The Complete Stories*. New York: Farrar, Straus & Giroux, 1977. 428–43.

———. "Some Aspects of the Grotesque in Southern Fiction." In *Mystery and Manners: Occasional Prose*. Ed. Sally and Robert Fitzgerald. New York: Farrar, Straus & Giroux, 1969. 36–50.

Poirier, Heather. "H. P. Lovecraft and the Dynamics of Detective Fiction." In Dennis P. Quinn, ed. *Lovecraftian Proceedings* 3. New York: Hippocampus Press, 2019. 115–34.

Spiegel, Alan. "A Theory of the Grotesque in Southern Fiction." *Georgia Review* 26 (1972): 426–37.

Walsh, Christopher J. "'Dark Legacy': Gothic Ruptures in Southern Literature." In Jay Ellis, ed. *Critical Insights: Southern Gothic Literature*. Ipswich, MA: Salem Press, 2013. 19–34.

Welty, Eudora. "Place in Fiction." In *The Eye of the Story: Selected Essays and Reviews*. New York: Vintage Books, 1978.

A Lover of Past Phantoms: Lovecraftian Reflections in R. H. Barlow's Life and Work

Thomas Schwaiger
University of Graz

Introduction: "Into the clear and jewelled heart of day . . ."

Robert Hayward Barlow was born in Leavenworth, Kansas, on 18 May 1918, and for the manifold and often considerable achievements of his all too short life, which he eventually would decide to end himself after not even thirty-three years on 1 or 2 January 1951, in Azcapotzalco, D. F. (Mexico City), he has been given many labels by various friends, teachers, colleagues, and admirers: "a writer, painter, sculptor in clay, pianist, landscape gardener, book collector, and scores of other things" (Lovecraft to Duane W. Rimel, 13 May 1934; *FLB* 171), most prominently among those scores "a born historian" (Alfred L. Kroeber, quoted in Bernal 301), a "romantic poet" but equally "one of the earlier Activist poets" (Hart 115), as well as "an anthropologist and linguist" (Smisor 97), in sum yielding "a picture of an extraordinary personality—a scholar, artist, and scientist—a solitary genius committed passionately to a solitary task for which there was 'never enough time'" (Mooser 5).

Although several scholarly works on Barlow exist now for quite a while, ranging from pioneering essays written in the late 1970s by the likes of George T. Wetzel and Kenneth W. Faig, Jr., to a book-length analysis of Barlow's fiction and poetry by Massimo Berruti published in 2011 and complemented by Marcos Legaria in an article-length study from 2017, many facets still remain understudied with respect to the child prodigy who at the age of only thirteen first contacted the nearly thirty-years-older Howard Phillips Lovecraft, and whom the latter surprisingly appointed to become his literary executor after his death a few months before the former's nineteenth birthday. Fortunately, recent years have seen a renewed and growing interest in the mutual literary and personal relationship between Lovecraft and Barlow, as evinced by Jarett Kobek's talk "A Closet Quetzalcoatl" at the Armitage Symposium 2015, Paul La Farge's novel *The Night Ocean* (2017), and Pierre Déléage's 2018 article in French on "La Transmigration de Robert H. Barlow." Nevertheless, with the exception of La Farge's semi-fictional account and certain sections of Déléage's essay, Barlow's further path after Lovecraft's passing in 1937 continues to be a less thoroughly investigated one.

Proceeding from the contemporary state of relevant research, this paper explores a hitherto relatively neglected avenue of inquiry, namely Lovecraft's possible posthumous influence on Barlow's notable character and career as steered toward becoming an outstanding specialist for Mesoamerican history, languages, and culture. Accordingly, the following sections try to retrace the most important steps of Barlow's brief but extraordinarily productive life—of which already in 1949, before his suicide, it was written that after "30 years he has accomplished and contributed to society what many men fail to achieve in a life time" (Fox 3)—by paying particular attention to what can be conceived of as likely Lovecraftian reflections in the later personality and occupations of Barlow. The goal is to show that Barlow's development from artist to scientist was more of a gradual metamorphosis than an abrupt change, with Lovecraft's impact on his young disciple and friend persisting long after the former had died and the latter had left the field of weird fiction and, ultimately, even the United States. Needless to say, the discussion heavily relies on the above-mentioned and other eminent studies of Barlovian scholarship, and it moreover draws on a number of Barlow's own fictional, poetic, autobiographical, and scientific writings as well as on pertinent letters from his extensive correspondence with Lovecraft.

Lovecraft Period: "I shall write until the wind is done scraping air . . ."

Barlow's childhood with his family—consisting of his father, Everett D. Barlow, his mother, Bernice Barlow, and his older brother Wayne—was somewhat nomadic due to the father's position in the U.S. Army. In addition, Lieutenant Colonel Barlow seems to have suffered from psychological problems: this much can be inferred from the subject coming up time and again in Lovecraft's letters to Barlow. However, statements in L. Sprague de Camp's biography of Lovecraft to the effect that Barlow's father was "something of a mental case" in that, for example, "he suffered from delusions of having to defend his home against the attacks of a mysterious Them" (393) have to be taken with a grain of salt, as the sources of such claims are not clear.[1] But in any case and whatever the exact reasons, at least as a child Barlow's relationship to his mother and brother appears to have been less strained than the one to the head of the family. Thus, combined with an ensuing lack of friends and proper school education, Barlow's relatively unstable early years soon made him turn to the largely introverted activity of reading and collecting fantastic fiction. Yet, at the same time it was precisely his bibliophilic pursuit of rare books, old magazines, original manuscripts, and writers' autographs that made him reach out to different authors whose works he admired. One of them, held in exceptionally high regard by the youth, was H. P. Lovecraft, who received the first letter from Barlow in 1931 after it was forwarded by the editor of *Weird Tales*. Barlow's family was then living at Fort Benning, Ga., but after the father's retirement would soon relocate to a Floridian homestead between the towns of DeLand (consistently spelled "De Land" by both Barlow and Lovecraft) and Cassia, where the most fruitful period of the Lovecraft–Barlow connection would begin to take its course, culminating in a several personal encounters in Florida, New York and Providence, R.I., that would cement their friendship for good.[2]

---

1. Déléage relegates them to a rather vague "tradition orale collectée tardivement" (125), i.e., to stories recorded orally (by and from apparently unidentified participants) at some unspecified later point in time.

2. Much about this amity can be learned from the nearly 160 surviving letters from HPL to RHB, collected and edited by S. T. Joshi and David E. Schultz, who state that, conversely, "[o]nly seven of RHB's letters to HPL survive" ("Introduction," OFF xxvn2). It seems, however, that this latter number needs to be corrected down to six, for the Howard P. Lovecraft Collection at Brown University's John Hay Library in Providence holds an undated typed letter to HPL from Stetson University in DeLand and attributed to RHB that in all probability actually came from Charles Blackburn Johnston, who together with his mother worked as the Barlows' housekeeper and whom HPL got to know when visiting the family in their Florida home for the first time in 1934. On the one hand, the writer of this letter expresses sorrow to learn that HPL is ill and provides information on some personal matters of a certainly strong Barlovian flavor, above all concerning an intended academic career in archaeology with pre-Columbian history as a special focus. On the other hand, the letter is signed in (for RHB) an uncharacteristically hard-to-read hand with the words "Lord Du-

It is hardly surprising that, in his memoir "The Wind That Is in the Grass" (1944), Barlow described Lovecraft as "the man who virtually moulded my intellectual life and many of my tastes and habits" (OFF xxxiii), for the two exhibited several commonalities basically from the out-set. Obviously, both "were true lovers of the weird tale" (Berruti 23), even if Lovecraft did not understand Barlow's attached proclivities of a bibliophile, but this by far did not exceed their common ground, which over a particular

---

nover" typed below and contains a passage that is less congruous with an authorship by RHB: "I have made arrangements with [astrophysicist] Dr. Cha[rle]s. [Greeley] Ab-bot [1872-1973], [fifth] Sec[retary]., of the Smithsonian Institution for six short arti-cles on the sun (you can see that I picked a worthy successor for you!) and some of the Teachers here at school will furnish the others needed" (letter to HPL, n.d.; ms., John Hay Library). However, all this does chime in quite well with the following passage from an unfinished letter of HPL (arguably his last one, found on his desk after his death and probably worked on during his final months from December 1936 to Feb-ruary 1937) to longtime friend James Ferdinand Morton, Jr.: "Down in De Land my friend Charles B. Johnston has become connected with Stetson University & its as-tronomical society, & asked me for a series of elementary articles on the heavens for the local paper. I had an old series—published twenty-two years ago—which seemed of about the right sort; but when I got them out, their obsoleteness completely bowled me over" (JFM 392). Apparently, HPL had planned to revise his own "Mysteries of the Heavens Revealed by Astronomy" (1915), a survey article series "designed for per-sons having no previous knowledge of astronomy" (CE 3.273), to comply with John-ston's request, but never got around to doing so. One could speculate that in the end HPL had to turn Johnston down for reasons connected to the former's terminal ill-ness, which would explain the latter's need to pick a successor in the first place. Addi-tionally, "Dunover" appears to have been the name of the Johnstons' new home after they at some point had moved out of the Barlows' place, which is corroborated in a letter from HPL to Robert E. Howard written on 11 July during HPL's second pro-longed stay with RHB's family in the summer of 1935: "The Johnstons have both moved to the cabin up the road ('Dunover')" (MF 860). In sum, it thus seems fairly safe to equate Lord Dunover with Charles B. Johnston and to date the Stetson letter to shortly before HPL's death. (Should this attribution be correct, HPL's letter of 25 October 1934 in OFF 184-86 was also addressed to "Dear Lord Dunover" Johnston and not to RHB. The slightly more distanced tone and some of the topics discussed in it seem to support this conclusion.) Also, an exciting issue for potential future re-search emerges: given the assumedly regular contact between RHB and Johnston over several years as well as their overlapping enthusiasm for things historic, a closer in-spection of this particular relationship is likely to shed a further revealing light on the shaping of RHB's teenage interests and adult career (see also note 6).

fondness for cats extended to all sorts of other self-sufficient inclinations as well as a literary-philosophical outlook on life characterized by a certain aloofness. As Lovecraft summarized it in one of his earlier letters to Barlow:

> Your detached sensation regarding the earth & your presence on it is something I can most poignantly share, though unimaginative persons probably lack such feelings. It is interesting to hear that your tastes & interests tend to remain stationary, as mine do. I can certainly equal your highest record for unpracticality & general uselessness! ([21 August 1933]; *OFF* 75)

Given Barlow's admiration and their huge difference in age (of which Lovecraft would become fully aware only when he first met Barlow personally in 1934), Lovecraft's impression on the teenager surely was pervasive in terms of influence and guidance, ranging from matters most mundane to the aesthetic and purely intellectual.

Concerning their first weeks spent together in Florida from 2 May to 21 June 1934, Barlow recalled the following in his 1944 memoir of Lovecraft: "He laundered his shirts thrice for every once he sent them to the laundry, and taught me the art of drying collars on a basin-edge to give the effect of ironing. (This I later put into practice as an art student.)" (*OFF* xxxi).[3] But immediately from the start of their almost six-year-long correspondence, it was first and foremost Barlow's literary aspirations, bibliophilic strivings, and overall restlessness that Lovecraft tried, often successfully, to act upon. In fact, Barlow "proposed such a welter of projects that Lovecraft had to advise him more than once to limit himself to one project at a time" (Faig, "R. H. Barlow" 202).[4] Apart from his ongoing

---

3. Practical household issues of this sort were humorously anticipated by HPL with respect to his travel preparations as described in a letter to RHB less than a month before the two would meet in person for the first time: "I carry no suit save the one on my aged carcass, & do a good deal of primitive linen-washing myself. Not very stylish—but I don't travel for style!" (10 April 1934; *OFF* 124).

4. To some degree, this oft-cited discrepancy between the two was perhaps a normal expression of how differently the passage of time is felt in teenage as opposed to adult life. In "[Memories of Lovecraft (1934)]," containing notes from a running journal on HPL's first Florida sojourn, RHB put it this way: "My quest for something to kill time was a source of perplexity to him, for he claimed that he never had to do anything to kill time, but was always rushed to get what was necessary done!" (*OFF* 406). HPL, in his characteristic self-styled-Grandpa manner, reinforced the point again in a letter to RHB the year after: "How the years do fly! A decade seems only a moment to an old man!" ([25 March 1935]; *OFF* 230).

reading and collecting, these plans especially comprised the writing of his own fiction, the composing of his own poems (literary activities that led to a handful of collaborations with Lovecraft over the years), drawing, painting, sculpturing, as well as the editing, printing, and publishing of his own amateur journal (*The Dragon-Fly*) and collections of various works (under the "Dragon-Fly Press" imprint) by people belonging to Lovecraft's circle of colleagues and friends.

During Barlow's affiliation with Lovecraft, writing certainly was a major occupation, and not only because of the correspondence he maintained with Lovecraft and others. Soon he began typing many of Lovecraft's stories in exchange for their original manuscripts (a fair deal, as Lovecraft loathed using a typewriter), of which several have survived only thanks to Barlow (Lovecraft often destroyed originals once a story had appeared in print), and he continued to pen his own little tales and short verse, often seeking Lovecraft's advice and opinion on them (which was generally quite high). In 1933, the tale "Eyes of the God" won him the story laureateship of the National Amateur Press Association, one of the organizations that grew out of the amateur journalism movement he had joined at Lovecraft's recommendation.

Yet one should not think that the Lovecraft–Barlow relationship was an asymmetrical one; as pointed out by Faig, it started out as "essentially one between teacher and pupil," but it developed "rapidly toward more of a dialogue than an instruction" ("R. H. Barlow" 196). Occasionally, this allowed for Barlow to bring hitherto overlooked works to Lovecraft's attention or to introduce him to a new future correspondent. With respect to fiction, "Barlow was able to push Lovecraft toward the inclusion of humorous elements in his work" (Berruti 287), exemplified by such of their collaborations as "The Hoard of the Wizard-Beast," "The Battle That Ended the Century," and "Collapsing Cosmoses."[5] Regarding Lovecraft's

---

5. RHB's achievement is all the more remarkable since, in general, "Lovecraft felt the urge to advise him in regard to the dangers of these sorts of inclusions" (Berruti 289). On the other hand, there is ample evidence that outside of his weird fiction HPL had a pronounced sense of humor. The following anecdote from RHB's "[Memories of Lovecraft (1934)]" should serve to illustrate: "When [HPL associate and Donald Wandrei's brother] Howard Wandrei mentioned, in a letter, his forthcoming story 'The Curse of the O'Mecca,' HPL observed, 'O'Mecca? It sounds like an Irish Arab'" (*OFF* 403).

poetry, it is noteworthy that "Recapture," poem number XXXIV in the *Fungi from Yuggoth*, "was written [. . .] well prior to the other sonnets in the cycle; it was only incorporated into the cycle in 1936 on the suggestion of R. H. Barlow" (*AT* 517).

One important commonality surfacing again and again in the letters between Lovecraft and Barlow pertains to the fascination that both held for various topics connected to history, the past, and "antiquarian exploration (my chief hobby)" (Lovecraft to Barlow, 17 September 1931; *OFF* 9). Early on, they exchanged information on diverse historical sites such as legend-enshrouded Glamis Castle in Scotland or "the presumably oldest house in America" (Lovecraft to Barlow, 16 November [1931]; *OFF* 14) located in Lovecraft's beloved city of St. Augustine, Florida. In January 1933, Lovecraft told Barlow about having visited New York's Metropolitan Museum during the post-Christmas season, to which Barlow replied that he had been at "the Smithsonian in Washington" and even "gave them a very peculiar hybrid butterfly, all the bugs did not devour of my collection in Benning, which, strange to say (also somewhat boastfully to say,) they did not have" (Barlow to Lovecraft, 10 February 1933; ms., John Hay Library). Lovecraft reacted with the following praise: "In many ways the Smithsonian is one of the most remarkable museums in the world. It is the only one to contain the colossal sculptures of mystery-fraught *Easter Island*—I suppose you paused with proper breathlessness before these reliques of a forgotten elder world!" (Lovecraft to Barlow, 18 February 1933; *OFF* 52; emphasis in original). This, in turn, sparked a discussion and swapping of newspaper cuttings on the probable age of ancient Polynesia and a possible prehistoric link between the Pacific civilization and the Indus Valley culture, leading Lovecraft to conclude: "What a strange Elder World must have existed around 10,000 B.C., before any of the known civilisations had developed!" (Lovecraft to Barlow, [29 November 1933]; *OFF* 87). Another repeatedly mentioned subject of historical and archaeological significance concerned excavations of Native Floridian burial mounds like the ones at Cassia, New Smyrna Beach, or "the newly discovered skeletons of Indians at the old village site" (Lovecraft to Barlow, 25 June 1934; *OFF* 141) north of St. Augustine (on the so-called "Fountain of Youth" property), the latter of which Lovecraft had inspected only a few days after his first stay with the Barlows.[6]

---

6. HPL also described his inspection of this cemetery in a postcard to the Barlows'

It appears apt to say that for both Lovecraft and Barlow "the search of the truth disclosed by the study of the past is indeed an unalloyed good" (Berruti 249), hence it was perhaps unavoidable that their common love for bygone eras seeped into much of their fictional output. In the case of Lovecraft, "[i]ts manifestations are almost too numerous to list, but consider for example that most of his horrors emerge from the past. There are those from the recent past ('Herbert West—Reanimator,' 'Cool Air,' 'The Colour out of Space'), the historical past ('The Tomb,' 'The Shunned House,' *The Case of Charles Dexter Ward*), and the incredibly distant past ('The Call of Cthulhu,' *At the Mountains of Madness*, 'The Shadow out of Time')" (Eckhardt 81). Similarly, in many of Barlow's stories "[t]he past turns into a sort of supernatural dimension and entity—and we must inevitably recall how Barlow might have been influenced, under this viewpoint, by Lovecraft's nearly idolatrous views on a multitudinous past" (Berruti 248), while on a formal level "the taste for lexical archaisms in Barlow's work (above all in fiction, but a few poetic examples are at hand) probably comes down to Barlow from Lovecraft's 'antiquarian' attitudes" (Berruti 341). So, in sum, although much was about to change dramatically in Barlow's life almost immediately after Lovecraft's untimely death at the age of forty-six on 15 March 1937, "[t]here seems to be little doubt that Lovecraft's morbidly fascinating tales, with their mixture of half-baked science and imaginative myth, had a permanent effect on his young admirer" (Mooser 7).

Battles: "Over me courses the mist, and the stars are obscured . . ."

Throughout their cordial correspondence and mutual visits (after their initial meeting in 1934, they met again briefly in New York at the turn of

---

hired handyman Charles B. Johnston (see note 2) postmarked 27 June 1934: "It is important that archaeologists from the Smithsonian Institution have been down to study the remains—complete skeletons with folded hands, evidently buried in the Christian manner. They are probably Indian converts of the Spaniards, interred in the late 1500's. There was an Indian village called 'Seloy'—today known as 'Nombre de Dios') on this site. [. . .] This is the only time I've ever seen exhumed skeletons in their original location" (OFF 417-18). Here, it is worth pointing out the coincidence that RHB's first academic book, published with George T. Smisor in 1943, was called *Nombre de Dios, Durango* (Sacramento, CA: House of Tlaloc).

the same year, once more in Barlow's Florida home from 9 June to 18 August 1935, and for the last time in Lovecraft's hometown Providence from 28 July to 1 September 1936), "Barlow's role as the principal trustee of Lovecraft's literary manuscripts was solidified" (Faig, "Executor" 55), and by way of the document containing the latter's "Instructions in Case of Decease," the former in the end became Lovecraft's literary executor. In view of Barlow's tireless accumulation of and intimate familiarity with all sorts of Lovecraftiana, Lovecraft's choice can be deemed very appropriate, if not almost imperative. Sadly, the handling of Lovecraft's literary estate quickly became conflict-laden for Barlow, mostly due to misunderstandings in dealing with Lovecraft's associates and family, particularly with such longtime friends as August Derleth, Donald Wandrei (the two had joint plans to preserve Lovecraft's works in book form under the "Arkham House" imprint and felt overlooked), and Clark Ashton Smith (who was another of Barlow's heroes in the weird fiction and painting scene) as well as with Annie Emmeline Phillips Gamwell, Lovecraft's younger aunt and sole heir (the unintentional discord with whom probably hurt Barlow the most). Most of these disagreements apparently were resolved at some point, but they nonetheless contributed considerably to Barlow's eventual retreat from the remaining Lovecraft circle and the world of fantasy fiction in general.[7] However, although it is true to a certain extent that "Barlow's professional and private life can be roughly split into two halves, the watershed being represented by Lovecraft's death" (Berruti 30), Lovecraft's presence in one way or the other would linger on until Barlow's suicide in 1951.

The hint of a possible career change was already in the air when the mentor was still alive, for in 1936 Barlow had begun to attend courses at the Kansas City Art Institute in Missouri to deepen his inclinations of a painter and sculptor.[8] But even after Lovecraft had died, Barlow "retained

---

7. In an "Autobiography" fragment from 1944, RHB put it this way: "After my third letter he [Clark Ashton Smith] wrote two lines, saying that he had no wish to hear ever again from a person who had acted so dishonorably in the estate of his dear friend H. P. Lovecraft. [. . .] If I had not received this letter, and other blows of the same sort, originating with the half-informed and antagonistic Wandreis [Donald and his brother Howard], and which continued for various years after, I should not have worked out new orientations" (OFF 410).

8. As of today, the following assessment by Faig still appears to hold: "Of all the phases of RHB's career, the least has been written about his artistic endeavors" (Faig 2009, 208). The present paper is no exception.

at least a loose connection with fandom for several years [. . .], despite giving up most of his collecting activities" (Faig, "R. H. Barlow" 204). On the one hand, he kept on writing and issuing weird fiction for a while. He finished his last story, "Return by Sunset" (based on a painting by Clark Ashton Smith), in 1939 (though it would not be published before 1943). Two issues of his new amateur magazine *Leaves* appeared in 1937 and 1938, respectively; the second issue "probably marks the definitive end of Barlow's activity within fandom as editor and publisher" (Faig, "R. H. Barlow" 204).[9] It furthermore contained the tale "Origin Undetermined," written by Barlow in August 1937, about an archaeologist who is driven to kill himself after being infected through contact with a supernatural plant discovered in an ancient Mayan urn. A large portion of this story can be interpreted "as a deliberate, posthumous homage to Lovecraft's literature" (Berruti 185n29),[10] but there is much reason for additionally reading it as an autobiographical reflection on Barlow's part regarding his personality, his feelings of loss, his being caught in-between authorship and scholarship as well as his imminent transition. Various of these aspects have been identified by Berruti, such as the main character's abrupt change of studies "from medicine to archaeology" (118), his "passion for the mysteries of Central America" (118n20), his "dreamy temper" that "valued imagination more than reality" (118) as well as his "physical description" (118n20): "a roundish head surmounting an awkward body; dark eyebrows and mustache; and a vaguely Oriental quality about the pale fleshy face, though he was Nordic enough in reality. His chin was not strong, and there was something weak about the corners of his mouth" (*EG* 121). But the list can be augmented further.[11] For one, the medical student turned archaeologist's full name, "Heywood Roberts" (*EG* 121), is a fairly

---

9. RHB's two early periodicals were recently issued by S. T. Joshi in a combined edition as *The Dragon-Fly & Leaves* (Seattle, WA: Sarnath Press, 2020).

10. RHB had dedicated the very Lovecraftian "A Dim-Remembered Story," published in the summer of 1936, to HPL during HPL's lifetime.

11. There are a few possible allusions to Lovecraft(iana) in the story; e.g., the mentioning of the main character's "incomprehensible breakdown" (*EG* 122)—HPL famously had a mysterious nervous breakdown in 1908 and withdrew himself to reclusion until 1913—, a nurse tellingly named "Miss Phillips" (*EG* 122), and a cat "called Arky" (*EG* 123)—a name perhaps hypocoristically derived from HPL's fictional town of Arkham, Mass.

obvious phonetic and sequential play on Barlow's two given names, Robert Hayward. It gains additional weight in light of Barlow's odd "discomfort with his own first name and the possibility it holds to be nicknamed" (Berruti 349). Then there is Heywood Roberts's former university, "Cassia Medical School in Detroit" (*EG* 121), incorporating a name closely connected to Barlow's Florida home in spite of being located in Michigan. Moreover, one of Heywood Roberts's statements toward the end of the tale, namely that "[a] horrible thing has begun to happen to my eyes" (*EG* 132), brings to mind Barlow's constant real-life troubles with his eyesight, a frequent topic in Lovecraft's letters to him.[12] Another statement of Heywood Roberts rooted in Barlow's biography is the following: "I was anxious to make certain that nothing of the plant survived. And then, having done these things, almost instinctively, as if a snake had slid into my path and I had clubbed it with the nearest stick until the fangs were hidden in its own dark gore, I began to reflect on what had just happened" (*EG* 127). Barlow was familiar with the killing of snakes because he used to hunt them so that he could utilize their skins as covers for his self-bound books, a practice that appears to have left an impression on Lovecraft.[13]

---

12. This condition is alluded to by the illness-stricken protagonist of "The Summons" (1935), another of RHB's tales: "This peculiar affliction had mystified the doctors, for it was neither epilepsy nor anything akin save in external appearances. It was connected with the visual trouble with which I had always been afflicted" (*EG* 66). This autobiographical clue is identified in Legaria's complementary follow-up article to Berruti's book, which also mentions RHB's father's "bouts of mental issues" (104n4) in connection with the following passage in "The Summons": "There was insanity in my ancestry, and because of this the subject was for me a field of morbid speculation. Brooding upon every fancied sign; ever watchful to find myself breaking down, I led an existence ceaselessly haunted by dread" (*EG* 66). Of course, there is a link to HPL's own biography here as well, his parents having died while institutionalized at Providence's Butler Hospital.

13. At least he must have told Robert E. Howard about it in a nonextant letter to which the Texan replied in late May or early June 1934: "No, I had not heard of Mr. Barlow's pursuit of reptiles for book-binding. Their hides ought to make good material. Rattlesnake skin belts used to be very popular in the Southwest" (*MF* 2.767). (Incidentally, Howard's prose-poem "With a Set of Rattlesnake Rattles" appeared posthumously in the first issue of RHB's *Leaves*.) RHB himself seemingly regretted his hunting deeds later on, as can be inferred from a poem like "Warning to Snake Killers," in which "the defense of nature (it is advisable not to kill snakes) is also justified

On the other hand, an even longer common thread is discernible in Barlow's poetic productions. In a self-belittling manner so typical of Lovecraft himself, Barlow once had written to him: "I rarely have the courage to attempt poetry, for it invariably ends in doggrel or jingle, even worse than my prose!" (10 February 1933; ms., John Hay Library). Lovecraft had usually reacted enthusiastically and encouragingly to Barlovian sonnets and "never failed to assist his pupil also in matters of poetic composition" (Berruti 334n1). He had especially praised Barlow's tribute to Robert E. Howard after the latter had shot himself: "Your sonnet-elegy is magnificent, & I hope you'll try it on W T. [. . .] Yuggoth, but I didn't know before what a poet you are!" (9 July 1936; *OFF* 350).[14] Now, stylistically, Barlow's poetry "can be roughly split into two phases, [. . .] one more classical and formal (dating approximately to the period Spring 1936–Fall 1939), and a second, 'Activist' phase, modernistic and experimental" (Berruti 333). The second phase began in 1939 when Barlow was living in San Francisco and consorted with a group of poets around the personage of Lawrence Hart. It is highly probable that this kind of verse would not have received Lovecraft's approval.[15] However, for these phases "a surprising thematic continuity can be detected [. . .], which connects one to the other and to the early fiction too" (Berruti 333), an overlap in Barlow's writings indicating "the cohesiveness of his overall literary output" (Berruti 336). Obviously, this long-lasting coherence is exemplified by the poetic tributes Barlow composed nearly every year to commemorate the anniversary of Lovecraft's death, for which he tended to return to a more classicist style even in his "most mature Activist phase" (Berruti 342). Yet, also as a non-classical poet, Barlow proved what could be called his occupational Midas touch, for he seemed to prosper in everything he tried, and in fact won a prize for his Activist poetry in 1942. Nevertheless, his "continual 'search' and striving for new and more challenging goals to achieve" (Berruti 309) was not over.

---

by the revenge that natural forces are capable of" (Berruti 387).

14. RHB did try "R. E. H." on *Weird Tales*, where it was accepted as his first and only published piece in that magazine.

15. In a letter to fellow Activist Rosalie Moore, RHB put the difference in a nutshell: "Lovecraft taught me to say exactly what I had in mind; Hart underlined that expression was strongest when put in retina and esophagus-twisting words" (15 May 1944; *EG* 179).

Mexico Period: "A gorgeous fruit can grow from boughs of pain . . ."

Prior to going to San Francisco in the spring of 1939 and a brief interlude in Lakeport, California, to work there in the small "Futile Press" during the previous winter, Barlow had left the Art Institute and Kansas City in 1938 and undertaken a first short trip to Mexico in the summer, which "seems definitely to have marked the end of his artistic studies" (Faig, "R. H. Barlow" 209). Already in his award-winning story "Eyes of the God," about a thief who breaks into a museum and apparently is killed by the idol of a god coming to life under the full moon, "[s]quat, grotesque pottery images of ancient Mexico" (*EG* 13–14) are mentioned in passing.[16] From late 1935 to early 1936, Lovecraft had kept Barlow in the loop on pulp writer Edgar Hoffmann Price's travels to Mexico[17] via Texas, visiting Robert E. Howard, and then back east. Lovecraft's hopes that Price would also visit Barlow in Florida were in vain, but he wrote the latter on 29 January 1936:

> Too bad Price didn't get as far east as Cassia. His limit in that direction was New Orleans. He reached home around the middle of November or a little later, and has been there ever since. His trip was magnificent, and I'll later lend you the travelogue he's circulating. He saw Two-Gun [Bob, that is R. E. Howard], and stood awed in the presence of Aztec antiquity. (*OFF* 315)

If said travelogue ever reached Barlow, it is likely to have additionally fueled his fascination for past and present Mexico, which subsequently could find its expression in such a tale as "Origin Undetermined."

In any case, the seeds were sown very early on, showed their first buds in the summer of 1938, and after a period of increasing dissatisfaction

---

16. Berruti goes as far as to say that "[w]e can here already detect, in a tale dating to 1933, the sense of profound respect Barlow was to nurture in his adult age toward the cultural and religious belief of the native peoples of Mexico (after all, that country is also mentioned in the tale)" (270).

17. HPL's excitement about Price's Mexican sojourn has been adduced as one of several arguments for the claim that "Amerind myths and knowledge of Aztec and other South American cultures certainly came within Lovecraft's sphere of general knowledge" (Blackmore 154), a fascination already manifest in the early tale "The Transition of Juan Romero" (1919) and said to have "stayed with Lovecraft as an appreciable element of his interest in world cultures" (Blackmore 155).

would begin to blossom in 1939 or 1940, when Barlow entered the Polytechnic Institute in San Francisco to begin prerequisite studies for his newly chosen career as an anthropologist. Attendance of a summer school in 1940 allowed him for the first time to study the Nahuatl (historically "Aztec," though Barlow would eventually take issue with that term) language in Mexico City and brought him into contact with fellow student, friend, and future literary executor George T. Smisor. The two would go on to Berkeley, California, in 1941, where Barlow studied anthropology proper under Alfred Louis Kroeber, eminent cultural anthropologist and father of science fiction author Ursula K. Le Guin.[18] He received his bachelor's degree in 1942, "the last degree that he ever bothered to obtain, although he did work equivalent to several Ph.D. dissertations" (Faig, "R. H. Barlow" 218). After working as a research assistant at Berkeley's Anthropology Department, Barlow permanently moved to Mexico at the end of 1943. There he continued his passionate study of Mexican culture and indigenous languages, at first supported by various teaching positions, a Rockefeller Foundation Fellowship in 1944 and a Guggenheim Fellowship from 1946 onward, finally becoming head of the Department of Anthropology at Mexico City College in 1948 until his death just a few years later.

Barlow's accomplishments as an expert in Mesoamerican history, philology, linguistics, anthropology, and archaeology are far too numerous, varied, and often specific for the non-specialist to be given adequate credit here. However, for someone also interested in Barlow's own history, the following oft-quoted reminiscence gives a revealing summary:

> He had an intellectual driving force that never seemed to relax, that picked me up and carried me along with it, as it likewise did later many others. He had a facility of expression that brought to life long-dead happenings. This happy facility was a carry-over from his years of reading and writing fantasy fiction and composing poetry. But there was nothing fantastic in this carry-over. He now insisted on accuracy of fact with brilliance of expression. (Smisor 99)

---

18. In his review of O Fortunate Floridian, Martin Andersson was amused "to note that there is apparently a connection—albeit extremely tenuous—between one of Lovecraft's foremost champions—Barlow—and one of his most famous detractors—Ursula K. Le Guin" (204), alluding to the latter's harsh criticism of HPL when she reviewed de Camp's Lovecraft: A Biography for The Times Literary Supplement of 26 March 1976.

This "carry-over" in a great measure can be attributed to the influence Lovecraft exerted on Barlow during the latter's formative teenage years. It surely does not stop at the "brilliance of expression," but rather extends to the insistence "on accuracy of fact," for "[i]t was a constant Lovecraftian preoccupation to search for the primal causes of phenomena, the 'ultimate reality': a scientific and positivistic attitude that is widely witnessed by the themes Lovecraft touched on in his letters" (Berruti 378n53). Consequently, Wetzel is only partly correct in saying about Barlow that "[f]rom what evidence we have, I should judge that he gradually lost interest in Lovecraft as his attention centered on his own developing career from the early 1940's on" (12).[19]

For a start, although "a break with the past was apparent almost immediately after Lovecraft's death" (Faig, "R. H. Barlow" 209), there were some Lovecraftian activities at least until 15 March 1947, the date of composition of the decennial and presumably last Barlovian Lovecraft tribute "Anniversary."[20] From 1937 to 1942, Barlow had sent the John Hay Library most of the Lovecraft material in his possession,[21] laying an important foundation for the present collection there. Over the next years, Barlow's Lovecraftian involvement by necessity decreased, but it was evident that Lovecraft had not been forgotten when "[i]n 1946 there arose a very peculiar exchange of correspondence between Barlow and the John Hay Library" (Joshi "Recognition" 50), in which the former offered his remaining Lovecraftiana (mainly books, letters, and manuscripts) in exchange for a printing press. Going back to his amateur roots, he needed the equipment to be able to publish fairly regularly a newspaper in Nahuatl.

---

19. It is possible that RHB himself denied links in his transformation from "[a]uthor, poet, painter" to "teacher, anthropologist, and linguistic expert" (Fox 3), for he, "according to one source, hated any connection between his anthropological research and his literary productions" (Mooser 6).

20. Traceable connections to HPL's hometown extend at least into the year 1948, a scientific note from which RHB opened with the following words: "This codex is preserved in the John Carter Brown Library in Providence, R.I." (RHB, "Techialoyan Codices" 383).

21. A notable exception was the manuscript of "The Shadow out of Time," which he kept until shortly before his death at the beginning of 1951 and which resurfaced only in 1994.

Furthermore, one is tempted to regard many aspects of Barlow's academic career as a subtle "carry-over" with respect to Lovecraft. Aside from reflecting Lovecraft's real-world rationalism and "attitude [. . .] of absolute materialism" (CF 2.43) in his scientific rigor, he took to heart at last also Lovecraft's gentle critiques and advice as to his notoriously starting more projects than he could finish, accomplishing a complete turnaround in this respect. He was moreover very Lovecraftian in his willingness to collaborate and support colleagues whenever and with whatever he could:

> He combined his zeal for search, his concern for detail, and his inexhaustible capacity for work by surveying and evaluating Mexican source material with the care and caution of a skilled detective. He published the results of his survey with acumen and insight. This task brought him to many important libraries or archives [. . .] Unselfishly he encouraged his colleagues and sponsored their publications. In this endeavor he was motivated by a genuine interest in the research of others and an enduring concern to make the many rare and unpublished documents available to all. Also testimony of his cooperative efforts is the long list of articles which he co-authored with his colleagues in colonial history, linguistics, codices, and archaeology. (Dibble 347)

Barlow's investigation into Mexico before the conquest and his collecting of ancient folktales are in perfect harmony with the affection for the past he shared with Lovecraft. As an outlet for pertinent source materials, Barlow and George T. Smisor had founded anthropological journal *Tlalocan* in 1943, named after Tlaloc, the Aztec god of rain, or, more specifically, after the "lugar del dios Tláloc" (Cabrera 147), meaning "the domain or kingdom of Tlaloc" (Barlow and Smisor 1).[22] Barlow described one of the journal's agendas thus:

---

22. An audience member at the Armitage Symposium 2019 pointed out to me an academic talk by John B. Carlson at NecronomiCon 2013 titled "Cthulhu? Who Knew? New Clues to His Name and 'Nature' from Pre-Columbian Art and Cosmovision." Unfortunately, I forgot to ask this audience member's name, but I nevertheless would like to express my deepest gratitude to him for calling my attention to Carlson's fascinating theory, summarized as follows by *LibraryThing* user bertilak: "Archaeoastronomer John B. Carlson presented his thesis that the name Cthulhu was at least partially suggested by the Aztec rain god Tlaloc. He remarked that Sonia Green [*sic*] gave HPL a copy of Herbert J. Spinden's *Ancient Civilizations of Mexico and Central America*, which mentioned Tlaloc. He also showed slides of images of Tlaloc as a crouching figure with something tentacular around the mouth (a representation of a beard?) and mentioned that HLP [*sic*] had access to these images. HPL also had access

In modern Mexican folktales one hears the same themes again and again, from different areas and different linguistic groups. An accumulation of these varied versions of certain basic themes (the Dog Wife, the Llorona, for example) is essential to the reconstruction of the prototype of each. [. . .] Tlalocan proposes to publish serialized collections of stories on certain themes [. . .] (Barlow, "Phantom Lover" 29)

When it came to foreign-language learning, Barlow was yet again a prodigy. His natural gift for languages enabled him to gain not only a flaw-less mastery of Spanish and a remarkable working knowledge of other In-do-European languages such as French or German, but also of genealogically and grammatically vastly different languages such as (Classi-cal) Nahuatl and, toward the end of his life, Mayan, including their noto-riously hard-to-decipher glyphs (*Bilderhandschriften*). In fact, it has been claimed that "Barlow learned to speak Náhuatl more fluently than any foreigner in Mexico today" (Smisor 101). Now, Lovecraft certainly had a soft spot for using linguistic terminology in relation to unknown languages in his stories,[23] something that many of Barlow's tales imitated by "intro-ducing a linguistic theme that echoes again a typical Lovecraftian concern" (Berruti 138). But in hindsight it is amusing to see that in their corre-spondence Lovecraft, who "could read only English and Latin fluently" (Joshi "Library" 49), had instructed Barlow in all sorts of questions con-cerning language, for example regarding the etymologies of "satyr" and "satire," English dialects and idioms as well as, curiously enough, the in-verted punctuation marks in Spanish orthography (which Barlow appar-

---

to Zelia Nuttall's works on Mesoamerica" ("NecronomiCon 2013 Friday"). Fully aware of the dangers of evaluating an argument solely based on a second-hand sum-mary, I would merely like to indicate briefly a potential problem for this theory as it per-tains to the study by Spinden: this is possibly the "fine book on primal American civilisations" (*JFM* 393) presented to HPL by a San Francisco librarian in October 1936, which, of course, would have been a decade too late for the naming of Cthulhu.

23. But note that an alleged HPL quotation describing a reptiloid individual express-ing itself through "a rapid succession of consonants that brought to mind certain pro-to-Akkadian dialects" (Houellebecq 75) could not be identified for the translation of Michel Houellebecq's *H. P. Lovecraft: Against the World, Against Life* from French into English. This appears to reflect a more general sloppiness of Houellebecq's scholar-ship, since S. T. Joshi "assisted the translator [. . .], Dorna Khazeni, and we were dis-concerted to find that a number of his citations of passages from Lovecraft could not be located" ("Houellebecq" 43).

ently had first come across when typing Lovecraft's "The Transition of Juan Romero").[24] In the preface to one of his most important works, *The Extent of the Empire of the Culhua Mexica* (1949),[25] Barlow shows a deep linguistic insight demonstrating his intellectual emancipation: "As for the translations scattered through the text, the author has chosen to make them loose, being aware that translations are at best worthless toys. No amount of ingenious paraphrase can possibly supplant the original documents, to which those wishing to investigate the problems of the paper will turn" (v).

In yet other ways, Barlow's path after 1937 can be viewed as a "carry-beyond" with respect to Lovecraft. In a sense, Barlow became what Lovecraft never could but what especially in the latter's "'great texts'" (Houellebecq 41) is one of the typical protagonists, who have sometimes been interpreted as "projections of the true personality of Lovecraft in much the same way that a plane surface can be the orthogonal projection of a volume. [. . .] Usually students or professors [. . .] who specialize in anthropology or folklore" (Houellebecq 68). Also, Barlow's studies and the Guggenheim Fellowship brought him as far as the libraries and archives of Paris and London, places that for lack of money and other reasons would always remain mere places of longing for Lovecraft, as would Europe as a whole. When it comes to Lovecraft's cultural biases and racial prejudices—unpleasant aspects of his complex character that can neither be denied nor "explained" by superficial kitchen sink psychology—Barlow truly went beyond him in candor and impartiality, not only in his professional but also in his private life, for "he did not stop at simply studying the native cultures at the time of the Spanish conquest: he became a friend of his contemporary Indians, among whom he spent most of the time during the Mexican period" (Berruti 392).[26]

---

24. Note also the incident that after his first Florida visit, HPL forgot a Spanish dictionary and learning manual at the Barlows, both of which RHB eventually found and sent after him back to Providence.

25. The publication process took a while: the study was already prepared between March and December in 1943, submitted on 27 May 1946, and finally issued on 25 March 1949. When interviewed for a *Mexico City Collegian* article the following April, RHB admitted that "525 footnotes in the book caused several printers to suffer nervous breakdowns" (Fox 3).

26. In total contradistinction, HPL once wrote: "Mexico or Cuba or South America

Finally, Barlow at times came full circle when translating certain of the legends he recorded into English in his very own characteristic "weird" style:

> The founders of Tlacotepec, Hueytlacatl and Ixquitotzin by name, explored a hill to the north of the present town, viewing snow-covered mountains from the summit. They remained atop the hill and ate *itacáte* ["Provisión de comida para el camino. Tortilla gruesa, redonda" (Cabrera 83), meaning "provisions for the journey" consisting of "thick, round tortillas"]. Hueytlacatl also found an egg in a hole in a rock and devoured it alone. That is why the hill is called Totoltepec ["Bird-Hill" (Barlow, "Migration Legend" 72n6)]. They slept there, but Hueytlacatl slept badly, and awoke with his body covered with eruptions. Ixquitotzin went back to the tribe and led its members to the hill, where they found Hueytlacatl transformed in the meanwhile into a scaly monster. His legs had merged, and his arms become little wings. The monster spoke to the tribe, telling them that they had found their home at last. Then this abnormality, which had clearly become a winged serpent, warned his tribesmen away because he was afraid he would eat them, and took wing. (Barlow, "Migration Legend" 71)

For one, this is reminiscent of "the hideous creature which merged something of the dog with something of the winged snake" (*EG* 29) from Barlow's "The Theft of the Hsothian Manuscripts" (*Annals of the Jinns* X, May 1934). Also, it is somewhat similar to a record in Barlow's "[Memories of Lovecraft (1934)]" of a dream as told to him by Lovecraft,

> in which he was one of a band of mediaeval soldiers [. . .] crawling over house-tops in search of a monster-thing concealed somewhere, that was not only menacing the lives of the villagers, but their very souls as well. The searchers were led by a man upon a black horse who encouraged them actively and spurred them on. Finally locating the Thing where it was behind a chimney, the men advanced [. . .] When it was cornered he saw for the first time it had wings like those of a flying-squirrel. It flew—or glided, and cast itself upon the man in the saddle upon the black horse, and looked up sardonically, for it had *merged* its identity and being with the man, and had the muzzle of the Thing in the armour of the knight. Then it laughed cacklingly and rode away. (OFF 402; emphasis in original)

And lastly, one cannot help but to envisage the flying-snake creature from "The Tlacotepec Migration Legend" as a distant—and more scrupulous—relative of the great Cthulhu himself.

---

don't lure me—what I want is the tropicks plus my own Anglo-Saxon civilisation" (14 January 1930; *JFM* 218).

Collapse: "The lash the heart endures or dies. . ."

The last months of Robert Barlow were marked by tragedy. The exact grounds for his final decision are still not clear, probably never will be, but in parallel to Barlow's newly found interest in the history and Mayan languages of the Yucatan some fatal disaster befell his soul. He was confronted with and had contemplated suicide more than once before, so it remains a mystery why he ultimately chose it during a period of his life in which on the surface everything seemed to play out in his favor.

Some have suggested blackmailing in connection with Barlow's homosexuality as the reason, as in the following passage taken from a commemoration by a former Mexico City College student who would go on to become a poet:[27]

> I didn't like him much
> but he was a human being,
> gave easy tests,
> and did not kill more
> than he had to, so I'm sad
> he died instead of his
> accuser: a student said he was
> a fairy and got expelled. (Dugan 98)

Others have referred to a "strain of overwork," such that already "in the summer of 1950 Barlow was given leave of absence because of health," added to by "[a] growing disillusionment with his life and career" (Faig, "R. H. Barlow" 226–27). Yet others have left the issue more open: "Never robust in health, sensitive to the world about him to an uncommon degree, unable to devote himself blindly and exclusively to his love of knowledge for its sake alone, he succumbed to the *mal du siècle* which in one way or another has touched us all" (McQuown 534).

But be that as it may, at the beginning of 1951, in his home in Azcapotzalco—which means "en los hormigueros; de *ázcatl*, hormiga, *putzalli*, terrero, y *co*, en" (Cabrera 38), that is something like "at the anthills," composed of the forms for "ant," "heap" and "at," respectively—he locked

---

27. Another of RHB's ex-students to achieve literary fame was William S. Burroughs, who alluded to RHB's death in a letter to fellow-writer Allen Ginsberg on January 11, 1951: "A queer Professor from K.C., Mo., head of the Anthropology dept. here at M.C.C. where I collect my $75 per month, knocked himself off a few days ago with overdose of goof balls. Vomit all over the bed. I can't see this suicide kick" (78).

himself in his bedroom from which he would never again emerge, his eyes forever closed to the "View from a Hill" that he had always admired from outside his house.

Conclusion: "Well I know the starless night awaiting . . ."

R. H. Barlow was a remarkable youth, artist, and scholar, and through the everlasting impact of Howard Phillips Lovecraft, among other things, developed a multifaceted personality that managed to leave a mark in many diverse fields and on many different people. As Lovecraft aptly remarked about Barlow to the editor of *Weird Tales* in a letter from DeLand written on 21 May 1934, during his first Florida stay: "In the course of time I think he'll be importantly heard from in one way or another" ("Letters to Farnsworth Wright" 40). One thus cannot but fully concur with S. T. Joshi's assessment that, considering Barlow's suicide at the mere age of thirty-two, "[i]t was a tragic waste, for—although not in the field of weird fiction—he had fully justified Lovecraft's predictions of his precocious genius, and would have accomplished far more had he lived" (*IAP* 1028).

Works Cited

Andersson, Martin. Review of H. P. Lovecraft, *O Fortunate Floridian*. *Lovecraft Annual* No. 2 (2008): 203–8.

Barlow, R. H. *Eyes of the God: The Weird Fiction and Poetry of R. H. Barlow.* Ed. S. T. Joshi, Douglas A. Anderson, and David E. Schultz. New York: Hippocampus Press, 2002. [Abbreviated in the text as *EG.*]

————. *The Extent of the Empire of the Culhua Mexica.* Berkeley: University of California Press, 1949.

————. "The Phantom Lover." *Tlalocan* 2 (1945): 29–34.

————. "The Techialoyan Codices: Codex N (Codex of Santa Maria Tetelpan)." *Tlalocan* 2 (1948): 383–84.

————. "The Tlacotepec Migration Legend." *Tlalocan* 2 (1945): 70–73.

————, and George T. Smisor. "Re-Introducing 'Tlalocan.'" *Tlalocan* 4 (1962): 1–2.

Bernal, Ignacio. "Robert H. Barlow (1918–1950 [sic])." *Boletin Bibliografico de Antropologia Americana* 13 (1950): 301–4.

Berruti, Massimo. *Dim-Remembered Stories: A Critical Study of R. H. Barlow.* New York: Hippocampus Press, 2011.

bertilak. "NecronomiCon 2013 Friday Part 2/3: Sessions Academics 1, 2, and 3." *LibraryThing*, 24 August 2013. www.librarything.com/topic /158021#4254327

Blackmore, Leigh. "Some Notes on Lovecraft's 'The Transition of Juan Romero.'" *Lovecraft Annual* No. 3 (2009): 147-68.

Burroughs, William S. *The Letters of William S. Burroughs: 1945-1959.* Ed. Oliver Harris. New York: Penguin Books, 1993.

Cabrera, Luis. *Diccionario de Aztequismos.* México City: Ediciones Oasis, 1988.

de Camp, L. Sprague. *Lovecraft: A Biography.* Garden City, NY: Doubleday, 1975.

Déléage, Pierre. "La Transmigration de Robert H. Barlow." *Les Temps Modernes* No. 700 (October-December 2018): 121-64.

Dibble, Charles E. "Robert Hayward Barlow: 1918-1951." *American Antiquity* 16, No. 4 (April 1951): 347.

Dugan, Alan. "In Memoriam. Unfinished. For Robert Barlow." *Iowa Review* 4, No. 3 (Summer 1973): 98.

Eckhardt, Jason C. "The Cosmic Yankee." In David E. Schultz and S. T. Joshi, ed. *An Epicure in the Terrible: A Centennial Anthology of Essays in Honor of H. P. Lovecraft.* 1991. New York: Hippocampus Press, 2011. 77-100.

Faig, Kenneth W., Jr. "R. H. Barlow." In *The Unknown Lovecraft.* New York: Hippocampus Press, 2009. 194-234.

―――. "Robert H. Barlow as H. P. Lovecraft's Literary Executor: An Appreciation." In *The Unknown Lovecraft.* New York: Hippocampus Press, 2009. 235-48.

Fox, Saul. "Many Talents in Diverse Fields." *Mexico City Collegian* 2, No. 3 (11 April 1949): 3.

Hart, Lawrence. "A Note on Robert Barlow." *Poetry* 78, No. 2 (May 1951): 115-18.

Houellebecq, Michel. *H. P. Lovecraft: Against the World, Against Life.* Tr. Dorna Khazeni. San Francisco: Believer Books, 2005.

Joshi, S. T. "Lovecraft's Library." In *Primal Sources: Essays on H. P. Lovecraft.* New York: Hippocampus Press, 2003. 47-50.

———. "R. H. Barlow and the Recognition of Lovecraft." *Crypt of Cthulhu* No. 60 (Hallowmas 1988): 45–51, 32.

———. "Why Michel Houellebecq Is Wrong about Lovecraft's Racism." *Lovecraft Annual* No. 12 (2018): 43–50.

Legaria, Marcos. "H. P. Lovecraft's Determinism and Atomism: Evidence in R. H. Barlow's 'The Summons.'" *Lovecraft Annual* No. 11 (2017): 101–9.

Lovecraft, H. P. "Letters to Farnsworth Wright." Ed. S. T. Joshi and David E. Schultz. *Lovecraft Annual* No. 8 (2014): 5–59.

McQuown, Norman A. "Robert Hamilton [sic] Barlow, 1918–1951." *American Anthropologist* 53 (1951): 543.

Mooser, Clare. "A Study of Robert Barlow: The T. E. Lawrence of Mexico." *Mexico Quarterly Review* 3, No. 2 (1968): 5–12.

Smisor, George T. "R. H. Barlow and 'Tlalocan.'" *Tlalocan* 3 (1952): 97–102.

Wetzel, George T. "Lovecraft's Literary Executor." In Wetzel's *The Lovecraft Scholar.* Ed. Sam Gafford and John Buettner. Darien, CT: Hobgoblin Press, 1983. 3–14.

American Frankensteins: George Porter and George Poe, and Their Attempts to Reanimate the Dead in New England

Michael J. Bielawa
The Barnum Museum

In Memory of Janice Bielawa
17 January 1964–22 April 2020
Inspired by Providence, Janice danced to
NecronomiCon's swaying chants

"West had already made himself notorious through his wild theories on the nature of death and the possibility of overcoming it artificially." (*CF* 1.292)
H. P. Lovecraft, "Herbert West—Reanimator"

Lovecraft's intriguing observations regarding "wild theories" and possibilities of artificially thwarting death are culled from one of his own least favorite works.[1] Serialized during 1922 in the magazine *Home Brew*, "Herbert West—Reanimator," aside from being an entertaining horror story, should be considered an important contribution to the Lovecraft canon. Not only did it introduce Miskatonic University, but more broadly it helped spawn the modern zombie genre. Beyond debating the literary merits of this particular work, a startling piece of historical context emerges: forty years before Lovecraft wrote the story, and only twenty years before West and his nameless narrator began their own experiments, southern New England was indeed home to two would-be reanimators: Dr. George Loring Porter and Prof. George Poe.

Well before the electro-alchemic creation of Victor Frankenstein—

---

1. S. T. Joshi has pointed out the extent to which HPL lamented the uninspired formula-based approach employed while composing "Herbert West—Reanimator" (*IAP* 411).

which Lovecraft admired, and long seen as an inspiration for Herbert West (*CE* 2.94; *LL* no. 864)—took to shambling through the countryside, medically trained individuals had been experimenting with electricity and dead things. Luigi Galvani in 1780 caused deceased frogs' legs to twitch, and afterward his inquisitive student-nephew, Giovanni Aldini, applied galvanism to a decapitated ox head during the first decade of the nineteenth century (Dougan 95-112). It was but the briefest hop, skip, and galvanic jump to arrive at the next phase of experiments. In 1818, Andrew Ure turned audiences pale by attaching electrodes to a recently executed convict and apparently awakened a cadaver. These exercises and others were conducted by scattered anatomists over a period of decades, each independently dabbling with galvanism (Mellor 106-7). By the time Porter and Poe began their own experiments, therefore, they were joining a long pedigree of serious researchers into the science of reanimation.

George Loring Porter was born in 1838 in the town of Concord, New Hampshire. A battlefield surgeon during the Civil War, Porter was a hero under fire. The first lieutenant had been a prisoner of war, participated in several major engagements, and aided both the Union and Confederate wounded. Strange events dogged Porter all his days, and the frontlines offered no exception. A lost order kept Porter unwittingly in Virginia just before the slaughter commenced at the Battle of the Wilderness. Instead of his returning to Washington, D.C., this delayed communication perpetuated the surgeon's presence at the battlefront, thus saving untold lives (Conn 451). Porter was clandestinely placed in charge of secretly burying the body of John Wilkes Booth; Porter also escorted Lincoln assassination co-conspirators to the island prison on the Dry Tortugas (George Porter 63-82). Stationed in the American West at the conclusion of the war, Dr. Porter was highly revered for his work treating both soldiers and Native Americans. After his military service the intrepid surgeon bravely set out alone to follow the wilderness path of Lewis and Clark to the Pacific Ocean (Bielawa 44). Eventually Porter relocated his family and medical practice to Bridgeport, Connecticut in 1868 (Mary Porter 44). His attempts at reanimation were merely a few years away. But before any such experiment could occur a corpse was required.

Unhinged by longtime alcohol abuse and sparked by a perceived family squabble over land and finances, thirty-six-year-old Edwin Hoyt, a resident of Sherman, Connecticut, jabbed a butcher knife into his father's jugular on 23 June 1878. During the subsequent trial held in Bridgeport, Hoyt's attorneys argued insanity. But two trials and a number of well-intentioned legal maneuvers could not postpone Hoyt's appointment with the noose. The date set for execution was 13 May 1880 (Bielawa 44–46). Hoyt was still hanging from the end of a manila coil when prison physician Dr. Robert Lauder pressed the condemned man's wrist while Dr. Porter counted the beats. At noon the two doctors, one after the other, placed an ear to the swaying man's chest. No heartbeat was detected. More time was allowed to fulfill the state's decree that Edwin Hoyt should "hang by the neck until dead." Hoyt remained dangling for 35 minutes in the green on the west side of the jail that to this day the prison staff still identifies as the "gallows yard."[2]

Removed from the scaffold, Hoyt's lifeless body was placed on a coffin lid and rushed to the jail's second-floor hospital facility. Upstairs the medical room had been carefully prepared according to Dr. Porter's wishes. The space was filled with twenty physicians, along with guards, ministers, and a number of wealthy merchants, many of whom were able to remain in the operating room only after being sworn in as special deputies ("The Great Problem of Life"). A plan had been set in motion to see whether Edwin Hoyt could be brought back to the living through the use of galvanism. Someone in the jostling throng postulated aloud, half-jokingly, that if the experiment proved successful, would Edwin have to be hanged again? A pall fell over the room. No one offered an answer.

An incision was made above Hoyt's clavicle and wires from "a single cell Kidder electro-galvanic battery, capable of giving a very powerful current" were applied to the phrenic nerve and diaphragm ("The Great Problem of Life"). Respiration was simulated. The doctors remarked how Hoyt seemed to be simply sleeping. The wetted electrodes were now attached to the muscles of the forearms, upper arms, and shoulders, causing the corpse's arms to thrash about and point accusingly at the merchants and holy men assembled. More startling were the facial expressions created by the galvanic charge; the doctors gasped when Edwin opened his eyes and stared. Dr. Porter noted in his official paper, read before the Bridgeport Medical Society, "the face produced expressions of joy and surprise, and anger and fright" ("Medical Manipulations of a Criminal's Cadaver"). Hoyt shockingly rolled his eyeballs at the assemblage, pausing to glare, and then "savagely frowned." However, hopes to restart the heart failed. An unnamed physician, in all likelihood Dr. Porter himself, remarked to reporters,

---

2. Anonymous Bridgeport corrections official in discussion with the author, 2016.

Could we have made the heart move we would have had some hope of being able to resuscitate the man. [. . .] We were at the very portals of the great mystery of life and death. [. . .] We had induced natural respiration. If we could have made the heart beat with the lungs doing their duty [. . .] it would have been actually raising the dead to life. ("The Great Problem of Life")

Undaunted, Dr. Porter's report concludes that the science of "reanimation may [still] be re-established [. . . by] mechanical revival" ("Medical Manipulations of a Criminal's Cadaver"). Viewing the results of the day's experiments, more than one doctor probably thought that the only thing needed to further explore galvanism was a fresh, untainted body. Herbert West would love this. In Lovecraft's story West is always musing how "a body must be very fresh indeed" (CF 1.298). But while West only required a wait of a single summer, Porter's work was ultimately delayed by eight years.

In a long-simmering fit of rage Philip Palladino killed his brother Francisco over a forty-dollar loan. Palladino was arrested, brought to trial, and later hanged 5 October 1888. Drs. Lauder and Porter were again part of the medical team (Bielawa 49–50). Everything proceeded as expected during and immediately after the execution—except that a fracas erupted when Palladino's body was lowered into the plain pine coffin. Lauder placed a hand on the dead man's neck to ascertain if it was broken and, according to the page one story of the 8 October 1888 *New York Evening World*, "a violent scene" ensued. Father Leo Rizzo da Saracena burst forward excitedly demanding that no one touch the body. The priest was intent on protecting the deceased from being experimented upon by means of galvanism.[3] To guarantee the body remained undisturbed, a sentinel was posted overnight at Palladino's grave.[4]

---

3. Rumors abounded regarding attempts to secure Palladino's corpse and repeat galvanic experiments: "Attempt to Rob a Grave," *New York Times* (7 October 1888); "Let the Dead Rest," *Bridgeport Daily Standard* (8 October 1888); and "Pallidoni's [sic] Grave: A Reported Attempt to Rob It—The Electrical Experiments That Were [De]sired," *Connecticut Courant* (11 October 1888).

4. Unnerving as it may sound, after his execution Palladino was reportedly seen alive and well in New York City and New Haven. According to reports, the convict was either buried alive and subsequently disinterred, or his execution was faked and he was rescued in an elaborate conspiracy set in motion by a secret society. Take your pick. "Was He Hanged? Some People Believe Palladoni [sic] Still Lives: Bridgeport Will Be Excited Until the Grave Is Opened," *New York Evening World* (8 October 1888); and "A Ridiculous Story [. . .] Is [P]alladoni [sic] Alive?" *Bridgeport Evening Farmer* (8 October 1888).

An anonymous city physician shared his thoughts on the matter with one of the local newspapers, the *Bridgeport Evening Farmer*. "Palladoni was a beautiful subject for an electrical experiment. [. . .] He was of robust body, and his neck not being broken there was excellent material for the galvanic battery to work upon. [. . .] Had it chanced by a bare possibility that our treatment brought him back to life, I presume he would have gone free, as the law had visited upon him the prescribed penalty" ("The Doctors Disappointed"). This unnamed reanimator's stoic perspective presciently channels Lovecraft's future aesthetic philosophy. As film scholar Jake Whritner observes, "Herbert West, with his belief that the soul is a myth and that life is essentially just a physical and chemical process that can be manipulated if one finds the correct formula, can be seen in one sense as springing from Lovecraft's worldview" (Whirtner 30).

While the uncredited quotation likely came from Porter, by 1888 there was another scientist in Bridgeport who would have been qualified to give his opinion on the process of resurrection. While surgeons had awaited Palladino's execution, a new prospective reanimator arrived in town: Professor George Poe. His interests were befitting his family name, for he was indeed related to the author who was such an influence on Lovecraft (*RK* 51), being the son of Edgar Allan Poe's second cousin. Nor was this relationship merely connected through a genealogy chart. Prof. Poe relished the opportunity to show colleagues an early handwritten copy of Edgar A. Poe's "The Raven." The scientist's life ambitions also brought him much closer to his macabre writer-cousin through their mutual appreciation for the bizarre. When Prof. Poe came to live in Bridgeport during 1888 he had already gathered the reputation as a celebrated chemist (Beckford 237). The study of oxygen and breathing disorders were a passion for the Victorian healer. George Poe was the first entrepreneur to make liquefied nitrous oxide commercially available; 5000 dentists nationwide employed his anesthetic. In addition to this business venture, Connecticut newspapers ran advertisements for an exotic-sounding "Poe's Volatilized Balsam of Tar," used to cure lung and throat problems.[5]

Poe's quest for a suitable laboratory where he could further his oxygen research came to fruition in Bridgeport's booming industrial complex;

---

5. One advertising example appears as "Compound Oxygen Treatment, Rational Cure for Chronic Diseases, also Poe's Volatilized Balsam of Tar [. . .] for Catarrh, Throat and Lung Troubles," *Meriden* [CT] *Daily Republican* (11 June 1887).

here Poe rented space in downtown's new Connecticut National Bank building. These rooms were in convenient proximity to the professor's residence on Madison Avenue. Strangely enough, his home was adjacent to the jailhouse.[6] Theoretically, in the event of a convict's sudden death, Poe's Madison Avenue home could allow the professor rapid entrance into the neighboring prison to employ the life-resuscitating device he was designing. But before Poe could apply his own wild theories to reanimating humans with the use of cylinders and bellows, he first needed to experiment on deceased animals. Unveiling his exceptional contraption to the world, Poe touted his lung machine and techniques on stage. Picture freakish Herbert West and his "immense numbers" of poor rabbits (CF 1.292). Shockingly, even to that era's blunt sensibilities, the chemist drowned a single rabbit eleven times and, eleven times, miraculously resuscitated the animal ("Prof. Poe of Bridgeport, Ct. is experimenting" 40). On another occasion audiences rose to their feet, astounded and shouting, as he suffocated a dog with noxious charcoal fumes and then, with the use of his remarkable engine, repeatedly restored life ("Smother Small Dog"). Bridgeport had established itself as the go-to destination for reanimating the dead.

It is difficult to imagine these two eminent men of science not meeting to discuss strategies. As further evidence, though circumstantial, Dr. Porter had indicated plans to acquire other corpses for galvanic experiments, including the body of Henry Hamlin, who was executed in Hartford, Connecticut, during late May 1880 ("Medical Manipulations of a Criminal's Cadaver"). Church officials thwarted Hamlin's use for medical tests. Even more damning, Poe would once again establish a future home near (as Herbert West so often morbidly intoned) an "exceedingly fresh" supply of doomed souls (CF 1.303–5). After living near the Fairfield County Jail in Bridgeport, Poe relocated to the neighborhood of the Hartford Retreat for the Insane. Was this an attempt on the part of Poe to experiment on unclaimed dead bodies? One fact, never before discussed, now comes to light: Porter served as the visiting physician at the Hartford Retreat for the Insane (Watson 508). It is entirely possible that Porter helped arrange Poe's Hartford move and allow secret access to the asylum.

Recognized around the world as the Bridgeport inventor who brought the dead back to life, Prof. George Poe died in Virginia on 3 February

---

6. *Sanborn Fire Insurance Map from Bridgeport, Fairfield County, Connecticut.* New York: Sanborn-Perris Map Co., 1898.

1914. He was sixty-seven years old. As for Dr. Porter, while vacationing in Florida on 24 February 1919, the stalwart surgeon-hero passed peacefully from this life. However, their tale does not end there.

Faye Ringel, the well-known Lovecraft scholar and noted weird fiction aficionado, suggested a separate path of inquiry with regard to this essay: one prompting a search for any possible link connecting the Bridgeport reanimation experiments of the 1880s with Lovecraft's writings. It is an outstanding hypothesis: was Lovecraft aware of Porter and Poe, or in any way influenced by the doctors' work? The question is not an outlandish one. Ringel herself has proposed that Lovecraft was inspired by seventeenth-century alchemical studies conducted in New London, just up the Connecticut coastline (142–43). Lovecraft passed through Bridgeport on his travels between Providence and New York, and his friend Robert Moe lived there (*ET* 300), as did Lovecraft's friend and occasional co-author Henry S. Whitehead. Both men lived in Bridgeport only subsequent to the writing of "Herbert West," but beginning in 1921 the latter began serving as acting archdeacon of the US Virgin Islands, leading to an interest in voodoo and obeah, including local zombie lore prior to its English-language popularization by William Seabrook (Barlow vii–x).

Research over a period of months has led to the conclusion that there is probably no direct relationship between Porter and West. Strangely enough, however, pursuing this course of investigation resulted in the discovery of several interesting coincidences concerning the reanimator doctor and the author of the Reanimator.

To begin with, Porter graduated from Brown University, Class of 1859 (Putnam x). He and his family resided in Providence until moving to Bridgeport, Connecticut. While attending Brown, Porter courted Catherine Maria Chaffee; they wed in 1862. At the time Maria lived at 91 Prospect Street in Providence (Providence Directory 1862 38). The Chaffee family were not without their own spectral lore. One night, seven years prior to the Porter wedding, Catherine's mother, Sarah, woke her from a deep sleep. Quite shaken, she explained to her daughter that she had just been visited by Catherine's brother, William, who for some time had been working in South America. The twenty-two-year-old man appeared at the foot of Sarah's Providence bed, and said, "Goodby mother." The family soon discovered that this was the exact day William died of yellow fever in Brazil (Mary Porter 3).

Sometime about the year 1870 Maria's family relocated down the road. Lovecraft was intimately familiar with the Chaffees' second home. Located at 140 Prospect Street (Providence Directory 1871 61), the Georgian architectural marvel is better recognized as the Thomas Lloyd Halsey Mansion. Discussing the ancient homestead with his aunt Lillian Clark, Lovecraft wrote: "And so the old Halsey house is haunted! Ugh! That's where Wild Tom Halsey kept live terrapins in the cellar—maybe it's their ghosts. Anyway, it's a magnificent old mansion, and a credit to a magnificent old town!" (24 August 1925; *LFF* 364).

The humorous reference to a nest of turtles wallowing in the Halsey basement refers to a tale recorded in a local history obviously consulted by Lovecraft, *Old Providence: A Collection of Facts and Traditions* (46–47).[7] Further evidence of intimacy with the Halsey house is provided when Lovecraft describes his immediate neighborhood to fellow weird author and confidant, Donald Wandrei: Just around the corner is the great double-bayed Halsey Mansion built in 1801 & reputed to be haunted, (I will enclose a snapshot of this & have also marked a picture of its classical late-Georgian porch" (27 March 1925; *DW* 76). The photograph mentioned in the Wandrei letter features Lovecraft's wife, Sonia Greene, and his aunt, Annie Gamwell, standing in front of the Halsey Mansion's snow-covered lawn.

Lovecraft proudly embraces an awe for and derives inspiration from "old New Englandism" (while reiterating a love for his Providence neighborhood and the Halsey Mansion) in a letter to Bernard Austin Dwyer of June 1927. The Halsey house was "just around the corner and now said to be *haunted*. Could a more fitting milieu be asked for a retrospective and archaistic fantaisiste?" (*MWM* 455).

Though the house was visited by Dr. Porter, S. T. Joshi postulates that Lovecraft may never have entered the Halsey place. However, the horror writer "had a clear view of it from 10 Barnes Street; looking northwest-

---

7. HPL was also familiar with another Providence history book that makes reference to the ghostly Halsey place. While living in Brooklyn, HPL wrote to Lillian D. Clark, "On Friday the 31st . . . evening went down to the library to read in that valuable volume, 'Providence in Colonial Times,' by Gertrude Selwyn Kimball" (6 August 1925; *LFF* 331). Kimball's book notes that "The old Halsey mansion boasts not only a well-developed ghost,—a piano-playing ghost!—but also a fine large bloodstain, which cannot be scrubbed from the floor, but which does not appear to all observers" (369). Kimball also indicates that superstitious folks in the neighborhood "objected to passing the [Halsey] place after dark."

ward from his aunt's upstairs back window, he could see it distinctly" (*IAP* 666). The Chaffees' onetime mansion would creepily serve as the fictional residence for Lovecraft's "essential saltes" conjuring magus, Charles Dexter Ward (*CF* 2.217). It is also interesting to point out that in "Herbert West—Reanimator" the name of the dean of Miskatonic University's medical school is Dr. Allan *Halsey*.

Connecting Lovecraft's extensive knowledge of historical Providence directly with the life of Porter might thus far appear anecdotal. Could Lovecraft have possibly stumbled across Porter's personal life, perhaps in old newspaper coverage? The 1880 reanimation attempt was detailed by the New York and Connecticut press and in papers across the nation. Theoretically Lovecraft might have read these decades-old accounts in the Providence Public Library, at Brown, or in the New York Public Library while he lived in Brooklyn.[8] As Porter died in 1919, did an obituary that Lovecraft read mention the Bridgeport reanimation experiment? The timeline would ostensibly conflate with Lovecraft's invoking the rudimentary existence of "Herbert West" as he commenced writing the reanimator story in 1921. A Bridgeport article appeared during the year of Porter's death, which does indeed note his galvanic attempts (Vickrey). Certainly such a newspaper discovery would have piqued Lovecraft's interest. Yet there is nary a mention of Porter in any of Lovecraft's voluminous correspondence.

In yet another stream of Porter-Lovecraft kismet, three years prior to the publication of "Herbert West" Bridgeport newspapers noted that Dr. Porter's State Street home remained brimming with a bewildering assortment of medical papers, Lincoln assassination documents, and historical artwork. "The whole of the lower floor of the Porter house is filled with not only interesting but highly valuable manuscripts, pictures, and books" (Vickrey). Local citizens demanded that this vast and unique collection be preserved and exhibited in Dr. Porter's adopted hometown of Bridgeport. Despite public outcry the Porter hoard documenting his extraordinary life was destined to be disbursed beyond Bridgeport's borders.[9] In one more tantaliz-

---

8. HPL might also have seen such old newspapers during a visit to the Hartford Public Library; however, that trip was made in 1933, too late to influence "Herbert West" (*IAP* 853).

9. There seems to be a good chance that Porter's collection included notes on his reanimation research. According to contemporary journalists, Porter had a penchant

ing bit of synchronicity some of Porter's material inevitably wound its way to Lovecraft's Providence. Unfortunately, the Porter family's donation to Brown University—consisting of 338 engravings celebrating the life of George Washington ("Brown to Get Gift")—was made in 1925, six years after the doctor's demise and three years after the writing of "Herbert West."

What was the fate of Porter's reanimation notes? Perhaps waiting in a forgotten archival box gathering century-old dust in the basement of John Hay Library? One person who might be capable of providing insight to their whereabouts is Marcia Maloney, the great-great-granddaughter of Dr. Porter. In recent conversations Ms. Maloney enthusiastically stated that the surgeon's diaries do exist. Marcia observed, "I lived with my great-grandmother and there were an assortment of family heirlooms collected in the house." Mulling over her great-great-grandfather's accumulated arti-facts, she offered, "There were a lot of papers, and actually, a lot of *things* in the attic." She continued, "I remember [. . .] even [Dr. Porter's] army uniform from the Civil War when I was growing-up [. . .] but it was pretty ratty and moth-eaten." As for the Porter diaries, they are in rather "poor shape and faded" but are silently biding their time, waiting to be exam-ined. Ms. Maloney promised to look through these tattered pages and see what might be uncovered. This writer asked her to especially pay attention for any mention of the word "reanimate."[10]

Vicariously these Victorian Connecticut reanimators would indeed have a passing strange bearing on Lovecraft. The Chaffee family and Dr. Porter are certainly a part of Providence's old New Englandism that Love-craft so absorbed; and Prof. Poe's own shocking experiments harkened to the terror tales of Edgar Allan Poe who poignantly influenced Lovecraft.

Did Porter and Poe collaborate on their reanimation work, perhaps on experiments which evaded reports in the press? Could a connection be-tween Porter and Lovecraft exist? Might Porter's family recall something

---

for acquiring "gory" mementos. Among his extensive inventory was an item newspa-pers relished highlighting, "the life blood of Lincoln, spattered upon the rich brocade of [Ford's Theater actress] Miss [Laura] Keene's dress and left there [the blood's] in-delible print. [. . .] The sanguinary relic of the assassination, reposed in a handsome box-like receptacle on the wall of Dr. Porter's dining room" ("Local Doctor Had Gory Lincoln Relic").

10. Marcia Maloney, great-great-granddaughter of Dr. George Loring Porter, in dis-cussion with the author, July 2019.

that illuminate on the matter? As Lovecraft states in the first paragraph of "Herbert West—Reanimator," "Memories and possibilities are ever more hideous than realities" (CF 1.291).

Works Cited

Barlow, R. H. "Henry S. Whitehead." 1943. In Whitehead's *Jumbee and Other Uncanny Tales*. Sauk City, WI: Arkham House, 1944. vii–xii.

Beckford, William Hale. *Leading Business Men of New Haven County; and a Historical Review of the Principal Cities*. Boston: Mercantile Publishing Co., 1887.

Bielawa, Michael J. "The Strange Notebook of Dr. George Porter: Reanimator." In *Wicked Bridgeport*. Charleston, SC: The History Press, 2012.

"Brown to Get Gift of Washingtoniana." *Providence Journal* (17 June 1925). Article from Bridgeport Public Library History Center, Newspaper Clippings File, "Porter, Dr. George Loring." And also, "College Gets Dr. Porter's Collections." June 1925. Unidentified article from Bridgeport Public Library History Center, Newspaper Clippings File, "Porter, Dr. George Loring."

Conn, Granville P. *History of the New Hampshire Surgeons in the War of Rebellion*. Concord, NH: Ira C. Evans Co., 1906.

"The Doctors Disappointed." *Bridgeport Evening Farmer* (6 October 1888).

Dougan, Andy. *Raising the Dead: The Men Who Created Frankenstein*. Edinburgh: Birlinn, 2008.

"The Great Problem of Life: Another Series of Scientific Experiments with the Dead." *New York Sun* (16 May 1880).

Kimball, Gertrude Selwyn. *Providence in Colonial Times*. Boston: Houghton Mifflin, 1912.

"Local Doctor Had Gory Lincoln Relic." Unidentified 1936 newspaper article from Bridgeport Public Library History Center, Newspaper Clippings File, "Porter, Dr. George Loring—Eminent Physician and Surgeon."

"Medical Manipulations of a Criminal's Cadaver: Experiments on the Body of Hoyt the Murderer." *Bridgeport Daily Standard* (10 June 1880).

Mellor, Anne K. *Mary Shelley: Her Life, Her Fiction, Her Monsters*. New York: Methuen, 1988.

Old Providence: A Collection of Facts and Traditions Relating to Various Buildings and Sites of Historic Interest in Providence. Providence, RI: The Merchants National Bank of Providence, 1918.

Porter, Dr. George Loring. "How Booth's Body Was Hidden: The True Story Told for the First Time in The Columbian, The Army Officer Who Hid the Body Relates the Grewsome [*sic*] Details." *Columbian Magazine* (April 1911): 63–82.

Porter, Mary W. *The Surgeon in Charge.* Concord, NH: Rumford Press, 1949.

"Prof. Poe of Bridgeport, Ct. Is Experimenting . . ." *Recreation: A Monthly Exponent of the Higher Literature of Manly Sport* (May 1889).

The Providence Directory for the Year 1862. Providence, RI: Adams, Sampson & Co., 1862.

The Providence Directory for the Year 1871. Providence, RI: Sampson, Davenport & Co., 1871.

Putnam, Eban, ed. "Dr. George Loring Porter." *Porter Leaflets* (May 1896): x–xii.

Ringel, Faye. "New England Gothic." In Charles L. Crow, ed. *A Companion to American Gothic.* Malden, MA: Wiley Blackwell, 2014. 139–50.

"Smother Small Dog to See It Revived: Successful Demonstration of an Artificial Respiration Machine Cheered in Brooklyn." *New York Times* (29 May 1908).

Watson, Irving A., ed. *Physicians and Surgeons of America: A Collection of Biographical Sketches of the Regular Medial Profession.* Concord, NH: Republican Press Association, 1896.

Whritner, Jake. "Method to the Madness." *Diabolique* (March–May 2015): 26–35.

Vickrey, Bab. "Why Should Not Bridgeport Keep Historic Collection of Dr. George Loring Porter?" Unidentified (4 May 1919) article from Bridgeport Public Library History Center, Newspaper Clippings File, "Porter, Dr. George Loring."

The author offers special appreciation to Edward Guimont, University of Connecticut, for lending a critical eye and especially for sharing his research concerning Lovecraft's Connecticut connections.

Encounters in the Mountains of Madness: H. P. Lovecraft and Werner Herzog at the World's End

Lúcio Reis-Filho, Laura Cánepa, and Jamer de Mello
University Anhembi Morumbi, São Paulo, Brazil

The most merciful thing in the world, I think, is the inability of the human mind to correlate all its contents. We live on a placid island of ignorance in the midst of black seas of infinity, and it was not meant that we should voyage far. The sciences, each straining in its own direction, have hitherto harmed us little; but some day the piecing together of dissociated knowledge will open up such terrifying vistas of reality, and of our frightful position therein, that we shall either go mad from the revelation or flee from the deadly light into the peace and safety of a new dark age.

H. P. Lovecraft, "The Call of Cthulhu" (1926)

For this and many other reasons, our presence on this planet does not seem to be sustainable. Our technical civilization makes us particularly vulnerable. There is talk all over the scientific community about climate change. Many of them agree, the end of human life on this earth is assured. Human life is part of an endless chain of catastrophes, the demise of the dinosaurs being just one of these events. We seem to be next.

Werner Herzog, *Encounters at the End of the World* (2007)

Introduction

In his career, especially in the past fifteen years, the German filmmaker Werner Herzog has developed a cinematic procedure characterized by the omnipresence of his voiceover. This allowed him to build up philosophical reflections endowed with a self-reflexive and self-representative rhetoric, which guides the debates surrounding his films. According to Les Blank's documentary *Burden of Dreams* (1982), the subject of these films is actually Herzog himself, driven by his own cinematic vision. "Taken together, the films of Werner Herzog can be seen as one long cinematic

161

quest for ecstasy through extremity" (Jirsa). In some of his last documentaries, a "Herzogian" vision stands out. Written and uttered by Herzog himself, his narration unveils predictions about human existence and experience in the world. As a result, Herzog's lines sparked the interest of the audiences, who eventually elevated him to the status of a "pop prophet."

"I believe the common denominator of the Universe is not harmony, but chaos, hostility and murder," Herzog claims in *Grizzly Man* (2005). The cynical, sometimes nihilistic judgments delivered by his voiceover, combined with other cinematic procedures, brings him closer to a philosophy very trendy nowadays. In a sarcastic tone very similar to Lovecraft's, the filmmaker evokes cosmicism, the literary philosophy that unveils the dark side of nature, a universe of appalling indifference and deliberate hostility toward humankind. We attempt herein to identify traces of this philosophy in *Encounters at the End of the World* (2007), relating the documentary film to Lovecraft's Antarctic novella.

Encounters at the End of the World is the register of Herzog's expedition to Antarctica. Published more than seven decades before the film, *At the Mountains of Madness* (1931) was set in the same location, in the environs of Mount Erebus. Written in the pseudo-documentary style that characterized Lovecraft's fiction, the short novel follows the disastrous incursion of a group of scientists and engineers into the frozen continent. Both the film and the text are part of a bicentennial tradition of Antarctic narratives. They evoke cosmic horror by miniaturizing humankind, conveying its insignificance in the gulfs of an infinite and hostile universe. This perspective creates fantastic and frightening visions that drive the characters mad in the face of the unknown.

In cinema, Lovecraft's horror stories have appealed to some well-known directors and writers. Among the exponents of Lovecraftian films, two stand out: Ridley Scott's *Alien* (1979)[1] and John Carpenter's *The Thing* (1982). Although they are not adaptations per se of Lovecraft's writings (Migliore and Strysik 11, 107), the first could be considered an appropriation of *At the Mountains of Madness* and the latter owes much to the main tropes of the novel: the setting (a research station in Antarctica), the science-world characters, and the shapeshifting alien creature. However, Lovecraft's vision should not be limited to horror fiction. As we suggest, Herzog's oeu-

---

1. Scott's *The Terror* (2018) is a series whose first season is a Gothic horror story set in the Arctic during the Heroic Era of Exploration, in the mid-19th century.

vre—which includes only one horror film, *Nosferatu the Vampyre* (*Nosferatu: Phantom der Nacht*, 1979), an adaptation of Bram Stoker's classic novel and its 1922 German version, directed by F. W. Murnau—also evokes cosmic horror, notably the documentary film *Encounters at the End of the World*.

Antarctic Exploration and Cosmic Horror in Lovecraft

Inspired by his bleak visions of a terrifying non-anthropocentric universe, Lovecraft conceived a complex cosmology. In his writings, a cosmic sensibility "keenly etches humankind's transience and fragility in a boundless universe that lacks a guiding purpose or direction" (S. T. Joshi, quoted by Steadman 264). A universe infinite in space and time, in which humanity and all terrestrial life occupy an insignificant place. This is the essence of Lovecraft's philosophy and the fulcrum of his mythology, which have come to be called Cthulhu Mythos. The Mythos could be closely related to Eugene Thacker's speculative category of "world-without-us" (9), developed in his book *In the Dust of This Planet* (the first volume in his *Horror of Philosophy* trilogy). The author adopts the perspective of the Universe, for which, as far as we know, the life and the nature of our planet have no cosmic relevance. Thacker's notion of horror fiction is tied to Speculative Realism, or "new materialism" (Shaviro i). This philosophical movement was quickly absorbed in the public debate, as Erick Felinto (2018) notes. He also points that, if there is still resistance to the movement in philosophy departments of North American or European universities, its resounding success in "alternative" spaces, such as the blogosphere, is worthy of mention. In some ways, it is related to Lovecraft's popularity nowadays, and with the popularity of Thacker's book as well. According to Shaviro, the central issue of Speculative Realism is "the anthropocentrism that has so long being a key assumption of modern Western rationality" (i). For Shaviro, questioning this is "urgently needed at a time when we face the prospect of ecological catastrophe and when we are forced to recognize that the fate of humanity is deeply intertwined with the fates of all sorts of other entities" (i).

As attested by Ian Fetters, Antarctica is a place of great importance in Lovecraft's Mythos (19), and a rich ground for explorations in the nascent field of science fiction. Analogous to another planet, the image of an icy desert has proven to be an efficient choice to create an atmosphere of cosmic horror and achieve the miniaturization of man in the universe. One of Lovecraft's longer prose works, *At the Mountains of Madness* follows the tragedy of a group of scientists and engineers from the fictional Miskatonic University into the hitherto mysterious continent. Lovecraft's characters see themselves in regions "never trodden by human foot or penetrated by human imagination" (CF 3.25), and the narrator describes the far South as an "austral world of desolation and brooding madness" (CF 3.58), a "treacherous and sinister white immensity of tempests and unfathomed mysteries" (CF 3.26).

Derived from expedition chronicles, the novella was set in 1931, when Antarctica was synonymous with a world of ice and death, a place where something alive could scarcely exist. Indeed, the cooler, stormier, and dryer continent used to devour the lives of the most experienced explorers. The geographic setting could not be more appropriate, since "Erebus" names the "Infernal Darkness" and its personification in Greek mythology (Grimal 143).

Lovecraft expressed early interest in the polar continent and its conquest. Before his birth in 1890, several expeditions had circled Antarctica, notably those of Cook, Ross, and Wilkes.[2] Others occurred in the first three decades of the twentieth century, and the writer was presumably aware of them (see Eckhardt). This brings us to 1928–31, a period of major expeditions. All the exploring activity must have provided Lovecraft with inspiration and a framework based in scientific fact. However, the Antarctic territory would remain stubbornly impervious, expecting safer and more efficient means for human crossing (Eckhardt 33). *At the Mountains of Madness* was written in February and March 1931.

Eckhardt defines the novel as "a monument to Lovecraft's imagination, his ability to capture the real and to make us believe the unreal" (38). The writer's source of inspiration could have been Edgar Allan Poe's *The Narrative of Arthur Gordon Pym of Nantucket* (1838); however, the influence is not clear. Despite Lovecraft's admiration for Poe and the many references to *Pym* in his own story, the narratives differ. According to Erik Davis, from the mid-1920s to the 1930s Lovecraft built a bridge between late nineteenth-century Gothic decay and "the more 'rational' demands of the new century's science fiction." In his mature tales, the writer adopted "a pseudo-documentary style that utilizes the language of journalism, scholarship, and science to construct a realistic and measured prose voice which then explodes into feverish, adjectival horror" (Davis). By adopting these same languages, Herzog would construct his own voice—the narration that

2. The Heroic Age of Exploration is taken up in detail by Fetters (26–29).

guides his documentaries and allows him to express a worldview endowed with cosmic horror.

Herzog's Eccentric Eye and the Imminence of Catastrophe

In the dialectics between human culture and the natural world, the general aspects of Herzog's prolific work rely on his search for the ecstasy or the sublime. His concept of cinema involves treating the medium as a physical, even athletic experience, an approach that can be observed in *Aguirre, the Wrath of God* (*Aguirre, der Zorn Gottes*, 1972) and *Fitzcarraldo* (1982). The physical presence of the camera and the subjection of the cast and crew to extreme conditions are expressive key elements in both films. Many of his more than thirty documentaries also address the struggle between man and nature—the latter depicted as hostile and dangerous. This is the case of *The White Diamond* (2004), in which Herzog and the British scientist Graham Dorrington fly to the Amazon rainforest in a prototype airship responsible for the death of another documentary filmmaker.

Herzog developed an intuition-based technique tied to a vital philosophy that pushes cinema away from its most common and obvious instances. This procedure is not about making a nostalgic or romantic cinema, preoccupied with personal dramas, or one that contemplates the world from a strictly aesthetic point of view. As defined by Albert Elduque, Herzog's style comprises a "cinematic and aesthetic discourse characterized by the imminence of the catastrophe, an imminence that [. . .] connects it with the prophetic tradition" (1). Commenting on this, Herzog considers himself not a nostalgic filmmaker, but someone who "contemplates disaster" (quoted by Elduque 2).

Elduque addresses the archetypal characters in Herzog's films, such as the visionary Hias in *Heart of Glass* (*Herz aus Glas*, 1976), who is endowed with a predisposition to foresee imminent catastrophes. Bill Jirsa mentions others. *Aguirre, the Wrath of God* is the chronicle of a Spanish conquistador's Amazonian search for the mythical El Dorado that ends in madness and violence. In *Fitzcarraldo*, an obsessive opera aficionado strives to build the first opera house in the Peruvian jungle and comes to calamity. "Both films are set in the wilderness of South America, displaying Herzog's attraction to frontiers-landscapes at the margins of civilization" (Jirsa).

Driven by his philosophical concerns, Herzog devotes himself to the idiosyncrasies of human life, to what in some extent was lost in modern times. As a filmmaker, he seeks to explore the inner part of the world, its depths, thus creating something capable of describing the ecstasy of truth before representing it. His work results in a process of documentary filmmaking with some particular features, such as his performative character, the omnipresence of his voiceover, and his search for unprecedented material—images never made before, never seen before. Other important features are Herzog's interest in extreme situations and the process of "mythologizing the landscape" (Ames 60), what he started in *Fata Morgana* (1971), an expression of his fascination with the sublime power of nature.

Herzog lends his wry voice to the narration of films such as *Grizzly Man* (2004) and *The White Diamond* (2005), the first being a milestone in his work. "In this phase of his filmmaking, Werner Herzog himself has become essential to Werner Herzog films" (Jirsa). The pursuit for hard-to-find images intensifies here, with the filmmaker now more interested in specific situations that grant recorded images a guise of rarity. In the making of *Cave of Forgotten Dreams* (2010), Herzog had exclusive access to the Chauvet-Pont d'Arc cave in southwestern France, where he recorded images of prehistoric paintings discovered in 1994 inside an underground passage, sealed for more than 30,000 years.

Jirsa points out that in *Encounters at the End of the World* Herzog's eccentric eye has supplanted the conventional doctrines of making films about Antarctica—tied to the principles of documentaries about nature: reverence for science and exploration, the nobility of human inquiry, and the anthropomorphized fauna. In turn, the filmmaker proposed a new cinematic representation of the continent. As Jirsa puts it, the film "is a travelogue, a loose concatenation of profiles collected during Herzog's six-week visit to McMurdo Station and vicinity, one that posits a human frontier populated by eccentric dreamers that only Werner Herzog could discover." Listening to the people settled in Antarctica, Herzog reflects on life in that great, mythic space: the last frontier on our planet.

Antarctica's Otherness in Lovecraft and Herzog

At the Mountains of Madness is a pseudo-documentary novel written as a compilation of reports by geologist William Dyer. The fictional character avows his intention of preventing a new expedition to Antarctica, since his own had ended in disaster. In his narration, he mentions the enormous obstacles faced by the pioneering explorers of the early twentieth century:

"Our sensations on first treading Antarctic soil were poignant and complex, even though at this particular point the Scott and Shackleton expeditions had preceded us" (CF 3.19). According to Fetters, Lovecraft sets up a "life-or-death tension" and demonstrates a "fundamental understanding of what makes Antarctica so averse to human life, what makes it unforgiving and horrific in the extreme—the vast distances between flights, the incalculable unknowns, the near impossibility of rescue in the middle of a blinding desert" (29).

Encounters at the End of the World, in turn, is the cinematographic record of a real expedition devoted to answering Herzog's particular questions about nature and his interest in finding out how people live in such a hostile environment. At the beginning of the film, Herzog warns the viewers that he and his crew are fleeing "into the unknown, a seemingly endless void." The documentary film also revisits the conquest of the South Pole by Robert F. Scott and Ernest Shackleton. Punctuated by Herzog's narration, which evokes the imminence of the catastrophe, a sequence of historical footage reveals the struggles of these pioneers, trapped in the unknown lands when their vessels ran ashore on the polar ice caps.

"On this very frozen ocean, the early explorer's ship got wedged into moving ice flows. Here, Shackleton's expedition evacuates their vessel, which would later come to ruin, leaving them stranded there," says Herzog, stepping on the exact spot where the forced landing took place. "Everything on this expedition was doomed, including the first ancestor of the *snowmobile* [. . .] At that time, every step meant incredible hardship."

After mentioning the early voyages to Antarctica, Herzog wonders: "What environment would the men of Shackleton's expedition encounter if they returned in a next life?" With this exercise, and by comparing the different representations of the frozen continent more than a hundred years ago and today, the filmmaker opposes fiction and reality. According to the glaciologist Douglas MacAyeal, one of his interviewees, Scott and Shackleton viewed the ice as a sort of static monster, a cold monolith that had to be crossed to get to the South Pole; this commentary evokes an image common in the Antarctic chronicles, the frozen continent devouring the lives of the explores. Unlike them, scientists today see the ice as a dynamic living entity that is producing change, even though the icebergs remain largely mysterious and poorly understood.

To some extent, the imagery of the "white immensity" with "unfathomed mysteries" still exists. MacAyeal points out that "[the iceberg] looks big and it looms above us. Even if we're on an aircraft flying above the iceberg, the iceberg is always above us. It's above us because it's a mystery that we don't understand." Bill Jirsa, computer technician working in the US Antarctic Program and a featured interviewee in Herzog's documentary, is sometimes tempted to think of the people who work in Antarctica as the twenty-first-century equivalent of the people on the eighteenth- and nineteenth-century voyages of exploration, "if you replaced the naval order of the day with today's corporate bureaucracy and government agency inefficiency."

As noted, the desolate atmosphere of the frozen continent makes it analogous to another planet. In Herzog's rumination, "Antarctica is not the moon, even though sometimes it feels like it. Yet, on this planet, McMurdo comes closest to what a future space settlement would look like." The physiologist Regina Eisert reinforces this sense of otherness by stating that many things about Antarctica are very unusual.

> [O]ne of the things that I find very fascinating is how quiet it gets. It's the quietest place. When the wind is down, when there's no wind, it wakes you up in the middle of the night because there's no wind, and there's no sound at all, and if you walk out on the ice, you can hear your own heartbeat, that's how still it is. [. . .] You can hear the ice crack, and it sounds like there's somebody walking behind you, but it's just the ice. (Herzog, *Encounters*)

While shooting the beauty and strange life forms of the frozen continent, Herzog is committed to investigate the people who live there, scientists and staff from McMurdo. Living in a region of hostile nature, they face unusual situations, such as the five months of cold summer without night. Affected by isolation at the edge of an inhospitable wasteland, they are archetypal Lovecraftian characters. Herzog asks himself about their dreams. One of his early interviewees, the philosopher and tractor driver Stefan Pashov, defines the McMurdo workers as "professional dreamers," through whom "the great cosmic dreams come into fruition, because the universe dreams through our dreams." Pashov concludes that reality manifests itself in many ways, "and dreaming is definitely one of these ways." The dreams and dreamlands also play a pivotal role in Lovecraft's fiction.

Another peculiar character is the biologist Samuel Bowser, who likes to show doomsday science fiction films to his colleagues. Many of these films express bad omens about our long-ranging presence on the planet. From Bowser's perspective, Antarctica can be a horrible place to be, and diving in the icy abyss is the strangest experience. It is obscure to humans because "we're encased in neoprene [. . .] if you were to miniaturize into that world, it'd be a horrible place to be. Just horrible" (Herzog, *Encounters*). The miniature scale amplifies the sense of cosmic dread, accentuated by the isolation.

Writing at the *Filmmaker Magazine* blog, Mike Plante concluded that "In Herzog's hands [. . .] the surroundings above and below the ice looks like outer space" (quoted by Jirsa). Under the sea ice, the divers find themselves in another reality where space and time take on a new and strange dimension. This perception evokes cosmicism, the central pillar of Lovecraft's philosophical thought. As defined by Joshi, it is both a metaphysical and an aesthetic stance, "an awareness of the insignificance of human beings within the realm of the universe," and "a literary expression of this insignificance, to be effected by the minimizing of human character and the display of the titanic gulfs of space and time" (*IAP* 484). Lovecraft's characters are inevitably faced with this harsh reality.

The Antarctic world precedes the human beings. Bowser and Herzog agree that the human race and other mammals fled in panic from the oceans and crawled on solid land to get out, to leave the horrors behind. This conclusion evokes fear of the unknown, referred to in Lovecraft's famous aphorism: "The oldest and strongest emotion of mankind is fear, and the oldest and strongest kind of fear is fear of the unknown" (*CE* 2.82). Also in "Supernatural Horror in Literature," Lovecraft reflects:

> The unknown, being likewise the unpredictable, became for our primitive forefathers a terrible and omnipotent source of boons and calamities visited upon mankind for cryptic and wholly extra-terrestrial reasons, and thus clearly belonging to spheres of existence whereof we know nothing and wherein we have no part. (*CE* 2.83)

At the Mountains of Madness brings even a warning: "Certain lingering influences in that unknown Antarctic world of disordered time and alien natural law make it imperative that further exploration be discouraged" (*CF* 3.94). It is not difficult to imagine these words being proclaimed with Herzog's halting Bavarian accent.

Entering the "mountains of madness" in Lovecraft's novel, the explorers figuratively return to a prehuman era. Old secrets lie in a monstrous lair, whose cavernous combs of masonry have been dead from time immemorial. The underground city is the work of "the Great Old Ones that had filtered down from the stars when earth was young—the beings whose substance an alien evolution had shaped, and whose powers were such as this planet had never bred" (CF 3.92). These powerful extraterrestrial beings rule over the shoggoths, "normally shapeless entities composed of a viscous jelly which looked like an agglutination of bubbles" (CF 3.103). In Herzog's documentary, the shrine-like subterranean catacombs are shown in one prolonged shot. We also learn that in recent years scientists discovered a whole world underneath the ice. Exploring the depths of the Antarctic Sea, they found creatures as scary and otherworldly as those imagined by Lovecraft.

According to Samuel Bowser, the frozen ocean inhabitants are like the creatures from science fiction films.

> They range in a way they would gobble you up from slime-type blobs, but creepier than classic science fiction blobs. These would have long tendrils that would ensnare you, and as you tried to get away from them you'd just become more and more ensnared by your own actions. And then after you would be frustrated and exhausted, then this creature would start to move in and take you apart.

Another example is the worm-type things with horrible mandibles and jaws to rend the human flesh. "It really is a violent, horribly violent world that is obscure to us," Bowser concludes.

Coming up through the icy floor, from the depths of the frozen ocean, a strange reverberation holds the attention of the scientists. It is the call of the seals, which sounds like a synthesizer or electronic transmission. Described as an "inorganic sound," it reminds the physiologist Regina Eisert of Pink Floyd. The impressive underwater recordings of seal calls contrast with the silent surface where the animals rest. "They [. . .] definitely don't sound like animals. It's really out of this world," she states (Herzog, *Encounters*). In Lovecraft, the surroundings of the mountains are described by the narrator as having a "touch of evil mystery," and the sound has a prominent role in his account for its "cloudy note of reminiscent repulsion" and the "dark impressions" it brings. "Even the wind's burden held a peculiar strain of conscious malignity; and for a second it seemed that the composite sound included a bizarre musical whistling or piping over a wide range as the blast swept in and out of the omnipresent and resonant cave-mouths" (CF 3.69).

In Lovecraft's novel, the explorers find gigantic, monstrous penguins inside the caves. When facing those "white, waddling thing[s . . . W]e were indeed clutched for an instant by a primitive dread almost sharper than the worst of our reasoned fears regarding those others" (CF 3.133). The birds were eyeless albinos of unknown species. Frightened, the explorers conclude "that they were descended from the same stock—undoubtedly surviving through a retreat to some warmer inner region whose perpetual blackness had destroyed their pigmentation and atrophied their eyes to mere useless slits" (CF 3.133).

The real-life penguins inhabit a colony in Cape Royds, where they live in isolation. Imbued with scientific curiosity, Herzog discovers that some of these birds could move away from the migratory flow, refusing to return to the group or even to their home colony. Seemingly disoriented and de-mented, they head for the mountains as if something were calling them, and there they disappear without a trace toward a future that will surely end in death. The images are disturbing. "They end up in places they shouldn't be, a long way from the ocean," explains the penguin expert Da-vid Ainley, a taciturn man who, in his solitude, rarely converses with hu-mans. Unfortunately, the researchers and the documentary team can do nothing to prevent the penguins' behavior, as they swore never to inter-fere. Even if they had, the birds would immediately leave the safe place and head back toward certain death at the mountains of madness. Her-zog's film presents this behavior as a symptom of depression. Until then, it remained unexplainable.

Speculative Exercises

To relate extensive artistic universes is a risky endeavor, as it requires us to compare particular cosmologies that have established eclectic dialogues with the arts and sciences. However, it seems that both authors analyzed here propose the speculative exercise of envisioning an experience that goes beyond the physical, objective world, as perceived by direct contact with the landscape, but never ignoring it. Lovecraft and Herzog sought to endow their work with scientific contemporaneity, drawing on the knowledge available in their times by using geographic, historical, and sci-entific information.

Therefore, both the writer and the filmmaker looked back to the tradi-tion of the Antarctic expeditions chronicles that preceded At the Moun-tains of Madness and extended toward the making of Encounters at the End *of the World.* Each within his historical context, they were able to point out the boundaries of science and philosophy they knew, constructing immersive artistic experiences endowed with an apocalyptic perspective. The relations we suggest go beyond the identification of Lovecraftian elements in Herzog's work. There seems to be a shared worldview, and even a procedure for unravelling what one cannot directly observe, that can be related to cosmicism and the trendy Speculative Realism. The common denominator is a catastrophic sensibility and the acceptance of mystery as an inescapable, constitutive element of human experience in the universe.

Works Cited

Ames, Eric. "Herzog, Landscapes and Documentary." *Cinema Journal* 48, No. 2 (Winter 2009): 49–69.

Davis, Erik. "Calling Cthulhu: H. P. Lovecraft's Magick Realism." In *Erik Davis' figments*. www.levity.com/figment/lovecraft.html. Accessed 19 July 2019.

Eckhardt, Jason C. "Behind the Mountains of Madness: Lovecraft and the Antarctic in 1930." *Lovecraft Studies* No. 14 (Spring 1987): 31–38.

Elduque, Albert. "As ruínas no cinema de Werner Herzog." In *Anais do XXVI Simpósio Nacional de História–ANPUH*, julho 2011. www.snh2011.anpuh.org/site/anaiscomplementares#E. Accessed 10 February 2020.

Felinto, Erick. "Realismo especulativo, comunicação e a lula-vampiro do inferno." *Revista ECO-Pós*. 21, no. 2 (2018). 10.29146/eco-pos.v21i2. 20494.

Fetters, Ian. "Lovecraft's Dark Continent: *At the Mountains of Madness* and Antarctic Literature." *Lovecraftian Proceedings* No. 3 (2019): 19–34.

Grimal, Pierre. *Dicionário da mitologia grega*. Rio de Janeiro: Bertrand Brasil, 2011.

Herzog, Werner, dir. *Encounters at the End of the World*. Discovery Films, 2007.

———. *Grizzly Man*. Lions Gate Films, 2005.

Jirsa, Bill. "Being Werner Herzog," 2012. www.bigdeadplace.com/being-werner-herzog. Accessed 10 February 2020.

Migliore, Andrew, and John Strysik. *Lurker in the Lobby: A Guide to the Cinema of H. P. Lovecraft*. 2nd ed. Portland, OR: Night Shade Books, 2006.

Shaviro, Steven. *The Universe of Things: On Speculative Realism*. Minneapolis: University of Minnesota Press, 2014.

Steadman, John L. *H. P. Lovecraft and the Black Magickal Tradition: The Master of Horror's Influence on Modern Occultism.* San Francisco: Weiser Books, 2015.

Thacker, Eugene. *In the Dust of This Planet: Horror of Philosophy,* Volume 1. Winchester, UK: Zero Books, 2011.

Fear and (Non)Fiction: Agrarian Anxiety in "The Colour out of Space"

Antonio Alejandro Barroso
Independent Scholar

H. P. Lovecraft wrote "The Colour out of Space" in 1927 after he returned to Providence, ending his days of living in New York. That same year, he took a very important trip to the rustic areas of New England. A letter to Maurice W. Moe summarizes the author's journey. Lovecraft describes the experience with exuberance: "Old New England forever!" (MWM 184). His trip is free of "[t]awdriness and commerce [. . .] urban smoke [. . .] ugly billboards" and instead is populated with "the recaptured beauty of vanished centuries" (235). He recalls one segment of his trip in a letter to Richard Ely Morse in 1935, though in a more somber tone:

> The trip through the doomed Swift River Valley must have held more than a slight touch of melancholy. I went through it 8 years ago, not long after its doom was first pronounced, & well-nigh groaned at the future destruction of exquisite old villages like Dana and its neighbours . . . We have had a similar experience in Rhode Island, where a vast amount of rural territory was flooded in 1926 for a reservoir. It was that flooding which caused me to use the reservoir element in "The Colour out of Space." (Lovecraft 60)

The Scituate Reservoir of Rhode Island was also an area Lovecraft visited, but it was on a separate journey in 1926 and after the program's completion (Joshi and Schultz 42). The Quabbin Reservoir was announced in 1926, but the valley was not depeopled and flooded until 1939, two years after Lovecraft's death (Lovecraft 60; Greene 84). The entry on "The Colour out of Space" in *An H. P. Lovecraft Encyclopedia* begins on the real-life influences of the story by stating that "[t]he reservoir in the tale is the Quabbin Reservoir," and then proceeds to share Lovecraft's information about the Scituate Reservoir's impact on his tale (Joshi and Schultz 42). The authors return to their initial point by claiming that Lovecraft "surely was thinking of the Quabbin" before using the similar location as support to his claim (42). In addition to borrowing and using the reservoir as an element in his short story, the terror felt by the rural inhabitants of the region is reflected as well. The dread experienced by the Gardners and Ammi Pierce in "The Colour out of Space" is the same as that of the residents of the Swift River Valley: total erasure by an outside force.

The cities of Dana, Enfield, Greenwich, and Prescott—along with several smaller villages—occupied the region of the Swift River Valley. Though it fit many of the pastoral and Puritan descriptions associated with rural cultures of the time and region, it was not without its own minor industrial boom. Overall, the economy of the nineteenth century was seen as prosperous. In Francis Underwood's *Quabbin: The Story of a Small Town with Outlooks upon Puritan Life*, a scenic description is given following the author's trip to the top of Delectable Mountain. He is sure to include that among the valley's sounds, one absent is the "hum of machinery" (3). This is not to say that the Quabbin region was completely free of industrialism; rather it had a complicated history, which Underwood addresses in the portentously titled chapter "Quabbin Loses and Gains." A sawmill, tanyard, and cotton, card, and linseed oil factories are listed as stand-out examples of larger scale operations and industry around the mid-nineteenth century. The success of these and other economic ventures drew people to the valley and inspired an increase in new housing. This minor industrial boom helped build the valley up, but as J. R. Greene points out, industrialism would also "spawn the instruments of the valley's decline" (5).

A series of economic depressions hit the region in 1873, 1885, and 1894, causing many once successful industries to either leave the valley or shut down entirely (Greene 6). The railroads caused income for smaller farming communities throughout New England to dip significantly in the 1870s. By opening access to cheaper sources of agricultural goods, the smaller farms simply could not compete. Furthermore, the lumber industry suffered from the increased use of coal. With all these factors stacked against them, the population of the Swift River Valley began to decline in the second half of the eighteenth century—a drop of nearly one-third of its total population—a significant number of which came from an agricultural background (Greene 7). Even Enfield, the most populous of the four villages, suffered significant loss during this time: "One of every thirteen acres of Enfield farmland had been abandoned by the turn of the century" (Greene 6).

Despite the devastation, further attempts were made to save the farm economies in the Swift River Valley. Right after the turn of the century, dairy farmers attempted switching from producing cheese to cream and whole milk in order to sell these products to communities in the surrounding area (Greene 6). However, new health standards regarding the production of milk ended up creating six state regulations, many of which challenged the traditional means of production. Two notable regulations were as follows: "Cows and horses must be kept in separate places" and "No pigs or manure should be kept under the barn" (Clark 17). These were especially difficult for the farmers of the valley, as the local practice was to use a single barn to house cows, horses, and pigs, with basement space for manure. In addition, all cows were to be tested for tuberculosis, and farmers were forced to purchase replacements for sick cows with little government compensation. These regulations were so taxing that by 1925 "only about six [farms] kept over twenty-five cows" (Clark 17). Thus, a once successful dairy industry—especially in Prescott, where dairy was the most successful agricultural item—was crippled by regulation (Greene 4). A similar disruption took place when the spread of bulk feed stymied the developing poultry economy in 1925 (Greene 6). Such losses to the economy were devastating, especially when considering how unemployment was treated then. In an interview with Myron Doubleday, whose father ran the grocery store in North Dana, Thomas Conuel discovered that "a man of forty-five who lost his job could not get another one" (8).

A few years following the passing of the dairy regulations, the Metropolitan District Water Supply Commission began to purchase lands from the people of the Swift River Valley. This, as well as all the aforementioned factors, led to a second great population decline in the early twentieth century. In 1900, the reported populations of cities were 790 for Dana, 1,036 for Enfield, 491 for Greenwich, and 380 for Prescott. For Dana, this was its highest population ever, and for Enfield, its third highest. By 1930, the numbers had dropped to 595, 497, 238, and 48 respectively, cutting the population in half (Greene 106).

News coverage and writings of the reservoir have a highly empathetic and at times maudlin tone. One article stated that the program will "drown out the historic old towns" ("Big Reservoir Dam Begun in Bay State"). F. Lauriston Bullard's article "Reservoir to Cover 3 Bay State Towns" serves as a particularly dramatic example. Opening his piece with the image of families "contemplat[ing] with sad forebodings the fate which has overtaken them," he then describes how the cities will be "obliterated" and that a long-suffered sense of "doom" will finally "befall" the inhabitants (Bullard). He takes stock of the beautiful natural resources and splendid man-made features of the area that will be lost forever before decrying the "waning" population—which he attributes to the "calamity, long apprehended and now imminent"—and the "empty" and "forlorn" houses they now leave "in their desertion" (Bullard).

A series of short articles titled "Letters from Quabbin" by Amy W. Spink and Mabel L. Jones were printed in the *Springfield Union* from 14 April to 19 July 1938. Over the course of the twenty-eight installments—an editing error made it appear that there were twenty-nine—the letters cover a range of topics and narrative tones. Topics include the dimensions of the then proposed reservoir, history of industry in the valley, final town meetings, relocation of buried residents, summer camps, historic churches, wildflowers, and notable individuals. Rarely did a single subject become the focus of multiple letters, with the exception of churches, which received coverage in issue 13 and 18, and notable individuals, which were in letters 24 and 27, though no one church or individual appeared in both. These letters provide brief snapshots of more than twenty distinct aspects of life in the Swift River Valley. With regard to the letters' varied tones, each lengthy subheadline previews the content and the narrative timbre. These range from straightforward pieces like "Swift River Chosen as Preferable to Merrimack . . . ," "Beautiful New Burial Ground Receives Thousands of Bodies . . . ," and "Huge Earthen Barrier, Half-Mile Long, Will Block Swift River Exit . . . ," to the more dramatic: ". . . Tragic Phase of Great Water Supply Project," ". . . Only Crumbling Walls Remain," and the headline to a picture series, which reads "Quabbin Villages Disappearing Forever."

Though the more obviously empathetic subheadlines occur in the earlier letters—the examples given being from numbers 3, 4, and 5—the sense of loss and fear permeate the bodies of the articles throughout. Letter 4, "The Exodus," covers the process of valley residents moving out of their homes, which is described as "heartbreaking" as many of those displaced knew no other home. Three people were interviewed in this installment. Two vowed not to move out until being physically forced to do so. Though accounts of residents resisting the move until the waters crept onto their lands exist are merely fiction, the *Ware River News* reported that in May 1939 one of the three remaining families attempted to continue their lives while "[a]ll around them burning debris were smoking" (Greene 84). Letter 19, "The Granges," laments the loss of the organizations that "touche[d] practically every phase of community life," and had "knit the friendship of the towns." Letter 22, "The Wild Flowers," mourns the "fate" of the region's beautiful flora, "to be drowned under the great reservoir." Letter 23, "The Camps," points out that in the Swift River Valley there were no longer hosts gardens, campers, or camps, "just the old chimneys standing deserted and alone."

Of all the letters, numbers 6 and 25 provide perhaps the most emotionally charged accounts of loss in the region. Letter 6, "Spring in Quabbin," establishes its somber mood with the opening sentence: "The usual pleasant bustle of spring activities is noticeably absent in the Quabbin area this year." Other things listed as absent include friendly farmers, complete with rake in hand, chatting with friends and exchanging gardening tips, flower enthusiasts exchanging resources, the pleasant sounds of livestock, and the scent of recently turned earth. Such an account makes sense when noting that this piece was written in 1938, the last spring before the region would be evacuated in April the following year.

Letter 25, "The Last Graduation," takes on a sentimental tone as it relates the tale of the three cities with remaining schools—Prescott having closed its schools years before the exodus—and their evening of graduation ceremonies. These ceremonies were held for the younger students, as the cities within the valley never had a high school and instead sent their older students to Athol, Belchertown, New Salem, or Ware. Despite the lack of high schools in the area, each city had consolidated its schools around the turn of the century, stepping away from the one-room-schoolhouse model and creating larger establishments. As a result, the closing of these widely shared spaces—especially in Greenwich, where the public building that housed the school also served as a grange hall—is depicted as resonating deeply with the locals. Spink and Jones set the scene by stating that the bells and buses have performed their final services and that the doors "are closed forever." The closing of the schools is seen as an ending not only for the children who studied there, but also for all who felt that the building was more familial than institutional. Brief summaries of the events are given, present faculty are acknowledged, and in the case of Dana the graduating class was listed, as it was small enough to fit within one sentence. Of all the schools, Greenwich is given the most attention, as it is described as a "typical scene" one would witness regardless of which graduation ceremony one attended. Though most of the events are summarized in a matter of a few sentences, special attention is given to the farewell song composed by one of the Greenwich teachers, the lyrics of which stuck with Evelina Gustafson in her travelogue *Ghost Towns 'Neath Quabbin Reservoir*, along with the audience's reaction to its conclusion: "Other organizations have danced themselves out, to the blare of horns and the thunder of drums," but for the residents of the doomed river valley, its "sweet and final benediction" would conclude the ceremony before the people left Quabbin, "once a valley of homes."

This sense of loss resonated even in schools outside the valley. In the 1927 edition of the Belchertown high school senior *Echo*, Madelaine Haesaert, an Enfield resident, had this to say about the fate of her hometown:

> Must be laid to waste, be uprooted, be destroyed, and be utterly removed . . . Where prosperity once reigned, ruin threatened [. . .] No matter what they pay us, they can never make suitable recompense [. . .] A pageant of many moods, but one theme: the eternal conflict between the old and the new, the struggles between the needs of the many and the rights of the few, the endless enigma of human existence. (Wilder)

Though the Metropolitan District Water Supply Commission offered comparatively good rates for the lands it purchased—$103.64 per acre compared to the $83.45 per acre in the nearby and also soon to be submerged Ware valley—Haesaert's essay echoes the sentiment heard from many residents of the area (Greene 69).

Elizabeth Rand of Enfield wrote essays and poetry expressing a similar sense of loss. Her poem "Reflections" was written in 1927 at the start of the official exodus. She wrote: "Before me stretches the valley which sooner or later will be the famous Swift River Reservoir as deep and as wide as the sea," then lists things that will be missed: "hilltops, trees, and flowers [. . .] many of the games of childhood, played about the old home door, many of the scenes of gladness," and ends on a similar point made by Haesaert by giving "the best we've got to Boston" along with the hope that its children will benefit from the valley's sacrifice (Wilder). Similar works of poetry and essays can be found scattered throughout Quabbin newsletters and archives, with most sharing the same bittersweet message with its hint of optimism. This sentiment is summarized well in Thomas Conuel's *Quabbin: The Accidental Wilderness*, in which he states that the problem of creating the reservoir was not logistics, but "the tricky emotional problem of [. . .] obliterating a whole community with its history and sense of shared lives" (11).

The residents of the Swift River Valley were understandably frustrated not only by the fate of their homeland, but also by their lack of representation in the decisions being made. The Metropolitan District Water Supply Commission, formed in 1926 as the result of the Ware River Act, managed construction of the reservoir project. Local resentment grew, as there were no members from the Quabbin region on the commission. Thus in the fall of 1926, a collective of representatives from the towns within the valley banded together and became known as the Swift River Valley Protective Association. Leslie Haskins, who had failed to be re-elected to the position of state representative despite support from the Swift River Valley, was the organization's chairperson. With the help of Haskins, the group created lists of demands and proposed amendments to a 100-page bill created by the commission (Greene 54). Nine amendments were created by the association, with the plan on settling on a deadline for ending local business at the forefront. This was a chief concern of the locals, as the commission had the legal right "to take over the towns at anytime" until their "final eviction"—an event that had no set date ("Hub's Water Need Doom Two Towns"). This is exactly what would happen to Prescott on 25 June 1928, when a vote by the dwindling population chose to turn management of the city over to "a half-dozen [. . .] agents of the commission" (Greene 61). Following an unhappy compromise that included some of the association's amendments, the bill was passed along to the Ways and Means Committee. There it met fierce resistance by the Assistant Corporate Counsel for Boston, Elijah Adlow, who disagreed with unemployment compensation for displaced people along with any other part of the bill he thought would increase the overall cost of the project and thus raise the cost of Boston's water supply. Following this, negotiations fell apart, and in the end very few amendments from any organization involved were accepted (Greene 57). In spite of their best efforts, the people of the Quabbin had failed to save their valley.

Despite local opposition, the Swift River Act of 1927 passed, setting in motion the funding and process of starting the reservoir program. Robert Wilder, a former resident of Enfield, claimed that he and those who lived in the valley were "driven away [. . .] just thrown out" without any kind of "safety net" and consequently "alienated" from Boston, as it was the city's need for water that caused the locals to lose their homes (*Inside Out Documentaries*). Further adding to this sense of resentment and powerlessness, the city of Boston chose to hire workers not from the valley, but from the capital itself. Strangers were now entering the lands of the Swift River Valley to cut down trees and dismantle homes. As the work continued, visitors and former and fleeing inhabitants experienced their last impressions of the region. On 22 April 1938, Enfield held its final gathering at the fireman's ball. This key event comes up time and time again as one reads about the demise of the Swift River Valley. Organized by the Enfield firemen, the event—which brought in nearly 1000 people—was meant "[t]o unofficially mark the end of the four towns as legal entities" (Greene 82). Due to the volume of attendees, the Enfield town hall had to host much of the gathering on its surrounding lawn. The scene was described as "bittersweet" as the people danced and sang "Auld Lang Syne" while "bawling their eyes out" (*Inside Out Documentaries*). Authors such as J. R. Greene felt that this single event was "the height of sentimentality" for the residents of the doomed river valley (82). A story in the *Springfield Morning Union* claimed the scene was "as dramatic as any in fiction or in a movie epic" (Conuel 10). The remaining cities of the Swift River Valley officially shut down six days later.

Over the course of the next year, the structures and trees of the area were cleared. Many locals would visit and watch the progress as it altered their former homeland. One witness described the newly barren land as "a moonscape. It was an awful looking mess" (*Inside Out Documentaries*). As disturbing as the vast openness of the land may have been, the last few efforts to destroy the towns' remains created responses that were more akin to the type of terror one could expect when reading a Lovecraftian tale. Robert Wilder and Lois Barnes described witnessing the burning of brush and demolished buildings as "like stepping into Hell, because the whole valley was fire [. . .] there was a real feeling of 'this is the end'" (*Inside Out Documentaries*).

Evelina Gustafson's *Ghost Towns 'Neath the Quabbin* was written during these end days of the Swift River Valley. The travelogue covers her time in the region as she observes the cities and speaks with the locals. As with Bullard before her, the tone of the piece is clearly sympathetic. Her account of an elderly resident weeping openly at the loss of his "narrow, wooded roads of the valley," the "whippoorwill that sang back of the old farm at night," and "meeting my old friends down at the General Store" sets the tone of the piece in its first chapter (16). She takes time to lament the towns that will be "condemned to obscurity," offering her "heartfelt sympathy" before going into summaries of her walking tours of each one (17, 20). Along the way, she collects the impressions of the locals as they prepare for their exodus. Stopping to chat with a shop owner in Greenwich, she asks where the young businesswoman plans to live once the valley is cleared, to which the woman "answered dryly 'I don't know. I have no place to go. This is my home.'" A similar sentiment is expressed by an unnamed citizen in letter 7 of the "Letters from Quabbin," as well as by Wallace Hunter in a 1938 interview with the *Boston Pictorial* (38; QCC). Gustafson's reaction to such an answer is as emotional as one would expect. In addition to the old country staple of the general store owner, Gustafson reports on a dialogue shared with two New England farmers as they discuss the virtues of an ox-yoke. She admires them for their "'down to earth' quality [. . .] which is so likeable" and "hope[s] that their type will always be with us" before reminding her reader that "the deathknell of this lovely, little countryside had now rung" (109).

One final summertime tour taken in 1939 is the subject of the book's final chapter. Gustafson notes the change that had come over the valley, stating that the "lovely valley" was "denuded of brush and trees," which she felt had been "sacrificed" to the reservoir program (120, 121). After pausing in the blank space that once was Greenwich, she recalls the lyrics to the class song performed the previous year during graduation exercises, which was also printed in full in the "Letters from Quabbin" series: "Our thoughts will linger here, tho waters flow / O'er all our homes and farms and schoolhouse too" (122). More signs of the end were spotted, including an abandoned buggy, houses in the process of being demolished, and the replacement of chimney smoke with that of sparse open fires within the valley. The book concludes with Gustafson making her work's intentions clear:

> I hope that I have succeeded in giving my readers a vivid description of this territory which is destined to lie evermore covered by the waters of the great Quabbin Reservoir. I hope that I have also succeeded in imbuing in your hearts some of the love for the old valley that I and many another possess [. . .] Once thriving little communities, they now lie forgotten—ghost towns. (125)

Both in tone and focus, *Ghost Towns 'Neath the Quabbin Reservoir* mirrors much of the coverage at the time of the clearing of the Swift River Valley by reporting the sense of dread felt by its inhabitants.

Given the distress felt by the people of Dana, Enfield, Greenwich, and Prescott, there are many points in "The Colour out of Space" that can be seen as expressions of their sense of dread. Lovecraft describes his landscape with precision. In the opening lines of the story we are given a snapshot of the location: "There are dark narrow glens where the trees slope fantastically [. . .] there are farms, ancient and rocky [. . .] brooding eternally over old New England secrets" (CF 2.367). When compared to Gustafson, Lovecraft's images are understandably much darker. The evidence of a community near its end is found in the works of both authors, but where Gustafson's imagery is lively, Lovecraft's is sinister. Gustafson's tragedy comes from the destruction of something beautiful and, in her eyes, very much alive. Rather than highlight the lively community about to be destroyed, Lovecraft's setting suggests an aura of decay, and the action follows accordingly. If Gustafson's work is meant to highlight "some of the love for the old valley" (125), Lovecraft's is meant to showcase the doom that came to the valley.

Gustafson's attempt to show the inhabitants of the Swift River Valley as an honest and simple sort of folk is done with the intent of helping them. The dismissal of their fears as a result of their perceived simplicity—as some characters do in Lovecraft's work—is a more accurate reflection of the consequences of such a depiction. Lovecraft, like Gustafson, also focuses on dialogue that expresses the locals' fear with simple speech, as is evident in this quotation from Ammi Pierce: "it come from some place whar things ain't as they is here . . . one o' them professors said so" (CF 2.388). Often they are ridiculed by the more academic and urbanized characters in his works. The newspapers surface at a critical moment at least twice in the story. The first is when Nahum Gardner is described in the newspaper coverage of the meteorite. Lovecraft mentions Nahum's newfound celebrity status and then immediately follows it with an economically worded description of the man as "genial" and "living [. . .] on the pleasant farmstead in the valley" (CF 2.375). This passage is in imitation of a newspaper article, and we are given an image of a man that the more metropolitan members of the Boston and Arkham communities could misconstrue as a simple country bumpkin. The second example, the article by a "city man" about the odd vegetation, focuses on mocking the "dark fears of rustics" and dismisses the alarming, unnatural events (CF 2.378). Even the narrator's prejudice toward the rural folk comes through with his first meeting with Ammi Pierce. Noting Pierce's surprising level of intelligence, which the author equates to that of "any man [. . .] in Arkham," and his lack of protest against the reservoir, the surveyor labels him as "not like other rustics [. . .] in the sections where reservoirs were to be" (CF 2.370).

Several other texts have been written on the subject of the Swift River Valley that connect the region to Lovecraft. Francis H. Underwood's *Quabbin: The Story of a Small Town with Outlooks upon Puritan Life* describes the Quabbin area as it was in the late nineteenth century. As "The Colour out of Space" takes place in 1882, Underwood's account provides the reader with a snapshot of the era Lovecraft attempted to emulate. A sense of unchanging and ancient lands is immediately impressed upon the reader, as the author states that little has been altered since the region's initial settlement a century and half before: "for the natural features are too marked to be affected by the superficial touches of men. Ploughs and axes do not disturb the eternal basis of landscape" (2). Attention then shifts to the many hills within the valley, including Great Quabbin, Delectable Mountain, and Ram Mountain. The areas where the land can be effectively cultivated are described as either having "thin" coverage of crops along with "poison ivy" and "skunk cabbage" infringing on "their pastures gray and brown," or as "prosperous" with "neat and comfortable" homes (18, 19). Regardless of the prosperity of the cultivated lands, all the farmhouses shared a unifying feature: the chimney. These immense structures were square, with openings on all sides, and centrally located so as to serve as a heat source for the whole house as well as an oven for the kitchen (19). One is reminded of Gustafson's idyllic scene of the family gathered around the hearth when reading Underwood's description of this staple of antique rustic architecture.

Like Gustafson, Underwood addresses the familial ties to their land. Of specific interest to our connections to Lovecraft, Underwood explains how the farms themselves came to be named after the families that occupied them. The tradition of keeping farms and their surrounding land within the families that started them was very much alive at the time in the Quabbin region. He provides the Estes Place, the Sherman Place, and the Deering Place as examples of such labels and notes that although many farms came to be owned—and thus renamed—by someone other than a family member, those possessing "a notion of permanency" kept their family farm's name (26).

Lovecraft re-creates Underwood's image of an unspoiled land filled with hills in the opening paragraph of his short story: "the hills rise wild, and there are valleys with deep woods that no axe has ever cut" (CF 2.367). Though the Gardner farm is initially described in a manner more befitting the healthy farmland in Underwood's account, the eventual state of the blasted heath resembles one of the poorer farms with its supernatural "fine grey dust" (CF 2.369) potentially drawing inspiration from the similarly colored lands of less fortunate but more natural Quabbin pastures. Among the natural features are similar flora mentioned in *Quabbin*, including skunk cabbage, which grows across the road from the Gardner farm (CF 2.376).

Likewise, chimneys are important features in the short story, just as they would have been in the lives of the people Underwood described. Not only do they function as recurring features of Lovecraft's signature atmospheric descriptions—"wide chimneys crumbling," "tumbled bricks and stones of an old chimney," "but there were not any real ruins [. . . o]nly the bricks of the chimney" (CF 2.367, 369, 397)—but the Gardner chimney plays a key role in the plot. Once Ammi Pierce notices no smoke coming from the Gardners' chimney he becomes "apprehensive of the worst," and upon entering the "deadly cold" farmhouse, he discovers that "the cavernous fireplace was unlit and empty" (CF 2.384). The disuse of the essential home feature, known both for its utility and use as a familial bonding place, indicates that something is gravely wrong at the Gardner Place. The fact that Lovecraft even uses the label "Gardner Place" throughout the short story taps into Underwood's point about vested farmland in rural New England (64, 72, 82, 94). Labeling the setting for his story as such reinforces the long-established tie that the Gardner family had to the land before the locals began to call it the blasted heath; a clear indication that the family's "notion of permanency" had expired (Underwood 26).

In addition to connecting to Lovecraft, Underwood writes about farther reaching economic aspects of the Quabbin region. In *Quabbin*, Underwood makes a clear distinction when comparing poorer farms to more successful ones. The former are described as surviving by means of subsistence farming, which leads to a "pinched and sordid" state of existence devoid of books and the ability to see nature as a kind thing (24). Underwood goes so far as to claim that life for such a farmer held "no hope except in the final rest from toil" (24). More prosperous farmers, though far from educated and often limited to reading the Bible and newspapers, had a much more comfortable and stable lifestyle; Underwood describes their lot as "fairer" and "better" when compared to their less fortunate neighbors (24).

This kinship with Gustafson and Underwood should come as no surprise, as Lovecraft's travelogues of the 1920s and 1930s were a significant part of his body of work. Starting in 1928, he began compiling annual travelogues that documented his journeys through New England, parts of the East Coast, and even parts of Canada. In addition to his annual travelogues, he wrote other accounts of his travels, such as his 1924 trip to Philadelphia and his final incomplete study of Rhode Island architecture (Evans 105). Structures were of chief interest to him, with antiquarian houses being his focus. It was Lovecraft's belief that homes "should never be *made*—they should be sown, water'd, weeded, tended, and allowed to *grow*" (SL 1.287). This idea, in addition to his growing concern for a landscape dominated by the aforementioned factories and accessible transportation, motivated Lovecraft to become part of a preservation movement that was taking place in New England. The "Colonial Revival Movement" worked to maintain the structures and heritage of the region, and was supported by organizations such as the Society for the Preservation of New England Antiquities and individuals such as Norman Isham (Evans 108).

In 1927, the year he visited the Swift River Valley and wrote "The Colour out of Space," Lovecraft began a campaign to save Providence's Brick Row, warehouses and buildings facing the Providence River that served as inspiration for settings in several of his horror stories, most notably in his novel *The Case of Charles Dexter Ward* (Evans 111). The city had decided to demolish the old buildings and replace them with a hall of records that would facilitate a newly constructed courthouse. Lovecraft, who had already made a name for himself as a staunch preservationist, increased his letter writing efforts, going so far as to write whole letters for others and urging them simply to sign their names before sending them to the *Providence Journal*. Despite his best efforts—including the publication of an essay-length letter in a 1929 issue of the *Providence Sunday Journal*—as well as the efforts of his colleagues, the preservation attempts failed and the buildings were razed. This was especially disappointing to Lovecraft, just as the neighborhood in Boston that inspired the setting for "Pickman's Model" had been demolished in 1927. Perhaps most upsetting of all was that because Brick Row was destroyed at the beginning of the Great Depression, the vacant land became a parking lot, since the city could not afford to make it anything else (112).

Losing such places was more than just a loss to a preservationist but to an author as well. Not only did Lovecraft use specific locations to evoke a sense of reality, his characters often are travelers who walk through the very places he encountered in his journeys, and the discoveries made there are what create the sense of horror. Timothy H. Evans points out that this is especially true of earlier works, which seem to follow a three-step system: 1. An "outsider" arrives in an unfamiliar place; 2. The setting is described "in picturesque terms"; 3. A deeper exploration takes place and horrors are discovered (114). This plays out in tales such as "The Festival," "The Outsider," "The Haunter of the Dark," "The Whisperer in Darkness," "The Shadow over Innsmouth," and At the Mountains of Madness (114).

In addition to being travelers, many of Lovecraft's protagonists are or become folklorists over the course of their travels. Like the character of the traveler, this trait can also be traced back to Lovecraft's personal life. An avid reader of folklore, his personal library contained volumes of tales from ancient Greece, the Middle East, Europe, and America. Like his characters, he collected and documented tales from the stops on his travels. Lovecraft reappropriated local folklore for "The Shunned House," which contains a ghost based on Rhode Island legend. This work is another example of a familiar location in action, as the setting is an amalgamation of two separate Providence homes: 135 Benefit Street and the Andrew Joline House in Elizabeth, New Jersey. "The Unnamable" also borrows from New England monster lore and even names the source—Cotton Mather's Magnalia Christi Americana (CF 1.400). "The Colour out of Space" provides the reader with locations based on Lovecraft's travels, which provide his traveling protagonist with terrifying folklore, all while expressing a sense of loss for a locale about to be consumed by industrialized progress. This work fits so neatly within the style of the author's work, and aligns so well with his personal fears of cultural loss, that it comes as no surprise that it is considered by many, including the author himself, to be his best work.

"The Colour out of Space" ends with its narrator voicing his lingering concern over Ammi Pierce, the one witness to the full extent of the colour's power. Such an ending is uncharacteristic of an author who was known for callously handing out gruesome fates to his characters. Accounts of Swift River Valley residents facing erasure in the wake of an incoming reservoir all leave us with our own Ammi Pierces. They are the ones who faced an outer force they could not comprehend; and despite the devastation they witnessed and were personally subjected to, they managed to tell their stories. What became of them is a question that gnaws away at us long after we have ceased our studies.

Works Cited

"Big Reservoir Dam Begun in Bay State." *New York Times* (23 May 1937): 37.

Clark, Walter E. *Quabbin Reservoir.* Athol, MA: Athol Press, 1994.

Conuel, Thomas. *Quabbin: The Accidental Wilderness.* Lincoln: Massachusetts Audubon Society, 1981.

Evans, Timothy H. "A Last Defense against the Dark: Folklore, Horror, and the Uses of Tradition in the Works of H. P. Lovecraft." *Journal of Folklore Research* 42 (2005): 99–135.

Gustafson, Evelina. *Ghost Towns 'Neath the Quabbin Reservoir.* Boston: Amity Press, 1940.

Greene, J. R. *The Creation of Quabbin Reservoir: The Death of the Swift River Valley.* Athol: The Transcript Press, 1995.

"Hub's Water Needs Doom Two Towns." *Boston Morning Globe* (28 January 1927): 16.

Inside Out Documentaries: Haunting the Quabbin. WBUR Boston, archives. wbur.org/insideout/documentaries/hauntingquabbin/index.php.html. Accessed 18 August 2017.

Joshi, S. T., and David E. Schultz. *An H. P. Lovecraft Encyclopedia.* 2001. New York: Hippocampus Press, 2004.

Lovecraft, H. P. *The Annotated H. P. Lovecraft.* Ed. S. T. Joshi. New York: Dell, 1997.

Quabbin Clippings Collection (MS 874). Special Collections and University Archives, University of Massachusetts Amherst Libraries.

Underwood, Francis H. *Quabbin: The Story of a Small Town with Outlooks upon Puritan Life.* Boston: Lee & Shepard, 1893.

Wilder, Robert. "Exodus From Enfield." *YouTube*, uploaded by Robert Wilder of Brookfield, 4 July 2014, www.youtube.com/watch?v =_4FNUvYhEww.

Nathaniel Hawthorne and Herbert S. Gorman's Shadows over Innsmouth

Jeremiah Dylan Cook
Independent Scholar

Introduction

H. P. Lovecraft's "The Shadow over Innsmouth" is a classic of horror fiction. In it, an outsider finds himself in a town where he is not wanted, and he soon discovers the residents are hiding a dark secret. The trope of a community with a dark secret has become increasingly popular in horror fiction and cinema. The folk horror film *Apostle* was released in 2018, followed by *Midsommar* in 2019. Both films concerned outsiders venturing to secluded locations ruled by secret cults. Folk horror makes particularly frequent use of this trope, as it tends to focus on "landscape[,] isolation[,] and skewed moral beliefs" (Paciorek 13-14). The trope of the community with a dark secret is now widespread throughout the horror genre, but when H. P. Lovecraft wrote "The Shadow over Innsmouth" it was still somewhat new. There were only two previous examples of its use before Lovecraft wrote the story. I employ close reading and the comparison of texts to illustrate how Nathaniel Hawthorne's "Young Goodman Brown" created the original town with a dark secret and inspired Herbert S. Gorman's *The Place Called Dagon*, which influenced "The Shadow over Innsmouth."

Peculiar Little Towns

The horror fiction genre comprises many works across multiple media that deal with isolated communities concealing dark secrets. There is the terrible ritual hidden by the pagan villagers who live on Summerisle in *The Wicker Man* (1973). In *The Stepford Wives* (1972) by Ira Levin, husbands ensure their wives do not discover the truth of what goes on in the town's men's club. As recently as 2019, Ari Aster's film *Midsommar* explored the mysteries of a remote Swedish commune and their midsummer celebration. The works employ what Stephen King calls the trope of the peculiar little town.

Having achieved both widespread critical and commercial success over his five-decade career as a horror writer, it is not surprising that King has both named and used this trope. In the notes for his short story collection *Nightmares & Dreamscapes* (1993) King coins the name for the "peculiar little town" trope discussing his tale "You Know They Got a Hell of a Band":

> There are at least two stories in this book about what the lead female character thinks of as "the peculiar little town." This is one; "Rainy Season" is the other. There will be readers who may think I've visited "the peculiar little town" once or twice too often, and some may note similarities between these two pieces and an earlier story of mine, "Children of the Corn." (883)

As King admits, he has used the "peculiar little town" trope at least three times in his fiction. "The Children of the Corn," was even adapted into a feature film in 1984, making that story one of his better-known works in popular culture. King observes: "There are certain horror-tale archetypes which stand out with the authority of mesas in the desert. The haunted-house story; the return-from-the-grave story; the peculiar-little-town story" (883). H. P. Lovecraft's "The Shadow over Innsmouth" stands out as focusing on a peculiar little town.

In that story, an unnamed narrator explores the Massachusetts seaport of Innsmouth as part of a "sightseeing, antiquarian, and genealogical" (CF 3.160) tour of New England. Once in the town, the narrator supplies Zadok Allen, the local drunk, with whiskey in exchange for information about how the town made a deal with "frog-fish monsters" (CF 3.188) to mix with their kind in exchange for gold and eternal life for the town's hybrid offspring (CF 3.184–201). Once the natives are aware the narrator knows Innsmouth's secret, they trap him in the town and attempt to capture him (CF 3.202–23). The narrator's last encounter with the residents of Innsmouth proves the validity of Allen's drunken claims because the narrator glimpses "blasphemous fish-frogs [. . .] living and horrible" (CF 3.223). In the closing pages of the story, the narrator discovers his great-grandmother hailed from Innsmouth (CF 3.227), and he "had acquired *the Innsmouth look*" (CF 3.229) of a fish-frog-human hybrid. After some convincing dreams, the narrator declares he plans to join "the Deep Ones" to "dwell amidst wonder and glory for ever" (CF 3.230).

Clearly, Innsmouth is a peculiar little town hiding a dark secret. "The Shadow over Innsmouth" shares the same trope as Stephen King's "Children of the Corn," "You Know They Got a Hell of a Band," and "Rainy Seasons" as well as *The Wicker Man*, *The Stepford Wives*, and *Midsommar*. Other works share this trope, but "The Shadow over Innsmouth" is one of the earliest examples of its implementation, having been published in 1936. There are only two examples of the peculiar little town trope's use before "The Shadow over Innsmouth." Herbert S. Gorman used it in his novel *The Place Called Dagon* in 1927, and Nathaniel Hawthorne created it in his short story "Young Goodman Brown." Both stories served to influence "The Shadow over Innsmouth."

Salem: The Original Peculiar Little Town

In his seminal essay "Supernatural Horror in Literature," Lovecraft describes American horror fiction as emanating from "an environment in which black whisperings of sinister grandmas were heard far beyond the chimney corner, and in which tales of witchcraft and unbelievable secret monstrosities lingered long after the dread days of the Salem nightmare" (CE 2.104). Lovecraft realizes that Salem is an especially important touchstone for the horror genre in America. He also realizes that Nathaniel Hawthorne, "scion of antique Salem and great-grandson of one of the bloodiest of the old witchcraft judges" (CE 2.104), is an important writer for the horror genre in America. Lovecraft says of Hawthorne:

> In Hawthorne we have none of the violence, the daring, the high colouring, the intense dramatic sense, the cosmic malignity, and the undivided and impersonal artistry of Poe. Here, instead, is a gentle soul cramped by the Puritanism of early New England; shadowed and wistful, and grieved at an amoral universe which everywhere transcends the conventional patterns thought by our forefathers to represent divine and immutable law. Evil, a very real force to Hawthorne, appears on every hand as a lurking and conquering adversary; and the visible world becomes in his fancy a theatre of infinite tragedy and woe, with unseen half-existent influences hovering over it and through it, battling for supremacy and moulding the destinies of the hapless mortals who form its vain and self-deluded population. The heritage of American weirdness was his to a most intense degree, and he saw a dismal throng of vague specters behind the common phenomena of life; but he was not disinterested enough to value impressions, sensations, and beauties of narration for their own sake. He must needs weave his phantasy into some quietly melancholy fabric of didactic or allegorical cast, in which his meekly

resigned cynicism may display with naïve moral appraisal the perfidy of a human race which he cannot cease to cherish and mourn despite his insight into its hypocrisy. (CE 2.104-5)

Lovecraft does not mention "Young Goodman Brown" in "Supernatural Horror in Literature," but the plot of the story conforms perfectly to Lovecraft's description of Hawthorne's prose. The tale starts when the protagonist, Goodman Brown, leaves his wife, Faith, and ventures into the woods outside "Salem Village" (24). On his way deeper into the woods, Brown contemplates the morality of his journey as he meets several people from Salem (24-31). Finally, he arrives at a Witches' Sabbath in the depths of the forest where "quivering to and fro between gloom and splendor, appeared faces that would be seen next day at the council board of the province, and others which, Sabbath after Sabbath, looked devoutly heavenward, and benignantly over the crowded pews, from the holiest pulpits in the land" (31). The Witches' Sabbath is led by a "dark figure" (32), who one could argue is similar to Nyarlathotep as depicted in "The Dreams in the Witch House," since that story drew as heavily on "Young Goodman Brown" as on the legends of Salem.

In the climax of "Young Goodman Brown," Brown and his wife, whom he is shocked to find at the ceremony, are baptized "by the shape of evil" (33). Goodman Brown tells his wife to "resist the wicked one" (33), but immediately after saying this, Brown "found himself amid calm night and solitude" (34), as the ceremony vanishes and he finds himself alone in the woods. Brown is left unsure whether his night was a dream or not, but the experience leaves him "a stern, a sad, a darkly meditative, a distrustful, if not a desperate, man" (34). Even his relationships with his wife and family are forever altered: "Often, awaking suddenly at midnight, he shrank from the bosom of Faith; and at morning or eventide, when the family knelt down at prayer, he scowled, and muttered to himself, and gazed sternly at his wife, and turned away" (34).

Hawthorne meant "Young Goodman Brown" to be interpreted in many ways. There is undoubtedly an allegorical reading by virtue of the protagonist being named "Goodman" and his wife being named "Faith," but the most basic, literal reading of the story tells the tale of a man who discovers that his hometown of Salem is populated by residents claiming to be Christians but who are actually witches. In other words, "Young Goodman Brown" uses the peculiar little town trope. In fact, because this is the earliest instance of the "peculiar little town" trope's use, it is highly probable that "Young Goodman Brown" is the wellspring for this trope, and that would make Salem the original peculiar little town. Of course Lovecraft never explicitly states that he read "Young Goodman Brown," but he does explicitly state he read a novel heavily influenced by it.

Young Goodman Brown's Influence on *The Place Called Dagon*

Herbert S. Gorman is certainly not as well-known as either Hawthorne or Lovecraft. Larry Creasy says of Gorman, "Only his non-fiction books [. . .] remain marginally available, having found safe havens from oblivion among the dusty shelves of university and high school libraries" (11). However, thanks to Lovecraft's writing a single sentence about Gorman in "Supernatural Horror in Literature," *The Place Called Dagon* continues to be read to this day. Lovecraft stated:

> A less subtle and well-balanced but nevertheless highly effective creation is Herbert S. Gorman's novel, *The Place Called Dagon*, which relates the dark history of a western Massachusetts backwater where the descendants of refugees from the Salem witchcraft still keep alive the morbid and degenerate horrors of the Black Sabbat. (CE 2.110)

Gorman's novel follows the protagonist, Doctor Dreeme, as he tries to discover what makes the residents of the town of Marlborough, Massachusetts, so odd. As Dreeme reflects, "An excessive reticence possessed these leather-skinned delvers in the soil, these small-shopkeepers, and even the scattering of professional men who conducted the affairs of Marlborough" (17). Dreeme is eventually filled in on the secrets of Marlborough by his predecessor, Humphrey Lathrop. He tells Dreeme that the witches who survived Salem settled in Marlborough, and "These farmers are the descendants" (134). Furthermore, he tells Dreeme that their ritual meeting location is called "Dagon" (134). Dreeme journeys to Dagon to rescue his love interest, Deborah, before the gathered residents can use her as a "sacrifice" (170). Unlike "Young Goodman Brown" and "The Shadow over Innsmouth," *The Place Called Dagon* has a happy ending with both antagonists dead and Dreeme happily engaged to marry Deborah (184).

It must be noted that in the text of *The Place Called Dagon*, the town of Salem is the direct progenitor of Marlborough. In the novel, one "peculiar little town" gave birth to another. The connections between "Young

Goodman Brown" and *The Place Called Dagon* do not stop there. Creasy explains most of the commonalities between the two works below:

> The theme of ancestral guilt, like that of the supernatural, is frequently an element in much of Hawthorne's work, and both are present in the story "Young Goodman Brown," which originally appeared in the collection *Mosses from an Old Manse* in 1846. We find in this tale the basis for *The Place Called Dagon*. The parallels are numerous and obvious [. . .] Suffice to say that Gorman's Dr. Dreeme is an extension of the impetuous Goodman Brown, as both are inexorably drawn into satanic confrontations through their own meddling–meddling that places both of them amidst the notorious Black Mass celebrations of witch-lore. Both characters must weigh their infernal temptations against the love of an innocent woman, and both are forced to make desperate journeys through primeval haunted woods, as they speed toward their respective destinies. (12–13)

There is also "the use of both Hawthorne and Gorman of the historical figure of Martha Carrier" (Creasy 13). In "Young Goodman Brown," the character appears bringing Faith to the accursed altar: "Thither came also the slender form of a veiled female [Faith], led between Goody Cloyse [. . .] and Martha Carrier, who had received the Devil's promise to be queen of hell" (32). As Creasy continues, "The *femme fatale* character Martha Westcott is the direct descendant of Martha Carrier in *Dagon*, and the specter of the ancestor witch makes an appearance in a flashback scene" (13). There are so many instances of continuity between "Young Goodman Brown" and *The Place Called Dagon* that it is reminiscent of the various Cthulhu Mythos pastiches written by subsequent scribes after Lovecraft's death.

Marlborough is not as iconic as Salem, and Gorman is not as widely read as Hawthorne, but *The Place Called Dagon* forms an essential link in the chain from "Young Goodman Brown" to "The Shadow over Innsmouth." It also forms an essential second instance of the use of the peculiar little town trope. In the conclusion to his introduction, Creasy remarks:

> And so, long before Stephen King's *Salem's Lot*, Thomas Tryon's *Harvest Home*, Charles L. Grant's *Oxrun Station*, or any of the other haunted towns, beleaguered villages, and conspiratorial communities that have become standard stomping grounds in modern horror fiction, Herbert S. Gorman's Marlborough [. . .] has existed as an unjustly neglected landmark. (14)

Hawthorne and Gorman's Influence on "The Shadow over Innsmouth"

It is certainly tempting to assume that the word "Dagon" in the title and story of *The Place Called Dagon* is an immediate connection to H. P. Lovecraft's work. "The author's decision to use the ancient Phoenician deity's name for the accursed gathering place of the witches in his novel is unclear" (Creasy 13). There are numerous other connections that can be drawn between *The Place Called Dagon* and "The Shadow over Innsmouth." Perhaps the easiest is the fact that both towns are described as decrepit. Gorman writes of Marlborough:

> There was no reason why the outer world should impinge too strongly on Marlborough, for, after all, the valley was a cul-de-sac, a cache into which the Past had thrust an untidy bundle of urges and traditions and left them there to rot in the sunlight. And Dreeme seemed to see the Marlborough of the future stretching out like a corpse in the bright sunlight of the valley and striving [. . .] striving [. . .] He shuddered at the picture so suddenly brought up before his mind, a picture of a white leprous mass struggling to live, dead and yet never dying, with closed eyes that continually quivered with blue lips rolling back over yellow decayed teeth, with long skeleton fingers opening and shutting and fighting against the *rigor mortis* of Time. (44–45)

Of Innsmouth, Lovecraft writes: "The vast huddle of sagging gambrel roofs and peaked gables conveyed with offensive clearness the idea of wormy decay" (CF 3.172). He continues, "The decay was worst close to the waterfront" (CF 3.173). The locations are described synonymously: Marlborough is likened to "rot" (Gorman 45) and Innsmouth to "decay" (CF 3.172).

The similarities between *The Place Called Dagon* and "The Shadow over Innsmouth" continue beyond the descriptions of the locations. Both stories contain two similar characters. The first similar character is described In the afterword to *The Place Called Dagon*, S. T. Joshi states:

> Lathrop appears to be the fount of all knowledge in the region [Marlborough]; and in this sense he bears a certain resemblance to Zadok Allen in "The Shadow over Innsmouth." Like Lathrop, Zadok is an aged toper who knows the ancient secrets of Innsmouth but will reveal them only when his tongue is sufficiently loosened by draughts of bootleg whiskey (Lathrop's preferred tipple is apple-jack). (186)

Lovecraft describes Zadok Allen thus:

> This hoary character, Zadok Allen, was ninety-six years old and somewhat touched in the head, besides being the town drunkard. He was a strange, furtive creature who constantly looked over his shoulder as if afraid of something, and when sober could not be persuaded to talk at all with strangers. He was, however, unable to resist any offer of his favorite poison; and once drunk would furnish the most astonishing fragments of whispered reminiscence. (*CF* 3.179)

Humphrey Lathrop is a respectable, retired doctor, but the following exchange between Lathrop and his wife shows the reader he does have his love of alcohol in common with Allen.

> "Lucinda," ordered Lathrop, "bring a bottle of apple-jack, and two tumblers."
> The vinegar face grew still longer. A thin mouth, a mere slit in the wrinkled face, shriveled in severe disapproval.
> "You had some apple-jack this mornin'," announced a high nasal voice.
> "I'm going to have some more now," answered Lathrop blandly. (Gorman 56)

In addition to their love of alcohol and providing vast swaths of vital background information for the stories, both Lathrop and Allen are tricked by the protagonists into drinking more than they should to get them to talk more openly. While Lathrop leaves his sitting room, Dreeme "poured out the amber liquor" he was drinking, and Dreeme accepts a subsequent glass, but while Dreeme takes a "brief swallow" of the next cup, Lathrop makes a comment before "draining off the tumbler" (57). This series of descriptions leads the reader to assume that Dreeme is maintaining his senses as Lathrop is getting drunk. Lovecraft has his protagonist perform a similar trick on Allen. As the narrator of "The Shadow over Innsmouth" says, "I began to dole out more liquor to the ancient tippler; meanwhile eating my own frugal lunch" (*CF* 3.186). This sentence makes it clear that the narrator is not getting drunk while Allen is. Both Allen and Lathrop serve similar purposes in the narratives of Lovecraft and Gorman.

The second duo of similar characters is Uriah Carrier in *The Place Called Dagon* and Obed Marsh in "The Shadow over Innsmouth." Both characters are sailors who founded the evil that has festered in their respective towns. Uriah Carrier's influence on the creation of Obed Marsh is particularly interesting because it creates a direct line from "Young Goodman Brown" to "The Shadow over Innsmouth" through *The Place Called Dagon*. This direct line exists because Uriah Carrier is a descendant of Martha Carrier, who appears in "Young Goodman Brown," and as Gorman says, Uriah Carrier "had been a ship-mate of Hathorne of Salem, the one who died of fever at Surinam and whose son wrote books" (59). That makes two connections from "Young Goodman Brown" to Uriah Carrier's character in *The Place Called Dagon*. The first is that he is a descendant of a character in "Young Goodman Brown," and the second is that he served with Nathaniel Hawthorne's father in the fiction of *The Place Called Dagon*.

Lathrop describes Uriah Carrier as follows: "He had hunted whales in the Pacific, had terrorized and robbed the natives of Tahiti, had black-birded off the African Gold Coast, had carried a Manchu woman about with him for mistress, had retired, returned to Marlborough" (59). When Lathrop informs Dreeme of the witch cult in Marlborough, he advises that "The black book they carried with them was the black book of old Uriah Carrier" (134). Lathrop finishes his explanation of Carrier by stating that "he [Uriah Carrier] was the last Black Man" (137), the man responsible for leading the Witches' Sabbath in Marlborough. That gives a clear picture of Uriah Carrier as both a sailor who traveled to the Pacific and a fountainhead for the cult that infected Marlborough through his "black book" (134), which was passed down from the original Salem witches and his ancestor Martha Carrier.

Compare Uriah Carrier with Obed Marsh. Marsh sailed to the "Saouth Sea Islands" and was "the only one as kep' on with the East-Injy an' Pacific trade" (CF 3.186-87). Both Carrier and Marsh are said to have sailed to the Pacific. Also, Allen says Obed called "folks stupid fer goin to Christian meetin' an bearin' their burden meek an' lowly" (CF 3.187). Marsh said that the residents of Innsmouth "orter git better gods like some o' the folks in the Injies—gods as ud bring 'em good fishin' in return for their sacrifices, an' ud reely answer folks's prayers" (CF 3.187). Later, Allen relays how "Obed he kinder takes charge an' says things is goin' to be changed . . . others'll worship with us at meetin'-time, an' sarten haouses hez got to entertain guests . . . they wanted to mix like they done with the Kanakys, an' he fer one didn't feel baound to stop 'em" (CF 3.196). Both Uriah Carrier and Obed Marsh are the reason the residents of their respective towns change religions and initiate the secret history at the start of both

The Place Called Dagon and "The Shadow over Innsmouth." Carrier is the fountainhead for the witch cult in Marlborough, and Marsh is the person who initiates Innsmouth's relationship with the Deep Ones.

The fact that both *The Place Called Dagon* and "The Shadow over Innsmouth" concern outsiders discovering a secret cult at the heart of their respective towns of Marlborough and Innsmouth cannot be over-looked. The ritual place in *The Place Called Dagon* is of particularly inter-esting focus in the passage below:

> One place they kept sacred. It was a hidden place, known only to the adepts. It was there that they buried the bones of the hanged witches, those poor bodies that they had carried for two hundred miles through the thick wilderness. There, too, they raised the Devil Stone upon which the Black Man stood during the great ceremonies. They called the place Dagon and strewed it with ashes. I can picture that place lighted by torches at midnight. I can picture the rapt faces of the witches and the compelling eyes of the Black Man as he stood above them and called on Satan, on Beelzebub, on Asmodeus, the fiends that he imagined served his purpose." (134)

As with Uriah Carrier, this is another way a direct line can be drawn from "Young Goodman Brown" to "The Shadow over Innsmouth." The ritual place description in "Young Goodman Brown" is remarkably like the description of Dagon. Hawthorne wrote, "At one extremity of an open space, hemmed in by the dark wall of the forest, arose a rock, bearing some rude, natural resemblance either to an altar or a pulpit, and sur-rounded by four blazing pines, their tops aflame, their stems untouched, like candles at an evening meeting" (31). Clearly, Gorman's Dagon is in-spired by the altar in "Young Goodman Brown."

In "The Shadow over Innsmouth," the ritual place of the residents is "Devil Reef" (CF 3.193). The reader never gets to visit Devil Reef in the text, but the fact that the "Devil Stone" (Gorman 134) shares the same first descriptor is an interesting observation. There are further similarities. Like the Devil Stone, Devil's Reef comes into existence because of a trans-fer of something with supernatural powers. In *The Place Called Dagon* this is the bones of the witches killed in Salem, and in "The Shadow over Innsmouth" it is a "funny kind o' thingumajig made aout o' lead or some-thing," that Obed is told to drop in the water to "bring up the fish things from any place in the water whar they might be a nest of 'em" (CF 3.191). Zadok Allen states that Marsh did summon the Deep Ones because "Cap'n Obed an' twenty odd other folks used to row aout to Devil Reef in the dead'o night an' chant things" (CF 3.193).

In addition to the other similarities, the ritual sites in "Young Good-man Brown," *The Place Called Dagon*, and "The Shadow over Innsmouth" all serve a sinister purpose. In "Young Goodman Brown," it is the devil's "baptism" (33); in *The Place Called Dagon*, it is to "cleanse [. . .] by charms and sacrifices" (170); and in "The Shadow over Innsmouth," it is "sacrific-ing heaps o' their young men n' maidens to some kind o' god-things that lived under the sea," (CF 3.188).

Regarding *The Place Called Dagon* and "The Shadow over Innsmouth," there is one final observation. In *The Place Called Dagon*, the initial repre-sentation of the primary antagonist of the novel, Jeffery Westcott, is simi-lar in detail to Lovecraft's description of a Deep One. Gorman writes of Westcott's face:

> It was curiously ridged in the center, as though the two sides of the skull had been pressed together while molten and so joined, leaving a cloven line where the bone had bulged upward on either side. The ears were long and rose thin and prominent on either side of the curious head. The broad brow slanted back at an obvious angle and the chin, blue also with incipient hair, thrust forward aggressively, the ensemble giving the impression of semi-malignant imperiousness. Westcott's nose was broken and this accident ac-centuated the curious profile which he presented when he turned his head, a profile almost ape-like but redeemed by a certain vitality of knowledge. (23)

Compare that monstrous description, especially the implication of Westcott's "ape-like" devolved features, to Lovecraft's description of a human–Deep One hybrid:

> His age was perhaps thirty-five, but the odd, deep creases in the sides of his neck made him seem older when one did not study his dull, expressionless face. He had a narrow head, bulging, watery blue eyes that seemed never to wink, a flat nose, a receding forehead and chin, and singularly undeveloped ears. His long, thick lip and coarse-poured, greyish cheeks seemed almost beardless except for some sparse yellow hairs that straggled and curled in irregular patches; and in places the surface seemed queerly irregular, as if peeling from some cutaneous disease. (CF 3.170)

Westcott is not revealed to be anything more than human, but it is still interesting how much his introductory description shares with Love-craft's presentation of a human–Deep One hybrid. Both have particularly monstrous visages, with unusual hair growth, and both have features that indicate they are a step down on the evolutionary scale, Westcott being compared to an ape, and the human–Deep One hybrid having actual gills, "deep creases in the sides of his neck" (CF 3.170).

If a reader were to keep probing into *The Place Called Dagon* and "The Shadow over Innsmouth," there are certainly more similarities to be uncovered, but those noted above are manifest. Lovecraft, whether consciously or unconsciously, was influenced by elements of *The Place Called Dagon*, and due to the influence of "Young Goodman Brown" on *The Place Called Dagon*, "The Shadow over Innsmouth" was also influenced by "Young Goodman Brown." S. T. Joshi states, "the novel may well have influenced Lovecraft, specifically in 'The Dunwich Horror' (1928), 'The Shadow over Innsmouth' (1931), and 'The Dreams in the Witch House' (1932)" ("Afterword" 185). Hawthorne and Gorman are certainly not the only influences on "The Shadow over Innsmouth"; Lovecraft was also inspired by the works of Irvin S. Cobb and Algernon Blackwood and by a trip to Newburyport (Joshi, "Headnotes" 195). It is undeniable that both *The Place Called Dagon* and (by extension) "Young Goodman Brown" also served as ingredients in the sauce of "The Shadow over Innsmouth."

Conclusion

H. P. Lovecraft did not invent the "peculiar little town" trope, but "The Shadow over Innsmouth" is one of the earliest uses of it in horror fiction. Nathaniel Hawthorne employed it in his story "Young Goodman Brown," in which the "grave, reputable, and pious people" (31) of Salem were revealed to be involved in a secret witch coven. In Herbert S. Gorman's *The Place Called Dagon*, Daniel Dreeme discovers "faces [. . .] once viewed in the quiet lanes of Marlborough" (160) engaged in "orgiastic liturgies of the Witches' Sabaoth" (161), continuing the "Salem coven" (133). Lovecraft read *The Place Called Dagon* before writing "The Shadow over Innsmouth," and as S. T. Joshi has observed, Lovecraft concluded it held his interest "because of the authentic New England colour & certain isolated bits of weird atmosphere whose merit is undeniable" ("Afterword" 183). *The Place Called Dagon* and "The Shadow over Innsmouth" share several similarities. Innsmouth is likened to "decay" (CF 3.172) and Marlborough is likened to "rot" (45). Each writer's respective description of their setting points to deteriorating towns. The characters Humphrey Lathrop and Uriah Carrier in *The Place Called Dagon* are replicated in Zadok Allen and Obed Marsh in "The Shadow over Innsmouth." The ritual locations of the "Devil

Stone" (*Dagon*) and the "Devil's Reef" ("Innsmouth") are similar in name, purpose, and origin. The antagonists in both tales share similarly devolved descriptions. Thus, the original "peculiar little town" of Salem had a direct impact on the creation of Innsmouth because Nathaniel Hawthorne's "Young Goodman Brown" was highly influential on Herbert S. Gorman's writing of *The Place Called Dagon*, which H. P. Lovecraft drew inspiration from to create aspects of "The Shadow over Innsmouth."

Works Cited

Creasy, Larry. "Introduction." In *The Place Called Dagon* by Herbert S. Gorman. New York: Hippocampus Press, 2008. 7–14.

Gorman, Herbert S. *The Place Called Dagon*. New York: Hippocampus Press, 2008.

Hawthorne, Nathaniel. "Young Goodman Brown." In *Young Goodman Brown and Other Short Stories*. Mineola, NY: Dover, 1992. 24–34.

Joshi, S. T. "Afterword: Gorman and Lovecraft." In *The Place Called Dagon* by Herbert S. Gorman. New York: Hippocampus Press, 2008. 185–87.

———. "Headnotes." In *H. P. Lovecraft: Great Tales of Terror*. New York: Fall River Press, 2012. 195.

King, Stephen. Notes. *Nightmares & Dreamscapes*. New York: Pocket Books, 2009. 883–84.

Paciorek, Andy. "Folk Horror: From the Forests, Fields and Furrows An Introduction." In Andy Paciorek et al., ed. *Folk Horror Revival: Field Studies*. 2nd ed. Morrisville, NC: Wyrd Harvest Press, 2018. 12–20.

Neo-Gothic Decadence as a Pervasive Challenge in the Works of H. P. Lovecraft, Arthur Machen, and Alexander Blok

Elena Tchougounova-Paulson
Independent scholar

"I am not mad, but soon shall be."
—Matthew Gregory Lewis, *The Captive* (1803)[1]

"The spirit made one with the spirit whose breath
    Makes noon in the woodland sublime
Abides as entranced in a presence that saith
Things loftier than life and serener than death,
    Triumphant and silent as time."
—Algernon Swinburne, "The Palace of Pan"
(September 1893) (Swinburne 178)

That the Decadent movement formed an image of Modernist culture in Europe and on the American continent at the end of the nineteenth century is not a foolhardy exaggeration and also not simplistic thinking: that is exactly how it has been developed and transformed in the most creative and interpretative ways. Since then, it has taken a variety of forms and representations, and it has gone through several phases, but there are two things that connect them all:

Validation of fear as a primal philosophical and aesthetical force.

Acknowledgment of the art of decay and the art of the unknown as a new cultural phenomenon.

That said, the new, Modernist culture was shaped so as to absorb the elements of Symbolism (primarily French), supernaturalism (i.e., mysticism,

---

1. HPL quotes this line in his letter to Maurice W. Moe of 17 May 1922 (MWM 90).

reframed Gnosticism, and other post-Hellenistic traditions), and the philosophy of pessimism (mostly established by Schopenhauer and Nietzsche), giving to the contemplative audience of the *fin de siècle* era a new, eschatological, and irrevocable outlook that we could define as Neo-Gothic Decadence.

While not always specifically *Neo-Gothic*, the actual term could be directly linked to the whole *fin de siècle* writing and art canon endowed with Gothic features: that is how, for example, *The Encyclopedia of the Gothic* (2016) reframes the glossary of the *fin de siècle* Gothic:

> Literally meaning "end of century," fin de siècle Gothic refers specifically to the Gothic literature of the last two to three decades of the 19th century. There is a pervading sense of instability and unease; an age was coming to an end and things would change, not necessarily for the better. This is reflected by the idea of human devolution or degeneration [. . .] Anxieties about the city and its future are also a feature, in the recurring image of a threatening cityscape that is always possessed of a dark underside capable of hiding characters like Stoker's Dracula and Stevenson's Hyde. [. . .]
>
> Broader artistic and literary movements also shaped fin de siècle Gothic literature. In Russia, for example, the prominence of symbolism prompted writers such as Anton Chekov to turn to Gothic expression (The Black Monk, 1894). The fin de siècle Gothic also served to denigrate French Decadence. (Hughes et al. 248)

This definition resonates perfectly with the paragraph dedicated to Decadance from another source on the same matter, *Encyclopedia of Gothic Literature* (2005):

> During the 1890s, languor, HYPERBOLE, theatricality, and bizarre themes infiltrated Gothic literature throughout Europe as artists extolled a self-indulgent philosophy of l'art pour l'art ("art for art's sake"). In France, disenchantment and libertinism overcame influential writers, notably the poets Stéphane Mallarmé and Paul Verlaine; Flanders produced its own Gothic specialist, Joris-Karl Huysmans, author of the black mass exposé in *Là-Bas* (*Down There*, 1891) and *Against the Grain* (1884), a novel chronicling an immersion in arcana that caught the attention of Oscar Wilde and H. P. Lovecraft.
>
> The last stage of European decadence produced some of its most controversial Gothic works. In England's fin de siècle ("end of the century") period, the short fiction and verse of Ernest Dowson and the writings of Arthur Llewellyn Jones-Machen and Wilde epitomized flamboyant decadence and a fashionable despair. Heavily castigated for unwholesomeness were Machen's *The Great God Pan* (1894) and *The Three Impostors* (1895). (Snodgrass 70)

So what is this Neo-Gothic/Decadent discourse that connects the works of H. P. Lovecraft, Arthur Machen, and Alexander Blok? First of all, let us look at the very definition of *Neo-Gothic* as we see it—mostly, for an opportunity to find an ontological resemblance between the aesthetics of the Western European/North American literature of the time and Blok's Symbolist literary insights.

According to one of the sources describing the Western (North American in particular) literary canon, a chronology of Neo-Gothic most likely refers to the middle 1950s:

> The term Neo-Gothic [. . .] designates all Gothic art forms subsequent to an originally Gothic phase. It is used more restrictively to refer to a phase opening in the middle years of the 20th Century. Primary features of the notion of New or Neo-Gothic are its resistance to clear-cut definition and a certain terminological instability. These stems at least in part from difficulties in end-dating and in adequately defining and circumscribing an original Gothic.[2]

However, other academic sources, such as *The Gothic Tradition in Fiction* by Elizabeth MacAndrew (1979), in which the author discusses the Gothic fiction of the end of the nineteenth century and the twentieth century in an epilogue; *The Gothic* by Fred Botting (1996),[3] or "The Gothic Heart of Victorian Serial Fiction" by Julia McCord Chavez (*Studies in English Literature, 1500–1900*, Autumn 2010) consider all late Victorian/Edwardian literature of the English-speaking world in general as the start of contemporary Gothic, or Neo-Gothic, which above all displays the unavoidable confrontation with the tragic, the inconceivable, the decayed, and the supernatural in multiple ways. In this regard, we also see the argument on the subject of the definition of contemporary Gothic depicted by Xavier Aldana Reyes[4] as very relevant to our research:

> Given the undecidability regarding the literary foundations of the Gothic, to attempt to provide an all-encompassing definition of the contemporary Gothic is a doomed endeavor. Current thinking in the area has tried to

---

2. E.g., www.arthistoryarchive.com/arthistory/gothic/Gothic-NeoGothic-Etymology. html Accessed 25 January 2020.

3. Specifically chapters 6, "Homely Gothic," and 7, "Gothic Returns."

4. Aldana Reyes is writing precisely about the most current works of the Gothic genre, but, in our opinion, everything that he has said in this article makes perfect sense concerning the broader chronological reframing of the *Neo-Gothic*.

overcome this problem by suggesting that the Gothic is "a mode rather than a genre," "mobility and [a] continued capacity for reinvention" being two of its "defining characteristic[s]." As the fragments of an already atomized type of literature, the contemporary Gothic is marked by its ubiquity: if a certain novel is not Gothic, it is bound to utilize motifs or to include literary aspects that have, at some point, been associated with the Gothic, from graveyards and ruins as memorable settings to rapacious monks, monsters, and ghosts as villains. Since these are very specific and no longer confined to narrative effect, it is possible to find the "Gothic" as an aesthetic or thematic qualifier in further subgenre hybrids [. . .]

Of course, the Neo-Gothic tradition covers and redefines many genres and subgenres, including classical literary works written by Bram Stoker, Algernon Blackwood, Ambrose Bierce, and others, and features common pulp fiction magazines that had evolved from the late half-folklore Victorian cheap storybooks, also known as "penny dreadfuls," to transform later into the whole weird fiction phenomenon. S. T. Joshi has described that very special role of horror literature as a strong reaction to the major and menacing challenges of history:

> it is undeniable that such writers as Lovecraft, Blackwood, Arthur Machen, Lord Dunsany, M. R. James, and a host of others not only gave voice to the myriad terrors facing a rapidly changing Anglo-American culture (the terror of the untenanted wilderness, the terror of unholy antiquity, and, perhaps most poignant of all, the terror of cosmic void suddenly emptied of its comforting and benevolent Creator), but also showed how weird fiction could be made to serve as the complex expression of the most intimate philosophical conceptions and a relevant commentary on social, cultural, and even political institutions. (Joshi, *Varieties* 17)

The main task in this paper is to reveal how the omnipresence of Neo-Gothic/Decadent ideas, reflections, and thoughts has appeared—and has been manifested—in the works of H. P. Lovecraft, Arthur Machen, and Alexander Blok. Each could be defined as a perfect type of Decadent author, with different backgrounds (American, Welsh, Russian) yet similar perceptions of the artistic dynamics. All three were ahead of their time with their pioneering writings: Lovecraft's weird/horror fiction, Machen's Edwardian supernatural works, Alexander Blok's mystical Symbolism.

If in the case of connections between Machen and Lovecraft we can definitely demonstrate the direct impact of one on the other ("Machen is a Titan—perhaps the greatest living author—and I must read everything of his," Lovecraft wrote to Frank Belknap Long on 3 June 1923 [*SL* 1.234]), Alexander Blok's name at first glance could be regarded as superfluous on this list. If we take a careful look at his poetry, essays, and correspondence, it becomes evident that he was part of the neo-Gothic/ Decadent league.

Common ground for our comparative research (also formalistic and hermeneutical in places) is formed by the philosophy of the *fin de siècle* era (first and foremost, reimagined antiquity, but let us not forget Nietzsche's works and post-Nietzschean nihilism; i.e., *transvaluation of values*, *ressentiment*, and *amor fati*) and also the turbulent social and political changes that were happening at the time all around the world. We will focus on the writings of the three authors.

The main thing that could unite the named authors is the deconstruction of the traditional literary paradigm, where the reaction at the supernatural is established by the narrative and is legitimized by it. We can say that the Neo-Gothic tradition verifies the whole spectrum of Decadent elements, such as reassessed archaic perception, mythopoeic ambiguity, and aesthetics of disintegration, and in this sense could be also taken as a valid extension of the classical Gothic model of thinking. In this sense we cannot but agree with Jeffrey Andrew Weinstock, who has pointed out that

> the Gothic portrait often stages the confrontation between past and present as long-dead ancestors exert their influence and, as Derrida suggests of ghosts in general in *Spectres of Marx* (1993), "hauntologically' interrupt the presentness of the present. (67)

It also exteriorizes the concept of fear and horror, taking its metaphorical structure "beyond comprehensible" and eliminating the most obvious ways of making an impact on the reader as obsolete. It has been perfectly defined James Kneale as follows:

> Allusion is central to fantastic writing, but "excessive allusiveness," merely saying that something "cannot be described," fails to conjure any sense of horror; it is the way in which the attempt of description fails that is significant. (47)

All Neo-Gothic authors implement an eschatological discourse in their writings based on views of the nature of fear as *Instrumentum Dei*. It is noteworthy that the genesis of horror per se in most Neo-Gothic works is inseparably connected with the philosophical and religious seeking of Modernism, and, especially with one of its main manifestations, *reinterpret-*

ed antiquity. In the case of Lovecraft, that would obviously be his undying interest in ancient Egypt, Greece, and Rome, which he put into a modern perspective: although he himself was an atheist and created the Great Old Ones, the origins of Lovecraft's outlook have strong connections with the renewed interest (in common with his time) in classical mythology. It would be justifiable to say that Lovecraft creates his famous anti-mythology reconsidering and reinterpreting in a sense the Nietzschean dichotomy of Apollonian/Dionysian, which makes the Lovecraftian canon at least partly descendant from the ancient sources through Modernist and *fin de siècle* (e.g., Nietzschean) sources. While deconstructing "musical" themes in Lovecraftian works, John Salonia has mentioned one of the earlier academic researches linked to the theme of the ancient Greek influence on Lovecraft:

> E. R. Dodds's *The Greeks and the Irrational* provides strong evidence that Lovecraft had excellent reasons for choosing the shrill shrieking of flutes and the hypnotic throbbing of drums. Dodds's treatise is a fascinating and sometimes chilling portrayal of the Hellenic rise from primitive superstition to supreme reason, and then the decline back into archaic irrationality. (This Spenglerian cycle of decay [. . .] is one of the basic themes of the Lovecraftian canon.) (96)

Taking the above into account, we dare to argue with S. T. Joshi in the part concerning Lovecraft's ties to Modernism. In one of his interviews Joshi has said in particular:

> Lovecraft himself was in some ways an aesthetic conservative, especially early in his career, but in the course of the 1920s and 1930s he evolved considerably. He never embraced Modernism [. . .]; but he thought of himself as a "prose realist," and his work—aside from its supernaturalism—bears striking affinities with regionalists or social realists such as Sarah Orne Jewett and Sinclair Lewis. (Michalkow)

Of course, we will not deny the obvious—Lovecraft did value realism in different forms—and we do remember what Lovecraft said about his literary preferences (which also confirmed Joshi's words). In his letter to Clark Ashton Smith of 17 October 1930, he points out that

> The basic essence of art is too subtle & elusive to be defined hastily, & I have a strong objective conviction that realism can be very great art. [. . .] But I think there is a profound aesthetic value in realism so developed as to give the reader a sense of the underlying rhyms of things—a realism which hints at longer

streams of essense & vaster marches of pageantry than the span & substance of the outward events, & in which detail serves either to indicate basic trends or to enhance the convincing lifelikeness of the foreground. (*DS* 247)

Even though we agree that Lovecraft's stylistic approach had always been rather purist and also held unmistakably recognizable features that marked his writings as distinctly old-fashioned and "conservative," as Joshi has pointed out, we claim that Lovecraftian narration toward the supernatural as chthonic *Dasein* (*being there-and-now*), on the contrary, can be regarded as new and exceptionally innovative; i.e., Neo-Gothic for that matter. One of the most evident confirmations of this Modernist and mythological side of the Lovecraftian lore can be found in the same letter to Smith:

> The true function of phantasy is to give the imagination a ground to limitless expansion, & to satisfy aesthetically the sincere & burning curiosity & sense of awe which a sensitive minority of mankind feel toward the alluring & provocative abysses of unplumbed space & unguessed entity which press in upon the known world from unknown infinities & in unknown relationships of time, space, matter, force, dimensionality & consciousness. [. . .] Well—as I have said, I think that in future the only readers of weird material will be people who are so organized as to feel this way. Formerly, the presense of nearer mysteries & the survival of religious feeling created a larger public for phantasy [. . .] (*DS* 248, 249)

Later, Tzvetan Todorov in his famous work *The Fantastic: A Structural Approach to a Literary Genre* also pointed out the evident links between Lovecraft's perception of myth/mythological and personal experiences, which can be considered as Modernist, by saying the following:

> Another endeavor to situate the fantastic, one much more widespread among theoreticians, consists in identifying it with certain reactions of the reader: not the reader implicit in the text, but the actual person holding the book in his hand. Representative of this tendency is H. P. Lovecraft, himself the author of fantastic tales as well as of a theoretical work devoted to the supernatural in literature. For Lovecraft, the criterion of the fantastic is not situated within the work but in the reader's individual experience—and this experience must be fear. [. . .] This sentiment of fear or perplexity is often invoked by theoreticians of the fantastic, even if they continue to regard a possible double explanation as the necessary condition of the genre. (34–35)

We can see traces and glimpses of those *fin de siècle* reflections elsewhere in the Lovecraftian universe—especially in his so-called Dream Cycle

("The Doom That Came to Sarnath," "The Cats of Ulthar," "Celephaïs," *The Dream-Quest of Unknown Kadath*, among others): Lovecraftian "Dreamlands," or places in an imaginary alternative dimension that could be reached in a dream state only, look very much like the settlements connected to the Eleusinian Mysteries of Orphic worshippers: macabre, menace, and decay in these stories combine with the splendor of a fantastic realm, and this amalgamation can be regarded as Decadent par excellence. The following fragment from "The Doom That Came to Sarnath" is a vivid example of it:

> Each year there was celebrated in Sarnath the feast of the destroying of Ib, at which time wine, song, dancing, and merriment of every kind abounded. Great honours were then paid to the shades of those who had annihilated the odd ancient beings, and the memory of those beings and of their elder gods was derided by dancers and lutanists crowned with roses from the gardens of Zokkar. And the kings would look out over the lake and curse the bones of the dead that lay beneath it. (CF 1.128)

To a certain extent, this fragment corresponds with an excerpt from a letter to Maurice W. Moe dated 17 May 1922:

> For us were the sinister wonders of Ægyptus—we entered the knighted womb of antique Perneb, transferred stone by stone from its age-long habitat beside the cryptical Nilus (in another place we saw the actual mummy of a priest of 2700 B.C.—the actual uncovered face, brown and withered, and the actual clawlike hands of a holy man who lived 4600 years ago!). (MWM 86)

This abundant language in the detailed description of an ancient Egyptian tomb is structurally similar to the opulent portrayal of Sarnath, a Decadent version of the Egyptian (or such) metropolis from an alternate dimension.

Lovecraft's aesthetic transition from a classicist perception (also including his perception of antiquity), which he had certainly acquired voluntarily in his early literary years, to a Decadent one had also happened by the time he created his most significant works, such as those quoted earlier. That is how Barton Levi St. Armand metaphorically describes it in his work dedicated to the Decadent features in Lovecraft as a New Englander:

> Lovecraft's taste in art, then, typically polarizes into the warm and the cold, the soft and the hard, the Decadent and the Puritan, which yield, alternately,

phantasmagoric details of an artificial paradise and "oneiriscopic[5] glimpses of other worlds." (45)

Accordingly, S. T. Joshi has pointed out that

> judged both from his letters and from his tales, the transformation from classicism to Decadence seems to have occurred around 1921 or 1922. But Lovecraft is certainly correct both in the delineation of these two phases of his aesthetic thought and in the admission that both gave way to—or, rather, their core components were integrated in—a different and more mature aesthetic theory. (Joshi, *Decline* 117)

We also agree with Joshi's concept that Lovecraft did not reject his anti-quarianism completely for the sake of being a Decadent:

> It should not be assumed that Lovecraft's adoption of Decadence meant the immediate sloughing off of classicism; rather, it meant the preservation of those tenets that were not in direct conflict with Decadence and also the transformation of classicism from a model to be slavishly imitated to an ideal to be selectively sought and, perhaps, to be used as a stick with which to beat the nineteenth century. (Joshi, *Decline* 121)

Despite his complex relationship with the changing perceptions of art, Lovecraft essentially gravitates toward Symbolist (overly Decadent, for sure) aesthetics (although he was not satisfied with it completely), questioning classical artistic cohesion:

> What is art but a matter of impressions, of pictures, emotions, and symmetrical sensations? It must have poignancy and beauty, but nothing else counts. It may or may not have coherence. If concerned with large externals or simple fancies, or produced in a simple age, it is likely to be of a clear and continuous pattern; but if concerned with individual reactions to life in a complex and analytical age, as most art is, it tends to break up onto detached transcripts of hidden sensation and offer a loosely joined fabric which demands from the spectator a discriminating duplication of the artist's mood. ("In the Editor's Study" [July 1923]; CE 2.71)

In our view, at a certain point this fragment could be recognized as Lovecraft's *Decadent manifesto*, especially as he insists that creative power is driven by subtle intuitive shifts of consciousness (let us not forget Bergson's work *L'Évolution créatrice*–widely popular at the time–with its main idea about *élan vital*).

---

5. I.e., dreamlike.

Of course, for Lovecraft and his literary circle, which became a creative force and also the center of *Weird Tales*, the re-evaluated view of antiquity was yet another way to construct new relationships with a reality that was becoming bizarre (the First World War, the October Revolution in Russia, postwar stagnation and uncertainty in Europe, the Great Depression in the United States). In this sense, Lovecraft's extraordinary view of the nature of chaos can be regarded as especially close to that of the author whom he had admired for most of his life in literature, Arthur Machen.

Machen's literary biography deserves to be thoroughly researched; fortunately, solid works on him are now available. This paper mentions the key points closely connected to our main subject, Neo-Gothic/Decadent discourse, and how it could be associated with Lovecraft and Lovecraftiana.

It is widely known that Machen was briefly a member of an occult organization, the Hermetic Order of the Golden Dawn, along with another prominent Neo-Gothic writer, Algernon Blackwood: Machen was of Welsh descent and is often called a writer of the Celtic tradition. It is understandable that he was heavily involved in paganism, mysticism, and occultism throughout his life (we all remember that young Lovecraft called himself "a pagan"), and his novella "The Great God Pan" is a vivid example of it:

> for one instant I saw a Form, shaped in dimness before me, which I will not farther describe. But the symbol of this form may be seen in ancient sculptures, and in paintings which survived beneath the lava, too foul to be spoken of . . . as a horrible and unspeakable shape, neither man nor beast, was changed into human form, there came finally death. (Machen 50)

Tessa Farmer has pointed out that

> Pan is the goat-foot pagan God of death and rebirth, the horned God of the wild places and father of all living things upon the earth who causes fear in the hearts of man and beast. Machen understood how paganism, driven underground by Christianity, could have become a force of evil. (49)

No wonder then that Machen's mysticism was the actual thing that attracted Lovecraft's attention:

> Lovecraft first encountered him rather late—in 1923—at a time when it might be expected that utter immersion in another author's work would be more difficult; and so it was. It is hard to point to tales of this immediate period that are slavishly Machenian; and even the later "Dunwich Horror" (1928), which strikes us as a clear imitation of the basic plot of "The Great God

Pan," offers much more than even an "unconscious" imitation of Machen. (Joshi, *Decline* 144)

Machen's stylistically exquisite stance toward the supernatural and phantasmagoria was framed by Lovecraft as a new approach to the weird as a whole in his iconic work "Supernatural Horror in Literature":

> Of living creators of cosmic fear raised to its most artistic pitch, few if any can hope to equal the versatile Arthur Machen; author of some dozen tales long and short, in which the elements of hidden horror and brooding fright attain an almost incomparable substance and realistic acuteness. [. . .] Of Mr. Machen's horror-tales the most famous is perhaps "The Great God Pan" (1894), which tells of a singular and terrible experiment and its consequences. (CE 2.116–17)

Lovecraft's admiration for Machen as the creator of "a masterpiece of fantastic writing, with almost unlimited power in the intimation of potent hideousness and cosmic aberration" (CE 2.118) is not random: he is fully aware that Machen, although he renews "The ancient wisdom, and the ancient pain,"[6] is actually modern and relevant. All these features definitely make him a proper Neo-Gothic writer, engaged with the Decadent movement. As Damien Walter once wrote in the *Guardian*,

> Many contemporary authors of weird fiction will see their own struggles reflected in Machen's life and career. Born into the social hinterland between the privileged upper classes and the poverty of the working class, he received an excellent early education but lacked the money to attend university. Nonetheless he pursued a career as a writer, working as a journalist and tutor and writing through the night, hard work that led in his thirties to Machen establishing himself as an author of "decadent horror."

On the basis of his folklore/mythological material, Machen intuitively reconstructs an utterly Nietzschean model of God-forsakenness, staying within his horror *fin de siècle* model of storytelling.

It is known that Machen's worldview had changed within his lifetime. Nick Freeman points out

> Finally, Machen possessed a robust common sense that would have made him skeptical towards some aspects of today's nature mysticism, let alone its

---

6. A quotation from Frank Belknap Long's sonnet "On Reading Arthur Machen" (cited in CE 2.117).

"workshops," tree hugging and "Iron John" "wilderness masculinity weekends" for stressed-out urban professionals. (110)

But did it really cancel everything that Machen created before? Of course not. As a decadent and Neo-Gothic author, Machen still holds his liminal place in the history of horror/supernatural/weird literature.

Now why have we considered the Russian Symbolist poet Alexander Blok. Because he clearly fits the named paradigm, featuring both the Neo-Gothic and the Decadent in his works. Before the actual comparative analysis, let us make a few remarks about him and the place he takes in the Russian literature of the early twentieth century.

Alexander Blok belonged to the second generation of Russian Symbolists (Junior Symbolists) and could be considered an older contemporary of Lovecraft (he was born in 1880). He thrived as a poet during the era that became an integral part of the social and aesthetic mainstream of Russian history at the very end of the nineteenth and the turn of the twentieth century. This era was later called the Silver Age, or Russian *fin de siècle*. For the first time in the history of Russian literature, the generally accepted realism had to share its influence over readers with representatives of Modernism, especially the most powerful and successful of its type: Symbolism.

Russian Symbolism absorbed the discoveries of Western art; unlike it, Symbolism strove toward universality. It became the leading artistic movement and the most striking aesthetic phenomenon of the first quarter of the twentieth century, defining the major philosophical achievements of this era. In their works, Russian Symbolists found original interpretations of the ideas of Schopenhauer, Nietzsche, Wagner, Bergson's intuitivism, Rudolf Steiner and his Anthroposophical doctrine, Christianity and Greek/Roman and Scandinavian mythology, modern scientific discoveries, and folklore. The *Philosophy of All-Unity* and the primarily Gnostic conception of the *Eternal Feminine* (*das Ewig-Weibliche*), created at the time by the prominent religious thinker Vladimir Solovyov, and his understanding of the role of the symbol in art were the theoretical basis and semantic impulse of Russian Symbolism. It defined its main tasks as cultural inclusiveness, synthesis of the arts, and the integration of actual reality with personal spiritual experience.

Usually Blok's poetry roughly divides into *three books* (periods), and the poet himself called it his *lyrical trilogy*. It is important to know that each book symbolizes a certain period in Blok's poetical biography; i.e., thesis-antithesis-synthesis. Blok proposed this conceptual division in 1910 when he was preparing his collected poems for publication in *Musaget,* a prominent Russian Symbolist publishing house and also a journal. The trilogy in its final state was republished in this exact way while Blok was still alive, and ever since it has been called a canonical trilogy.

According to Blok, it looks like the following:

thesis, or the very first stage of Blok's poetic route, is "the spell of chaos, *The Verses on a Fair Lady*"[7] (Blok, *Zapisnye Knizhki* 168),[8] where the Fair Lady is the main poetic symbol of Blok's lyrical universe, his own version of the Gnostic conception of Sophia and the *Eternal Feminine;*

antithesis, or "world as chaos: would you accept it? [. . .] For me, darkening the image of the Fair Lady" (Blok, *Zapisnye Knizhki* 168);

synthesis, or "appeal to a canon. This is the third period of Symbolism" (Blok, *Zapisnye Knizhki* 168).

One could argue that nothing mentioned above has anything to do with our main subject—and would be mistaken: for a long time Blok was regarded as the most Decadent poet in the Russian cultural landscape, one who described the fear of the unknown exhaustively, although he did not care to call himself a "proper Decadent." The elements of fear and horror in his poetry, especially in his poetic collections of different years, such as *The City (Город,* 1906), *Mask of Snow (Снежная Маска,* 1907), *The Terrible World (Страшный Мир,* 1909–16), *Danse Macabre (Пляски смерти,* 1912–14), and *The Life of My Companion (Жизнь моего приятеля,* 1913–15), his essays "Stagnation" («Безвременье,» 1906), "Nature and Culture" («Стихия и культура», 1907), and "On the Modern State of Symbolism" («О современном состоянии русского символизма,» 1910), his plays *The Puppet Show (Балаганчик,* 1906) and *The Rose and the Cross (Роза и Крест,* 1913), and his correspondence make him one of those literary figures who are inevitably Decadent—and Neo-Gothic for that matter. Blok's prose, including his autobiographical pieces such as diaries and notebooks, is Symbolist and Modernist par excellence and can be defined by the term that S. T. Joshi has used toward Blok's Irish contemporary,

---

7. The very first and profound collection of Blok's poems (including the earliest ones, "Ante Lucem," 1899–1904).

8. All translations of quotations herein are by the author.

Lord Dunsany, who "infuses his new realm with his own philosophical predilections, and these predilections—although expressed in the most gorgeously evocative of prose-poetry—are of a very modern, even radical, sort" (Joshi, *Varieties* 192).

As T. J. Binyon has noted in his review "Alexander Blok's Beautiful Lady" on the most famous biography of Blok in English,[9]

> 'By the will of fate (and not by my own feeble strength) I am an artist— that is, a witness,' he [Blok] wrote in 1917. His viewpoint was always an idio- syncratic one. Ratiocination was alien to him: he experienced rather than thought. 'It would be wrong to say that he was out of touch with real life; still less that he was "not clever", yet at the same time everything we call philoso- phy, logic, metaphysics, simply bounced off him; it was not applicable to him,' wrote Zinaida Hippius. He saw life in terms of mystical colours, ele- mental sound. 'I . . . was drawn into the grey-purple, the silver stars, mother- of-pearl and amethyst of the blizzard' is his description of the Revolution of 1905.

Let us take a brief look at a few short excerpts from Blok's prose, which will give readers a proper impression of his representation. In one of the earliest entries in his notebooks, made on 13 August 1902, Blok wrote:

> This man wasn't an ordinary one. God, when creating, wrapped his heart in dark fabrics: once they fell, he would feel that glare and couldn't stand his love. Now, he was called an egoist. And sometimes he has visions. (*Zapisnye Knizhki* 35)

We see it as a clear indication that Blok, like Lovecraft and Machen, is try- ing to perceive a chthonic, seditious part of his inner manifestation, claim- ing this duality (*dark fabrics* vs. *glare*) as a necessary performance of his aesthetics. This, yet again, makes us think of it as a part of the Gothic na- ture (or, as judging the timeline, the Neo-Gothic). Later, Blok described similar reflections in numerous letters to his correspondents—and to his friend and literary rival, another Symbolist poet, Andrei Bely:[10]

> The main point of the drama of my worldview (I am not fully grown up

---

9. Avril Pyman, *The Life of Aleksandr Blok: Volume 1: The Distant Thunder 1880–1908* (Oxford University Press, 1979).

10. Andrei Bely (pseudonym of Boris Nikolaevich Bugaev, 1880–1935), Russian poet- Symbolist, novelist, essayist, literary critic, and philosopher.

for tragedy) is that I am a lyric. It is both uncanny and joyful to be a lyric. There is an abyss behind horror and joy where you could fall, and nothing would be left. Joy and horror is a dreamy veil. If I had not held this dreamy veil over my eyes, had not been called by *Indescribable Fear* (from which my only soul protects me), I could not have written any poems that you could value. (Bely and Blok 325)

The structure of this fragment is surprisingly Lovecraft-like, featuring the main elements of his writings, such as weakness of descriptive language, which is unable to define the ultimate horror, and ambiguity of named feelings (uncanny/supernatural/joyful), which means that from the onto-logical point of view they are incredibly close to each other.

His famous essay "The Poetry of Magic and Spells" («Поэзия заговоров и заклинаний,» 1906) has the very same Neo-Gothic tendency. Here Blok presents his own (Symbolist to the core) interpretation of how mystery, which is created by primal subverted fear and elemental charms, reaches its peak in folklore-ritualistic mythology, and what impact it has on a person.

Next to these domestic and mundane news there are those that are dedicated to certain colossal entities, commanding respect to them-selves by their dimension and remoteness.

The place of the deceased god Pan was replaced by a belittled, persecuted magician and healer, whom people still visit, but secretively, not openly, ask-ing for his intercessions in front of the dark forces of nature; the very same nature, which he majestically bewitched and thus subdued. [. . .] He is a mys-terious bearer of those spells that were put on people's everyday life; and once bewitched, this domesticated life turns into something else, non-mundane, glowing with magic light and a threat to that other, casual, life, as it its full opposite. (Blok 5.39, 43)

Basically, by arguing that every folklore myth preserves its ritualistic trans-gressive origins, Blok reveals its chthonic nature, which can be easily jux-taposed with both the chaotism of the Lovecraftian Great Old Ones and the Machenian demonic entities.

The ambivalent and eerie elements of the Neo-Gothic and Decadence and the mythopoeics of horror and grotesque par excellence, which pre-vailed in the *fin de siècle* ontological landscape as a transformative power, can in fact unite writers and thinkers such as H. P. Lovecaft, Arthur Ma-chen, and Alexander Blok despite different enthocultural backgrounds, as the main fears and eschatological uncertainties of the twentieth century were about to appear. This paper is a first attempt to define Neo-Gothic Decadence in the works of these three writers as a much broader theoretical problem than has been done before, and we hope to continue our research in the future.

Works Cited

Aldana Reyes, Xavier. "The Contemporary Gothic." In *Oxford Research Encyclopedia of Literature*. Oxford: Oxford University Press, 2018. DOI link: 10.1093/acrefore/9780190201098.013.187. Accessed 12 August 2020.

Bely, Andrei, and Alexander Blok. *Correspondence: 1903–1919*. Ed. A. V. Lavrov. Moscow: Progress-Pleiada, 2001.

Binyon, T. J. "Alexander Blok's Beautiful Lady." *London Review of Books* 2, No. 15 (7 August 1980). Accessed 9 August 2020.

Blok, Aleksandr. "Poeziya zagovorov i zaklinaniy." In Blok's *Polnoye sobraniye sochineniy v vos'mi tomakh*. Vol. 5. Moscow-Leningrad: GIKHL, 1962. 36–65.

———. *Zapisnye Knizhki. 1901–1920*. Moscow: GIKHL, 1965.

Farmer, Tessa. "An Exploration Beyond the Veil, Guided by Arthur Machen." In *Faunus. The Decorative Imagination of Arthur Machen*. London: Strange Attractor Press, 2019. 39–55.

Freeman, Nick. "A Longing for the Wood-World at Night: The Sylvan Mysteries of Arthur Machen." In *Faunus. The Decorative Imagination of Arthur Machen*. London: Strange Attractor Press, 2019. 101–10.

Hughes, William; David Punter; and Andrew Smith, ed. *The Encyclopedia of the Gothic*. Hoboken, NJ: Wiley Blackwell, 2016.

Joshi, S. T. *H. P. Lovecraft: The Decline of the West*. 1990. Rockville, MD: Wildside Press, 2003.

———. *Varieties of the Weird Tale*. New York: Hippocampus Press, 2017.

Keane, James. "Ghoulish Dialogues: H. P. Lovecraft's Weird Geographies." In Carl H. Sederholm and Jeffrey Andrew Weinstock, ed. *The Age of Lovecraft*. Minneapolis: University of Minnesota, 2016. 43–62.

Machen, Arthur. *The Great God Pan*. Oxford: Oxford University Press, 2018.

Michalkow, Steven A. "A Literary History of Weird Fiction: An Interview with S. T. Joshi." formerpeople.wordpress.com/2013/10/30/a-literary-history-of-weird-fiction-an-interview-with-s-t-joshi/ Accessed 17 February 2020.

St. Armand, Barton Levi. *H. P. Lovecraft: New England Decadent.* 1979. Providence: WaterFire Providence, 2013.

Salonia, John. "Cosmic Maenads and the Music of Madness: Lovecraft's Borrowings from the Greeks." *Lovecraft Annual* No. 5 (2011): 91–101.

Snodgrass, Mary Ellen. *Encyclopedia of Gothic Literature: The Essential Guide to the Lives and Works of Gothic Writers.* New York: Facts on File, 2005.

Swinburne, Algernone Charles. "The Palace of Pan." In *Astrophel and Other Poems. The Collected Poetical Works of Algernon Charles Swinburne.* Vol. 6. London: William Heinemann, 1917. 178.

Todorov, Tzvetan. *The Fantastic: A Structural Approach to a Literary Genre.* Tr. Richard Howard. Cleveland: Press of Case Western Reserve University, 1973.

Walter, Damien G. "Machen Is the Forgotten Father of Weird Fiction." *The Guardian.* (Tuesday 29 September 2009). www.theguardian.com/books/booksblog/2009/sep/29/arthur-machen-tartarus-press?fbclid=IwAR1clRg_enE1QmRHTP09hn3tWozmXZ7iCaYRtQtCGvR6XlKfAh0lUASdca8 Accessed 23 January 2020.

Weinstock, Jeffrey Andrew. "Lovecraft's Things: Sinister Souvenirs from Other Worlds." In Carl H. Sederholm and Jeffrey Andrew Weinstock, ed. *The Age of Lovecraft.* Minneapolis: University of Minnesota, 2016. 62–79.

Lovecraft's Accursed Share in Bataille's General Economy: Antiutilitarian Cosmologies and Anti-capitalist Social Visions

Christian Roy
Independent Scholar

There is a surprising amount of common ground to be found between H. P. Lovecraft and Georges Bataille (1897–1962). Most likely, Lovecraft never heard of the seminal thinker for French theory (who must however have known of him by the 1950s; see Huling 78). Nevertheless, Bataille's daring explorations of humanity's engagement with the mind-canceling formlessness and excess of a chaotic universe of uncontrollable forces are often strikingly adumbrated in Lovecraft's fiction, despite their opposite aesthetic and political sensibilities (Roy, "Fascination" 2017). Even so, not only Lovecraft's cosmic horror but also his social views lend themselves to a close reading in light of Bataille's theorizing of a cosmic economy of gloriously fascinating waste. The latter's political implications and anthropological assumptions may in turn be interrogated by taking seriously the final stage of Lovecraft's own articulation of an anti-utilitarian social stance, in tune with man's precarious situation in the universe.

Already locating horror in the vastness of space in his early mythological writings posthumously collected in *The Solar Anus* (1927–31), Bataille fantasizes a reversal of all verticality into terrifying abysses that stand for the depths of the sky as the foul, bottomless pit of wasteful expenditure of the universe's chaotic energies. Their vortex issues in an obscene rotting sun that cannot be gazed at without dying or at least going blind or mad. To translate these poetic insights into concepts, in a series of essays on economics writ large, from his article on "The Notion of Expenditure" (1933) to his book *The Accursed Share* (1949), Bataille appropriates Albert Einstein's distinction between general relativity and special relativity for a

non-anthropocentric recasting of cosmology and sociology. Bataille contrasts a "general economy" of the physical universe with the "special economy" of living entities, organized as they are for self-preservation and self-
perpetuation amidst the wider world's irreducible turmoil. Their "*économie
restreinte*" is patterned on "*relativité restreinte*," but is best translated as a
"limited economy." Human organisms are aware of—and even drawn to—
excessive states of free self-expenditure beyond their limited forms. However, they remain bound for most of their lives by the imperatives of calculative utility for individual and collective survival and security. I would
argue that it is helpful to view Lovecraft's once-and-future gods, indifferent
or hostile to mankind, moving in deep time on unimaginable scales, as
standing for Bataille's general economy. In both cases, organic life as we
know it appears as an insignificant marginal phenomenon, "a very rare
form of death," as Nietzsche put it ("Let us beware of saying that death is
opposed to life. The living is only a form of what is dead, and a very rare
form": Aphorism 109 of *The Gay Science*, Nietzsche 110).

There is a Lovecraft story in which this little eddy of biological partiali-
ty that is human life amidst the cosmic flow of energetic unraveling is
neatly portrayed in terms of this continuum of organic life and post-
mortem decay. We may see it in the greasy puddle to which the life scientist Dr. Muñoz is reduced at the end of his doomed effort to preserve his
individual form from death and dissolution as the default way of all things
at the end of "Cool Air" (1926). In this race against time that is utilitarian
reason's enterprise of preserving organic forms and organized selfhood, it
is fair to say that Bataille is on the side of the puddle that always wins out
in the end, and always lurks and lures with an obscene grin on the way
there. For Bataille ascribed to such abject refuse the same ultimate sovereignty as Hegel did to the lowly slave who has nothing to lose, in contrast
to the master whose lofty status depends on the exploitation of other people's servitude for its maintenance and recognition. In the general economy of the cosmos, what Bataille still calls "evil" must likewise prevail
sooner or later. It is the very principle of utter waste as the underlying energy of the world, from its origin in the sun's blinding radiance to its en-
tropic decay in local or universal heat death, and every accidental
complication of chance in between. The narrow "good" of particular entities is always a provisional diversion from the relentless mainstream of
blind explosive and diffusive momentum from which they derive the at-
tenuated forms of their limited economy, like the swirls and bubbles gen-

erated by the countercurrents of an impetuous river. "Evil" in this sense is not a moral category as opposed to "good" so much as a dramatic expression of what Lovecraft means by the "cosmic horror" of the world's senseless, boundless, essentially formless agitation.

The way that Bataille highlights this economic dimension in cosmic horror finds a kind of literal illustration in "The Shadow out of Time" (1934–35). For one thing, in its depiction of the Great Race's social system, this mature novella reflects Lovecraft's interest in the New Deal, with its Keynesian emphasis on expenditure over savings, which would also later fascinate Bataille in the post-war Marshall Plan as a focus of his book *The Accursed Share*. But leaving aside Lovecraft's incidental political commentary for the moment, it is no coincidence that this story's protagonist is an economist. For he is ravished to a different mode of awareness and connection to space-time by the consideration of the general economy of the cosmos, in its unthinkable connection to the limited economy of human exchange that is his scientific focus.

Nathaniel Wingate Peaslee, full professor of political economy at Miskatonic University, loses his mind to an alien entity in mid-sentence during a lecture in 1908. Lovecraft deliberately chose for his narrator's period of amnesia the dates of the long bout of depression when he was no longer quite himself. Peaslee therefore comes back to his senses five years later. He then completes in mid-sentence the thought that had sent him into an altered state, taken over by a non-human, cosmic form of awareness. The interrupted sentence was about William Stanley Jevons (1835–1882), an actual logician among "orthodox economists," who gave the discipline—especially the theory of utility—its mathematical features and thus "typifies the prevailing trend toward scientific correlation" (CF 3.372). In contemporary discussions of the Anthropocene era when human activity is subsumed under blind geological forces, the "Jevons paradox" is sometimes invoked as sealing mankind's doom, as it points out that technological efficiency gains in resource use only ever lead to their accelerated depletion. Lovecraft sounds as if he sensed these cosmic implications of the "dismal science" of economics when he portrays Jevons as having brought it to is "apex" by connecting "the commercial cycle of prosperity and depression with the physical cycle of the solar spots" (CF 3.372). Echoing Bataille, Lovecraft uses Jevons to explicitly inscribe the limited economy of human affairs within the heedless general economy of the sun and stars.

The real-life timing of this fictional account of reason derailed in its reductive academic work also shows that the black sun of psychological depression as experienced by Lovecraft is also implicitly involved in Peaslee's mind-blowing realization of the full implications of taking economics to its cosmic (absence of) limit. The point of Lovecraft's mind-swapping tale, as stated from the outset, is that "man must be prepared to accept notions of the cosmos, and of his own place in the seething vortex of time, whose merest mention is paralyzing" (CF 3.363), and likely to induce depression. To avoid such melancholy, Bataille embraced a radical defamiliarization of thought, in a switch of allegiance to the sun's mad self-expenditure and the swirling movement of the galaxies. This was his way of taking the leap of Nietzschean *amor fati* from limited human economy to general cosmic economy. Conversely, when Lovecraft writes to Frank Belknap Long on 7 February 1924 that "I consider anything connected with man as sadly cramped and wanting in universality," one is also reminded of Bataille's limited economy. Yet Lovecraft parts company with him in adding: "I think anything based on low instinct necessarily tawdry, local and limited to a vast degree" (SL 1.305). By contrast, in striving to unleash man's basest instincts in all their mindless savagery, Bataille expected to commune with the "blind, idiot god" of wildly excessive cosmic immanence, rather like the cultists plotting humanity's overthrow by immemorial alien forces from below in Lovecraft's stories.

Their respective imaginaries thus keep on intersecting at specific points of opening to that larger economy of groundless inhumanity. In Lovecraft's story "From Beyond" (1920), it is with the "preternatural eye" of his pineal gland (CF 1.198) that the mad scientist Crawford Tillinghast has learned to see whatever lay beyond the limitations of the human, organic viewpoint, by attuning himself to the general flow of all things into outer space. In the late 1920s, Bataille too fantasized in great detail about a pineal eye on top of the skull. In his musings on this theme, he maintained that such an organ would have been the only justification for man's erect station, turned away from the horizontal plane of animality. For instead of bottling him up inside/under his head, the pineal eye would have enabled a direct erotic discharge of the earth's metamorphic energy into the unbounded void of the sky, pierced by the blind spot of an obscene, putrid sun exceeding vision at the far end of its bottomless well.

We find an analogue to Bataille's para-evolutionary speculations in *The Solar Anus* in Lovecraft's collaborative story "The Crawling Chaos" (1920/21). There, a plague patient's drug overdose induces in him an outer-space falling sensation, "curiously dissociated from the idea of gravity or direction" (*CF* 4.30)—as in the condition resulting from the death of God as lamented by Nietzsche's Madman in aphorism 125 of *The Gay Science*:

> What were we doing when we unchained this earth from its sun? Where is it moving to now? Where are we moving to? Away from all suns? Are we not continually falling? And backwards, sidewards, forwards, in all directions? Is there still an up and a down? Aren't we straying as though through an infinite nothing? Isn't empty space breathing at us? Hasn't it got colder? (120)

For Lovecraft's dreamer, as in the endless thrownness of particular beings within Bataille's atheistic general economy, it is "as though the universe or the ages were falling past me," with "a subsidiary impression of unseen throngs in incalculable profusion, throngs of infinitely diverse nature, but all more or less related to me" (*CF* 4.30). This may sound a lot like the feeling Bataille cultivates of communicating at the lowest common denominator of a generic discharge that pries discrete selves away from their separate prisons. But such communion with the multitude of beings elicits both visceral revulsion and weird aesthetic fascination in Lovecraft's "The Crawling Chaos." In the end, his narrator's pounding head has morphed into "the pounding sea," "afraid of dark gods of the inner earth that are greater than the evil god of waters" (*CF* 4.36). Similarly, in Bataille's erotic cosmology of *The Solar Anus*, the earth's masturbatory frenzy overtakes the regular coital motion of tides and waves in volcanic eruptions as explosive diarrhea, likened to the revolutionary upheaval of society's lowest strata. One may even speak with Ray Huling of Lovecraft's "thalassophobia" in connection with Bataille's glorification in his 1936 manifesto "Popular Front in the Street" of the "ALL-POWERFUL multitude" of demonstrating workers. "That image of a 'human ocean' would have disgusted Lovecraft, as would have much else in this passage: the violence from below, the undifferentiated masses, the very notion of revolution" (Huling 74-75), all connected to the horror of fusional states of mind, society and phenomenal reality at the heart of his writings as of his psychology.

In "The Crawling Chaos," the raging sea swallows all land, only to be itself consumed in super-volcanoes that tear the globe apart, as "a cloud of steam from the Plutonic gulf [. . .] sped outward to the void [. . .] in one delirious flash and burst," leaving, "against the background of cold, humorous stars" (a favorite symbol of blind chance for Bataille), "only the dying sun and the pale mournful planets searching for their sister," the disintegrated Earth (CF 4.36). By taking it all the way to global destruction, Lovecraft here radicalizes Nietzsche's imagery of Earth stripped of its sun and of gravity, orientation, and all direction. Like Bataille, he conflates the psychological and the geological in the monstrous rush of wild expenditure, spewing forth from the Earth's incandescent depths to dissipate in the astronomic outer darkness revealed by Nietzsche's "death of God." This is for Lovecraft the realm of "a dread not of this or any world, but only of the mad spaces between the stars," celebrated in "The Festival" (1923; CF 1.414). The narrator also writes under the spell of the pounding sea and the inspiration of the infinite space outside his little head, abysses above and below being ultimately the same.

If we take Bataille's cue in seeing celestial and chthonic abysses as interchangeable, it may not matter much that, in "From Beyond," the current seems to flow the other way, from outer space to Earth. For thanks to his pineal vision, Tillinghast has "harnessed the shadows that stride from world to world to sow death and madness" (CF 1.200). Among these may well be counted Nyarlathotep (in the 1920 prose poem of that title) walking the earth during "a season of political and social upheaval," amidst a horrible "general tension" and "the brooding apprehension of hideous physical danger" (CF 1.202). This is precisely the kind of social climate Bataille sought to cultivate in order to bring about a general panic experience of "death and madness" for their own sake, as the incandescent touchstones of a common ecstatic breakdown, convulsively joining individuals at their exploded edges, in atheistic religious response to the blinding glory of careless cosmic excess. There is thus a discreet, unwittingly Bataillean social dimension, brought out elsewhere in Lovecraft's fiction (e.g., "The Call of Cthulhu"), to the disintegration of reality that the mad scientist of "From Beyond" wants his former friend to experience, coming "down" to him from unfathomable cosmic dimensions.

The phrase "the Crawling Chaos," most often used by Lovecraft about Nyarlathotep as messenger of Azathoth, also echoes Marx's image of the "old mole" of revolution undermining the foundations of established order. This is a metaphor that Bataille deploys in 1930 against civilization's elevated conceits in both its bourgeois and fascist forms, with relish at its implications of a blind, subterranean, relentlessly vermin-like impulse that "hollows out chambers in a decomposed soil repugnant to the utopians" ("The 'Old Mole'" in *Visions* 35; Parkinson 137–38). Such underground chambers crawling with foul things abound in Lovecraft's fiction, precisely because they are even more repugnant to this conservative aesthete, who was nevertheless perversely drawn to such territory as a literary subject. The "old mole" image thus even applies to the cosmic deity Azathoth himself, "who gnaws hungrily in inconceivable, unlighted chambers beyond time amidst . . . detestable pounding and piping" and the absurd dance of "the blind, voiceless, tenebrous, mindless Other gods whose soul and messenger is the crawling chaos Nyarlathotep" (CF 2.100).

In the eponymous tale, Nyarlathotep gains his following by showing a film of "the world struggling against blackness; against the waves of destruction from ultimate space" (CF 1.204), beneath which "unsanctified temples [. . .] reach up to dizzy vacua above the spheres of light and darkness" (CF 1.205). Related to the shameful self-consciousness of individuated beings who, as such, can never measure up to the infinite excess of Bataille's godlessly divine universe, "a sense of monstrous guilt was upon the land, and out of the abysses between the stars swept chill currents that made men shiver in dark and lonely places." (Compare above the "mad spaces between the stars" in "The Festival.") All the while, "a demoniac alteration of the seasons," with fearsome "autumn heat," brought on a general sense "that the world and perhaps the universe had passed from the control of known gods or forces to that of gods or forces which were unknown"—or from an earthbound limited economy to a vaster, more chaotic general economy, "whirling, churning, struggling around the dimming, cooling sun" (CF 1.204). We are again reminded here of Nietzsche's astronomical allegory for the death of God and the attendant chill of guilt and disorientation.

Lovecraft often depicted mad scientists and crazed cultists as living out the consequences of this inner collapse of post-Christian culture amidst dim intimations of dark new deities sweeping down "from beyond" human scale. But unlike Bataille, he still stood firmly on the side of civilization against both its bourgeois decadence and its barbarian overthrow. In "The Shadow out of Time," the Great Race's "fascistic socialism" reflects Lovecraft's own stoical, gentlemanly response to the general economy of the cosmos his alien scholars are clearly attuned to, but which they manage to transfigure in more soberly genteel ways than other races of the Mythos pantheon. In that society, "industry, highly mechanised, demanded but little time from each citizen; and the abundant leisure was filled with intellectual and aesthetic activities of various sorts" (CF 3.404) that creatively expend the energies thus reclaimed from utilitarian pursuits tied to survival. The mature Lovecraft likewise wished to save civilization by spreading its energy gains so as to make non-calculative activity more of a norm across society, once it moves in the "*unqualifiedly desirable* direction [. . .] of lessened emphasis on property & wealth & acquisitive ability, & greater emphasis on personal excellence" (22 April 1935, *ET* 305).

In those same years, Bataille was still seeking convulsively explosive outlets for the energies monopolized by the limited economy of capitalist accumulation. However, by the time the Cold War set in and he wrote *The Accursed Share*, Bataille seemed content with tamely redistributive macroeconomic extrapolations from the current use of energy gains. It is in the interval that Bataille's views on these matters approach a happy convergence of bold originality and relative sanity. In the rest of this article, I will concentrate on probing some surprising overlap and revealing contrasts they suggest between Lovecraft's final social views and those articulated by Bataille just a few years later during the war in *The Limit of Usefulness*. For there is more to compare with Lovecraft in the latter book as a more balanced, alternate early draft of what would in 1949 become *The Accursed Share*. This was Bataille's own summation of two decades of reflection on a general economy on the scale of the universe as senseless waste, as opposed to the political economy of limited human self-perpetuation.

Both Lovecraft and Bataille are driven by a fundamental aversion for the utilitarian assumptions of such political economy, which is not unrelated to their fascination with the splendor and horror of the vast, indifferent physical cosmos. The connection is explicit and direct in Bataille's wartime draft: "My life takes place within a huge universe," inducing a sense of both anguished grandeur and risible smallness.

> For nothing is more closed to the obvious divinity of night than this world that is accountable for work without which it gives us over to cold and hunger. The myriad stars of heaven do not work, not doing anything that would subordinate them to any *employment*: but the earth demands the toil of every man, forcing him to wear himself out in unfinishable labors. (*Limite* 36)

Yet, insensitive to the stars' useless allure, today's earthbound massman relies on utilitarian morality, raising about even the most commonly recognized values what is to him the ultimate question:

> What is the use of it? (he is content with vague answers but to have peace, confusions have to be introduced: between technique and disinterested

culture, between pleasure and needful relaxation). What is of no use is held to be base, devoid of value: and yet what is of use is but a means. Utility has to do with acquisition, with the increase of products or of the means to produce them: it is opposed to unproductive expenditure. Insofar as man accepts utilitarian morality, it can be said that the sky is closed to him: he has no sense of poetry, of glory, the sun to him is but a source of calories. (*Limite* 37–38)

Bataille is moved by nostalgia for a glory that only belongs to the sky, with the sun as model of naïve expenditure that knows no tomorrow. He contrasts this premodern festive economy driving life beyond its basic maintenance with capitalism's methodical avoidance of play and chance to harness all life to a productive project.

Lovecraft too puts above all else the "sense of poetry, of glory," the latter however being understood not as a sacrificial religious impulse to emulate the sun's self-expenditure, but as the aestheticization of human experience of the world through culture. As he explained at length in a letter to Clark Ashton Smith dated 28 October 1934, his "lifelong and directly anti-Marxian conception of *cultural* values as distinct from *economic* values" (*DS* 579) assumed that "the best of culture *has always been non-economic*. Hitherto it has grown out of the *secure, non-struggling* life of the aristocrat. In future it may be expected to grow out of the secure and not-so-struggling life of whatever citizens are personally able to develop it. [. . .] With *economic opportunities* artificially regulated, we may well let other interests follow a natural course," generating "different social-cultural classes: less tied to the holding of material resources" (*DS* 582). From his current standpoint as a rational socialist as before from than of an agrarian feudalist, Lovecraft despises the "old petty-bourgeois concept of *acquisitive power* as the only ultimate measure of human quality," not seeing in *"the absence of insecurity anything to deplore"* (*DS* 581). "Better far to be 'decadent' than to tolerate such a brutish waste of human energy" as a deliberately maintained "state of constant anxiety & threatened starvation on the part of every ordinary citizen" (*DS* 581).

The truly pointless waste is the one that channels "human energy" to self-preservation in thrall to large-scale commerce and manufacture that corral for useless private gain resources and profits which rightfully belong to the public for social use (CLM 208).

Such social use, however, was for Lovecraft not so much an end in itself as a general condition for enabling the glorious individual pursuit of disinterested encounters with the nobler anxiety of conscious existence. Having often made very similar-sounding statements, Bataille likewise maintains that

> if each being on earth is of necessity greedy, it is as a glorious being who cannot escape the hard law of earth: that you cannot spend anything without having first acquired something. But having turned the means of greed into an end, capital, being impersonal, lacking an existence of its own, was able to turn away from glory. (*Limite* 92)

As such, it always came into conflict with Lovecraft's "ideal of life, which is *nothing material or quantitative*, but simply *the security & leisure necessary for the maximum flowering of the human spirit*" (DS 580):

> It is that of the gentleman as opposed from that of the tradesman [. . .] because of its repudiation of *calculativeness* & *ulterior motivation* inseparable from the acquisitive character. That everyone could not feasibly pursue it in the agricultural age of scarcity was a source of genuine regret to me. [. . .] *Too much energy was wasted in the mere scramble for food & shelter. The condition was tolerable only because inevitable in yesterday's world of scanty resources.* Millions of men must go to waste in order that a few might really live. Still—if those few were not upheld, no high culture would ever be built up. (DS 580, 579–80)

"I never had any use for the American pioneer's worship of *work and self-reliance for their own sakes*," says Lovecraft, not minding if he may sound un-American, though he likes to think his "ideal has flourished naturally in many parts of America—Virginia, South Carolina," and even pre-revolutionary New England (DS 580). "Thus I have no fundamental meeting-ground with the rugged Yankee individualist. I represent rather the mood of the agrarian feudalism which preceded the pioneering & capitalistic phases" (DS 580).

This is a sentiment Bataille largely shares, except that he lays the blame squarely at the feet of the Puritans whom Lovecraft proudly claims as his forebears. He denies that the spirit of capitalism born of their sect according to Max Weber met with any resistance in America, being un-checked by the prejudices of nobles and their contempt for trade. "The grasping businessman who devotes all waking hours to work and the growth of his enterprises was to the New World what the saint or the man of honor were to archaic Europe" (Bataille, *Limite* 60). "The world was never so needy as under the grey cloak of utility" spread by the Refor-mation, so that "nothing is more opposed than Puritan morality to the festive spirit" of medieval and even Counter-Reformation Europe that Bataille celebrates for its baroque excess and exposure to loss of self unto death. Lovecraft is certainly more ambivalent as a cultural Protestant, fascinated and repelled at once by the wild festive abandon he portrays in fiction as the province of Bataille-like cultists. He holds up the (eighteenth-century) English gentry's life of leisurely self-cultivation. This marks a different anti-capitalist path than Bataille's retrieval of the (seventeenth-century) continental nobility's reckless cult of glory as a new "religious" performance of sovereign self-expenditure, deliberately courting disaster.

Lovecraft's attitude is the more detached yet aesthetically appreciative one of the antiquarian devotee of tradition, who recoils at the crude pioneer, without condoning "aimless idleness"; he is merely questioning the "savage & feverish scramble for bare necessities, *made artificially hard after machinery has given us the means of easier production*" (CLM 180). This of course fails to consider the Fordist twist of consumer society's addiction to widely available, endlessly varied creature comforts as the main driver of economic growth in developed societies. No better at discerning the traps of economic abundance and commercialized hedonism, Bataille would add that "capitalism must rigorously make men starve, since it could not deliver to them the products available without betraying its own greedy end of relentlessly increasing productive power" (*Limite* 92). For Lovecraft as well, it is a matter of channeling energy away from its stockpiling and reinvestment as (to use Heideggerian language) "standing reserve" for its ongoing mobilization as potential for further quantitative increase, i.e., as capital. As he writes in October 1936 to C. L. Moore, "invention & discovery are meant to make living as easy as possible for everyone in order to liberate energies for the real development of human personality," in contrast to the dominant utilitarian philosophy of life "which urges that the struggle of the jungle be prolonged—life being made very hard for those not happening to inherit resources, so that the less shrewd will be forced into an intolerable position . . . while the shrewd and calculative . . . cultivate an ideal of dominant shrewdness, . . . trampling down the non-calculative" for the sake of national success in the "world-struggle" (CLM 179) of competitive production and financial asset-building as ends in themselves.

Lovecraft believes that "until capitalism is really shaken, it will make no concessions, but will simply wait till a revolution blows the whole civilisation up" (DS 579). This is why he favors a gradual path to socialism, which can maintain "complete continuity with the Western-European mainstream" and "mean a return to art impulses typically aristocratic (that is disinterested, leisurely, non-ulterior)," as "there is nothing in *bourgeois* culture which need be mourned. It was cheap & contemptible from the start" (*DS* 582). But now that

> we live in an age of easy abundance which makes possible the fulfilment of all moderate human wants through a relatively slight amount of labour. [. . .] there must be a *fair & inclusive allocation of the chances to perform work & secure rewards*. When society can't give a man work, it must keep him comfortable without it; but it must give him work if it can, & must compel him to perform it when it is needed. (*DS* 580–81)

With "*regulation* [of] industry to afford every citizen a decently compensated situation" (*SL* 5.390), Lovecraft clearly has in mind something like the federal job guarantee favored by many progressive Democrats today. But like those who favor instead an unconditional basic income as a corollary of citizenship—unhitched from employment-dependent earnings, Lovecraft could write to R. H. Barlow on 27 January 1937 that "a certain minimum will be absolutely guaranteed whether or not employment can be provided" (*OFF* 396). He had recognized "technological unemployment" as the paramount social issue of industrialized societies "long before the depression." Initially, "as a convinced feudalist," he thought "corporations would overtly control government and, to avoid revolution, *voluntarily* curtail profits enough to spread work among more men" along with social welfare. Speculating (like Tocqueville in *Democracy in America*) about how aristocracy might eventually arise from industry in new feudal forms, he "assumed that the *funded proprietor* of the future would come to feel the same basic responsibilities as those felt by the *landed proprietor* of the past— & that eventually the great accumulations of wealth would once more breed a *real gentry* with non-acquisitive interests & a true ability to use cultivated leisure to advantage" (*DS* 581–82).

Having jettisoned even this inventive paleoconservative revision of the "naïve Republican orthodoxy" he had inherited from his family (*DS* 582), Lovecraft still felt equally remote from his friend Frank Belknap Long's naïve Marxism (*DS* 582). He would have agreed with Bataille that "the terror drumbeats of revolutions only sounded to ensure an even narrower dedication of human energy to industry" (*Limite* 94), Lovecraft therefore could not abide extreme radicals' "savagely uncivilized depreciation of intellectual and aesthetic activity for its own sake." Dead set against such an "attempt to drag culture down to the level of crude minds" (DS 582), Lovecraft did not feel "any cultural upheaval" was necessary to attain a "new feasible economic equilibrium" in "light of modern machinery, modern knowledge & revised values & objectives which spring from these things." The collective mind just needed to be molded very gradually in a country where the word "socialism" and the idea of public ownership were largely anathema (SL 5.390).

Lovecraft's gradualism, that allowed him to see in fledgling Scandinavian social-democracy "a very hopeful sign" (letter to Kenneth Sterling, 16 September 1936, RB 282), stood in sharp contrast to Bataille's own religious cult of sacrifice for its own sake, which, through the 1930s, he had hoped to unleash across Europe. His revolutionary vision then sounded like a kind of anarchic, Sadean anticipation of China's later Cultural Revolution, without much of an agenda beyond competing with fascism for the same sacred ground of mystico-political atheology. For he saw fascism as still not violent *enough* to do away with the profane orderliness and limited economy of militarism and the State. If Surrealism's leader André Breton could famously call this position a "surfascism" aiming to outdo its rival at its own game, by wartime Bataille's sacrificial impulse of intimacy with death in violent ecstasy eventually became largely privatized in literary approaches to an "inner experience" of self-expenditure in crime, sex, and mysticism amidst workaday productivist society.

Lovecraft's priority was precisely to avert the destruction of civilization in a flash of barbaric frenzy, such as the global orgiastic rapture Cthulhu's followers were looking forward to as the return of a barely human primitive scene. Like them, Bataille located humanity's dignity in just such ecstatic debasement of human forms. As his loyalty also lay with the earth and stars rather than with anything containable within territorial boundaries, it is something remarkably similar that he wished to let loose upon the modern world in a messianic cult of his own, chiefly aimed against fascism. However, had it ever been allowed to leave the realm of confidential literary myth-making, as his Acéphale secret society purported to accomplish in its detailed planning for human sacrifice, was it not more likely to make fascism look comparatively attractive? For fascism could appear to provide at once satisfying collective ecstasies and the bulwark against social chaos Lovecraft had long seen in it, with efficient enough crowd control to also keep trains running on time instead of allowing public order to disintegrate. Since Bataille's ambition already in 1930 was to realize the long-repressed "possibility of a humanity entirely suffocated by horror" ("The Modern Spirit and the Play of Transpositions," tr. Krzysztof Fijalkowski and Michael Richardson, in Ades and Baker 242-43), it is hard not to recognize the fictional achievement of this very possibility in many passages of Lovecraft's stories, starting with his famous depiction of "The Call of Cthulhu" to a life "free and wild and beyond good and evil, with laws and morals thrown aside and all men shouting and killing and revelling in joy" (CF 2.39-40).

Lovecraft was keen to rescue Western civilization from this kind of contagious, riotous vandalism, but also from bourgeois society's "cheap ideals of speed, quantity, ostentation, surface amusement, &c." (CLM 210), as some of the "worst influences" of commercialism (CLM 210), even if it meant checking both anarchy and decadence with fascist lawless violence, as he had often mused (see Huling). For as he writes in October 1936 to C. L. Moore, "the chief indictment of a capitalistic ideal is perhaps something deeper even than humanitarian principle,—something which concerns the profound, subtle & pervasive hostility of capitalism, & of the whole essence of mercantilism, to all that is finest & most creative in the human spirit," since its real beneficiaries are *not* the truly superior (e.g., the likes of Poe, Spinoza, Baudelaire, Shakespeare, Keats), "but merely *those who choose to devote their superiority to the single process of personal acquisition rather than to social service or creative intellectual or aesthetic effort*" (CLM 182-83).

These three kinds of non-acquisitive pursuit happen to align closely with those an anti-utilitarian reorganization of industrial society was meant to support through a combination of basic income and civic service (redistributing across all classes any menial tasks in the public interest not yet obsolesced by ever-increasing automation) in the personalist social schemes of Arnaud Dandieu (1897-1933). This close colleague of Georges Bataille at the Bibliothèque Nationale sought like him to draw revolutionary lessons from sociologist Marcel Mauss's *Essay on the Gift* (1922), without however succumbing to Bataille's mysticism of violence and the abject as means of communing with a godless cosmos. For not unlike Lovecraft, some social thinkers thought they discerned constructive ways out of the limited economy of technocratic productivism undergirding both capitalist democracy and communist dictatorship. In other words, then as now, there must be better choices than the one between nationalist personality cults and the critical "dark mass of human evil that, Bataille thought, alone could allow humanity to overcome the crisis of fascism," and of which many of Lovecraft's vividly depicted objects of disgust afford us a taste (Huling 93).

As more of a pragmatic reformist by the end of his life, Lovecraft would already have been happy to see some significant strides taken toward the promotion of cultural pursuits at odds with the profit motive and mass culture, along the lines of a socialist development of New Deal policies. As he writes on 7 February 1937:

> Under a better-controlled economic system, with Federal encouragement of mass-education [. . .], an appreciable rise in public taste may well be expected. It is probably as subsidized projects of some sort—governmentally subsidized or otherwise—that really meritorious magazines in fields as narrowly specialised as the weird will exist . . . . if they ever do exist. Capitalism had no place for this kind of thing—& in pre-capitalist ages such special products depended upon the caprice of royal or other powerful patrons. The war between honest human expression & the profit motive is eternal & truceless. (CLM 210-11)

This conflict finds an echo in Bataille's wartime description of the daily debate between one's isolated existence as a tiny enclosure of self-awareness and the free space of an exuberant world that is uncaringly poised to annihilate it. This debate of limited and general economy begins between other men and oneself, between generosity and greed. "But to go from within to the outside, one must go through the narrow pass whose name is Anxiety" (Bataille, *Limite* 142-43)—a mortal anguish that comes along with the gift of self life demands to be worthy of the name. "I am one of those people who believe men are meant for other things than ever-growing production, things that instill in them a sacred horror" tied to the stars (Bataille, *Limite* 133). And this is of course what weird fiction was all about for Lovecraft, as erotic literature was for Bataille, as steeped in evil's dark sacrificial excess as any blasphemous Mythos cult. Lovecraft's own ethos of *noblesse oblige* was no less anti-utilitarian, however, in graciously cultivating whatever contributed to an otherwise meaningless world's wonder and beauty. For it assumed "*a psychology of non-calculative, non-competitive disinterestedness, truthfulness, courage, & generosity fostered by good education, minimum economic stress, & assumed position, &* JUST AS ACHIEVABLE THROUGH SO-

CIALISM AS THROUGH ARISTOCRACY," as he wrote to C. L. Moore in mid-October 1936 (CLM 179).

With this final creative version of the anti-utilitarianism running through all successive iterations of his worldview, Lovecraft was closer in inspiration than Bataille to democratic socialist Marcel Mauss's original retrieval for social science of the gift economy. He seems to have had some anthropological sense that giving is primarily relational, as an open-ended circulation process. It is this giving back and forth or forward that weaves the fabric of cultures. This cohesive bond of social graces and folkways is inscribed within the larger—symbolically cosmic—dynamics of a gift economy that relies on human scale and connection, while shunning narrow self-interest. To refocus anti-utilitarian giving on the useless waste of the abject sacred as one-sided expenditure, Bataille had to emphasize ethnographic reports of the potlatch (made when this festival of formal giving was probably already destabilized by the colonial money economy), singling out the escalation and breakdown of competitive exchange in deliberate ruin. He was obsessed with how Northwest Native chiefs would sometimes crush social rivals by tauntingly destroying their own prized possessions, and portrayed such behavior as a model of insuperable personal sovereignty to be emulated by going all the way to self-destruction.

Unlike Bataille, Lovecraft realized that human generosity and the immanent grace to be found in the world's beauty involved more than the mere reversal of anal retention into generic diarrhea. He reserved for the waking dreams of weird fiction this accursed share at the formless fount of cosmic horror. For all his literary dallying with the latter, he was also able to overcome some of the social and racial prejudice with which it was long intertwined in his mind. By the end of his life, Lovecraft appeared moved by remarkably humanistic sentiments. His reasoned articulation of them may well have more to offer contemporary post-industrial society than Bataille's pursuit of a general economy of sacrifice to cruelly inhuman powers of mindless rapture, akin to Mythos gods. Compared to Lovecraft's belatedly achieved social insights, Bataille's visions of excess in fusional community, which have come to fascinate many in academic and cultural circles, can even appear as a self-defeating sideshow to global capitalism's limited economy, including, as I hope to have shown, on the anti-utilitarian terms they shared with the austere, distant, yet generous gentleman-writer aptly identified with Providence.

Works Cited

Ades, Dawn, and Simon Baker. *Undercover Surrealism. Georges Bataille and DOCUMENTS*. London: Hayward Gallery; Cambridge, MA: MIT Press, 2006.

Bataille, Georges. *The Accursed Share, Volume I: Consumption*. New York: Zone Books, 1991.

———. *La Limite de l'utile*. Foreword by Mathilde Girard. Paris: Lignes, 2016.

———. *Visions of Excess. Selected Writings, 1927–1939*. Tr. Allan Stoekl. Minneapolis: University of Minnesota Press, 1985.

Huling, Ray. "Fascism Eternal Lies: H. P. Lovecraft, Georges Bataille, and the Destiny of the Fascists." In Dennis P. Quinn, ed. *Lovecraftian Proceedings No. 3*. New York: Hippocampus Press, 2019. 70–96.

Mauss, Marcel. *The Gift: Forms and Functions of Exchange in Archaic Societies*. London: Routledge, 1990 (Taylor & Francis e-Library, 2002, libcom.org/files/Mauss%20-%20The%20Gift.pdf).

Nietzsche, Friedrich. *The Gay Science*. Tr. Josefine Nauckhoff. Cambridge: Cambridge University Press, 2003.

Parkinson, Gavin. *Surrealism, Art and Modern Science. Relativity, Quantum Mechanics, Epistemology*. New Haven, CT: Yale University Press, 2008.

Roy, Christian. "Transpositions of Mauss' Theory of the Gift in the Personalist Social Critique of Arnaud Dandieu (1897–1933)." In Antoon Vandevelde, ed. *Gifts and Interests*. No. 9 in the "Morality and the Meaning of Life" series edited by Albert W. Musschenga & Paul J. M. van Tongeren. Leuven, Belgium: Peeters, 2000. 177–89.

———. "Civilian Service for Social Security? Basic Income and Labor-Sharing in the Thought of Arnaud Dandieu." The Seventh Congress of the U.S. Basic Income Guarantee Network, as part of the Eastern Economic Association Conference at the Boston Park Plaza Hotel, Boston, MA (7–9 March 2008). www.usbig.net/papers/183-Roy-BIGServiceDandieu.doc.

———. "H. P. Lovecraft, Georges Bataille, and the Fascination of the Formless: One Crawling Chaos Seen Emerging from Opposite Shores." In Dennis P. Quinn, ed. *Lovecraftian Proceedings No. 2*. New York: Hippocampus Press, 2017. 189–207.

Weber, Max. *The Protestant Ethic and the Spirit of Capitalism*. Tr. Talcott Parsons. Intr. Anthony Giddens. London & New York: Routledge, 1992.

(Taylor & Francis e-Library, 2005. is.muni.cz/el/1423/podzim2013/ SOC571E/um/_Routledge_Classics___Max_Weber-The_Protestant_ Ethic_and_the_Spirit_of_Capitalism__Routledge_Classics_-Routledge__ 2001_.pdf).

A Sequence of Paintings So Horrible: Montage in Visual Adaptations of "Pickman's Model"

Nathaniel R. Wallace
Independent Scholar

Early twentieth-century author H. P. Lovecraft sought to disrupt time and space through his distinct brand of supernatural fiction. Notably, in his short story "Pickman's Model," the reader is presented with such disruption through the descriptions of ten paintings representing members of a fictional race, the ghoul, throughout the history of colonial New England, and in contemporary locations in Boston. Each painting's description is fairly brief, a mere fragment of text embedded within the protagonist's commentary, and documents a separate event involving the subject of the ghoul. One can associate this sequence of repetitive imagery with the technique of montage, a term defined by the film theorist André Bazin, as "the ordering of images in time" and "the creation of a sense or meaning not objectively contained in the images themselves but derived exclusively from their juxtaposition" (24, 25). Lovecraft employs a technique similar to montage in "Pickman's Model" by including individual textual fragments depicting distinct times and locations in an intentional sequence to create a juxtaposition of texts that leads to a "shock-like disruption," as Mario Slugan describes the effect (18).

In examining "Pickman's Model," this analysis traces the original montage-like techniques to those realized in visual adaptations, as their respective media contain different levels of complexity regarding modalities of engagement. Significantly, the distinct nature of the printed word leads to a singular source of communication for the audience as the information processed by the reader occurs one word, phrase, or sentence at a time, while relationships with words immediately before and after allow the reader to render meaning to the text. When this same technique of montage is employed by an artist, the fragments of paintings described in "Pickman's Model" may gain extra modalities and more complicated internal and external juxtapositions when adapted into visual form. The significance of this study is to isolate key theories Lovecraft championed regarding disruptive elements of literature in visual contexts as they contain possibilities for artists not only to associate visual fragments sequentially in time, but also to stack multiple visual texts within a shot or frame, a process conceived by Lev Manovich known as spatial montage (Betancourt 51). To help categorize these transitions, this analysis employs certain terminology used by comic book theorist Scott McCloud in his book *Understanding Comics: The Invisible Art* in order to classify the juxtapositions among images. Key visual adaptations of the story to be evaluated in this analysis for their use of both temporal and spatial montage include Jack Laird's segment for the television show *Night Gallery* (1971), Herb Arnold's illustrated comic book story "Pickman's Model" (1972), and Horacio Lalia's comic book segment "Pickman's Model" (2001).

Literary Montage

The application of montage theory to Lovecraft's work is complicated by the origins of the epistemology of the practice, given that the author would not have been familiar with the discourse surrounding the term due to its later popularity. Indeed, David Trotter, in his essay "T. S. Eliot and Cinema," makes the case that while many of the theories of montage arose from film practice and from the work of Soviet filmmaker Sergei Eisenstein, a similar development had occurred within literature previously that followed a comparable track, or "parallelism" as he refers to the phenomenon. Later, through explicit crossovers between the two media of literature and film as employed by novelist John Dos Passos, theorists would bridge these media together despite their separate, though similar, progressions. Lovecraft was aware of Modernist writings employing such techniques at the time, such as Eliot's *The Waste Land,* published in 1922, but found their style objectionable and chaotic (*ES* 27).[1] Despite his consistent objections to their approach, Lovecraft was familiar with a literary work that predated the Modernists which he would come to replicate in several of his stories—Bram Stoker's *Dracula,* published in 1897. Dracula is considered an epistolary novel in that most of the proceedings are told

---

1. According S. T. Joshi, HPL owned a copy of the novel *Dracula*, though it is unknown when the copy was acquired or the edition number (Joshi 132).

through assumed letters addressed to other characters within the narrative. The novel contains multiple fictional texts of this type, and their accumulation and relationship within one another provide additional validity to events, such as Jonathan Harker's imprisonment in Dracula's castle.

Lovecraft would use this technique of bridging textual fragments together in service of a narrative in stories such as "The Call of Cthulhu," "The Whisperer in Darkness," and At the Mountains of Madness. Lovecraft used this type of photomontage to portray different aspects of a fictional creature or race, affording it further depth within the larger text with the inclusion of each consecutive fragment.[2] Indeed, Sean Elliot Martin in H. P. Lovecraft and the Modernist Grotesque has pointed out that "The Call of Cthulhu" employs a "modernist use of collage," a practice related to photomontage, and "revolves entirely around the collaged documentation" (19, 84). Significantly, Lovecraft fashions these relationships among fragments explicit in a way that yields a particular narrative outcome, and Martin's reference to the opening passage in "The Call of Cthulhu"—"the inability of the human mind to correlate all its contents" (CF 2.21)—is relevant to this analysis, as the placement of fragments with the aid of Thurber's commentary leads the reader to formulate certain conclusions about the material. In "Pickman's Model," Lovecraft distilled his approach by concentrating text fragments in the form of paintings into ten paragraphs located toward the end of the story rather than distributing them throughout the text. This configuration of fragmentary texts is in essence very similar to the sequential process of montage, which also is connected to how Lovecraft evaluated works of literature. For instance, Lovecraft, after having read August Derleth's novelette "The Early Years," focused on fragments of imagery it contained and their sequential arrangement, stating, "isolated fragments [. . .] arranged in a proper organic relationship" and "There is profound and subtle beauty, splendidly modulated, in this sequence of dream-glamourous pictures. [. . .] You are equally felicitous in arranging these things in a

---

2. See HPL's essay "A Living Heritage: Roman Architecture in Today's America" (1935), in which he appears largely to reject the use of Modernist approaches in the extreme to break with traditional notions of art and beauty. Specifically, he held that "no work of art ought to be encumbered with excrescences wholly alien to its purpose, or to counterfeit—beyond certain bounds and without power and instinctive associative reasons—objects of alien function or alien workmanship" (CE 5.121). One can deduce that Modernist aspects in art could be paired with tradition for contrast, but he did not view works that were completely Modernist to be encouraged or celebrated.

significant, revelatory, and aesthetically satisfying form" (*ES* 258). Clearly Lovecraft understood the significance of potent imagery and its sequencing within a given work.

Montage through Fragmentary Painting Descriptions

"Pickman's Model," written in 1926 and published in *Weird Tales* in 1927, assumes the first-person perspective of Eliot, who engages in a one-way conversation with his friend Thurber at an unnamed club in Boston (Joshi and Schultz 204). Structurally, the story uses what is known as a wraparound narrative, a framing device that provides context to the multiple fragments constituting the body of content. Recounting scandals involving the artist Pickman, Thurber describes to Eliot the Boston Art Club's response to his work, how Thurber came to know Pickman, and particularly his trip to Pickman's secret studio in an obscure part of Boston. After describing his trek to the studio, Thurber recounts his experience of viewing ten paintings, divided into two categories. The first, identified by the author as "Colonial Studies," accounts for five paintings, in contrast to the second group of five, which Thurber explicitly refers to as "Modern Studies." To help map these paintings, this analysis uses a slightly modified form of Marie-Laure Ryans's technique of mapping narrative boundaries, featured in Exhibit 1, with "Ghoul Feeding" featured on the far left (Ryans 366).

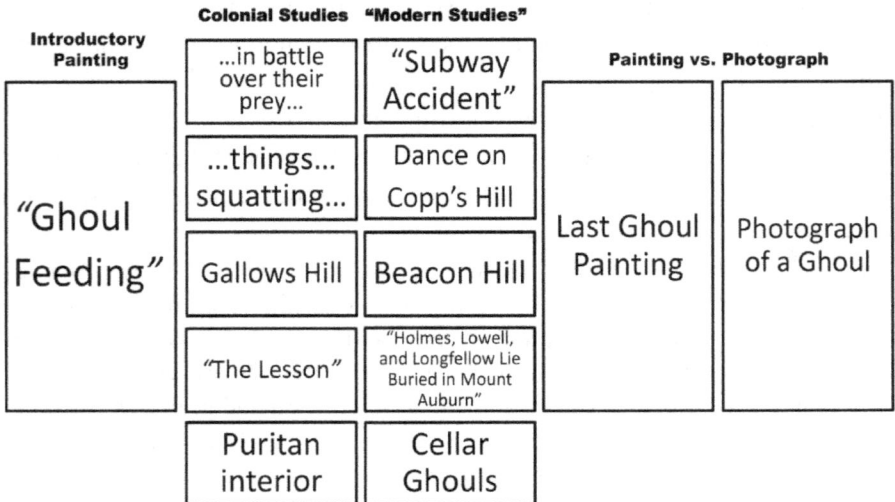

Exhibit 1. Diagram of the narrative in "Pickman's Model."

Both sets of studies include depictions of Copp's Hill, an actual location in Boston, but the first includes paintings of a ghoul attacking someone in a bedchamber, a witch hanging from Gallows Hill in Salem, a small child in the cemetery learning from a pack of ghouls how to consume human flesh (this painting is entitled "The Lesson"), and finally a colonial interior in which a Puritan family listens to a father reading from the Bible while a feral young man looks on. The "Modern Studies" include five named or described paintings. "Subway Accident" depicts a scene from the present with subway-goers attacked by ghouls. Others depict scenes of ghouls dancing at Copp's Hill, ghouls crawling through the honeycombed chambers underlying Beacon Hill, a group of ghouls laughing uproariously as they read a Boston guidebook, and finally a ghoul waiting in a cellar to attack an unlucky passerby. Notably, six of the paintings are described in a single sentence and the most detailed descriptions are connected with "The Lesson" and the Puritan interior. Some sentences in this section could easily function as modern-day one- or two-sentence horror stories as one might find in an Internet Creepy Pasta or Two-Sentence Horror Story on a subreddit. Others make historical connections, and some are didactic in demonstrating how ghouls indoctrinate human children. These short descriptions are embedded in Thurber's anxiety-ridden analysis of the paintings and comments on Pickman's style, but because of their shortness, the focus is never long on one painting, and the effect of ten brief fragments of descriptions of different paintings leads the reader to consider the meaning of their totality and connections between them.

Adaptations of Pickman's Paintings in the Visual Arts

Since the initial publication of "Pickman's Model," adorned with Hugh Rankin's illustration of a ghoul, and since Lovecraft's sketch included in a letter,[3] this segment of the story has been adapted a dozen or more times through the media of comic books, television, and short film (see Exhibit 2).

---

3. See *FLB* 95, image dated 28 July 1934.

Exhibit 2. Visual Adaptations of "Pickman's Model": 1952–2016

Date	Creators	Story Title (length in pp.)	Publication Title	Medium and Notes
Sept. 1952	Rudy Palais (art)	"Portrait of Death" (7)	*Weird Terror* (Vol. 1, No. 1); rpt *Horrific* #8 (Nov. 1953)	Comic book story (color); cover story in *Weird Terror*?
May 1970	Larry Woromay (art)	"Demons and Vampires" (7)	*Tales of Voodoo* (Vol. 3, No. 3); rpt *Weird Worlds* (Apr. 1971) and *Terror Tales* (Oct. 1972)	Comic book story (b/w)
Jan. 1971	Roy Thomas (script), Tom Palmer (art), & Sam Rosen (lettering)	"Pickman's Model" (7)	*Tower of Shadows* (Vol. 1, No. 9); rpt *Masters of Terror* #2 (Sept. 1975), (b/w); *L'Echo des Savanes Spécial U.S.A.* #21, 4e trimestre, 1981 (France)	Comic book story (color)
1 Dec. 1971	Jack Laird (direction), Alvin Sapinsley (script)	"Pickman's Model" (27 min.)	*Night Gallery* (Season 2, Episode 11)	Television series episode
May 1972	Herb Arnold (script & art)	"Pickman's Model" (8)	*Skull* (No. 4)	Comic book story (b/w)
2000	Ricardo Harrington	*Chilean Gothic* (43 min.)	*H. P. Lovecraft Collection Volume 4*	Short Film
2001	Horacio Lalia (art)	"Il Modello di Pickman" (12)	*Gli Incubi di Lovecraft: Il richiamo di Cthulhu e altri racconti dell'orrore*	Comic book story (b/w)
2007	Giovanni Furore (director)	"Pickman's Model" (33 min.)	*H. P. Lovecraft Collection Volume 4*	Short film (color)
2012	Jamie Delano (script) & Steve Pugh (art)	"Pickman's Model" (11)	*The Lovecraft Anthology: Volume II*	Comic book story (b/w)
2012	Kim Holm (art)	*Pickman's Model*	Self-Published	Comic book story (b/w)
2015	Bethesda Softworks LLC	Side quest	*Fallout 4*	Video game. Released PlayStation 4 and Xbox One
2015	Pablo Angeles (director)	*Pickman's Model* (11 min.)	Self-published	CGI animated short film

Date	Creators	Story Title (length in pp.)	Publication Title	Medium and Notes
2016	Brandon Barrows (script), Hugo Petrus (art), & Diana Leto (art)	"Pickman's Model"	*Mythos: Lovecraft's Worlds, Volume 1*	Comic book story (b/w)

See also "Granny Gumshoe," an obvious send-up of "Pickman's Model," *National Comics* #58 (February 1947), story and art by Gill Fox, 7 pp. Source: Grand Comics Database (www.comics.org/ issue/5712/#58834). The full story in at Comic Book Plus (comicbookplus.com/?dlid=20116).

When the painting sequence described in "Pickman's Model" is adapted into the visual arts, the nature of the paintings' representation moves from second hand, that of telling, to that of actually showing, and the demarcation of what was once in the form of sentence structure through words, punctuation, and paragraphs finds its expression in frames, shots, and panels. Indeed, Scott McCloud states that "[t]he panel acts as a sort of general indicator that time or space is being divided" (99). That the paintings have frames that divide them from the greater reality of a given scene that is also demarcated with a frame or shot allows the artist to manipulate these differences in their visual adaptations, further disrupting the *viewer's* sense of time and space. Linda Hutcheon, a noted theorist regarding adaptation studies, has stated that "The adapted text . . . is not something to be reproduced but rather something to be interpreted and recreated, often in a new medium" (84). Similarly, in recreating these fictional paintings in their adaptations, writers and visual artists have taken on the role of curator in choosing which of Pickman's paintings to depict. In so doing they intentionally create relationships among these paintings in order to tell a parallel narrative regarding a race of ghouls in Lovecraft's fictionalized New England. The literary montage contained in the original story is translated visually with each iteration in a way that emphasizes the loose connection between the original fragments, depicting an intentional sub-narrative, or represent the fragments simultaneously in a manner that is more conducive to the visual media in which it is expressed.

Transitioning from the literary to the pictorial also affords extra dimensionality to the relationships of each painting to each other, and the wider reality depicted in a given frame. The written word is largely "sequential in time," as McCloud indicates of film, except that the reader controls the speed and focus of the translation from word to thought, whereas comics also have the ability to be sequential within space (7). This analysis goes further in suggesting that the format of sequential pictorial media such as comic books and film creates meaning not only between the juxtaposition of panels or scenes, but also within a given panel among the objects it contains. In other words, meaning is imparted through montage based on time, whereas these same images also have the ability to contain multiple fragments within themselves, offering juxtapositions within single shots or images, known as spatial montage (Betancourt 3). For instance, the paintings from "Pickman's Model" set in colonial New England represent a different time from the space in which they are displayed, just as paintings with ghouls displayed in contemporary Boston represent a distinction in space from their setting. As the term *montage* applies to the visual arts examined here, Scott McCloud's "scene-to-scene" transitions best apply in that each fragment depicts the subject of the ghoul in a different time and location (71).[4] However, when these fragments are viewed and understood in totality, they depict a much larger history, geography, and interconnectedness to humanity than can be presented in an individual panel. Indeed, a single image attempting to convey this complex and seemingly disjointed information can be overwhelming to the viewer, as seen in the tableau-style adaptation of these ghoul-related subjects in Fig. 3. One can see that beyond the ability to create disruption, montage can also be a way of organizing visual information to present to the viewer.

"Ghoul Feeding" as Exemplar

The first painting cited by Thurber during his discussion with Eliot is "Ghoul Feeding," a work that exists merely as a title referenced twice near the beginning of the story.[5] Unlike the later sequence of paintings, no de-

---

4. McCloud's transitions include panel-to-panel, which signifies different moments in time; action-to-action to show an action developing in real time; scene-to-scene, which depicts different times and spaces; subject-to-subject, which tends to show elements in a single scene or event but makes direct connections, such as cause and effect; aspect-to-aspect, which represents different perspectives of a central idea or thing using a "wandering eye"; and finally, non-sequitur, which doesn't offer a logical connection between panels but can set a mood (70–72).

5. The word *ghoul* is referenced only three times in the story, and most references to the creature are through associations and direct descriptions of their bodies and actions.

scriptions are given here of the work; rather, the reader is told only about the negative responses of members of the Boston Art Club. The title itself suggests the subject, the ghoul, and its ghoulish activity, which is about "feeding."

The term *ghoul* refers to a mythological race of creatures with cultural origins in Mesopotamia, later popularized and given cultural currency within Arab culture in the Middle East (Al-Rawi 2009).[6] Borrowing the creature from these previous Middle Eastern cultural contexts, Lovecraft, through his reference to the ghoul in the painting, establishes the "model" that later descriptions of paintings would incorporate through a multitude of representations. In terms of the actual paintings created by the character Pickman in the story, it is positioned at the beginning of the text, hence is depicted in Exhibit 3 at the extreme left, and can be designated in

Exhibit 3. "Pickman's Model" (2019) by Ramiro Roman. Used by permission of the artist.

6. HPL became aware of the mythological ghoul in his childhood during repeated readings of his grandfather's copy of *One Thousand and One Nights*. HPL read the English version, also called *Arabian Nights*, when he was five years old (Joshi 22). The structure of "Pickman's Model" is similar to that of a tale from *Arabian Nights*, as both employ a framing device.

this analysis as the *exemplar*, defined as "a model or pattern to be copied or imitated" (Dictionary.com 2020).

Notably, "Ghoul Feeding" has not been consistently represented in many of the visual adaptations of "Pickman's Model" listed in Figure 2. Indeed, in later adaptations by Horacio Lalia (2001), Kim Holm (2012), and Jamie Delano and Steve Pugh (2012), the painting is referenced in dialogue between Thurber and Eliot but never shown, a situation much in line with the original story. If titles serve as maps to the viewer, i.e., a means of interpreting what is seen, as is suggested by researchers Margery Franklin, Robert Becklen, and Charlotte Doyle, the absence of the visual in this instance would probably cause the viewer initially to attempt to depict the image mentally (108). Such an exercise prepares the viewer for what might be seen later, as in Horacio Lalia's version, but remaining unrealized in the adaptation by Kim Holm, which does not feature any images of the paintings, in accordance with Thurber's emphasis on Pickman's detractor's reactions to his work, rather than on their actual content.

Explicitly featured in the *Night Gallery*'s adaptation of "Pickman's Model," "Ghoul Feeding," inexplicably renamed "Ghoul Preparing to Dine," becomes central to the narrative, especially within the mise-en-scène. *Night Gallery*, the creation of the writer and host Rod Serling, ran on NBC-TV from 1969 to 1973.[7] The adaptation of "Pickman's Model," directed by Jack Laird and scripted by Alvin Sapinsley, aired on 1 December 1971 (Skelton and Benson 206). It was produced with a keen awareness of temporal issues contained within the original text, as it uses montage in an innovative manner, both spatially and temporally.

In *Night Gallery*, "Ghoul Feeding" is linked with specific cuts in video footage that assume transitions within time and space. The painting is shown by Serling in his introduction, in which he says, "It's a painting that tells a story of a young artist who recruits his models from odd places—and the models are very odd indeed" (*Night Gallery* 1971). This synthesis of the show's format, the staged gallery where Rod Serling introduces each segment, with the actual painting associated with "Ghoul Feeding," is one of the most potent uses of art in the show since the series' initial segment, "The Cemetery."[8] Laird cuts to a close-up of the painting within the cam-

---

7. *Night Gallery* also featured an adaptation of HPL's "Cool Air."

8. "The Cemetery" contains a painting that depicts the recently murdered character of William Hendricks digging out of his fresh grave and approaching his former

era's frame; it remains there as the credits appear. The segment then begins with the audio of a conversation taking place in the assumed present between two men, Eliot and Larry, who are discussing the work. During their conversation, they give the painting the much less menacing title "Ghoul Preparing to Dine." As the camera pulls back from the painting, a significant change in time and space is revealed, distinct from the gallery space in which Rod Serling's introduction took place.

The conversation between Eliot and Larry continues until the camera cuts to a close-up of the painting again. As the two men finish their conversation, Pickman's voice transitions from the status of non-diegetic, a source external and from the past, to one that is diegetic as the camera pulls back to reveal that Pickman is teaching a women's painting class, and "Ghoul Preparing to Dine" is on display at the front of the room. Despite its occurrence in distinct temporal moments in the narrative, the painting's presence in each segment, which largely uses subtle cuts and camera movements to create a spatial montage between the paintings and the reality of the narrative, ties these distinct scenes together. Compared to the other visual adaptations examined here, "Ghoul Preparing to Dine" almost transcends the state of exemplar to be a driving force in the segment. Laird's use of temporal montage, moving as it does from the present to the past, largely disguises this cut and demonstrates an ability to engage in the medium of film to provide it qualities that would be difficult to replicate in literature.

Pickman's "Sequence of Paintings"

Lovecraft was fond of characterizing climaxes in his stories as the "high point," and one such moment in "Pickman's Model" occurs once Thurber is taken into Pickman's studio on the north end of Boston and shown a sequence of paintings (CF 2.57). Once in the studio, Thurber is exposed to a variety of paintings that expand upon the ghoul first introduced with the reference to "Ghoul Feeding." As noted, there are two groups of paintings contained within this sequence, those that center on the history of the "forefathers" within the region of Boston and those regarded by the artist as his

---

house menacingly. With each viewing of the painting by Hendricks's nephew, the recently deceased comes closer and closer to the house, creating an increasingly desperate situation. This approach to depicting sequential action in an image can also be found in M. R. James's short story "The Mezzotint" and in the film *In the Mouth of Madness* (1994).

"modern studies" (CF 2.65). Lovecraft references ten specific paintings in "Pickman's Model," with only three being titled. The reader's understanding of the ghoul race expands and accumulates with the description of each painting, hastened along with Thurber's increasingly anxious commentary on what the paintings mean. The transition of describing one image to another repeatedly is done out of an almost panicked state of the narrator, but the effect it has is still the same in that his telling of his experience on this point is dependent on the segments that comprise the overall scene.

As expressed through this series of paintings, the repetition of time and space is representative of the technique of montage, both spatial and temporal. Through repeated reference to each distinctive painting, Lovecraft uses montage to bring time and space together in a manner that elicits greater meaning than the sum of individual reference. Further, the function of montage in this example is to disrupt linear time through the use of multiple image fragments within the narrative. Montage, through its particular use of time manipulation, allows an artist the ability to foreground certain relationships among separate scenes or elements. Indeed, Lovecraft's use of montage within his fiction is very similar to the process of quotation that Peter Wollen ascribes to directors Dušan Makavejev and Jean-Luc Godard, as such references "impose a new meaning on material by inserting it into a new context" (125). Through a repetitive process of representing disparate scenes, which all involve an object or category of objects, an artist may suggest a greater meaning concerning the object utilizing that process. Each scene or image then elaborates a distinct quality of the object, which results in a cluster of related qualities attributed to said object that is subsequently come to be held by the observer. An object's significance increases through repeated reference, as gaps in knowledge are constantly filled with the addition of new qualities or sets of behaviors.

Within "Pickman's Model" the visual adaptations of this sequence of paintings vary from medium to medium, and some artists, in not revealing too much about the monstrosities, opt not to include any direct depictions of the ghouls. Comic artists, such as Kim Holm, have completely left out the sequence of ghoul paintings or changed their content to remove references to the creature in their adaptations, diminishing the importance of the paintings while emphasizing Thurber's reactions.[9] Other comic book adap-

9. Indeed, Holm, in his graphic novel, only depicts Thurber and Pickman looking at

tations, such as Jamie Delano and Steve Pugh's, feature Pickman's paintings decentered on the walls of his studio in the background of a few panels, and some close-ups of particular paintings with little association with the paintings named and described in the original text beyond featuring ghouls. Indeed, their first panel containing paintings in the story depicts Thurber looking in particular at one ghoul with large teeth, and another on the next page shows a man being bitten on the thigh by a ghoul, with his hands flailing in the air. Considering their lack of ties to the original text and nonspecificity, they represent a view into the danger ghouls present to humanity, but do not necessarily convey additional context such as specific locations or historical events.

Studio-to-Painting Transitions

One technique of montage employed, as demonstrated in the Brandon Barrows and Hugo Petrus adaptation, is to depict the studio from a distance within a single image that includes the numerous paintings created by Pickman. This approach uses the conventional format of a gallery or studio, such as Giovanni Paolo Panini's painting *Modern Rome* (1757), which depicts a large decorated hall with the presence of practicing artists among a great multitude of landscape and architectural paintings from the region. Although the painting represents an indoor space, most of the paintings are of the outdoors, providing a conflict that undermines the orientation of the viewer.

In much the same way, in the Barrows and Petrus adaptation of "Pickman's Model," the studio section of the narrative is dominated by a

---

the works, not the works themselves. The film *Chilean Gothic* (2000) similarly refrains from showing the sequence. The comic adaptations "Demons and Vampires" (1971), "Portrait of Death" (1952), and Jamie Delano and Steve Pugh's version from *Lovecraft Anthology Volume 1*, this last title being a collection of comic book adaptations, contain a multiplicity of paintings but do not explicitly contain images relating to the original text. "Portrait of Death" features representations of the creature but lacks any narrative context beyond merely depicting its physical features. "Demons and Vampires" tracks closely with "Portrait of Death" but contains only one image portraying the creature, not named within the story, attacking a scantily clad female. The *Tower of Shadows* version of "Pickman's Model" (1971) also contains various depictions of paintings and a few of the actual ghoul, but they are not connected in any logical manner.

Exhibit 4. "Pickman's Model" by Brandon Barrows, Hugo Petrus, and Diana Leto. *Mythos: Lovecraft's Worlds*. Used by permission of the artist.

wall of unframed ghoul paintings, again rendered using much softer line work (Exhibit 4). The violence against humans on display in the paintings, as Thurber is shown viewing them as a museum patron in a gallery, direct-ly undermines this conventional relationship of viewer and paintings. These images take a single subject, in this instance the ghoul, and repeat it in space in a way that overwhelms the initial instance, not in an overly mechanical way, but rather one that has divisions among fragments, gain-ing a disruption through the relations of images punctuating the cellar wall. In McCloud's account of such transitions, the focus of this multitude of images is subject-to-subject and it becomes a clear example of spatial montage in stacking simultaneous images within a single panel, in a way similar to "the singular screen that displays multiple images," as Michael Betancourt refers to it in *Beyond Spatial Montage* (55). As Thurber is over-whelmed, so are readers as their gaze turns from one image to the next in order to make sense of the sea of representations, in contrast to the constructed reality of the narrative.

An image on the far right of the multitude of canvases in Barrows and Petrus's adaptation appears to reference a passage from the painting sequence of the story: "Occasionally the things were shewn leaping through open windows at night, or squatting on the chests of sleepers, worrying at their throats" (CF 2.64). In this representation of a painting, a ghoul is depicted hovering over a sleeping individual lying in bed, with the ghoul's arms outstretched. Another in the center right depicts a scene in a forest where ghouls are "in battle over their pretty—or rather, their treasure-trove." Immediately below this scene, a panel offers a close-up of the painting, representing three ghouls consuming a distressed human pressed to the forest floor. Pickman mentions in the panel below that the name of the painting is "Ghouls Feeding," a variation of the title of the initial painting referenced Lovecraft's story. In the next panel, Pickman approaches a painting standing on an easel that is shown at the top of the subsequent page, a close-up of the painting entitled "The Lesson." Here a sequence of juxtaposed images of paintings and the men present in the studio emphasizes interior space against that represented by the paintings, as the artificial images displace those that depict the constructed reality of the narrative.

In much this same way, the *Night Gallery* adaptation generally uses spatial montage to document the numerous compositions existing in parallel in the studio space, while cutting to shots that take the subjective view of the protagonist, emphasizing these works as paintings whereas director Jack Laird uses a subjective shot to depict different modes of experiencing them. The show's resident artist, Tom Wright, produced the paintings featured in this segment, all characterized by Scott Skelton and Jim Benson, authors of the book *Rod Serling's Night Gallery: An After-Hours Tour*, as "dread-inspiring renderings of Pickman's ghoulish, Goya-esque oeuvre" (209). Upon entering Pickman's studio alone, the character Miss Goldsmith alternates between looking at individual canvases and pulling them out from a larger stack to place them on easels. Within this sequence, six paintings generally lack clear division between the past and present sequences, leading the audience to believe that these were made during the Pickman's lifetime. With each movement and new painting displayed by Goldsmith, Laird cuts the scene, creating individual fragments of film devoted to each painting arranged in time through the use of montage. This effect is used to highlight both Goldsmith's act of looking at these paintings through the first-person point of view and her movement and interactions with the paintings through the third-person point of view.

Subject-to-Subject Transitions

Herb Arnold, in his Skull Comics adaptation of "Pickman's Model," differentiates the studio portion of the narrative, using repetition to create a bridge between the format of comic books and an artist's studio gallery. Indeed, for much of the adaptation Arnold aligns his comic panels in a manner that is asymmetrical, with a panel or two always taking up or leaving space in a way to distinguish each page. Not so once Thurber enters Pickman's studio and casts his eyes on the first painting, an adaptation of the passage, "They were sometimes shewn in groups in cemeteries or underground passages, and often appeared to be in battle over their prey" (CF 2.64). Here, as in Petrus's adaptation, Thurber is shown in third person looking at the framed image, sequestered from the rest of the image. As a spatial montage of these two elements, there is a clear distinction between the reality of the story, and the image contained within that reality. In the subsequent panel the frame assumes the entirety of it, and everything beyond this constructed reality is cut out, almost as if it is a subjective view comparable to Laird's shots in his *Night Gallery* adaptation. This second image features a ghoul gnawing at a human slumbering in bed, similar to the passage in the short story.

On the next page, Arnold's novel formatting of panels becomes a distinguishing feature in their staunch regularity. Lovecraft's original text is largely quoted verbatim, and over the course of the next six panels, "The Lesson," the colonial interior, "Subway Accident," a ghoul in a cellar, Beacon Hill, and "Holmes, Lowell, and Longfellow Lie Buried in Mount Auburn" are all represented within this sequence.

This section of the comic mimics the original text, through a scene-to-scene montage, placed largely within a subject-to-subject sequence that loses the painting frames of the previous panels and become separate panels unto themselves. Each panel is essentially a frame, marking a point where the implied medium of paintings is conjoined with the very format of comics. In *Understanding Comics: The Invisible Art*, Scott McCloud indicates that "[c]omics panels fracture both time and space, offering a jagged, staccato rhythm of unconnected moments" (67). As it applies to this sequence, Arnold's representation of Pickman's paintings are used to fracture the events represented from one another in a very symmetrical pattern, a marked departure from the attempted reproduction of Pickman's studio. Indeed, looking at the entirety of the page of painting representations is more visually symmetrical than any other representation of the story examined here.

Photomontage

In Horacio Lalia's version of "Pickman's Model," the painting sequence begins with Pickman lighting a gas lamp, revealing Thurber sitting as he stares at the wall. From here, a large composition extending over the entire page is revealed with elements that do not seem to have clear boundaries. A large tree overwhelms the upper part of this image, while a human face blends with that of a ghoul in the middle of the page, and a cemetery studded with gravestones adorns the bottom. Four paneled images are dispersed among the body of the image, with one featuring ghouls in the ravine next to a field, another with twisted vegetation, with three ghouls facing one another at the bottom of the composition, a giant hole in the ground with seven figures standing at the edge, and finally Martin Van Maele's 1911 illustration of a black mass in the lower right corner.[10]

On the next page, Lalia represents the Gallows Hill painting referenced in Lovecraft's story with a witch hanging from a noose in front of an enlarged moon amidst a circle of howling ghouls. To the right of that panel is one with Thurber looking at a depiction of the colonial family gathered around a father reading from the Bible. At the lower right corner, the image is truncated to make way for a panel depicting a close-up of one of the children gathered at the father's feet, an image that bears a striking resemblance to the Pickman character featured in this particular adaptation.

Finally, at the top of the next page are two horizontally oriented panels, with the uppermost depicting Thurber's face in various stages of duress, and centered between the middle and rightmost depiction are two overlapping paintings of ghouls. The left image depicts a hairy, bearded ghoul stepping on a human's back, while the image on the right depicts a female ghoul appearing to eat a mutilated section of meat. The horizontal panel below best expresses this montage of images, with completely differ-

---

10. Note that witches are referred to on nine occasions in the story.

ent ghouls appearing to be cut out of their original images, overlapping in a way that gives the impression that the panel is a product of photomontage. Photomontage, a practice developed and coined by German artists in the early twentieth century, involves the appropriation of existing images by an artist, their removal from their original context, and their recontextualization in a new composition. The fragments in Lalia's panel clearly combine in a way that privileges the novel assemblage of images that does not reveal a narrative, but rather an excess of abject imagery. The manner by which Lalia rendered it, highlighting each ghoul as a separate piece of the assumed collage, reinforces the notion that the ghoul has been encountered by multiple artists and captured in a distinct manner with each depiction; the result is an image comprising distinct experiences, yet coming together in a way that universalizes the encounter between ghouls and humanity. The implied method of appropriation and synthesis demonstrated here maintains the experience of multiple encounters by reducing it for the audience into a singular image while preserving the distinctions in terms of each image's source.

The Use of Individual Paintings in Adaptations of "Pickman's Model"

The introduction of the ghoul and its continuous presence through a variety of contexts in adaptations of "Pickman's Model" are very much like what Fritz Leiber labeled as "orchestrated prose" (57). The essence of this style of writing is to take an object or location and describe it using slightly different sets of adjectives or wording, or what Leiber referred to as "sentences that are repeated with a constant addition of more potent adjectives, adverbs, and phrases" (57). The result is to grant these objects additional qualities with every new reference and subsequent context. When applied to a visual narrative, which similarly is bound with temporal progression, a time-dependent concept is established within the proceedings of the narrative through citation related to an object or set of objects. The introduction of the painting "Ghoul Feeding" in "Pickman's Model" is similar to what Leiber described as establishing a melody in a song that is later reworked and elaborated upon (57). The continuous citation within the narrative is expressed in the form of paintings that all take the ghoul as subject and depict it in different spatiotemporal contexts, elaborating on the initial theme. In *Night Gallery's* adaptation of the story, the female character, Goldsmith, a student in Pickman's class, refers to these paintings as "a series of canvases." Together with Pickman, she regards them as a "sequence of paintings so horrible that they would turn a man to stone."[11] Considering the many visual adaptations of "Pickman's Model," one finds three common approaches to representing this sequence of paintings.

The first involves an artistic attempt to replicate each painting and photo and its corresponding subject matter. This approach varies on a spectrum that runs from the maximalist approach of Herb Arnold's comic adaptation, which shows more of Pickman's paintings than any other (eleven in all), to Barrows, Petrus, and Leto's four, Horacio Lalia's three, and Laird's and Angeles's two each. Such an approach is faithful to the original text and emphasizes the ghouls' connection with history by the inclusion of the Gallows Hill painting and the passage of ghouls and humans into one another's culture through the "The Lesson" and the Puritan interior. At the same time, there is an emphasis on ghouls trespassing in the colonial past into humanity's territory, as aggressors or predators, and in the story's present day. Overall, it is fairly uncommon for many of these visual adaptations to take such an approach, with a vast majority of them either not adapting them or keeping the adaptations to a minimum. Considering the sheer number of paintings, it is understandable that a comic adaptation, especially within a collection of multiple stories, would need to be more economical in incorporating them in that particular format.

The second approach incorporates paintings in a way that emphasizes a certain parallel narrative or concept. For example, the *Night Gallery* adaptation contains two paintings in Pickman's studio that actually implies mating between ghouls and humans. After the audience is presented with a various paintings depicting the ghoul eating dead bodies in cemeteries, Goldsmith picks up a painting of a ghoul carrying a woman, who is wearing a white dress, through a cemetery. After Goldsmith places the painting

---

11. The "Pickman's Model" sequence of *Night Gallery*, which functions much the same way as the original story, focuses on the horrors of the creatures and their constant efforts to capture women and to mate with them. There is a particular panel that seemingly shows Pickman as a child with his mother. Seen in the shadows behind Pickman is the image of a ghoul, possibly indicating that the creature is the artist's father.

on the floor, she discovers another painting featuring a boy next to his mother, who is wearing the same white dress. Behind the boy, who is likely Pickman himself, is the faded image of a ghoul, implying that the woman in the previous painting is his mother. To emphasize this connection, the director includes a voiceover of Pickman's former recounting of the backstory behind the ghouls: "It became a fanatical obsession, especially those whose womenfolk had disappeared in the dead of night. They believe that these creatures had carried them off to their subterranean dwellings for purposes of procreation." Thus, these two images are clearly attempting to provide a specific backstory to Pickman, rather than a history of the ghoul in New England, and serve less to offer a parallel narrative that has implications on the one in the foreground in that it potentially explains Pickman's origins.

The third approach to incorporating the images from "Pickman's Model" is to render paintings that emphasize a certain grisly and sensationalist aspect. Generally, the paintings described by Lovecraft in "Pickman's Model" involve repeated aggressions by the ghouls against humans, leading to a domination of humanity within the sphere of multiple representations. All the referenced scenes, such as the child learning to consume human flesh in "The Lesson," break social boundaries and as a result, as art theorist Anthony Julius finds of disruptive art, lead to a "panic we can experience when they are transgressed or muddled" (134). Indeed, Thurber states of Pickman: "The fellow must be a relentless enemy of all mankind to take such glee in the torture of brain and flesh and the degradation of the mortal tenement" (CF 2.67). Bruce Kawin, noted scholar in film studies, has stated that "[r]epeated enough, a word or idea or phrase or image or name will come to dominate us to such an extent that our only defenses are to concede its importance or turn off the stimulus completely" (50). This idea of the ghouls' consistent subjugation of humanity, depicted in these scenes, comes to overwhelm the audience through constant repetition within the visual space of Pickman's paintings, which can particularly be seen in Lalia's and the Barrows and Petrus versions. Lalia's version especially contains depictions of multiple paintings beyond references to a few of Lovecraft's original descriptions.

Conclusion

This analysis focused on visual adaptations of the paintings from H. P. Lovecraft's story "Pickman's Model" and the manner in which images can be multiplied in ways that are innovatively suited to the medium in which they are adapted through the use of temporal and spatial montage. The temporal montage afforded by stacking descriptions of paintings one upon the other in the original text allows a similar sequencing of images in time, whereas a spatial montage allows multiple ideas to be expressed simultaneously within a single image. The combination of both methods of montage, at their most disruptive, can further complicate the original without compressing it back to the singular. This survey of adaptations of "Pickman's Model" demonstrates how a story so dependent on its relationship with the visual, when adapted into visual media such as comics and film, can become even more potent in its ability to displace the audience.

In regard to the patterns of montage explored within these adaptations, perhaps it is significant to return to Lovecraft's own theory of how art works on the audience. Elaborating on his views regarding the use of repetition and symmetry, Lovecraft stated:

> art is a very complex matter, with diverse roots drawing upon sources as widely separated as abstract rhythm or symmetry, & certain types of imaginative association which vary with the individual & the civilization. The two extremes are connected, however, by the essential identity of rhythm with repetition—the latter being the crux of the matter of imaginative association. Art must cause certain nerves in the brain to repeat a former pattern. (ES 185–86)

Whether repeated in a temporal sequence or shown simultaneously, the representations of Pickman's art demonstrate a clearly visual interpretation of this theory. Left unexplored is the manner by which such methods are used in new visual media, such as the digital arts. As artists turn toward creating new iterations of "Pickman's Model" in virtual reality and video game versions, such as in *Fall Out 4*, it should prove instructive to see how the paintings' relationships further become complicated.

Works Cited

Al-Rawi, Ahmed. "The Mythical Ghoul in Arabic Culture." *Cultural Analysis* 8 (2009). socrates.berkeley.edu/~caforum/volume8/ vol8_article3. html. Accessed 10 December 2013.

Arnold, Herb. "Pickman's Model." *Skull Comics* No. 4 (May 1972): 25-32.

Barrows, Brandon. "Pickman's Model." In Michael Hudson, ed. *Mythos: Lovecraft's Worlds 1.* Wayne County, MI: Caliber Comics, 2016. 5-16.

Bazin, André. *What Is Cinema? Volume 1.* Berkeley: University of California Press, 1997.

Betancourt, Michael. *Windowing; or, The Cinematic Displacement of Time, Motion, and Space.* New York: Routledge, 2016.

Delano, Jamie. "Pickman's Model." In *The Lovecraft Anthology, Volume II.* New York: Abrams Books, 2012. 9-19.

Franklin, Margery B.; Robert C. Becklen; and Charlotte L. Doyle. "The Influence of Titles on How Paintings Are Seen." *Leonardo* 26 (1993): 103-8.

Holm, Kim. *Pickman's Model.* Bergen, NO: Den Unge Herr Holms Tegnede Tjenester, 2012.

Hutcheon, Linda. *A Theory of Adaptation.* New York: Routledge, 2006.

Joshi, S. T., and David E. Schultz. *An H. P. Lovecraft Encyclopedia.* Westport, CT: Greenwood Press, 2001.

Julius, Anthony. *Transgressions: The Offenses of Art.* Chicago: University of Chicago Press, 2002.

Kawin, Bruce F. *Telling It Again and Again: Repetition in Literature and Film.* Ithaca, NY: Cornell University Press, 1972.

Laird, Jack, dir. "Pickman's Model" by H. P. Lovecraft. Adapt. Alvin Sapinsley. *Night Gallery.* NBC-TV. 1 December 1971.

Lalia, Horacio. "Il Modello di Pickman." 2001. In *Gli Incubi di Lovecraft: Il richiamo di Cthulhu e altri racconti dell'orrore.* Rome: Magic Press Edizioni, 2017.

Leiber, Fritz, Jr. "A Literary Copernicus." 1949. In S. T. Joshi, ed. *H. P. Lovecraft: Four Decades of Criticism.* Athens: Ohio University Press, 1980. 50-62.

Martin, Sean Elliot. *H. P. Lovecraft and the Modernist Grotesque.* n.p.: CreateSpace Independent Publishing Platform. 2008.

McCloud, Scott. *Understanding Comics: The Invisible Art.* New York: HarperPerennial, 1994.

Online Etymology Dictionary. www.etymonline.com/word/montage Accessed 2019.

Palais, Rudy. "Portrait of Death." *Weird Terror* 1, No. 1 (September 1952): 17-23.

Petrus, Hugo; Brandon Barrows; and Diana Leto. "Pickman's Model." In Michael Hudson, ed. *Mythos: Lovecraft's Worlds, Volume 1.* Wayne County, MI: Caliber Comics, 2016. 5-16.

Ryans, Marie-Laure. "Stacks, Frames and Boundaries, or Narrative as Computer Language." *Poetics Today* 11 (Winter 1990): 873-900.

Skelton, Scott, and Jim Benson. *Rod Serling's Night Gallery: An After-Hours Tour.* Syracuse, NY: Syracuse University Press, 1999.

Thomas, Roy. "Pickman's Model." *Tower of Shadows* 1, No. 9 (January 1971): 1-3, 5-7, 10.

Trotter, David. "T. S. Eliot and Cinema." *Modernism/Modernity* 13 (April 2006): 237-65.

Willersley, Rane, and Christian Suhr. "Montage as an Amplifier of Invisibility." In Christian Suhr and Rane Willerslev, ed. *Transcultural Montage.* New York: Berghahn Books, 2013.

Wollen, Peter. "Godard and Counter-Cinema: Vent d'est." *Afterimage* 4 (Autumn 1972). In Philip Rosen, ed. *Narrative, Apparatus, Ideology: A Film Theory Reader.* New York: Columbia University Press, 1986.

Woromay, Larry. "Demons and Vampires." ("Pickman's Model.") *Tales of Voodoo* 3, No. 3 (May 1970): 11-17.

Contributors

Robert Landau Ames is a lecturer in New York University's Global Liberal Studies program. He received his doctorate from Harvard's Department of Near Eastern Languages and Civilizations in May 2018 and specializes in the study of religion and literature in Early Modern and Modern Iran. His articles have appeared in *Comparative Islamic Studies* and *Sufi Studies*. *The Many Faces of Iranian Modernity: Sufism and Subjectivity in the Safavid and Qajar Periods*, his first book, is forthcoming from Gorgias Press.

Antonio Barroso is a high school English teacher in his hometown of Marshall, Michigan. He specializes in early twentieth-century American literature. He obtained his master's degree in Literature from Eastern Michigan University, where he wrote his thesis on the Swift River Valley and its connections to "The Colour out of Space" (available through Digital Commons @ EMU). He is continuing his studies of industrialism's impact on small communities, with a shift in focus from reservoir programs to railroad systems. In addition to academic writing, he has also published short stories, including "Haberdashers and Shoggoths" for Insomnia Press. Barroso is currently preparing a collection of his short stories that he intends to submit for publication.

Michael Bielawa is an award-winning author and historian and is well versed in New England's paranormal heritage. His explorations to northeast America's most mysterious and sacred sites have resulted in numerous books and articles, including *Wicked New Haven* and *Wicked Bridgeport*, which received the first ever New England Paranormal Literary Award. Bielawa's work has appeared in the *Edgar Allan Poe Review*, *Fortean Times*, *FATE Magazine*, *Connecticut Magazine*, the *Christian Science Monitor*, and even in a Major League Baseball's All-Star Game Program. Michael's engaging efforts in actively preserving New England history has been featured in the *New York Times*, the *Washington Post*, and the *Wall Street Journal*.

Laura Loguercio Cánepa received a Ph.D. in Multimedia (Unicamp, Brazil, 2008). Currently, she is professor in the Post-Graduate Programme in Communication at Anhembi Morumbi University (Brazil). She has published several works on Brazilian horror films, including "Erotic Brazilian Movies of Female Killers" in *A Panorama of Brazilian Porn* (2018); "José Mojica Marins versus Coffin Joe: Auteurism and Stardom in Brazilian Cinema" in *Stars and Stardom in Brazilian Cinema* (2017); and "Panorama histórico del horror en el cine brasileño" in *Horrofílmico: Aproximaciones al cine de terror en Latinoamérica y el Caribe* (2012).

Jeremiah Dylan Cook is a horror writer with a Master of Fine Arts in Writing Popular Fiction from Seton Hill University. While attending St. John's University for his undergraduate degree, he received the Mario Mezzacappa Memorial Award for Outstanding Achievement in Poetry and Prose. He is a member of the Horror Writers Association and is the managing editor of *New Pulp Tales*. His story "The House Flipping Find" was featured in Season 14, Episode 8 of *The No Sleep Podcast*, and his story "Lost Vintage" appeared in *Castle of Horror Anthology, Volume 4: Women Running from Houses*.

Benjamin Davis is an independent scholar in Washington, D.C., specializing in Central Asian politics and history. He received his M.S. in Defense and Strategic Studies from Missouri State University and works as an analyst on physical and IT infrastructure.

Cole Donovan is an English instructor in rural south Georgia. A recent graduate of both the University of Georgia and the University of Chicago, he pursues research in early English medieval literature and instances of medievalism in twentieth-century pulp fiction. In addition to his medieval interests, he is also interested more generally in weird fiction and folk horror. As a high school teacher, he has taught courses on British and American literature and medieval philosophy.

Lúcio Reis Filho (Ph.D., University Anhembi Morumbi) is a film critic and historian specializing in the relationships between cinema, history, and literature, with a focus on the horror genre. Addressing the echoes of H. P. Lovecraft in Clive Barker's works, he wrote "Demons to Some, Angels to Others: Eldritch Horrors and Hellbound Religion in the Hellraiser Films," in *Divine Horror: Essays on the Cinematic Battle Between the Sacred and the Diabolical* (McFarland, 2017). His award-winning essay funded by

CAPES (Coordination for the Improvement of Higher Education Personnel, Brazil), "Lovecraft out of Space: Echoes of American Weird Fiction on Brazilian Literature and Cinema," was published in *Lovecraftian Proceedings No. 3*. He has also written several essays on zombies in contemporary Latin American films, published in journals such as the SFRA Review and horror-themed anthologies, and the entry "Cloverfield," in *Aliens in Popular Culture* (Greenwood, 2019). Currently, he investigates the works of Lovecraft and its cinematic adaptations in the late twentieth century.

Kyle Gamache is an adjunct professor and clinician at the Community College of Rhode Island. He is a licensed mental health counselor specializing in severe and persistent mental health issues as well as risk assessment. Kyle holds a master's degree in Forensic Psychology from Roger Williams University and an advanced graduate certificate (CAGS) in mental health counseling from Rhode Island College. He is completing his Ph.D. in Education at the University of Rhode Island. Kyle's research has appeared in the *Applied Journal of Communality College Research* and *Applied Psychology in Criminal Justice*. Kyle is from Rhode Island and has been interested in weird fiction since childhood, voraciously engaging with Lovecraft's works and home city ever since.

Edward Guimont received his Ph.D. in history from the University of Connecticut. His dissertation focused on settler colonialism in Africa and the creation of mythical alternate histories to justify imperialism, using the city of Great Zimbabwe as a case study. His current primary research is on the history of Flat Earth belief in the British Empire, and he teaches as an adjunct professor at the University of Connecticut's Stamford campus. His scholarship has been published in the *Tufts Historical Review*, the *Block Island Times*, *Contingent Magazine*, *Lapsus Lima*, *Dead Reckonings*, *Lovecraftian Proceedings*, *Lovecraft Annual*, and *Quest: The History of Spaceflight*.

Jamer Guterres de Mello earned his Ph.D. in Communication (Federal University of Rio Grande do Sul, Brazil, 2016). He is professor in the Post-Graduate Program in Communication at Anhembi Morumbi University, Brazil, where he develops research on the micropolitical dimensions in contemporary documentary. He has published the book *A(na)arqueologias das Mídias* (2017) and was a member of the production crew of the Cine Esquema Novo Festival in Porto Alegre, Brazil. He is coordinator of the Thematic Seminar Theory of Filmmakers, linked to the Brazilian Society of Cinema and Audiovisual Studies, and author of several articles mainly on the themes of documentary cinema, experimental cinema, aesthetics of communication, visual arts, media archaeologies, digital technologies, and Big Data.

Paul G. Neimann, Ph.D., teaches at the University of Colorado Boulder. His background in eighteenth-century literature informs his interest in the Gothic and weird in book and film. He has taught courses on horror genres, popular culture, and related theory. His research often focuses on Enlightenment and religious toleration, and he has published work on Jonathan Swift. Neimann's essay "Naming the Unnamable: Lovecraft's Return of the Text" appeared in *Lovecraftian Proceedings 3*.

Heather Poirier is a writer/editor living in Washington, D.C. After teaching at the university level for ten years and working at a biomedical research center with a world-class researcher for five years, she moved to Washington and worked as a senior editor at a scientific journal for twelve years. She is writing on two books, one of which explores Lovecraft's relationship to Southern literature, *The King in Yellow*, and the detective in popular culture.

Dennis P. Quinn earned his Ph.D. in Religion at Claremont Graduate University with an emphasis on the history of early Christianity, and is Professor and Chair of the Interdisciplinary General Education Department at Cal Poly Pomona. Dr. Quinn is Chair of the Armitage Symposium, NecronomiCon Providence and has been editor of *Lovecraftian Proceedings* since vol. 2.

Christian Roy (Ph.D., McGill, 1993), based in Montreal, is an independent scholar in intellectual history by calling, a multilingual freelance translator by trade, and an art and film critic. He has written numerous papers, articles, book chapters, and dictionary entries on twentieth-century thought (many available at roychristian.academia.edu), including for NecronomiCon Providence since 2015, exploring parallels between H. P. Lovecraft and Georges Bataille. He is working on a book about the latter's connections to Bernard Charbonneau, an overlooked existential thinker he has recently been trying to introduce to the Anglosphere; e.g., by translating his *The Green Light: A Self-Critique of the Ecological Movement* in 2018 for Bloomsbury, the publisher of a forthcoming book on post-humanism on science fiction cinema to which Roy contributed an analysis of *Annihilation*. Since 2007, he has been co-curating a film-based psychoanalytic seminar on the historical anthropology of modern culture. Roy is also the author of *Traditional Festivals: A Multicultural Encyclopedia* (ABC-Clio, 2005), sampling rituals and folklore from all continents and periods. He contributes to the blog TheSymbolicWorld.com. Roy is finishing the first of several planned photo books illustrating Lovecraft's travel writings, starting with one about his native Quebec City.

Thomas Schwaiger received a master's degree and a Ph.D. from the University of Graz, Austria, where he is working as a post-doctoral researcher at the Institute of Linguistics. Next to his teaching of courses in core linguistic areas such as morphology, syntax, and semantics, and his ongoing research on grammatical topics such as reduplication, serial verbs, and the theory of Functional Discourse Grammar, he is also involved in a historiographic project dedicated to the life and work of the eminent linguist Hugo Schuchardt (a voluminous letter-writer not unlike H. P. Lovecraft). While he has worked on cross-linguistic aspects of human grammar and the history of linguistics with scholarly articles in pertinent journals, handbooks, and edited collections, the contribution in the present volume is his first Lovecraftian publication.

Elena Tchougounova-Paulson obtained her Ph.D. at the Department of Theory and Methodology of Philology and Art (A.M., Gorky Institute of World Literature, Russian Academy of Science, Moscow). Her degree is in twentieth-century Russian literature, dedicated to the theoretical analysis of Russian Symbolist poet Alexander Blok's poetry and prose. She has worked as Head of the Communications Department and later as a Research Fellow and publisher at the Research Information Centre at the Russian State Archive of Literature and Art, Moscow. As a textual scholar and translator, she took part in several editorial projects, such as: *Alexander Blok–L. D. Mendeleeva-Blok: Correspondence (1901–1917)* (IMLI RAN, 2017). Dr. Tchougounova-Paulson is an independent researcher, resident in Cambridge, who takes part in various literary projects and translations. As a scholar of Lovecraftian studies, she took part in some related academic events (conferences and workshops).

Nathaniel R. Wallace is an independent scholar living with his wife, son, and two very spoiled cats in Athens, Ohio. He received his Ph.D. from Ohio University's Interdisciplinary Arts program in 2014 and wrote his dissertation *H. P. Lovecraft's Literary "Supernatural Horror" in Visual Culture* on visual adaptations of the author's work. Nathaniel has appeared at the Armitage Symposium at the NecronomiCon for the past three events and previously contributed essays to *Lovecraftian Proceedings* 2 and 3.

Appendix: Abstracts from the Fourth Biennial Dr. Henry Armitage Memorial Scholarship Symposium of New Weird Fiction and Lovecraft-Related Research, Providence, RI, 23–25 August 2019

Dennis P. Quinn, Chair
Cal Poly Pomona

The Dr. Henry Armitage Memorial Symposium aims to foster exploration of Lovecraft's elaborate cosmic mythology and how that mythology was influenced by, and has come to influence, numerous other authors and artists before and since. The Lovecraft Arts & Sciences Council (which established NecronomiCon Providence) organizes the symposium of new academic work to explore all aspects of the writings and life of H. P. Lovecraft, including the influence of history, architecture, science, and popular culture on his works, and the impact he has had on culture. The Armitage Symposium consists of the latest cutting-edge research on Lovecraft, topics related to Lovecraft, and his circle.

Robert Landau Ames
Independent Scholar
"Żaḥḥāk Beside Cthulhu: Philosophizing with Monsters in
Persian Mythology and American Horror"

This paper applies the terms in which recent exponents of speculative realist tendencies in (post-)continental philosophy have analyzed horror and monstrosity to the study of classical Persian literature. Just as Graham Harman adopted Lovecraft as the poet laureate of his philosophical project (*Weird Realism*, per the title of his book of 2012), this paper asks what positions might result from a similar attempt to philosophize with Żaḥḥāk, the serpent-shouldered king who features prominently in the Iranian national epic, the *Shāhnāmah* (*Book of Kings*) of Firdawsī (d. 1019 or 1025), rather than Cthulhu. As the *Shāhnāmah* tells the myth, Żaḥḥāk is an Arab prince whom the devil convinces to commit patricide, invade and conquer Iran, and kill its king (Jamshīd). Following Żaḥḥāk's conquest of Iran, the devil appears again and kisses Żaḥḥāk's shoulders. After the kiss, a voraciously hungry serpent grows from gus Żaḥḥāk's shoulders, and he rules over Iran for a millennium, attempting to sate the snakes' hunger by feeding them the brains of Iranian youths. A rebellion led by the blacksmith Kāvah eventually overthrows Żaḥḥāk and restores a native Iranian, Faraydūn, to the throne. Most interpretations of this myth tend to focus on its apparent nationalist dimensions by dwelling on Żaḥḥāk's role as a tyrannical foreign king, but I aim to use Żaḥḥāk's monstrosity, and not his Arab origins, as the basis for my analysis. Applying the method Harman uses with Lovecraft (a close reading of the primary source's specific descriptive language) does not necessarily imply the same philosophical priorities. Although Harman's Cthulhu points to an ontological project, I argue that Żaḥḥāk ultimately points to an ethical one.

Lars G. Backstrom
Independent Scholar
"In Search of the Lost Kitab *Al Azif*"

According to H. P. Lovecraft, Abdul Alhazred, the mad poet of Sanaá, wrote the *Necronomicon* (under the title *Al Azif*) in Arabic in the years before 738 C.E. in Damascus. At the time, Damascus was an economic hub, important religious center, and capital of the Second (Umayyad) Caliphate. The caliphate was vast, stretching from Morocco and Portugal in the west to China's T'ang Dynasty in the Transoxiana region in the east, but in 750 it was replaced by the Abbasid Caliphate. This began an extremely dynamic period in world history as the Abbasid Caliphs ordered the translation of books of knowledge into Arabic, the Far East entered a Golden Age under the T'ang Emperors, and the Byzantine Empire revived intellectually and culturally after the great iconoclasm. It was during this revival that in 950 Alhazred's work was translated into Greek and given the name of *Necronomicon*. Many years later, around the time Olaus Wormius translated the text into Latin in the early thirteenth century, the Arabic original was lost, according to the "History of the 'Necronomicon'"

(1927). Or was it? Could it not be so that this most dreaded tome still exists? In the first part of my presentation, I give a very brief overview of the world of the *Al Azif* between the eighth and the thirteenth centuries C.E. In the second part, I carry out a literary critical analysis of "History of the 'Necronomicon'" to show that it cannot be treated as a reliable source, nor does it tell the complete history of the *Necronomicon*. Based on this I present a number of locations, some quite surprising, where intrepid, foolish, or just plain unlucky investigators might find a copy of this abominable work.

Antonio Barroso
Independent Scholar
"Fear and (Non)Fiction: Agrarian Anxiety in
'The Colour out of Space'"

This literary and sociological study examines H. P. Lovecraft's "The Colour out of Space" alongside New England agricultural societies in the late nineteenth and early twentieth centuries as their members faced sociopolitical change. Anxieties expressed in the story reflect fears of communities facing change at the hands of a reservoir project. Lovecraft's status as a literary reactionary is on full display in this short story, as his activities with historical conservation and his travels along New England made him acutely aware of this problem. One community in particular, the Swift River Valley, caught Lovecraft's attention, as it was facing not merely change but complete erasure. Though the region was once a promising agricultural community, nearby metropolitan expansion and industrial progress doomed the towns of Dana, Enfield, Greenwich, and Prescott. Boston's need for water necessitated the construction of the Quabbin Reservoir, which would displace the people of the valley, destroy their homes, and irreversibly alter their culture. The particular strain of fear that Lovecraft addresses in "The Colour out of Space" can be found when reading newsletters, interviews, and essays describing the plight of the denizens of the Swift River Valley. By analyzing the story together with a culture that experienced this kind of fear, we can discover how the Swift River Valley's fate inspired Lovecraft to write a tale that resonates with many cultures similarly menaced by forces beyond their control. Patterns of historical American rural communities facing destruction in the name of progress as well as modern communities facing similar threats show the endurance of Lovecraft's specific brand of fear.

Michael J. Bielawa
The Barnum Museum, Bridgeport, Connecticut
"American Frankensteins: The Magnificent Nightmare
of Dr. Porter and Prof. Poe and Their Attempts to Reanimate
the Dead in Victorian New England"

H. P. Lovecraft's name has long embraced a shuddering association with the ghoulish imagery of reanimation. Rightfully so. What acolytes of the horror master may not realize is that the midnight exploits of Lovecraft's fictional reanimator, Herbert West, have a very real foundation in bizarre research conducted in nineteenth-century New England. Well before Herbert West's, or even Victor Frankenstein's, undead monstrosities took to menacing the countryside, scientifically trained individuals had been dabbling with electricity and dead things. Following an overview of the origins of galvanism in late eighteenth- and early nineteenth-century Europe, this presentation provides an in-depth look at the lives and experiments of Dr. George Loring Porter and Prof. George Poe. Though largely forgotten, reanimation experiments were conducted by these extraordinary Victorian gentlemen while they resided on the shores of Long Island Sound. George Poe actually succeeded in raising deceased animals while George Porter focused his attentions solely on reanimating a human being. But an even more astounding story arises when pondering how Porter and Poe, so preoccupied with the mechanisms of reviving the newly dead, somehow simultaneously arrived in Bridgeport, Connecticut. Were Porter and Poe on a clandestine mission to convert this New England city into a realm for the reanimated? Murder trials, the morbid task of securing corpses, and strange experimentations in front of terrified audiences all swirl around the lurid tale of Porter and Poe, the American Frankensteins who attempted to reanimate the dead in Victorian New England. This true-life adventure would certainly shock Herbert West's own pulse to pound all the faster.

Cole Donovan
Independent Scholar
"Mad Poets and Howling Daemons: The Anglo-Saxon and
Nordic Ancestry of Lovecraft's Grimoires"

Foundational to Lovecraft's core mythology is the fictional grimoire the *Necronomicon*. Though the content of the text remains largely obscure in Lovecraft's own work, its nature is clear: it is an account written by a "mad Arab" of dark and hidden forces that lie just beyond the horizons of understanding and the grasp of sanity. As a literary invention, the *Necronomicon* is a unique and powerful unifying device for Lovecraft's mythos; however, despite its seemingly singular nature, it has clear roots in reality. Taking a cue from Lovecraft's essay "Supernatural Horror in Literature," in which he describes the Anglo-Saxon epic *Beowulf* as a text "full of eldritch weirdness," my research looks carefully at the weirdness, both literary and cultural, of the early medieval period as a means of understanding Lovecraft's own fictional texts. My research seeks to orient Lovecraft's work within a larger cultural tapestry that, for the purposes of this project, begins with some of the very earliest texts of the European Middle Ages. Drawing parallels between the fractured and often self-contradictory world of the Norse and Anglo-Saxon peoples with that of the American Modernists, I critically compare the mythos with both literary and quasi-scientific sources including *Beowulf* and *The Wonders of the East* respectively. Drawing on contemporary Lovecraft research, I identify links between the Christian/Pagan dissonance of early England with that of the Pentecostal/Scientific dissonance of Modernist America and the Orientalism that pervades Lovecraft's fiction and medieval texts alike. I conclude that despite Lovecraft's seemingly radical departure from the Gothic and supernatural fiction that immediately preceded him, his understanding and use of the "weird" is not exclusively a twentieth-century phenomenon and has a tangible heritage in medieval literature.

Philip Chang
University of Colorado Boulder
"The Farnese Settings of 'Mirage' and 'The Elder Pharos'"

After receiving Lovecraft's permission in July 1932, Harold S. Farnese composed musical settings for the sonnets "Mirage" and "The Elder Pharos" from *Fungi from Yuggoth*. In a letter to Elizabeth Toldridge of August 1932, Lovecraft wondered what Farnese might do "in a musical way, with my fantastic images." Over the decades, Kenneth Faig, Jr., James Wade, and S. T. Joshi have addressed partial reproductions of the music. Recordings of the songs were released for the first time in 2015 by publisher Fedogan & Bremer, and in 2017 the complete scores became more available in *The Annotated Fungi from Yuggoth*, edited by David E. Schultz. We can now address Lovecraft's curiosity and more fully examine the songs' text/music relations, a longstanding practice in music theory and musicology. According to August Derleth, Farnese's perspective was to create a musical atmosphere to "exude" the "fragrance" of Lovecraft's poetry. This audiovisual presentation shows how Farnese's compositional strategies, from the immediately hearable to more long-range subtleties, illustrate or enhance the meaning of Lovecraft's lines. In addition, we can see that the songs are not, per Wade, entirely "inept" and "sub-professional." Indeed, the texts seemed to have determined a marked musical contrast: "Mirage," which hearkens back to Romantic *Sehnsucht*, demonstrates fairly conventional compositional practice, whereas the bizarre imagery of "The Elder Pharos" provokes modal chords, unusual key relations and harmonic shifts, and whole-tone scale ambiguity.

Jeremiah Dylan Cook
Independent Scholar
"The Shadow over Horror Tropes: An Analysis of the
Blighted Location Trope Pioneered by H. P. Lovecraft"

Horror is a genre of tropes. There are haunted houses, dark forests, clowns, creepy gas station attendants, and countless more. H. P. Lovecraft contributed a vast number of tropes to popular horror fiction. One that is particularly interesting but seldom discussed is the blighted location trope. In this trope a protagonist visits a location, such as a town, city, or even a space station, only to discover the inhabitants are hiding a dark secret, and the discovery of that secret puts the protagonist in mortal danger. While endeavoring to prove that Lovecraft's "The Shadow over Innsmouth" pioneered the blighted location trope that runs through popular culture today, I analyze the trope from its birth to modernity. My research delves into Lovecraft's seminal "Supernatural Horror in Literature," Nathaniel Hawthorne's classic "Young Goodman Brown," and of course a textual analysis of "The Shadow over Innsmouth." When my studies move closer to current popular culture, I examine the blighted location trope's impact on James Cameron's *Aliens* and Capcom's *Resident Evil* franchise. In addition to these works, I delve into traditional academic books and essays dissecting Lovecraft's fiction. I believe this research illustrates that Lovecraft's influence on horror tropes is even greater than many realize. Casual fans of Lovecraft, horror writers, and academics may find this topic interesting as it blends literary analysis with popular culture. I hope this subject encourages other fans and scholars to continue expanding this line of research to illuminate the many ways Lovecraft's imagination inspired a diverse array of tales across every form of entertainment media.

Anthony Conrad Chieffalo
Independent Scholar
"Sword-&-Sorcery, Gender-&-Genre: Non-Binary Heroism of
C. L. Moore's Jirel of Joiry"

Catherine Lucille Moore, better known as C. L. Moore, created the first female sword-and-sorcery hero in Jirel of Joiry. "The Black God's Kiss" (1934) presents Jirel's journey through a hellscape of hyperbolic contrast constituting a metaphor for twentieth-century gender binarism. The tale features a revenge plot centered on a patronizing villain. Jirel's quest takes her through a vibrant setting capitalizing on Moore's motif of brightness and darkness. Moore's metaphor for twentieth-century gender binarism presents a world of incessant conflict due to conventional conceptions of gendered identity and heteronormativity. Moore's sword-and-sorcery inscribes a figure of heroism upon the consciousness of her readers transcending phallocentric precedents of the genre. Revolutionary perspectives on masculinity and femininity have been addressed in American pulp fiction since the 1930s, but these texts are rarely read as transcending gender binary. They are rarely read as challenging patriarchy and sexism. However, Moore's tales of Jirel of Joiry combat exploitation and oppression while envisioning a form of heroism regardless of sex or gender. Her fiction constructs a poignant critique of heteronormative notions of "masculinity" and "femininity" predating cultural critic and theorist Judith Butler and her seminal work Gender Trouble (1990). The Jirel of Joiry series stemming from "The Black God's Kiss" challenges rigid notions of representation and identity while positing gender as both socially constructed and performative in nature. C. L. Moore's sword-and-sorcery forms a feminist critique of normative heroism and an evolution of the subgenre into one disrupting social prerogative. Rather than phallocentric heroism or even gynocentric heroism, Jirel of Joiry is a manifestation of non-binary heroism born from literature that challenges systemically imposed and policed gender binary.

Benjamin Davis
Independent Scholar
"The Influence of The Great Game on the Writings of
H. P. Lovecraft: From Tibet to the Mountains of Madness"

In numerous letters H. P. Lovecraft wrote about his love and use of geography and architecture in his works. The modern exploration of Tibet, especially its geography and architecture, provided indirect and direct influences on Lovecraft. It began with the closing of Tibet to outsiders in 1792, sparking a desire to explore and encounter the unknown. In the mid-nineteenth century, at the height of "The Great Game" between Imperial Russia and the British Empire, explorers from both countries raced to be the first to explore, map, and possibly claim Tibet. Stirred by initial reports from Tibet, private citizens across Europe and America became determined to be the first Westerners to reach the capital, Lhasa. The extreme lengths required to access such a remote and inhospitable place, along with the Tibetan's overly polite methods of turning away travelers, only fueled the desire. All these stories drove speculation and excitement, providing ample material for newspapers, books, and paintings. Weird tales began to emerge from Tibet, from the true (the seemingly cannibalistic drinking from skulls and sky burials) to the false (flying monks). Though the Treaty of Lhasa in 1904 opened Tibet to the world, it continued to inspire the imagination of artists and authors. Some of these include Alexandra David-Néel, whose book *Magic and Mystery in Tibet* inspired ideas Lovecraft recorded in his commonplace book. Nicholas Roerich's strange paintings of "forbidden and half-fabulous" Tibet directly inspired Lovecraft. Ruled by a god-king and isolated for decades, Tibet became a place of speculation and mystery, and for Lovecraft possibly a place harboring forbidden knowledge. The wild and rugged geography, lore, and architecture influenced Lovecraft's use of setting and scenery in *At the Mountains of Madness* and the Plateau of Leng.

Ian Fetters
Robert E. Kennedy Library, San Luis Obispo
"Icy Portents of Doom: Clark Ashton Smith's Hyperborean Cycle
and the Polar Myth"

Clark Ashton Smith's Hyperborean Cycle, a thematic collection of prose tales set on the northernmost continent of Earth in the earliest days of mankind, is considered a lesser myth cycle in the poet's prolific catalogue. Smith scholars tend toward the consensus that the Hyperborean tales are at best a mixed bag of sardonic prose and poetry fragments that are more amusing than vital—a minor speed bump on the road to Averoigne and Zothique. Yet this critical diagnosis ignores a crucial element of the cycle: the Arctic setting of the Hyperborean continent. And beyond setting, the cycle's "Arctic-ness"—the collective sense of space, time, and historical and mythological context of the far North—has the potential to illuminate a greater significance for the Hyperborean tales in Smith's oeuvre. To fully understand this new context, one must delve into the foundational myths and apocryphal histories of the Arctic region, defined here collectively as the Polar Myth, in an effort to reimagine the cycle not as a lesser work but a new centerpiece of the rich and long-standing tradition of Arctic myth in literature. With the help of archival materials from the Bancroft Library's Clark Ashton Smith collection, this paper employs textual analysis and close reading of Hyperborean Cycle manuscripts, as well as Smith's personal correspondence, to peer into the writer's creative mindset. Analysis of "The Coming of the White Worm" and the mythopoetic fragment "Ultima Thule" reveals Smith's obsession with the interdependent motifs of coldness and doomed civilizations that recur across the cycle. Contextualizing these motifs against the backdrop of the Polar Myth imparts a new characterization on the Hyperborean Cycle and its "Arctic-ness" that bridges the gaps between myth, history, and fiction.

Shawn Gaffney
Suffolk County Community College
"Hideous Writing Systems in Lovecraft Country"

Lovecraft and his contemporaries regularly refer to sources of obscure knowledge in the form of ancient books, manuscripts, and tablets in Latin, Greek, Arabic, Coptic, and also R'lyehian, Aklo, Tsath-yoan, and Naacal. These languages were written in the Roman, Greek, Arabic, and Coptic scripts, as well as R'lyehian and Naacal hieroglyphs. Several other stories reference writing, including an alphabet in "The Nameless City," the "cryptic writing" in "The Call of Cthulhu," the hieroglyphs in the library in "The Shadow out of Time," and the elaborate historical record depicted visually in At the Mountains of Madness. Numerous authors and illustrators have used these texts, languages, and orthographies in their own works as well as creating new systems. Though connected to Lovecraft's original works these new pieces often reflect the changing understanding of his works, as well as evolving ideas regarding Lovecraftian imagery, relationships, and languages. Many of the newly invented systems show similarities, sometimes related to the descriptions that Lovecraft gave but also because the media of writing and visual communication have their own limitations. Additional imagery from grimoires, television, and video games, as well as the constructed-language community, appear to influence much of the art. This paper examines some of the newer imagery and hieroglyphs, attempts to connect them, when possible, to previous works, and discusses the divisions between Lovecraft's descriptions and the adapted works. I identify some of the less explored areas, and those areas that have various overlapping interpretations, including insight from the artists. The goal is to examine the expanding nature of the visual elements of "cosmic horror" and its ability to work inclusively, bringing in new interpretations and understandings of how to represent the weird, and how to communicate the uncommunicable.

Kyle Gamache
Community College of Rhode Island
"Ebb of Sanity: 'The Night Ocean' and Bipolar Disorder"

H. P. Lovecraft and R. H. Barlow's collaborative work "The Night Ocean" is one of the more poignant and atmospheric pieces in early weird fiction. It is a simple piece about an artist spending a lonely, late summer in a small seaside town. Compared to other works, there are limited supernatural occurrences, but the weird world is alluded to peripherally. The strength of the story is in its subtlety and milieu. The premise of this paper is to explore a deeper meaning present within the story. The tale of the artist exploring the town can be seen as a metaphor for bipolar disorder. Mental illness perseverated in Lovecraft's life and fiction, and it would not be surprising if mental illness were a theme in "The Night Ocean." The cluster of bipolar disorders share similar symptomology: the presence of depressive states, with spikes of elevated manic episodes. This ebb and flow is explored directly in the piece with great attention placed on the passing of the tides and seasons within the setting. The nameless narrator also describes frenzied activity followed by melancholy and disinterest, common staples of bipolar disorder. The limited supernatural experiences in the piece are indirect and murky, possibly able to be explained by paranoid delusion and brief hallucination. The paper presents an overview of the story, and argue that the symptoms of bipolar disorder are present within the mood and action of the piece, intending to show that "The Night Ocean" is more about bipolar disorder than cosmic entities.

Edward Guimont
Independent Scholar
"The *Necronomicon Yalensis* and Lovecraft in Connecticut"

At the 1990 H. P. Lovecraft Centennial Conference, Will Murray noted that in Lovecraft Country, "all the great fictitious cities are in Massachusetts . . . certainly not Connecticut—I don't think Lovecraft ever wrote of Connecticut." This presentation refutes that assertion, integrating Connecticut back into the New England of Lovecraft Country alongside Massachusetts, Rhode Island, and Vermont. When Connecticut is mentioned in relation to Lovecraft, it is typically done in one of three ways: the influence on legends from the town of East Haddam on "The Dunwich Horror"; Hartford being the final meeting place for Lovecraft and his wife Sonia Greene; and the possibility that one of several Connecticut rivers was the inspiration for the Miskatonic. This paper explores the extent of Lovecraft's exploration of Connecticut and his friends (and distant family) who resided there, and take a position in the river debate in favor of the Connecticut River, while then primarily making four arguments. First, the Arkham Sanitarium of several of Lovecraft's stories, and the wider pastiche Mythos, may have been inspired by two Connecticut hospitals he became aware of in his travels. Second, Lovecraft may have drawn inspiration from Connecticut megaliths or that Miskatonic University was inspired by Yale have no merit; but that Yale does have a subtler influence. Third, in *At the Mountains of Madness*, both Professor Pabodie and the discovery of the fossilized Old Ones have Connecticut links. And finally, a number of legends specific to southwestern Connecticut have parallels to elements from "The White Ship," "The Outsider," "The Shunned House," and "The Shadow over Innsmouth," indicating that Lovecraft may have at least partially drawn influence for those stories from the Connecticut legends, just as it is widely accepted that he did for "The Dunwich Horror."

Daniel J. Holmes
Independent Scholar
"The Shadow Over Cyrodil: Elder Things and *The Elder Scrolls*"

One of the more engaging topics at the intersection of religious studies and the digital humanities is what theorist Robert Geraci has termed the "virtually sacred," or the incorporation of mythological and spiritual themes in video games (and especially in fantasy role-playing games). The advent of electronic entertainment media has created a participatory mode of mythic storytelling, allowing players to immerse themselves in supernatural and fantastic narratives. An especially exciting (and so far entirely unexplored) expression of this phenomenon can be found in the wide variety of games to draw upon H. P. Lovecraft's Cthulhu Mythos—a catalogue of titles stretching from "Alone in the Dark" (1992)—often considered the first survival horror game—to the electronic adaptation of the classic *Call of Cthulhu* tabletop RPG. This paper seeks to open a new discussion on Lovecraftian gaming by adapting the concept of the virtually sacred to explore Cthulhoid influences on the popular Elder Scrolls series of RPGs, published by Bethesda Softworks. The lore of the Elder Scrolls games is heavily influenced by Lovecraft (a debt openly acknowledged by designer Todd Howard in a discussion regarding the "Dragonborn" expansion to "The Elder Scrolls V: Skyrim," which features a tentacled, entirely amoral elder god whose holy text—bound in human flesh, of course—drives readers mad with forbidden knowledge). Although this paper touches upon the entire Elder Scrolls series, its particular focus is be "The Elder Scrolls III: Morrowind" (2003). This title not only incorporates aesthetic elements of Lovecraft's work, it also directly reflects upon the metaphysical tension between materialism and supernature that underpins the entire Cthulhu Mythos—thereby providing an especially dynamic case study in how the "virtually sacred" can offer players a sense of mythic participation entirely distinct from literary narratives.

Ray Huling
Independent Scholar
"Lovecraftian Georgics: Horror, Disgust, and the
Ecology of Agriculture"

The most dire threats of our times are environmental, and the most dire environmental threat lies in farming. A Lovecraftian sensibility, attuned to the horror and disgust that ecological knowledge should evoke, has an important role to play in practical responses to these threats, especially with regard to those found in agriculture. Ecologically minded thinkers have confronted environmental catastrophe in a Lovecraftian mode: Eugene Thacker and Ben Woodard have done so straightforwardly; Donna Haraway has done it coyly. John Michael Greer has addressed environmentalism in a series of Mythos novels. All these authors have applied Lovecraft to ecology generally. This paper considers a particular case, that of agriculture, and, even more particularly, William Vogt's work on guano. In 1948, Vogt's book *The Road to Survival* was a sensation, a bestselling environmentalist screed that decried material growth and inspired action at all levels of governance. The intensity of his warning came from his experiences researching Guanay cormorants for a Peruvian guano company. From 1938 to 1941, Vogt lived in a hut on a guano island, to discover how to improve this crucial agricultural resource. There, he witnessed the abandonment of millions of Guanay chicks by adults whose fishing grounds had been depleted by El Niño. He recorded their starvation and analogized their circumstances with humanity's. He knew the horrible and disgusting truth of how his civilization fed itself. Horror and disgust aroused by science form the emotional core of Vogt's work, and, alongside hope, these feelings should lie at the heart of all efforts to make agriculture sustainable—once we refine our sense of them by reflection on the work of one of their most sensitive connoisseurs. Lovecraft's infamously stunted emotional range nicely plugs the hole left by an equally stunted ecological optimism. This paper argues that Lovecraft's fixations can play a crucial role in developing the emotional wholeness necessary for realistic environmental action.

Karen Joan Kohoutek
Independent Scholar
"'An Almost Unparalleled Influence':
Horace Walpole through a Lovecraftian Lens"

This essay looks at the pioneering work of Horace Walpole (1717–1797), generally acknowledged as the founder of Gothic literature, by way of the critical perspective given by H. P. Lovecraft in his essay "Supernatural Horror in Literature" (1925–27; revised 1933–35), and explore the common threads between the two writers. Informed by, but diverging from, Edith Birkhead's less well-known *The Tale of Terror* (1921), Lovecraft's analysis was for many years one of the few significant works on the Gothic that were readily available to scholars. He filters his overview of the Walpole's eccentric writing through his own highly personal ideas about cosmic horror, acknowledging Walpole's immense significance within the genre, at the same time deeming his work "tedious, artificial, and melodramatic" and full of "intrinsic ineptness." Despite their differences in style and intent, and a distance of two centuries, the writers have a surprising amount in common: antiquarians interested in past times and archaic architecture, they both followed their idiosyncratic tastes, with a sense of confidence in their aesthetic beliefs. Significantly, both also attempted to free themselves, in actuality or at least conceptually, from the inhibiting constraints of the marketplace. This was easier for Walpole, an independently wealthy nobleman of leisure with his own printing press, but Lovecraft's efforts in small-scale self-publishing, and the important role of amateur journalism in the development of his art and professional career, point in a similar direction, which led them to write weird fiction that would exert "an almost unparalleled influence" on the genre.

James C. Lethbridge
Independent Scholar
"A Realism so Hideous:
Reflections of Heidegger in H. P. Lovecraft"

This essay employs the phenomenology of Martin Heidegger, particularly his conception of Being and truth as found in *Introduction to Metaphysics*, to construct a three-part framework for interpreting the horror fiction of H. P. Lovecraft. Drawing on Heidegger's distinctions between Being and otherness, truth and appearance, and grounding and concealment, I construct three phenomenological/literary lenses or moods by which Lovecraft's horror fiction can be interpreted. The first of these, which I term "the deception of appearance," involves the crucial difference in Heidegger between Being and seeming/appearance, under which distinction human beings are often liable to error owing to failures do appreciate the ways in which the appearances of Being can color our conception of its truth. The second, "uncovering the deception," relates to Heidegger's conception of both rational inquiry as "unconcealment" or a clearing away of false appearances, and human beings' natural and insatiable drive to do so. The third and final lens I term "the horror of truth," which involves the often shocking results of clearing away false appearances and observer biases, and the horror of confronting the truth of Being. Having reconstructed these three aspects of Heideggerian phenomenology, I then apply them to Lovecraft's stories "The Call of Cthulhu" and *At the Mountains of Madness*, interpreting them as following a similar literary structure, including a process of passing through each of the three Heideggerian moods. The paper closes with some suggestions regarding how this interpretative framework can be applied to a large portion of Lovecraft's horror corpus, and offers some conjecture as to how these three lenses might be strengthened and refined to create a strong critical tool for Lovecraftian literary analysis.

Jennifer Loring
Seton Hill University
"Eldritch Calling: Examining the Influence
of Cosmicism on Black Metal"

Black metal is a genre of extreme heavy metal characterized by its ideology, primarily in terms of anti-religion and trenchant misanthropy, almost as much as its musical style. It comes as little surprise, then, that the themes of human insignificance prevalent in cosmicism resonate with many black metal artists. These artists often engage with not only cosmic horror and the weird in general but with Lovecraft's work in particular. Bands such as Obed Marsh, Crafteon, and The Great Old Ones, for example, have constructed their entire raison d'être around Lovecraft's original characters and locations. Lovecraft famously stated that "The oldest and strongest emotion of mankind is fear, and the oldest and strongest kind of fear is fear of the unknown." Cosmic horror, in short, uses the unknowable to create a pervasive sense of fear, particularly that of humanity's meaninglessness on a universal scale. As Thomas Ligotti explains, Lovecraft insisted that "[I]n the case of weird art the emphasis must fall upon ... *the mood of intense and fruitless human aspiration typified by pretended overturning of cosmic laws and the pretended transcending of possible human experience.*" Thus, lacking characters the reader can relate to or care about, the weird tale by Lovecraft's definition must rely on atmosphere, and here too we find a corollary in black metal, which among its other essential characteristics emphasizes atmosphere. That atmosphere is usually cold, bleak, and in the language of music and lyrics, conveys the same sense of cosmic hopelessness.

Fred S. Lubnow
Independent Scholar
"The Lackey/Fifer Hypothesis: The Weakness of the Old Ones"

Many entities described by H. P. Lovecraft were originally regarded as gods but over time, as his tales became more ingrained in science rather than the supernatural, the entities were more appropriately described as aliens. Initially these extraterrestrial or extradimensional beings were thought to have incredible powers, manipulating energy, matter, and even time. Critical review of Lovecraft's stories reveals that in spite of being extremely powerful, some Lovecraftian entities can be considered weak in some capacity, particularly entities not endemic to our universe.

The H. P. Lovecraft Literary Podcast, created in 2009 by Chris Lackey and Chad Fifer, has been reviewing Lovecraft's work and other weird fiction for a decade. When it began, it reviewed all Lovecraft's work in sequential order. Reviewing Lovecraft's fiction in this young media format has identified an interesting pattern in Lovecraftian entities. That is, those that are not native to our universe can be easily defeated. Examples include the death of Wilbur Whateley and some members of the Mi-Go, both as a result of dog attacks, the destruction of Cthulhu by a ship, and the dissipation of the flying polyps through electrical discharge. Using information outlined in the H. P. Lovecraft Literary Podcast, this paper presents the pattern of powerful extradimensional entities being easily destroyed in our universe. It also presents possible explanations for this seemingly contradictory situation of powerful entities that can be easily defeated.

Tonya Maynard
Independent Scholar
"Phantom Normalcy: The Threat of Discreditable Social Stigma
in the Works of H. P. Lovecraft"

What horrors are lying in wait just past the threshold of social acceptance? In this paper, I endeavor to connect the depictions of the insane and asylums in the works of Howard Phillips Lovecraft with theories of stigma and identity in the social constructionist school of thought. Erving

Goffman's *Asylums* (1961) and *Stigma* (1963) put forth the most in-depth analyses of social stigma and spoiled identity seen in sociology or any social science at the time. By looking to the ways in which many characters in the works of H. P. Lovecraft are depicted in their disturbing and fascinating descents into madness, we can understand better how the social foundation of interpersonal contact and identity management served to inspire terror in Lovecraft's time, as well as in Goffman's, and still now in our own. Beginning with an overview of Goffman's theories on stigma and insanity, my piece continues with a brief survey of Kirkbride asylums and their powerful impression on the mind of the American public (Lovecraft himself included), and finishes with an application of Goffman's theoretical framework to characters from "The Call of Cthulhu," "Pickman's Model," "The Outsider," and "The Shadow over Innsmouth," among other works. "Pickman's Model" in particular explicitly equates madness with a lack of humanity—something Goffman considered a social truth and often acknowledged in his discussion of those attempting to manage a hidden, or discreditable, stigmatized identity. Where do we find ourselves when the veneer of sanity has been socially stripped and our madness is lain bare, subject to the scrutiny of others, others who are undoubtedly shielding their own dark secrets from the public that they, themselves, compose? Lovecraft and Goffman both assure us that this all-encompassing shame and terror of social stigma lies sleeping, waiting only for our foolishness and mortal incompetence to rouse its grand and furious power.

Ann McCarthy
Independent Scholar
"Weird Christmas (with *Krampus*, Ligotti, Lovecraft, and Spark)"

I explore the genre of Christmas stories to determine recurring themes and features of its weird subgenre, through close readings of H. P. Lovecraft's "The Festival," Thomas Ligotti's "The Christmases of Aunt Elise," Muriel Spark's "The Seraph and the Zambesi," and Michael Dougherty's film *Krampus*. Recurrent themes among these works include: masks, torment by ancestors, the horror of the enforcement of ritual, and the powerful role of sound. In "The Festival," ancestors distantly, mutely impel the vulnerable narrator to a Yuletide celebration in the town of his people, and the experience leaves him briefly hospitalized. A relation leads him down into the earth, where he hears lunatic piping, and realizes his guide's true face is covered by a waxen mask. In "The Seraph and the Zambesi," sound is dulled and deformed by the intense Zambian December heat. The performance the protagonist attends is repeatedly referred to as a Nativity "masque," a particular word choice that emphasizes the ancientness of the undertaking. The events that follow are definitely weird, but any horror is evaded by the extreme aridity of the characters. Ligotti's narrator in "The Christmases of Aunt Elise" is being directly tormented by the eponymous ancestor; the whole narrative is revealed at the end to be dead Elise invading his brain to replay his Christmas memories over and over again for her entertainment. Part of his dislike of the holiday is conveyed by his revulsion at certain sounds in the story. *Krampus* tells the story of a family punished for not being happy enough about Christmas, for not observing its secular, social rituals adequately. Krampus, his toys, and his elves all wear really magnificent masks. The film's sound design is extremely rich and central to its effect.

Sean Moreland
University of Ottawa
"From Beyond the Pleasure Principle: Freud, Lucretius,
Lovecraft, and *The Locomotive-God*"

In a letter to August Derleth, Lovecraft acknowledged professor, poet, memoirist and translator William Ellery Leonard as "A character, & a figure of real importance in American letters." This paper explores Leonard's importance for Lovecraft, focusing on two intersections between their work crucial to Lovecraft's developing conception of cosmic horror. The first is between Leonard's translation and interpretations of Lucretius' *On The Nature of Things* (1916) and Lovecraft's early expression of cosmicism with the 1918 poem "The Poe-et's Nightmare." Analysis of a number of significant imagistic and verbal parallels between Leonard's translation and Lovecraft's poem provides insight into one of the sources of Lovecraft's early cosmicism, while also illuminating aspects of his reception of both Lucretius and Edgar Allan Poe. The second intersection is between Leonard's 1927 psycho-biographical account of his phobic obsessions, *The Locomotive-God*, and a number of Lovecraft's post-1929 fictions. Lovecraft's letters praise the penetrating psychology of traumatic obsession that *The Locomotive-God* offers; for example, he recommends it to Robert E. Howard as essential reading for anyone interested in psychobiography. *The Locomotive-God* was crucial to Lovecraft's conception of the power of atmosphere, the sine qua non of cosmic horror; he writes to Maurice W. Moe, "Unless one is steeled against the ascendancy of the capricious and meaningless subjective feelings, he is lost so far as the power of rational appraisal of the external world is concerned. Thus poor W. E. Leonard sees and feels things that aren't there—and knows he does—yet continues to see and feel them just the same. That shows the power of irrational mood over rational perception." In conclusion, I explore how the traumatic temporality and alien entities at the heart of *At the Mountains of Madness*, "The Whisperer in Darkness," and "The Shadow out of Time" represent Lovecraft's attempts to formulate this power in a fictional framework, one significantly informed by Leonard's phobic autobiography.

Paul Neimann
University of Colorado Boulder
"The Other Others: Mapping Lovecraft's Loathing"

H. P. Lovecraft's ethnic and national prejudices have received considerable attention. This essay takes a broader look at his animosities, as he mapped them on a range of characters: from benighted rustics to Victorian prudes to degenerate aristocrats and provincials. These suspicious personae recur frequently, in similar stories, often set on a cosmic timeline that suggests Western history. But Lovecraft's fictional schemas rarely reveal clear values. His tales contrast undesirable qualities with positive traits, like curiosity and imagination; but these accounts sometimes fit poorly with his usual preferences for high culture and tradition over modernity. One might ask, then: Who is the real Lovecraftian villain? Instead of piecing together a unified cosmology, I explore a pattern-seeking or folkloric approach to repeated narrative units. Early works, for example, furnish different iterations of one or two underlying templates or ur-stories. These arguably have some final expression in efforts like "The Rats in the Walls" (1923) and "He" (1925). Looking for common elements yields a sense of Lovecraft's peculiar triangulation between patrician elites, mass culture, and pulp fiction. Finding "other others" does not imply obscuring specific prejudices and looking for a general misanthropy. Instead, we might see how Lovecraft used different kinds of outsiders to stand for different cultural dangers he perceived.

Heather Poirier
Independent Scholar
"The Weird within the Real: Common Territories
in Lovecraft's Fiction and Southern Literature"

H. P. Lovecraft famously argued that William Faulkner's story "A Rose for Emily" could not be considered weird fiction because, despite its bizarre events, the story was plausible and thus did not liberate the imagination. Indeed, weird fiction would not seem to have much in common with Southern literature, especially that of Southern literature written during and just after Lovecraft's life. Probably because of this, literary critics do not offer much analysis of Lovecraft's weird fiction and Southern literature, which prevents us from understanding their commonalities. The lack of research is understandable. Lovecraft's devotion to New England would distract most scholars, while researchers in Southern literature rarely concern themselves with weird fiction. The barriers to research begin with the conceptual: for instance, Lovecraft's New England seems quite distant from the South. Elements such as cultural divergences, images of conflict and war, and assumptions about the inhabitants of both New England and the South present other obstacles. This paper addresses and explores some of the implications of common territories in Lovecraft and Southern literature. Lovecraft's immersive world-building in New England renders it as vivid as Faulkner's Yoknapatawpha County, and both Lovecraft and Southern writers are concerned with matters such as family lineage; the almost mythical power that the land holds over its inhabitants; religious strangeness; perversity; murder; and weird locals mixed with backwoods degeneracy. After moving toward a definition of Southern literature, this paper examines the common ground of realism, communal knowledge, and communal truth-telling, including how the grotesque becomes a fluid capacity derived from abjection that merges and overlaps the works of various authors. The truth-telling mechanism of the grotesque bridges the common characteristics found in Lovecraft's fiction and Southern literature. The paper concludes with a discussion of its implications and possible directions for future research.

Lúcio Reis-Filho (Laura Cánepa, and Jamer de Mello, coauthors)
University Anhembi Morumbi, São Paulo, Brazil
"Encounters in the Mountains of Madness:
H. P. Lovecraft and Werner Herzog at the World's End"

The documentary film *Encounters at the End of the World* (2007) is the record of Werner Herzog's expedition to Antarctica. There, the German filmmaker and his crew attempted to capture the beauty and the strange life forms of the polar continent, and to investigate the human characters who inhabit it—members of the community of scientists and workers at McMurdo Station. Published seventy years earlier, H. P. Lovecraft's novel *At the Mountains of Madness* (1931) was set in the same place, in the surroundings of Mount Erebus. Written in the pseudo-documentary style that characterizes Lovecraft's fictional texts, the novel narrates a disastrous incursion of a group of scientists and engineers into the mysterious Antarctic continent. The proposal of our ongoing research is to suggest an approximation between Herzog's documentary film and Lovecraft's pseudo-documentary novel, based on the premise that they are part of a bicentennial tradition of narratives about Antarctica, many of them fictional reports inspired by historical expeditions. Not coincidentally, both Herzog and Lovecraft make references to some of these expeditions in their works. The analysis also seeks to observe the philosophical ground that underlies Herzog's and Lovecraft's worldview, since both authors represent Antarctica as a place that miniaturizes human life, reducing it to its insignificance within an infinite and hostile universe, about which very little is known. Such a perspective, tied to Lovecraft's cosmicism, creates not only fantastic environments, but also ends up leading the characters to the brink of sanity and eventually to madness in the face of the unknown.

Troy Rondinone
Southern Connecticut State University
"The Horror of 'White Trash' in H. P. Lovecraft's Work"

In his short story "Beyond the Wall of Sleep," H. P. Lovecraft references a mental patient named Slater, a "typical denizen of the Catskill Mountain region, who corresponds exactly with the 'white trash' of the South." These degraded people exist without "laws and morals," their low "mental status" even making them susceptible to alien occupation. In this essay, I focus on a less-analyzed aspect of Lovecraft's racialized horror landscape; i.e., monstrous whiteness, or "white trash." Like others of his day, Lovecraft was preoccupied with racial degradation. Poor rural whites figure as touchstones of horror in several of his stories. Incorporating recent scholarly studies of racial formation, including the landmark book *White Trash* by Nancy Isenberg, as well as the work of horror theorist Noël Carroll, I examine some of the ways that Lovecraft demonized "inferior" whites and incorporated the terrors of racial decline into his stories.

Christian Roy
Independent Scholar
"Anti-Utilitarian Economics and Post-Capitalist Social Visions
in Lovecraft and Bataille"

Surprising overlap and revealing contrasts can be found between Lovecraft's later social views and economic thought and those articulated by Georges Bataille a few years later during the war in *The Limit of Usefulness*. Both are driven by a fundamental aversion for the utilitarian assumptions of political economy, which they historicize in reference to pre-capitalist ways of life, particularly those of landed aristocracies. Bataille expresses renewed appreciation for their ethos as he moves away from his previous calls for revolutionary extremism. Lovecraft hopes to avoid its attendant cultural ravages by articulating a gradual path to socialism as a way to generalize conditions of freedom from toil and insecurity once reserved to the agrarian elites he had long revered, as the happy few alone able to develop disinterested pursuits amidst pre-industrial conditions of scarcity which the easy abundance of the machine age had since made untenable. But too much energy was wasted in the calculative struggle for necessities, while untrammeled accumulation only served socially useless gain, instead of liberating energies for the real development of human personality through good education and minimum economic stress for all as conditions for creative leisure. Lovecraft's ideal was thus one of humanistic *Bildung*, while Bataille's aim was to lavish human energies in glorious self-destruction on the pattern of the sun and galaxies: a sacrificial impulse of intimacy with death in violent ecstasy, by then however largely confined to erotic literature. Similar cosmic horror was also the stuff of weird tales Lovecraft hoped to see flourish through grants to non-profit presses, free from pulp's commercial imperatives. The eighteenth-century gentry's life of genteel contemplative self-cultivation held up by Lovecraft as a model yet marks a different post-capitalist path from Bataille's retrieval of the seventeenth-century nobility's reckless "religious" performance of sovereign self-expenditure, deliberately courting disaster.

Michael-Paul Schallmo
University of Minnesota
"Abnormal Perception and Mental Illness in Weird Fiction"

Mental disorders can dramatically affect how people perceive the world, but only recently have scientists begun to understand the physiological basis of these sensory abnormalities. However, abnormal perception in people with mental health conditions has been a topic of interest for fictional authors for more than a hundred years. In particular, short stories in the horror, science fiction, and weird fiction genres have described in remarkable detail how perception may be disrupted by mental illness, and in ways relevant to modern science. Abnormal sensory experiences occur with some frequency in certain mental disorders. For example, people with schizophrenia may experience hallucinations—hearing or (less often) seeing things that are not present in the external environment. It is difficult to study hallucinations in a controlled, scientific way, but researchers have developed other methods to investigate abnormal perception in psychiatric conditions. Using images that evoke visual illusions, research from myself and others has shown that people with schizophrenia have trouble integrating and organizing information in laboratory tests of visual perception. When combined with measurements of neural physiology, such as brain imaging, this research gives us clues about the biological basis of abnormal perception in these disorders. Weird fiction stories from the late nineteenth and early twentieth centuries include many characters whose mental illness affects their sensory perception. The works of H. P. Lovecraft are notable in this regard; in tales such as "The Rats in the Walls" and "The Colour out of Space" the author details how characters with troubled minds see and hear things that others cannot. Well-known works from other authors, such as Charlotte Perkins Gilman's "The Yellow Wall Paper" deal deftly with the same subject. Drawing from knowledge gained first hand, these stories give the reader insight into the subjective experience of disordered perception in mental illness.

Daniel Schnopp-Wyatt
Lindsey Wilson College
"Lovecraftian Silver John: Wellman, Lovecraft,
and the Appalachian Occult"

By virtue of his prolific publication history in *Weird Tales,* a single story written as a Lovecraft tribute, and themes found in some stories, Manly Wade Wellman's Silver John stories are sometimes considered "Lovecraftian." Both authors present cohesive mythologies built around an occult worldview in which supernatural powers can be summoned and exploited. Wellman's mythic world is, however, explicitly Christian. That said, Wellman's Christianity is not that of the church or the theologian; it is the Christianity of the isolated quasi-pagan frontier. It is a Christianity of magic words, sacred metals, and ritual magic. Just as Lovecraft did, Wellman referenced many a quaint and curious volume of forgotten lore. Unlike Lovecraft, the books Wellman referenced were actual texts, in the pow-wow tradition, used throughout Appalachia for occult purposes. This paper takes the form of an essay examining approaches to the topic, Wellman's life context, points of comparison and contrast with Lovecraft's work, the pow-wow tradition as an enduring influence on Wellman's writing, and ends with an argument for considering Wellman's work as a parallel to Lovecraft's and as an exemplar of the Appalachian folk horror tradition.

Erica Sumrall
Independent Scholar
"'His Active and Enthralled Assistant'":
Homoromanticism in the Works of H. P. Lovecraft"

Male friendships dominate and shape the tales of H. P. Lovecraft. Male companions are the primary emotional touchpoints for his characters. Familial ties have diminished importance compared to intense friendships. His male characters trust each other with eldritch secrets and fears, in addition to their own lives. The ardor and passion of Lovecraft's friendships are transgressive to the twenty-first-century mores of male affection. Stories such as "Herbert West—Reanimator," "The Thing on the Doorstep," and *The Case of Charles Dexter Ward* have uncommonly involved protagonists. The unnamed narrator of "Herbert West—Reanimator" dedicates his life to West's obsession. They live and work together; the bond is so impenetrable that it continues throughout military service. Even as the narrator becomes fearful of West, he still stands by his side. Only West's shocking death is sufficient to break the spell of the relationship. A more positive example of Lovecraft's male relationships would be that between the characters of Dr. Willett and the titular character of *The Case of Charles Dexter Ward*. Dr. Willett's friendship with Ward leads him into macabre but ultimately heroic circumstances. In comparison, the relationship between Daniel Upton and Edward Derby in "The Thing on the Doorstep" is perhaps the most poignant and tragic friendship in Lovecraft's entire canon. Upton has such belief in Derby that he is willing to kill at his imploring. Lovecraft himself had intense correspondences and friendships with other male figures. Without these connections, Lovecraft would have lost much of his support and inspiration. Male trust and bonding are the pillars on which H. P. Lovecraft's stories stand.

Elena Tchougounova-Paulson
Independent Scholar
"Neo-Gothic decadence as a pervasive challenge in works of
H. P. Lovecraft, A. Machen, and A. Blok"

The Decadent movement of the late nineteenth and early twentieth centuries has evolved from different sources, it has had a variety of forms and reflections, it has gone through several phases, but there are two things that connect them all: validation of fear as a primal philosophical and aesthetical force, and acknowledgment of the art of decay as a new cultural phenomenon. Since then, the new Modernist culture was shaped in such a way that it absorbed the elements of Symbolism (primarily French), supernatural (i.e., mysticism and reframed Gnosticism, alongside other post-Hellenistic traditions), and the philosophy of pessimism (mostly established by Schopenhauer and Nietzsche), giving to the contemplative audience of the *fin de siècle* era an absolutely new, eschatological, and irrevocable outlook, which we could define as Neo-Gothic Decadence. The object of this paper is to reveal how the omnipresence of Neo-Gothic/Decadent ideas, reflections and thoughts has appeared—and has been manifested—in the works of H. P. Lovecraft, Arthur Machen, and Alexander Blok. Each could be defined as a perfect type of a Decadent author with different backgrounds (American, Welsh, Russian) but similar perceptions of artistic dynamics. All three were ahead of their time with their pioneering writings (Lovecraft's weird fiction; Machen's Edwardian supernatural works; Alexander Blok's mystical Symbolism). In the case of connections between Machen and Lovecraft, we can definitely demonstrate the direct impact of one on the other ("Machen is a Titan—perhaps the greatest living author—and I must read everything of his," wrote Lovecraft wrote to Frank Belknap Long in 1923); Blok's name might seem out of place in the list. That perception will change as we look carefully at Blok's poetry, essays, and correspondence and prove that he was one of the neo-Gothic/Decadent league.

Thomas Schwaiger
University of Graz, Austria
"A Lover of Past Phantoms: Lovecraftian Reflections in
R. H. Barlow's Science"

Recent years saw a growing interest in the mutual literary influence and personal relationship between H. P. Lovecraft and R. H. Barlow (e.g., Jarett Kobek's talk at the Armitage Symposium 2015 and Paul La Farge's novel *The Night Ocean*). However, apart from La Farge's semi-fictional account, Barlow's path after Lovecraft's death in 1937 is less investigated. This paper explores a hitherto neglected avenue: Lovecraft's possible posthumous influence on Barlow's distinguished career as an outstanding Mesoamerican anthropologist and linguist up to his suicide in 1951. George T. Smisor, his co-founder of anthropological journal *Tlalocan*, reminisced about Barlow in 1952: "He had an intellectual driving force that never seemed to relax, that picked me up and carried me along with it, as it likewise did later many others. He had a facility of expression that brought to life long-dead happenings. This happy facility was a carry-over from his years of reading and writing fantasy fiction and composing poetry." The present contribution aims to show that this carry-over was additionally a "carry-on" and even "carry-beyond" with respect to Lovecraft's influence. While the young Barlow notoriously started more projects than he completed—for which he received a mild rebuke but also advice by Lovecraft—the later scholar underwent a considerable turnaround and eventually, according to Lovecraft biographer S. T. Joshi, "fully justified Lovecraft's predictions of his precocious genius, and would have accomplished far more had he lived." This transformation is clearly reflected by Barlow's studies in anthropology and linguistics (e.g., his recording and editing of old Mexican folktales such as "The Phantom Lover"), revealing a rationalism akin to Lovecraft's and their shared interest in the past, which ultimately brought him as far as the libraries of Paris and London—destinations that had always remained mere places of longing for Lovecraft.

Michael A. Torregrossa
Independent Scholar
"Cthulhu and King Arthur?: Lovecraft's Knowledge and
Use of the Matter of Britain"

In roughly forty texts produced from the 1960s to at least 2017, creators have co-opted themes from the writings of H. P. Lovecraft and combined them with motifs from the Matter of Britain, the millennium-and-a-half-old conglomeration of stories about King Arthur and those associated with his court at Camelot, to create a series of innovative sub-traditions within the larger Arthurian tradition that I have elsewhere referred to as Lovecraftian Arthuriana. Initially, I thought these mash-ups of the Cthulhu Mythos and the Arthurian legend to be original contributions to each tradition with no direct connection to Lovecraft. However, further research into Lovecraft's nonfiction and letters, and interpretations of his fiction, offer a potentially deeper connection, suggesting that Lovecraftian Arthuriana might be an authorized tradition. This paper traces Lovecraft's use and knowledge of the Matter of Britain by looking closely at his references to Thomas Malory's *Le Morte d'Arthur*, Thomas Bulfinch's *The Age of Chivalry*, and Lord Tennyson's Arthurian poems in Lovecraft's "Supernatural Horror in Literature" (1927), "Suggestions for a Reading Guide" (1936), and his correspondence, and highlights recent scholarship on his work by fellow medievalists to evaluate what and when Lovecraft may have known about Arthur and events at Camelot.

Lucas Townsend
Independent Scholar
"Who Is Lovecraft's True Protagonist?:
The Oriental Semiotician and His *Necronomicon*"

Abdul Alhazred, whom Stephen King in *Danse Macabre* calls "that quaint pre-OPEC Arab," is perhaps H. P. Lovecraft's most conspicuously present character from across his entire body of work. My question is why—why should a mad Yemeni scholar and his notorious *Necronomicon* be the mediator through which no fewer than nineteen of Lovecraft's tales are negotiated? While Lovecraft's narrators are often pastiches of himself and his life, Alhazred is an enigma. Given the early views of a Spengler-inspired Lovecraft, it is quite surprising that a dead eighth-century poet from the Orient is as influential, multilateral, and convincingly well developed as he is. The author of the *Necronomicon* exists as the filter through which Lovecraft's pastiche-narrators interpret the sign systems of inhuman alien identities, giving Alhazred nearly limitless power within the available textual space. His position therein as subaltern intermediary between human and alien of disparate metaphysical aeons offers commentary on his capability as hermeneutic interpreter for both worlds; in the case of the Anglo-American–Aryan Lovecraftian narrator, said narrator often goes insane upon interaction with the Oriental sign systems presented by Alhazred's forbidden tome. This paper discovers the etymological and conceptual origins behind Alhazred, delves into the true textual and semiotic significances of the *Necronomicon* using Jacques Derrida's notion of iterability, and uncovers the answers as to how the Yemeni scholar accepts, rejects, or converses with the characteristics of other Modernist narrators and protagonists. The significance of an Orientalized character existing as perhaps the most memorable takeaway from Lovecraft's work—possibly more so than even his pantheon of alien entities or his cosmic indifferentist philosophy—cannot be understated, as this interpretation opens up Lovecraftian studies to even greater postcolonial conversations than have been previously realized.

Nathaniel R. Wallace
Independent Scholar
"A Sequence of Paintings so Horrid:
'Pickman's Model' Visual Adaptations"

Like many of H. P. Lovecraft's well known tales, such as *At the Mountains of Madness* and "The Nameless City," the short story "Pickman's Model" includes numerous descriptions of visual images that, when collated, tell a history of the immediate events in the main story; namely the relations the fictional race of ghouls have with the residents of Boston. These descriptions serve as a network of cursory fragments highly associated with the technique of montage within the greater narrative. Noted film theorist

André Bazin defines montage as "the ordering of images in time" and "the creation of a sense or meaning not objectively contained in the images themselves but derived exclusively from their juxtaposition." Through montage, the fictional history communicated within "Pickman's Model" is strongly connected with these textual fragments' orientation and relationship to each other through their placement within the overall text, but also the spatio-temporal qualities attributed to the subject matter they depict. When adapting "Pickman's Model" into a visual medium dependent upon sequences, whether in film or comics, an artist serves as curator in selecting which descriptions to render visually and what aspect of this fictional history from the original texts they wish to communicate to the audience. It is this juxtaposition of montage fragments in visual adaptations of the short story that is analyzed in this presentation for the formal qualities by which they disrupt the narrative through their orientation in the text. Many such adaptations commonly include a photograph or film footage of a ghoul to serve as the climax of the narrative, but more significant to the notion of montage are the contrasting images in these adaptations that require the audience to make associations between two or more images which are bound up with the relations between ghouls and humans. This presentation chronicles the various comic, television and film adaptations of "Pickman's Model" and focuses primarily on the *Night Gallery* (1971) television adaptation of the story and Herb Arnold's comic "Pickman's Model" (1972).

Index

Abbot, Charles Greeley 129n2
Accursed Shore, The (Bataille) 219, 221, 226
Adlow, Elijah 180
Aguirre, the Wrath of God (film) 165
Ainley, David 171
"Alchemist, The" 86, 92
Aldana Reyes, Xavier 204-5
Aldini, Giovanni 150
Alhazred, Abdul 56, 57, 268, 293-94
Alien (film) 162
"Alone in the Dark" 278
American Gothic Fiction: An Introduction (Lloyd-Smith) 114-15
American Psychological Association 103-4, 108, 109
Ames, Robert Landau 13
Ancient Wisdom Revealed (Campbell) 43
Andersson, Martin 139n18
"Anniversary" (Barlow) 140
Annotated Fungi from Yuggoth, The 272
Apostle (film) 189
Aretaeus of Cappadocia 103
Aristotle 103
Arnold, Herb 238, 252-53, 255
Arthur, King 293
Askari, Nasrin 29, 36
Aster, Ari 190
At the Mountains of Madness 13, 47, 51, 61, 63-64, 73-74, 80-81, 116, 122, 162-65, 166-67, 169-72, 274, 275, 277, 281, 287
Azathoth 53, 224-25
Azif, Al (Alhazred) 70, 268-69

Backstrom, Lars 57
Bakhtin, Mikhail 118-19

Barlow, Bernice 127
Barlow, Everett D. 127-28
Barlow, R. H. 13, 14, 100-109, 115, 126-48, 230, 276-77, 292-93
Barlow, Wayne 127
Barnes, Lois 181
Barroso, Antonio Alejandro 13
Barrows, Brandon 249-51
Battaile, Georges 13-14, 219-36, 288-89
Bazin, André 237
Bear, Elizabeth 65
Bely, Andrei 215-16
Benson, Jim 251
Beowulf 271
Bergson, Henri 210
Berruti, Massimo 126, 135
Betancourt, Michael 250
Beyond Spatial Montage (Betancourt) 250
"Beyond the Wall of Sleep" 90, 115, 287-88
Bibliography of the Negro in Africa and America, A (Work) 76
Bielawa, Michael J. 13, 54
Binyon, T. J. 215
Birkhead, Edith 280
Biltmore Hotel (Providence, R.I.) 12
"Black God's Kiss, The" (Moore) 273
Black Metal music 281-82
Blank, Les 161
Blavatsky, Helena P. 13, 43-44, 50
Bloch, Robert 73
Blok, Alexander 205-6, 213-17, 291-92
Book of Dzyan 50
Book of Eibon 57

"Books That Never Were" (de Camp) 55
Booth, John Wilkes 150
Borges, Jorge Luis 72, 75
Boston Pictorial 182
Bowser, Samuel 168-69, 170
Branch, Mark 61
Branford Review and East Haven News 60
Braune, Sean 74, 75
Brennan, Doris 59
Brennan, Joseph Payne 53, 54, 58-59
Breton, André 231
Bridgeport Evening Farmer 153
Brookshaw, Dominic Parviz 28-29
Brown University 10, 155, 158
Buddhism 44
Bullard, F. Lauriston 176-77, 181
Bundahišn 24, 26, 37
Burden of Dreams (film) 161
Burke, Edmund 97
Burnaby, Frederick 42
Burroughs, William S. 145n27
Butler, Judith 273

"Call of Cthulhu, The" 21-22, 81, 97,
    108, 116, 224, 232, 239, 275, 281
Call of Cthulhu (RPG) 278
Cameron, James 272
Campbell, Bruce F. 43
Cannon, Peter 54
Carlson, John B. 141n22
Carpenter, John 162
Carroll, Noël 288
Carter, Lin 56
Case of Charles Dexter Ward, The 54,
    76, 77, 156-57, 186, 291
Casey, Samuel, Jr. 62
Cave of Forgotten Dreams (film) 166
Chaffee family 155-56, 157
Charles W. Morgan (ship) 55
Chartier, Roger 79
"Children of the Corn, The" (King)
    190
"Christmases of Aunt Elise, The"
    (Ligotti) 283, 284
Chua, Kendrick kerwin 57
Clark, Fraser 27

Clark, Lillian D. 10, 156
Clinton, Jerome 27
Clore, Dan 57
Colavito, Jason 57
"Colour out of Space, The" 21, 53,
    174-75, 183-88, 269-70
"Coming of the White Worm, The"
    (Smith) 275
Conover, Willis 60
Conuel, Thomas 176, 179-80
Cook, Jeremiah Dylan 13
"Cool Air" 220
"Crawling Chaos, The" (Lovecraft-
    Jackson) 222-24
Creasy, Larry 193, 194
Cross, Cameron 27-28
Crowe, John H., III 53-54
Cthulhu 17, 22-23, 38, 268
Cthulhu Mythos 163, 278, 293
Cult of Alien Gods, The (Colavito) 57
Cyclonopedia (Negarestani) 23-24, 35

Dādestān ī dēnīg 26
"Dagon" 108
Dandieu, Arnaud 232
Dante Alighieri 36-37
David-Néel, Alexandra 44, 49, 274
Davies, Owen 60-61
Davis, Benjamin 13
Davis, Dick 18, 32
Davis, Erik 164
de Camp, L. Sprague 55, 57, 58, 59,
    127
de Certeau, Michel 80, 81
De Vermis Mysteriis (Prinn) 73
Decadent movement 202, 206, 209-
    10, 212, 291
Dee, John 57, 75
Déléage, Pierre 127, 128n1
den Uijl, Sebastiaan 27
Dēnkard 26
Derleth, August 46, 60, 84, 239, 272,
    284
Derrida, Jacques 75, 294
"Dim-Remembered Story, A" (Barlow)
    135n10

Dodds, E. R. 207
Donovan, Cole 13
"Doom That Came to Sarnath, The"
  209
Doubleday, Myron 176
Dougherty, Michael 283
Dracula (Stoker) 238-39
Dream-Quest of Unknown Kadath, The
  79
"Dreams in the Witch House, The"
  192
"Dunwich Horror, The" 53, 54, 64,
  74, 75, 76, 81, 115, 277
Dwyer, Bernard Austin 156

"Early Years, The" (Derleth) 239
Eckhardt, Jason 52, 164
Effinger, George Alec 57, 65
Einstein, Albert 219-20
Eisenstein, Sergei 238
Eisert, Regina 168, 170
"Elder Scrolls III: Morrowind" 278
Elduque, Albert 165
Eliot, T. S. 238
Ellis, Jay 112
Emerson, Ralph Waldo 112
Encounters at the End of the World (film)
  162, 166, 167-72, 287
England 41-43
Engle, John 73n3
Essay on the Gift (Mauss) 232
Evans, Timothy H. 187
"Everything That Rises Must Con-
  verge" (O'Connor) 120-22
Évolution créatrice, L' (Bergson) 210
Extent of the Empire of the Culhua Mexica
  (Barlow) 143
"Eyes of the God" (Barlow) 131

"Facts concerning the Late Arthur
  Jermyn and His Family" 86-87, 90
Faig, Kenneth W., Jr. 126
Fantastic, The (Todorov) 208
Farmer, Tessa 211
Farnese, Harold S. 271-72
Fata Morgana (film) 166

Faulkner, William 111, 114-15, 120,
  286
Felinto, Erick 163
Fetters, Ian 163, 167
"Festival, The" 224, 225, 283
Fifer, Chad 282
Firdawsī 17-20, 24-38, 268
Fisher, Mark 38
Fitzcarraldo (film) 165
Fort, Charles 53
Freeman, Nick 212-13
Freud, Sigmund 117
Friedrich, Markus 72
"From Beyond" 86, 222, 224
Frye, Mitch 113-14
Fungi from Yuggoth 132, 271-72

Gafford, Sam 54, 65
Galvani, Luigi 150
Gamache, Kyle 13
Gamwell, Annie E. P. 62, 134, 156
Gay Science, The (Nietzsche) 223
Gencarella, Stephen Olbrys 54
Gender Trouble (Butler) 273
Geraci, Robert 278
Ghost Towns 'Neath Quabbin Reservoir
  (Gustafson) 179, 181-82
Gibson, James 72-73
Gilman, Charlotte Perkins 289
Glasgow, Ellen 116-17
Godard, Jean-Luc 248
Goetsch, Paul 71
Goffman, Erving 282-83
"Good Country People" (O'Connor)
  119
"Good Man Is Hard to Find, A"
  (O'Connor) 120
Gorman, Herbert S. 189, 191, 193-
  201
Gothic Tradition in Fiction, The
  (MacAndrew) 204
"Great God Pan, The" (Machen) 211
Greeks and the Irrational, The (Dodds)
  207
Greene, J. R. 175, 181
Greene, Sonia H. 12, 53, 54, 156, 277

Greer, John Michael 279
Greimas, A. J. 91, 92
Grizzly Man (film) 162, 166
Guimont, Edward 13
Gustafson, Evelina 179, 181-83, 184, 186

"H. P. Lovecraft: The Books" (Carter) 56
H. P. Lovecraft Encyclopedia, An (Joshi–Schultz) 174
H. P. Lovecraft Historical Society 10, 12
Haesaert, Madelaine 179
Hamlin, Henry 154
Harman, Graham 17, 21-23, 25, 30, 37, 267, 268
Harms, Daniel 57, 58, 60, 61, 65
Hart, Lawrence 137
Haskins, Leslie 180
"Haunter of the Dark, The" 50
Hawthorne, Nathaniel 189, 191-94, 197-201, 272
Hayes, Edmund 28
"He" 93, 95-97
Heart of Glass (film) 165
Heidegger, Martin 280-81
"Herbert West—Reanimator" 13, 62, 86, 87, 88, 95, 149-50, 152, 153, 154, 155, 157-59, 270, 290-91
Herzog, Werner 161-72, 287
Hippocrates 103
"History of the 'Necronomicon'" 56, 268-69
Hobbs, Niels-Viggo 14
Holm, Kim 246, 248
Home Brew 149
Homer 103
"Horror at Red Hook, The" 90, 97, 116
Houellebecq, Michel 142n23
"Hound, The" 48
House of Nodens, The (Gafford) 54, 65
"House on Stratford Lane, The" (Crowe) 53-54
How to Do Things with Books in Victorian Britain (Price) 79

Howard, Robert E. 136n13, 138, 284
Howard, Todd 278
Hoyt, Edwin 150-51
Huling, Ray 223
Hunter, Wallace 182
Hurston, Zora Neale 114n4
Husserl, Edmund 22
Hussey, Derrick 14
Hutcheon, Linda 243

Iliad (Homer) 103
In the Dust of This Planet (Thacker) 21, 163
Inferno (Dante) 36-37
"Instructions in Case of Decease" 134
Introduction to Metaphysics (Heidegger) 280
Isenberg, Nancy 288
Isham, Norman 186

"Jendick's Swamp" (Brennan) 53
Jevons, William Stanley 221
Jirsa, Bill 165, 166
Johnson, Charles Blackburn 128n2
Jones, Mabel L. 177, 178
Joshi, S. T. 14, 48, 85, 98, 112n1, 135n9, 142n23, 146, 149n1, 156, 169, 195, 200, 205, 207, 210, 214-15, 238n1, 292
Julius, Anthony 256

Kawin, Bruce 256
Kim (Kipling) 41
King, Stephen 190, 191, 293
Kircher, Athanasius 60
Kline, Otis Adelbert 60
Kneale, James 206
Kobek, Jarett 127
Kraepelin, Emil 103
Krampus (film) 283, 284
Kristeva, Julia 121
Kroeber, Alfred Louis 139

La Farge, Paul 127, 292
Lackey, Chris 282
Laird, Jack 238, 251

Lalia, Horacio 238, 246, 253–54, 256
Lauder, Robert 151, 152
Le Guin, Ursula K. 139
Leaves 135
Legaria, Marcos 126
Leiber, Fritz 254
Leonard, William Ellery 284–85
Lévi-Strauss, Claude 84
Levin, Ira 189–90
"Library of Babel, The" (Borges) 72, 75
Ligotti, Thomas 281, 283
Limit of Usefulness, The (Bataille) 226, 288
Lipetz, Ben-Ami 58
Literary Swordsmen and Sorcerers (de Camp) 55
"Living Heritage, A" 239n2
Lloyd-Smith, Allan 114–15
Locomotive God, The (Leonard) 284–85
Long, Frank Belknap 46, 206, 222, 230
Loucks, Donovan K. 60
Lovecraft Chronicles, The (Cannon) 54
Lovecraft Lexicon, The (Pearsall) 61
Lucretius (T. Lucretius Carus) 284
"Lurking Fear, The" 90

MacAyeal, Douglas 167
MacAndrew, Elizabeth 204
McCloud, Scott 238, 243–44, 250, 252
Machen, Arthur 205–6, 211–13, 291–92
Magic and Mystery in Tibet (Néel) 44, 274
Magnalia Christi Americana (Mather) 64, 76, 187
Mahallati, Mohammad Jafar Amir 28
Makavejev, Dušan 248
Maloney, Marcia 158
Manovich, Lev 238
Marsh, Othniel Charles 62–63
Martin, Sean Elliot 122, 239
Marx, Karl 224, 230
Mather, Cotton 64, 187
"Maureen Birnbaum at the Looming Awfulness" (Effinger) 57
Mauss, Marcel 232, 234

Melville, Charles 29
"[Memories of Lovecraft (1934)]" (Barlow) 131n5, 144
Mencken, H. L. 115
Merritt, A. 61
Midsommar (film) 189, 190
Modern Rome (Panini) 249
Modernism 202–3, 206–8, 238–39, 291
Moe, Maurice W. 62, 174, 209, 285
Moe, Robert Ellis 53, 55, 155
Moghadam, Nahid 119
"Moon-Bog, The" 86
Moore, C. L. 117, 229, 232, 234, 273
Murnau, F. W. 163
Murray, Will 52, 277
Musaget 214
Myths and Legends of Our Own Land (Skinner) 53, 64

"Nameless City, The" 275
Narrative of Arthur Gordon Pym, The (Poe) 164
Natsoulas, Thomas 72–73
Nature (Emerson) 112
Necronomicon (Alhazred) 13, 55–61, 65, 70, 72, 73–75, 77, 79–82, 268–69, 271, 294
Necronomicon, The (Price) 57
Necronomicon: A Study, The (Owings) 56
Necronomicon Files, The (Gonce–Harms) 57, 58
"NecronomiCON REFerence file" (Chua) 57
Negarestani, Reza 23–25, 35
Neimann, Paul 13
Neo-Gothic 203–17, 291
New Lands (Fort) 53
New York Evening World 152
Nicholas I (Tsar of Russia) 42
Nietzsche, Friedrich 206, 207, 212, 220, 222, 223, 224, 225
Night Gallery (TV series) 238, 246–47, 251, 252, 254–56
"Night Ocean, The" (Barlow–Lovecraft) 13, 100–109, 276–77

Night Ocean, The (La Farge) 127, 292
Nightmares & Dreamscapes (King) 190
Nosferatu the Vampyre (film) 163
"Notion of Expenditure, The" (Bataille) 219
Nyarlathotep 192, 224-25

O'Connor, Flannery 116, 118-22
Off the Ancient Track (Eckhardt) 52
Olcott, Henry 43-44
Old Providence: A Collection of Facts and Traditions 156
On the Nature of Things (Lucretius) 284
O'Neill, Eugene 53
Oriental Tales 50
"Origin Undetermined" (Barlow) 135-36, 138
"Outsider, The" 92
Owings, Mark 56

Pabody, Frederic J. 63
Palladino, Philip 152-53
Panini, Giovanni Paolo 249
Pashov, Stefan 168
Peabody, George 63
Peacock, A. C. S. 29
Pearsall, Anthony B. 61
Pedersen, Nate 57
"People of the Pit, The" (Merritt) 61
Petrus, Hugo 249-51, 252
"Pickman's Model" 14, 186, 237-59, 294-95
"Picture in the House, The" 76, 90, 94, 122-23
Pierce, Laurie 27, 31
Pigafetta, Antonio 123
Place Called Dagon, The (Gorman) 189, 191, 193-201
Plante, Mike 169
Plato 103, 108
Pnakotic Manuscripts 73, 79
Poe, Edgar Allan 112-13, 153, 158, 164, 284
Poe, George 149, 153-55, 158, 270
"Poe-et's Nightmare, The" 284

"Poetry of Magic and Spells, The" (Blok) 216
Poirier, Heather 13
Poliakova, E. A. 27
Porter, George Loring 149-55, 156-58, 270
Powers of Horror (Kristeva) 121-22
"Preface to the Al-Azif" (de Camp) 57
Price, E. Hoffmann 138
Price, Leah 79
Price, Robert M. 57
Providence Gazette and Country-Journal 77
Providence Journal 77-78, 186

Quabbin: The Accidental Wilderness (Conuel) 179-80
Quabbin: The Story of a Small Town with Outlooks upon Puritan Life (Underwood) 175, 184, 185
Quabbin Reservoir 174-75, 269

Rand, Elizabeth 179
Rankin, Hugh 241
"Rats in the Walls, The" 86, 92, 93-95, 119
"Raven, The" (Poe) 153
"Recapture" 132
Regnum Congo (Pigafetta) 76-77, 78, 123
"Return by Sunset" (Barlow) 135
"Return of the Lloigor, The" (Wilson) 60
Ride to Khiva, A (Burnaby) 42
Ringel, Faye 54, 155
Rizzo da Saracena, Leo 152
Road to Survival, The (Vogt) 279
Rod Serling's Night Gallery (Skelton-Benson) 251
Roerich, Nicholas 44-48, 50-51, 274
Roosevelt, Franklin D. 45-46
"Rose for Emily, A" (Faulkner) 111, 286
Roy, Christian 13-14
Russia 41-43
Ryans, Marie-Laure 240

St. Armand, Barton Levi 209-10
Salonia, John 207
Sapinsky, Alvin 246
Schultz, David E. 14, 272
Schwaiger, Thomas 14
Scituate Reservoir 174
Scott, Ridley 162
Scott, Robert F. 167
Seabrook, William 155
Secret Doctrine, The (Blavatsky) 50
"Seraph and the Zambesi, The" (Spark)
    283-84
Serling, Rod 246, 247
Shackleton, Ernest 167
"Shadow out of Time, The" 64,
    140n21, 221-22, 225, 275
"Shadow over Innsmouth, The" 62,
    108, 116, 189-201, 272
Shānāmah (Firdawsī) 17-20, 27-38,
    268
Shaviro, Steven 163
Shea, J. Vernon 62
"Shoggoths in Bloom" (Bear) 65
"Shunned House, The" 187
Simon 59, 73n3
Simpson, Marianna S. 27
Skelton, Scott 251
Skinner, Charles M. 53, 64
Slugan, Mario 237
Smisor, George T. 139, 141, 292
Smith, Clark Ashton 46, 49, 135, 207,
    208, 227, 274-75
Smithsonian Institution 129n2, 132
Solar Anus, The (Bataille) 219, 222, 223
Solovyov, Vladimir 213
Sound and the Fury, The (Faulkner) 120
Spark, Muriel 283
Spiegel, Alan 117
Spink, Amy W. 177, 178
Springfield Morning Union 181
Springfield Union 177
Stanley, Joan L. 56-57
Starry Wisdom Library, The (Pedersen)
    57
"Statement of Randolph Carter, The"
    87

Stepford Wives, The (Levin) 189-90
Stoker, Bram 163, 238-39
Stowe, Harriet Beecher 112
"Street, The" 88
"Summons, The" (Barlow) 136n12
"Supernatural Horror in Literature"
    21, 86, 169, 191, 193, 212, 271,
    272, 279, 293
Swift River Valley 175-88, 269

Tale of Terror, The (Birkhead) 280
Tales of the Cthulhu Mythos (Derleth)
    60
Tavakoli-Targhi, Mohamad 27
Tchougounova-Paulson, Elena 14
"Temple, The" 108
"Terrible Old Man, The" 90
Terror, The (TV series) 162n1
Thacker, Eugene 21, 36, 163, 279
"Theft of the Hsothian Manuscripts,
    The" (Barlow) 144
Theosophy 43-45, 50
Thing, The (film) 162
"Thing on the Doorstep, The" 291
Tibet 41-43, 44-45, 49, 274
"Tlacotepec Migration Legend, The"
    (Barlow) 144
Todorov, Tzvetan 208
Toldridge, Elizabeth 10
"Tomb, The" 86
"Transition of Juan Romero, The" 90,
    142-43
Trotter, David 238

"Ultima Thule" (Smith) 275
Uncle Tom's Cabin (Stowe) 112
Understanding Comics (McCloud) 238,
    252
Underwood, Francis 175, 184-86
"Unnamable, The" 187
Ure, Andrew 150

van Zurphen, Marjolijn 28
"Virtual Objects" (Natsoulis) 72-73
Vogt, William 279
Voynich Manuscript 60-61

Wade, James 271, 272
Wallace, Henry 46
Wallace, Nathaniel R. 14
Walpole, Horace 279-80
Walter, Damien 212
Wandrei, Donald 156
Ware River News 177
Warner, Harry, Jr. 56, 59, 60
Waste Land, The (Eliot) 238
Weber, Max 228
Weinstock, Jeffrey Andrew 206
Weird Realism (Harman) 17, 21-22, 267
Weird Tales 128, 146, 211, 240, 290
Wellman, Manly Wade 290
Welty, Eudora 113
Wetzel, George T. 126, 140
"Whisperer in Darkness, The" 52
White, Michael 53
White Diamond, The (film) 165, 166
"White Ship, The" 64-65
White Trash (Isenberg) 288
Whitehead, Henry S. 53, 155

Whritner, Jake 153
Wicker Man, The (film) 189
Wieland, George 63
Wilder, Robert 180, 181
Wilson, Colin 60
"Wind That Is in the Grass, The" (Barlow) 129
Winthrop, John, Jr. 54
Wollen, Peter 248
Wollheim, Donald A. 59-60
Woodard, Ben 279
Woodward, Walt 54
Work, Monroe 76
Wormius, Olaus 268
Wright, Tom 251

Yale Alumni Magazine 61
Yale University 55-64, 65, 277
"Yellow Wall Paper, The" (Gilman) 289
"Young Goodman Brown" (Hawthorne) 189, 191-94, 197-201, 272

www.ingramcontent.com/pod-product-compliance
Lightning Source LLC
Chambersburg PA
CBHW060952030726
47503CB00003B/837